ACCLAIM FOR
DANIEL WOODRELL

"Daniel Woodrell is that infrequent thing, a born writer. His is a style both brutal and touched with poetry. And it's very much his own. Don't miss it." — *Philadelphia Inquirer*

"Daniel Woodrell writes with insistent rhythm and an evocative and poetic regional flavor." — *The New Yorker*

"Daniel Woodrell has quietly built a career that should be the envy of most American novelists today." — *Washington Times*

"Put Woodrell on the shelf alongside Faulkner, Jim Thompson, and Cormac McCarthy.... Mr. Woodrell has earned himself a piece of immortality." — George Pelecanos

"A backcountry Shakespeare.... The inhabitants of Daniel Woodrell's fiction often have a streak that's not just mean but savage; yet physical violence does not dominate his books. What does dominate is a seasoned fatalism.... Woodrell has tapped into a novelist's honesty, and lucky for us, he's remorseless that way." — *Los Angeles Times*

"Daniel Woodrell writes in sentences that could be ancient carvings on a tree." — *Chicago Tribune*

"Daniel Woodrell is stone brilliant—a Bayou Dutch Leonard, steeped in rich Louisiana language." —James Ellroy

"Daniel Woodrell is the least-known major writer in the country right now." —Dennis Lehane, *USA Today*

"Woodrell writes books so good they make me clench my fists in jealousy and wonder, both at his talent and because nobody seems to have heard of him." —*Esquire*

"A master craftsman....Daniel Woodrell is one of the very few I refer to again and again to learn how true poetic writing is achieved....I would love to devote a whole novel to just quoting from his work. There are crime writers...literary writers...and then Daniel Woodrell. Nobody comes near his amazing genius and I very much doubt anyone ever will." —Ken Bruen

ACCLAIM FOR
UNDER THE BRIGHT LIGHTS

"Sly and powerful." —John D. MacDonald

"Poetic prose and raw dialogue...dark-hued suspense." —*Washington Post Book World*

"A gritty, atmospheric slice of crime fiction....As steamy as the bayou country that is its setting....A superior piece of narrative noir." —*Kirkus Reviews*

"A flawless novel....Vitality pulses from this perfectly paced book." —*San Francisco Examiner*

THE
BAYOU
TRILOGY

UNDER THE BRIGHT LIGHTS

MUSCLE FOR THE WING

THE ONES YOU DO

DANIEL WOODRELL

MULHOLLAND BOOKS

LITTLE, BROWN AND COMPANY

NEW YORK   BOSTON   LONDON

Mulholland Books
Little, Brown and Company
Hachette Book Group
237 Park Avenue, New York, NY 10017
www.hachettebookgroup.com

First omnibus edition, April 2011

Mulholland Books is an imprint of Little, Brown and Company.
The Mulholland Books name and logo are trademarks of
Hachette Book Group, Inc.

Library of Congress Cataloging-in-Publication Data

Woodrell, Daniel.
 The Bayou trilogy : Under the bright lights, Muscle for the wing, The ones you do /
Daniel Woodrell.— 1st omnibus ed.
  p. cm.
 ISBN 978-0-316-13365-4
 1. Shade, Rene (Fictitious character)—Fiction.   2. Saint Bruno (La. : Imaginary place)—Fiction.
3. Detectives—Louisiana—Fiction.   4. City and town life—Louisiana—Fiction.
5. Louisiana—Fiction.   I. Woodrell, Daniel. Under the bright lights.   II. Woodrell, Daniel. Muscle
for the wing.   III. Woodrell, Daniel. The ones you do.   IV. Title.
 PS3573.O6263A 2011
 813'.54—dc2   2010045419

10 9 8 7 6 5 4 3 2 1

RRD–C

Printed in the United States of America

CONTENTS

UNDER THE BRIGHT LIGHTS

To Katie, for all the reasons

"You can map out a fight plan or a life plan, but when the action starts, it may not go the way you planned, and you're down to your reflexes— that means your [preparation]. That's where your roadwork shows. If you cheated on that in the dark of the morning, well, you're going to get found out now, under the bright lights."

—JOE FRAZIER

1

JEWEL COBB had long been a legendary killer in his midnight rev-
eries and now he'd come to the big town to prove that his upright
version knew the same techniques and was just as cold. He sat on the
lumpy green couch tapping his feet in time with a guitar he scratched
at with sullen incompetence.

It was hard to play music in this room, he felt. There was a roof but
it leaked, and great rusty stains spread down the corners of the apartment. The walls were hefty with a century's accumulation of layered
wallpaper bubbled into large humps in their centers. The pipe from the
stove wobbled up to and through a rip in the ceiling where some indus-
trious derelict had tried to do a patch job by nailing flattened beer cans
over the gaps. It was altogether the sort of place that a man with serious
money would not even enter, a man with pin money would not linger
in, but a man with no money would have to call home. For a while.

"Suze," Jewel called. "Bring me a cup of coffee, will ya?"

"What?" Suze yelled. "I can't hear you, I'm in the john."

After a few more slashing strums Jewel gave up on trying to bully a
song from the flattop box. He shoved the guitar under the couch. He
wore a stag-cut red shirt, shiny black slacks, and sharp-toed cowboy boots.
His bare left bicep exposed the wet-ink blur of a cross with starlike points
jail-tattooed into his pale skin. His long blond hair was combed up and
greasy, sculpted into a style that had been the fashion at about the time of
his birth. Jewel, however, had divined an image of himself in his nocturnal wonderings and the atavistic comb work was the key flourish in it.

He called to Suze again. "Well, get out of the john! And bring me a cup of coffee, hear?"

"A cup?"

"Yeah! A cup of coffee, damn it."

Maybe he should have left her back home, Jewel speculated. Let her dodge grease splatters at the Pork Tender Stand for the rest of her life. Give joy to pig farmers at drive-ins on Saturday night and wonder why she'd ever let Jewel Cobb slip away. That would be fitting. He was bringing her along in the world, taking her to Saint Bruno, a city where things can change, but was she grateful?

Not by a long sight. She'd rather paint each of her toenails a different color, or count the pigeons under the bridge, than learn how to cook him a decent meal. Lots of women knew things that she didn't and he might not put up with just a whole lot more of her laziness before he picked up his walking cane and strolled out to pluck some daisies.

Ah, but he couldn't leave her now. He'd come to Saint Bruno to change his life, dip a great big spoon into the fabled gravy train of the city, and if cousin Duncan hadn't been greening him, then tonight could be the first little taste of how sweet that new life could be.

Jewel stood up and looked out the window onto Voltaire Street, a street of front-room appliance repair businesses, discount clothing shops, a pool hall called the Chalk & Stroke, a bail bondsman's office, and two hair salons that promised summer cuts and granite perms.

"I let it cool for you, Jewel." Suze's voice entered the room before her loose-jointed shuffle that advertised her dissatisfaction with mundane physical processes. This body was meant for finer things, she seemed to mime, and fine things could happen with a body like that. She was still prey for pimples, and several smears of pink makeup marked the scenes of the latest attacks. Her hair was black and fell in a tangle past her shoulders, front and back, the longer strands flirting with the deep neckline of her floral-print, showtime summer dress.

She sat the cup on the arm of the couch. "Most like it hot. You must've bit a nerve in your mouth when you was drunk or something. It's just the other way about with you."

"I like to drink it, darlin' girl, not sip it. Not slurp around at it like my teeth was loose and I can't wander too far from the front porch rocker no more."

"Some folks put ice in it. Like a Coke."

"No kiddin'," Jewel said. "I think I've heard of that. Must've saw it on Walter Cronkite."

Suze's shoulders slumped beyond their normal depth. "You shouldn't make fun of me," she said. "Everybody makes fun of me."

"Hmm," Jewel grunted, raising the cup of coffee and draining it in one long pull. But then he remembered Duncan.

"You got the time?" he asked.

Suze smirked at him, her hands on her hips in the pose of a barn-dance coquette. "You got the nerve, hillbilly?"

"You got to ask that?" Jewel said with a smile. He patted his hair, still smiling. "Nobody's got to ask that. But could be I ain't got the time."

"It's about quarter past eight."

Jewel glanced out to the street where the buildings blocked what was left of the sun, giving an extra dose of gloom to the scene.

"That about makes it time," he said as he walked to the dresser that buttressed the far wall. He opened the top drawer and raised a short, evil-looking knife with a bumble-bee-striped handle and stuck it, sheath and all, into his rear pocket. "You know my business?"

"It's got to do with Duncan, I would guess."

"Well, you can't know that. Forget you do. It's not something you can know."

He started dealing through the few rags in the drawer until he came to a red towel that was wadded in a ball. When the towel was unwadded he lifted a .32 Beretta from it and holstered it inside his waistband. He pulled the tails of his shirt out and let them dangle.

"Oh, fudge," Suze said. "I see it's still going to be *that* kind of business."

Jewel shrugged, then started toward the door.

"It's still *that* kind of life, darlin' girl."

★   ★   ★

Jewel was to wait for Duncan on the corner of Napoleon and Voltaire, so he stepped into the Chalk & Stroke and bought a couple of bags of Kitty Clover potato chips and a six-pack of tall-boys. He would, given the choice, rather eat potato chips than steak, and since there was rarely such a choice to ponder, he pretty well lived on Kitty Clover.

He stood inside a phone booth and opened a beer, then began to eat the chips. The street was now awake, busy with people going toward taverns and others staggering home, all of whom avoided the younger denizens, bare-chested in satin jackets, who kicked down the streets waiting for something funny to happen at which they could snort and guffaw, or for something mean to pop up so they could prove meaner and stomp it down. If boredom gave way only to more boredom then, perhaps, they would take it upon themselves to borrow something shiny and custom upholstered in which to escape that chronic state.

No one paid any attention to Jewel Cobb.

Duncan was just on time. He pulled up in a long blue Mercury that was past its prime but still flashy enough for a Willow Creek boy to take horn-honking pride in.

Jewel slid in on the passenger's side.

"Hey, cousin Dunc," Jewel said with a nod. "Nice wheels."

Duncan regarded his younger cousin with some disdain. The boy was country tough, but hillbilly tacky. That shirt was an open admission to cops, citizens, and marks—watch out, I'm trouble.

"You settled right in the middle of it," Duncan said as he pulled into traffic, heading north on the cobblestone street. "Frogtown."

"The price is right."

Duncan was in his late twenties with a neatly molded pot belly and thick, strong arms. There was a placid quality about his pale, sagging features that the ambitious glint of his green eyes served to counterpoint. His clothes were simple: open-necked blue knit shirt, a cream sports jacket, and gray slacks. His wheat-straw hair was cut short but not freakishly so. By careful design there was very little that would cause him to be remembered in a crowd of three or more.

"It's called Frogtown," Duncan said, "because it was French folks who settled it. Run into lots of Frogs hereabouts."

Jewel had gorged on the chips and swallowed most of the beer. He finished it, stuffed the empty under the seat, and opened another.

"Frogs, huh? Why do they call 'em Frogs?"

"I can't say I know. They seem to like water, swamps, and such like. I don't know. It's a saying, like coon, you see? Maybe like redneck." He caught Jewel's eye. "You don't call 'em Frogs to their face, though. If you ain't one, too. You see, it's not as bad as nigger, but it's not good."

"Huh," Jewel said. "I'm always learnin'."

As they traveled, they left the close-in, crowded jumble of buildings and entered an area that was more spacious but no less grim. The river was in sight, a huge presence to the east, and trailers and wooden houses on stilts were flopped as near to the water as possible. They had come only four blocks but it could have been miles.

"This looks like Willow Creek, only with water instead of rocks," Jewel said.

"Only it ain't. And the people in them places ain't Willow Creek kind of folks."

They passed under a railroad bridge as the light faded into dark. Once beyond the bridge Duncan began to count the slim dirt lanes. At the third he turned toward the water. On either side of the lane was a tangled, belching, smelly swamp. Soon a yellow light was seen, then another light that bounced on the water from a dock.

"That's it," Duncan said. He turned off the car and headlights, then faced Jewel. "Now leave the beer here. Pete Ledoux, he's a grown man and won't go for that joyriding style of yours. If I had to bet, that's what I'd bet, anyway."

"Fuck 'im, then."

"I'd rather camp under the outhouse than fuck with Pete Ledoux, boy. You keep that attitude, Jewel. You keep it." Duncan sighed, a troubled man. "If you wasn't kin I'd deal you out right now."

"I need the dough, that's all."

"Then act like you deserve the chance to get it. Opportunity's knockin' on your thick skull, boy. This ain't the annual Willow Creek–Mountain Grove dustup, Jewel. We're fixin' to tree a fella and tack his hide on the side of the barn. There's folks that won't like that, don't you know? You can't be lousin' it up."

"Yeah," Jewel said. His jaw jutted defiantly, as if this were a commonplace enterprise for him. "Don't be tellin' me what's wrong with me, Dunc. You know and I know why I'm in on this."

"Run that by me again."

"'Cause I shoot to hurt and I come to shoot, that's why."

Duncan stared at Jewel, then smiled proudly.

"You ain't smart, Jewel, but I can't say as you're dumb, neither." He opened the car door. "Let's go."

Ledoux's house was a sturdy, winterized weekender's cottage bordered by screened-in porches. From the rear door a planked walkway curved down to the dock about fifty feet away.

Duncan knocked on the door.

A woman with a pretty face that had begun to bloat and tousled blond hair swung the door open, revealing a porch overrun by fishing poles, milk cartons, and sporting magazines. She had the expression of one who is intent on being constantly disappointed, and held a can of beer in her hand. She looked at Duncan, then Jewel.

"My word," she said. "We don't often get encyclopedia salesmen out here."

"I expect not," Duncan said. "I've come to see Pete."

"I wouldn't've bought none anyway, just cut out a few of the pictures." The woman gestured with her head, snapping it toward the light that shone on the water. "Saint Francis of the Marais du Croche is down there rappin' with the fishes."

Duncan smiled at her. She was a drinker with good looks picking up speed downhill, which was his usual game, but she was Pete's woman.

"Thanks."

"You fellas want a beer, or anything?"

"No thanks."

"That's good, 'cause we ain't got enough to share, anyhow," she said as she closed the door.

The walkway swayed underfoot as they crossed it to the dock. The needle of light was playing on the water, illuminating a great bog of murk and brackish water.

"Say, Pete," Duncan called. "I got my cousin, Jewel, here to meet you."

"Hiya," Pete said, then stuck the beam of light in Jewel's face.

Jewel tried to screen his eyes, then turned his face away.

"Say, hey, man! You learn that trick in the cops, or what?"

Pete aimed the light between himself and Duncan.

"Nasty lookin' pup, ain't he?" Pete said.

These fellas aren't handing me much respect, Jewel thought. He'd whipped two men at a time who were bigger than them before. That time in Memphis there'd been three bargemen on a spree and he'd come out of that one pretty good, too, once his tongue had been stitched back together.

"I ain't a pup," Jewel said. He raised his shirttails and exposed the handle of the pistol. "See that there? That's what says I ain't. It can say it six times, too."

Ledoux exchanged glum glances with Duncan. He then walked to a pillar of the dock and flipped an unseen switch. Lights lit up the dock and the men. Ledoux motioned for the others to follow him as he ambled to the edge of the dock.

"I got some catfish to tend to," Ledoux said. He was a short man, well into middle age but still supple and quick. His skin was tanned to match mud, and his brown hair had fingers of gray running through it. He bent to one knee and reached over the edge of the dock to the water. When he stood he pulled a stringer of channel cat and bullhead up. The fish made a weighty, wet splat when he tossed them onto a wooden bench beneath the brightest light.

Without looking away from the fish, he asked Jewel, "You know what you're supposed to do?"

"Sort of. I'm gonna cool out some kind of a porn king."

Ledoux slowly swiveled to face Duncan. When their eyes met he nodded once, then grinned snidely, as if some little-believed prediction of his had come true.

Duncan lowered his eyes, inspecting the toe of his shoe. "He ain't king of his own cock, Jewel. He just owns a theater."

Ledoux spat on the dock near Duncan's feet. "What you're supposed to do, which you 'sort of' know, is kill a nigger and get away with it. 'Sort of' gettin' away with it used to be good enough, back in '37 or so, but the Kennedys and ol' Johnson done shit in that bowl of soup. So, you see, mon ami, 'sort of' wasn't the way I'd planned it to be."

"I went over it with him," Duncan said. "He's game. More than game, ain't you, Jewel?"

"I'm a Cobb, ain't I?" Jewel replied with tremulous bravado.

Ledoux had taken the fish off the stringer and now, one by one, he began to drive nails through their heads, tacking them to the bench. There were a few odd grunts from the fish, which Ledoux seemed to echo. He then raised a knife and inserted the tip beneath the tail fin of each, and, with short, gentle strokes, gutted them. The guts drooped over the side of the bench and hung toward the deck.

Ledoux looked up from his work. "I like fish," he said.

Jewel's head bobbed. "No shit," he said.

Duncan gave Jewel a rough shove. "Tell him what you're going to do, boy! You can come up tough on your own time, but now you're making *me* look bad, hear?"

After straightening himself, as if considering revolt, Jewel relaxed slightly.

"Right," he said. Reality seemed to hug his thoughts and he smiled at the comfort of the embrace. "Sure. This is business. I'm *all* business."

Ledoux was bent over the fish, sticking his hands into their body cavities and ripping out the clinging organs.

"Now you're talkin', mon ami," he said as he flipped a handful that splashed in the darkness beyond the arc of light.

"Duncan told me everything. About twenty-seven times, at least. I got it down, man."

"It really ain't all that involved," Duncan said. "Point it and go boom. He ought to have it down."

"That's very comforting," Ledoux said. "That is very comforting. I'll have that to cherish, for about a quarter-to-life over in Jeff City, there. 'Point it and go boom.' It's good to know we got us such a simple murder, 'cause I can name eight or ten other fellas I know who must've drew tougher jobs. Mon Dieu, if they only saw it as clear as you do, they wouldn't be pressin' boxer shorts for the state."

"Geez, Pete," Duncan said, his voice flat, with only his lips moving. "You don't have to make a speech out of it. You got concerns, then you mention 'em."

"Why, thank you," Ledoux replied, as if honored by some rare privilege. "I do believe I have a concern or two, there, Judge Cobb." He pointed a finger at Jewel. "For instance, does he know this deal cold?"

"No," Jewel said, and swaggered forward. "Look at my ears, buddy. They're too small to be on a dog, see? That means I can talk for myself. And now you bring it up, there is one important thing I don't know cold." He jabbed a finger at Ledoux's chest. "What'm I gettin' exactly? Duncan here, cousin Dunc, he's been a little confusin' with the numbers."

"Well," Ledoux said, "this is beginnin' to make some sense. You're just getting started with us. Fifteen hundred bucks is what you get. That's about ten times what I got when I decided to grow up. It'll all be hidden on the Micheaux Construction payroll."

"I won't do any of that kind of work, though," Jewel said. "I didn't bus up here to strain and sweat for no paycheck."

"This *kid,*" Ledoux said, tapping a finger to his temple, "he's really ready for a step up from stealin' eggs from chickens?"

Duncan shrugged, impassive and bored. Ledoux turned back to Jewel.

"You. You're a tough kid, right, mon ami? I'm just curious about the generation gap, you know, that sort of thing. I was wonderin' — what've you ever *done?*"

"Nothin' that ain't strictly my own business, that's what. Mainly."

After nodding, Ledoux returned to the task of cleaning the fish.

Duncan walked over and stood next to Jewel, then began to jab him in the short ribs with his finger. Jewel walked away.

"Okay," Ledoux said. "I've got instincts that it don't pay to fight. You could be right for us, Cobb. Everybody deserves a chance, you know." Ledoux sat on a bloodless section of the bench. "Now the reason you get a payroll check is so we can all run fakes on the taxman, see? He's worse than any cop you ever saw. Any *six* cops you ever saw. I ever get got, it's goin' to be some Kraut with an addin' machine, not some Mick with a badge who does it to me."

Slowly, Jewel nodded. He'd seen that on TV. IRS. Capone, seems like they did it to him. And most of the other big boys went up when their math became criminally inaccurate.

"That's smart," Jewel said, finally. The sophistication of such financial transactions increased his attraction to this line of work.

"I want to tell you one thing first," Ledoux said. He picked up a squat flashlight and began to shine it across the water. The outlines of trees, tips of floating logs, undulations of green scum that roiled on the water's surface, and phantom eye reflections were caught in the beam. "That there—you know what it is?"

"I just hit town," Jewel said. "I ain't learned every backwater."

"That's a hell of a backwater, mon ami. It's the Marais du Croche. That means 'Crooked Swamp' in the tongue. It's a big, endless black bugger, too. Full of sinkholes and slitherin' things and sloughs that go in circles, and every part of it looks so much like every other part of it that most folks, they can't remember which is which, or which way is out, or nothin'. So they get confused. Many times they get confused unto death, mon ami, then in the spring they wash down and land at the dam, bone by bone."

"I been in woods before, with big trees and hooty owls and all that shit, man."

"Not like that." Ledoux flashed the light high and low, slowly displaying a great meanness of which he had somehow grown fond. "You know who knows their way around over there, Cobb?"

Jewel looked at Duncan, then at Ledoux's weathered face.

"I'm goin' to guess *you*."

"Très bien." Ledoux shone the light on Jewel once more. "Me and two or three other old Frogtown boys. That's it. You get in there, no one else can help you but them and me, and they don't know you."

Jewel folded his arms across his chest, then rocked back on his heels and squinted into the light.

"I ain't got no plans to go in there."

"I know. And as long as you do right, I won't ever have to *put* you in there, either. Understand what I'm sayin'?"

Jewel nodded solemnly but did not reply.

"So you're goin' to cool that coon, Crane, on Seventh outside of his theater. Tomorrow afternoon, am I right?"

"As rain and mother-love," Jewel replied.

"This is our special secret, right, Jewel?" Duncan said. "That juggy gal of yours ain't clued in, is she?"

"Are you kiddin'? You got to be kiddin'."

Duncan stepped up and heartily slapped Jewel on the back.

"Oh, yeah, now we're in business. What say you run up to the car and break out that beer you been savin', cuz? We'll cement this deal."

"That's a hell of a notion," Jewel said, and started up the wooden walkway to the car.

Duncan and Ledoux watched him. When the overhead light in the Mercury went on, Ledoux nudged Duncan.

"Him bein' your cousin—that a problem for you?"

"No," Duncan replied, shaking his head. "He's an asshole."

Ledoux began to pile the skinned fish in order to carry them to the house.

"Wonderful," he said. "We've got to be on time and I think he might be one peckerwood who's just barely dumb enough to pull the trigger when we want him to."

"When it comes to dumb, bet on him," Duncan said, as he watched Jewel coming back down the walkway. "If you had a Sears catalogue of dummies you couldn't order a better one. I mean, the punk's just perfect for us."

2

Detective Rene Shade, dressed casually in a black T-shirt and jeans, sat on a stool in the corner of the room and contemplated the patrons of Tip's Catfish Bar. He saw red-faced men with untamed cigarettes bucking their hands through the air; squinty-eyed men who huddled in booths and had professional flinches that drew their heads to the side; white-haired men with fists as gnarled as ancient roots and with expressions mutely wise and unafraid. Few women and no squeamish men gathered here.

Shade's brother owned the bar, and this, too, was on his mind. It had sometimes been an embarrassment at Headquarters for Shade, having to admit that, yes, the Tip Shade who ran the Catfish Bar and welcomed felons, petty thieves, and their apprentices was his older brother. He had tried to explain that the bar was the center of the neighborhood in which they had grown up, and the regulars were neighbors first and threats to society second. It was more personal, not at all clear-cut, where the line could, or even should, be drawn. Such explanations were regarded as suspiciously metaphysical by his superiors. It did not help that his father, the regionally notorious John X. Shade, was prominent in what he insisted upon calling sporting circles, and others, with equal insistence, termed the gambling fraternity.

The bar was built of rough wood on a mound overlooking the river. Oak beams pressed the roof above their heads, while fishnets with cork floaters, a mystifyingly fey decorating touch, dripped down between the beams. The chairs and tables were all wooden, and squeaked with use. There were athletic prints on the walls and photos of local champions. A large mural of Tip hung behind the bar. In it he was poised to hurl his two hundred and thirty some pounds into a spider-legged half-back; holding an intercepted ball aloft in the end zone; and snarling down at a shell-shocked fullback whom he'd crumbled on the one yard line. There was a team picture of the Saint Bruno Pirates, the local minor league baseball team, and a small picture of Eldon Berenger, who'd played one season of basketball in the Continental League. There were several boxers represented. Just to the rear of one stout oak pillar there was a small photo of Rene Shade, gloved hands held above his head as he celebrated a victory in the early, hopeful days of his former career. Near the entrance there was a larger picture of Shade, one taken near the end of the night that the Light-Heavy Champ, Foster Broome, had chased him with a posse of left jabs until his face split up and retreated in different directions to elude pursuit. Shade could not avoid looking at this reminder of his almost glorious past, but every time he did so his stomach tightened up. The picture was one of Tip's attempts at rugged good humor, but Shade rarely managed to smile at it.

As Shade watched, Tip poured a double shot of bourbon and pulled a draw for a lanky hustler named Pavelich, who'd once bowled the best game in town, but now regularly bowled the second best for better side money. Tip shoved him his change, then walked down to Shade's end of the bar.

"Another rum, li'l blood?" Tip asked in his slow but somehow belligerent voice.

"But of course. Put it on your bill."

Tip smiled and raised a bottle of Jamaican dark and poured a healthy dollop into Shade's glass.

"Free rum is one thing, drivin' my business away would be another. You lookin' for somebody, or just lonesome to mix with your peers?"

"Have I ever busted anybody in here?"

"Thankfully, no. Or I'd have to bust you."

There was more in that comment than sibling rivalry, Shade thought.

Tip always had acted as if he could punish Shade whenever there was a need to. Shade conceded that it could be true. At one seventy, he was outweighed by about sixty pounds, had an advantage in speed but none in unrefereed experience, and knew that their battle hearts were of equal girth.

Shade smiled and nodded.

"I haven't busted any of this crowd, but I could easy enough." He turned on his chair to view more of the room. "I could make six busts on my way to the pisser."

"And lose the goodwill of your neighbors and childhood playmates, li'l blood."

"I could probably pop you, Tip, if I spent ten or twelve minutes in the effort."

Tip began to nod, then shook his head. "I could be eight kinds of crooked, there, piglet, but I ain't never been no kind of dumb."

Shade wondered, for perhaps the thousandth time, what his older brother might've become had his knees held out for more than two memorable seasons of college ball.

"Genes will tell," Shade said.

"What's that mean?"

"Ah, I can't be sure, but I'd be a more confident man if I was."

Tip moved down the bar to tend to a group of men who'd begun shaking their empty mugs at him.

Shade returned to his contemplation of the clientele. He'd known many of them since his childhood, had teamed with them in sandlot games of every sort, sparred with them beneath the elms of Frechette Park on cool summer mornings, and clustered with them at Catholic Church dances where they shared whiskey cleverly secreted in Coke bottles. He'd fought them in the crowded-alley scraps of youth that still seemed more important than those of adulthood, run errands for the older men, and watched as their daughters were happily married off to outsiders, returning to Frogtown only for very short holidays and funerals.

A compact hand nudged him on the shoulder, rousing him from a nostalgia he wasn't sure he believed in.

"Rene. Don't see you much these days. What're you up to tonight?"

It was Wendell Piroque, a keg-shaped teamster who had probably steered more blackjacks than trucks. Shade had known him since grade school, when Piroque had hung out at his mother's poolroom.

"Just drinkin' on Tip."

"Lucky for you," Piroque said, resting on the next stool. "A good brother to have, a bartender is." Piroque had a sweet, round face, with dark features, and his smile was all innocence. "And your mother runs a poolroom. Must be the Irish half of you, gives you that luck."

"Must be. There are no famous sayings about Frogs having it."

"Not in this town, anyhow," Piroque said as he tapped a finger on the bar surface. He suddenly pointed toward the pool table at the rear of the room, a table that was mysteriously underused. "Shoot a game?"

"You got the table roll figured or something?"

"Would I do that to you?" Piroque asked in mock horror.

"You'd do it to yourself, I think, if you could be two chumps at once."

Shade led the way through the maze of tables, nodding at those who nodded at him, saying hello twice, and being stared down once.

"Nine ball?" Piroque asked when they reached the table.

"If you insist," Shade said. "But you might as well just hand me your cash."

Piroque was bent over the green felt, his tongue peeking from the side of his mouth, studiously racking the balls.

"I think different," he said.

"That's good," Shade said. He was a broad-shouldered, dark-skinned, chronically fit man, not youthful but still young, and his blue eyes lit up with the prospect of competition. "That's what keeps me interested enough to hang on to the planet."

The two uniformed patrolmen entered the Catfish at a few minutes past 1 A.M. The larger of the two was a black man who loomed over his squat partner. As they approached the bar the squalling conversations dropped to a whisper, then silence. The patrolmen attempted to meet the glares of the patrons to show command of the situation, but found that two pairs of eyes cannot upstage thirty, and that their erect postures and imitative confidence were seen as comic acting rather than cool control.

The bartender stood with his arms folded, his upper lip hidden by his lower in a warning pout.

"Hey, Shade," the squat patrolman said. "Your brother here?"

Tip sneered, then swung his head upward, indicating the back of the room.

"There he is," the black patrolman said. "At the pool table."

Shade leaned on his cue as he watched the blue aliens approach. He scanned the layout on the table, then turned to meet them. Before they could speak, he said, "One more inning and I got it bagged."

The smaller patrolman shook his head. "Captain Bauer says now."

Piroque overapplied English and threw off an attempted combo of the six-nine. He straightened, scraped chalk on the cue tip, and smiled at Shade.

"You could forfeit," he said. "If duty calls."

"No," Shade said. He stepped up to the table, calculated the odds on his running out, then bent over to shoot. With his left arm bulging lean muscles like twisted brown taffy he poised to stroke. "Six ball," he said, and sank it, the high left on the cue ball carrying it to the far rail.

"Captain's waitin'," the short beat man said. "What's it goin' to cost you?"

"Nothing," Shade said. He had a hope, and it involved a bank shot combination, for a run-out was stymied by the far-flung eight ball. "Seven-nine. In the corner, just in case I make it I'll have witnesses." He positioned himself for the shot, stroked the cue ball dead on, with no English, and watched as the seven ball banked across the table and did just what it was meant to do — kick the nine ball gently into the pocket.

He turned to Piroque, whose hand was already in his wallet.

"Save it, Wendell. Get your kid a model airplane."

"Uh-uh," Piroque said, shaking his head. "When you come up short, you got to shell out." He handed Shade a five-dollar bill without ceremony. "You shoot decent stick, Shade. I'll give you that. But I got to tell you, you still ain't good enough to hold your old man's chalk, you know?"

"Thanks, Wendell," Shade said.

"Detective," the talkative patrolman said, his foot leaving the ground in a weak stomp of insistence. "It shouldn't be takin' us this long."

Shade followed the uniforms toward the door, conscious of the near silence, and the truculent presence of Tip's eyes upon him. At the bar Tip beckoned to him by crooking a finger.

"Yeah?" Shade said.

Tip leaned toward him, then did a threatening flex of his massive arms. "Keep your new friends out of here." Tip's blunt-featured, pock-marked face was expressionless, but his brown eyes were flat with anger. "You can play with them in the street, but not in the house, understand?"

"Why don't you bounce them?"

Tip glared at Shade. "You owe me for the rum now, smart-ass," he said, rearing back. "It decided not to be free."

"I got business," Shade said and walked toward the door.

Tip came around the bar like it was a pudgy high school lineman and Shade a passing quarterback. The two patrolmen dropped their fingers onto the handles of their street-issue pacifiers. They looked around nervously as the brothers confronted each other.

"Stay the fuck out of here if you're goin' to cause me trouble," Tip said. He clenched his fist and waved it vaguely in Shade's direction. "I told you, you cost me business and I'll drop-kick your ass, brother or not."

After scraping his fingers beneath his chin, an ancient taunt, Shade said, "When you feel froggy, start jumping, bro."

Tip opened his mouth to retort, then looked at the uniforms and took a backward step. He nodded several times.

"Been a pleasure seein' you, Rene. Drop me a postcard along about Armageddon, hear?"

Shade turned away, then paused before the large, prominent picture of himself in a bruised and humbled state.

"Next time I come callin', Tip, it'd be good if that was gone."

"Naw. It's my favorite," Tip said in a strained whisper. "'Cause it's you to a tee, li'l blood. It's you to a tee."

Shade looked back at the picture and studied it complacently. Finally he shrugged and threw up his hands. "It's everybody once in a while," he said, then walked out the door.

Some of the blood had splattered the television set. Detective How Blanchette craned his neck over the expensive RCA and looked on the table behind it. There were flecks of gray and chunks of white visible in the smears of red.

"Looks like he was turnin' the channel or somethin', is what would be my guess," he said. "If I was paid for guessin' I'd be done."

The patrolman to whom he'd spoken did not respond. He was transfixed by the crumpled body of a middle-aged black man, a man who'd been ruined by the sudden excavation of the back of his head.

"You spot any clues in the body language, there, Cooper?" Blanchette asked. Blanchette was sandy-haired and fat, and he insisted on wearing, at almost all times, a black leather trench coat that he believed slimmed his image by twenty pounds. "Maybe Rankin died in the shape of a letter of the alphabet to tip us off, huh? That look like an 'm' or a 'z' to you?" Cooper looked away. "Could be, though, that he was usin' deaf-talk sign language, huh, Cooper? All the politicians use it now."

Cooper finally met Blanchette's eyes.

"You got a soft heart, How," Cooper said. "Almost squishy." Cooper held his hands up, then began to wander about the room. It was nicely decorated, a den with ornate lamps and polished mahogany furniture. He shook his head. "I knew this man. I was on his stinkin' bodyguard detail, you know, back when that busin' thing got nasty." He paused with his back to the body. "He treated me pretty fuckin' decent. Not like a butler who carries a gun, you know. Fuckin' decent."

Blanchette nodded, apparently in sympathy. "Somebody didn't think him so decent, though, is what I would think. What with my nine years' experience and all, I'd have to say that could be a fact. I'd say you should get out your black notebook, there, the one full of blank pages, and start one of 'em out with—Alvin Rankin, city councilman, was whacked in the head by someone who didn't think he was so fuckin' decent."

"I'll be outside," Cooper said. "You miserable tub of guts."

Blanchette held up a hand to halt him.

"That'll be Detective Sergeant miserable-tub-of-guts to you, there, patrolman."

"Check," Cooper said and went outside.

Blanchette surveyed the room, his dark eyes taking in the scene, his thick brows flexing as he concentrated. The room was a reluctant witness. For a crime scene, which it indisputably was, it set new levels of tidiness. Other than the blood and body fallout necessary to qualify it, Blanchette thought, the place could win a Good Housekeeping Seal for most meticulous murder site. The only thing out of place besides the wrecked remains of Alvin Rankin was the *TV Guide* that had landed about two feet to the right of Rankin's outstretched hand.

As Blanchette speculated on the possibilities offered by the slim clues on the scene, the door from the main room opened and Captain Karl Bauer entered the den, followed closely by a pack of crime specialty men.

Bauer was a large, square man with hair the color of carp scales, still loyally fashioned into a flattop. He had stern features, and knobby fists, but many of his subordinates believed him to be an incompetent police officer. His talent as a political infighter, however, was undeniable, and he was a truly gifted backslapper.

Captain Bauer walked past Blanchette and stood with his back to him.

"The wife and the girl are across the street, at 605. Neighbors named Wilkes. Give them time to have a shot of whiskey or some coffee, then get over there."

"Right," Blanchette said. "She say anything else?"

"I wouldn't keep it a secret if she did, Detective. She came home from seeing *Raiders of the Lost Ark* with the girl—" Bauer flipped through his notepad to find the daughter's name. "Janetha, aged seventeen. It was about eleven forty-five or so." Bauer closed the notepad and put it in his breast pocket. "End of dialogue."

"I think maybe his wallet is gone," Blanchette said. "It ain't layin' around nowhere."

"His wallet? You break in a house, kill a city councilman with a Mercedes and a stash of chink vases, and you just take his wallet? That make sense to you? I mean, the rest of the house hasn't even been walked through, from the looks of it."

"Well," Blanchette said. "Guys who ain't used to splatterin' people's brains, they do funny things when it finally happens, sir. The French have a word for it, but I don't know it, so I call it freakin' out."

"That's one possibility," Bauer said. He turned toward the other officers in the room and held both hands pointed at them, then began to click his fingers. "You guys get busy. Fariello, get plenty of shots," he said to the photographer. Bauer had watched this scene in many movies and directed the rest of the crime squad action in a Rich Little–type whirl of unconscious imitation.

Blanchette shook his head as he watched his captain. He nodded his treble-chinned moon face whenever he noted obvious influences on Bauer's behavior. That's Broderick Crawford, there. Oh, that bark's familiar, there's more than a hint of Bogart in it. That steely glare, seems like Matt Dillon traded on it for a fortune in reruns. Where's Kojak?

Finally Bauer returned to Blanchette.

"Where's Shade?" he asked.

"I'm not on Shade watch this week, Captain."

Bauer stared down at him. "You know, Blanchette, for a short guy you're awful fat—anybody ever tell you that?"

"No person now living, sir. A gentleman wouldn't say it anyway, I know that from reading the 'Dear Abby' in the paper."

"So, you're a literate man, Blanchette. Have another doughnut and you'll be two of them." Bauer started toward the door, then stopped. "I'm going over to the mayor's house. He'll want to be kept informed by the tick-tock on this. When Shade manages to get here you and him talk to the wife and girl, then meet me on Second Street."

"Sure, Captain."

In the front room, between the den and the main door, was a large, overstuffed, underused leather chair. Blanchette sank into it, then lit a cigar and waited for Shade. As he smoked he thought about Alvin Rankin. About forty-four, forty-five, a product of Pan Fry, Saint Bruno's historically black section; smart and tough, blessed with the rare talent to know who to be tough to and who to outsmart; a coming power of the Democratic Party, with increasing clout as Pan Fry residents began to actually vote, rather than put X's where told to and stay quiet the rest of the decade. Alvin Rankin could have been, Blanchette knew, the first black mayor of Saint Bruno. That was motive number one in flashing neon. The banner of social advancement did not wave at the head of a unanimous throng, and Saint Bruno was, and had long been, a city of tenacious suspicions and disparate convictions. Saint Brunians were imbued with an unfriendly blend of ancestral pride, selfish toughness, and purposeful ignorance that served to produce succeeding generations of only slightly less narrow views than the generation that had laid the bricks that still paved the streets.

Blanchette stared toward the room in which Rankin's future had been diverted. Yes, he could've made it, all right, Blanchette thought. Not with his next breath or two, but by the time he was fifty, fifty-five. It was up to someone else now.

The end of his cigar had a thumb of ash on it, so Blanchette flicked it on the rug, then rubbed it in with his foot. He looked around the room, feeling slightly outclassed by the numerous objets d'art and fashion that he could not even name. Yup, pretty swell place for a smoke who'd never moved away to sing in falsetto or shoot balls through hoops. Hard hustle to get here in this hometown.

Shade walked in and Blanchette stood up.

"Glad you could make it, Shade. Didn't interrupt you in something important, I hope. You know, like a date with that slinky brunette you been seein', there—the one who moves like her back ain't got no bone. What's her address again?"

Shade moved past Blanchette without an answer and entered the den. At the sight of Rankin's body there was a tremor of weakness through his legs. It was unprofessional, he knew, but the shockingly limp postures of the dead were something he would never be hardened to. To make this one more meaningful was the fact that he'd known Rankin slightly.

"Didn't take any chances, did they?" he said.

"No," Blanchette said. He moved with a pugnacious waddle that had a limber grace to it, despite his build. "Two bullets—zip, zip—in the back of the head. That usually turns the trick."

"Who found him?"

"His wife and daughter. They're across the street."

"Bauer been here?"

"Just left. He went to hold the mayor's hand till the bogeyman leaves his dreams."

Shade examined the room, stepping around the photographer and the fingerprint boys.

"Damn clean piece of work," Shade said. His brown hair was long, combed back on top, and he brushed at it with his hand, a habit he had when distracted. "It must've been a friend, huh."

"That's a sickeningly liberal definition, there, Comrade Shade, for a guy pumps two bullets in the back of your head."

"It's point-blank," Shade said. "In his den, watching TV. That sounds like they knew each other to me. Knew each other well enough that old Alvin could relax with him. Or her."

Blanchette picked up the *TV Guide* and scrutinized it.

"I'd say he was changin' channels," he said. "He's only been dead an hour, maybe two. That'd be my guess, and from what the wife says it's pretty close."

Shade was listening with only a fraction of his attention. Alvin Rankin's house, his death, his limp body, all put Shade in mind of the Rankin he'd admired since youth. He was much younger than Rankin, but he clearly remembered the audacious teenaged Rankin who'd boldly made the trip down the ridge from Pan Fry toward the river and Frogtown. He'd come alone, and he'd had a proposition for the Frogtown boys: if we all quit pounding each other for sport we'd have less cops around and more spaciousness, you know, and then we could all take care of business. The Sadat of Pan Fry had had a vision and the nerve to give it a try. Shade had been impressed. Of course the older Frogtown boys had stomped the uppity smoke into a near sludge and dumped him from a Chevy at the foot of the Pan Fry hill, but ever since then Shade had paid attention to Rankin's career. He had been a man to watch, always.

Blanchette tapped Shade on the shoulder.

"Looks to me like he was turnin' from 'Nightline,' there. Must've got bored hearin' how the Israelis and PLO still won't kiss and make up, even though we're all anxious for the wedding party. So he gets up to turn to something else." Blanchette flicked a thumbnail on the guide. "I'd say he was switchin' over to forty-one for the late movie, which was *The Good Humor Man.*"

"Why do you figure that? Or is it just a chubby guy's intuition?"

Blanchette held his hands to the sky and shrugged.

"That's what I'd've turned to. I loved that movie when I was a kid. 'Niat pac levram.' Saw it at the old Fox, you know."

"I'd forgotten that, How," Shade said. "That was 1953, wasn't it? I remember I went to the library that day, instead."

"Yeah," Blanchette said. "You got that book, *101 Bad Jokes,* didn't you? Then you memorized it."

Shade began moving the furniture, searching for shell casings. He was getting the details of the room straight in his mind.

"There's no sign of forced entry?" he asked.

"None. Not unless a delinquent genie misted through the keyhole. No scratches on the locks, no crowbar work."

The intimacy of such crimes, the friend with a gun, a grudge, and the natural opportunities to get even, gave them an aspect of tragedy that other crimes lacked.

"It had to be someone he knew and trusted."

"Rene," Blanchette said, "he was black, but he was still a pol, you know. They play the game just like Irish ward bosses, or German congressmen, buddy. It's their job to be approachable by people with a vote. That's why they get the vote. All that does, far as I can see, is narrow it down to members of his own party."

"That," Shade said, "is a suggestion that will no doubt have the county chairman giggling shrilly into his brandy snifter."

With her hands spread on either side of herself, Mrs. Cleo Rankin leaned back on the couch, her head held high, and met Shade's gaze with unmistakable suspicion. Her hair was feathered at the sides and back, with a wave on top. Mocha skin was contrasted skillfully with red glossy lipstick and white jewelry.

"That's everything I told the captain. That's all there is."

"Did Janetha notice anything?" Shade asked.

"She came in behind me. I'm not certain that she even clearly saw — what I saw. She's upstairs now."

"Alvin carry a lot of cash on him?" Blanchette asked abruptly. "Was it a habit of his to flash a roll down at the corner store, places like that?"

Cleo's eyes darkened.

"After he'd parked his pink Cadillac, you mean?" she asked.

"I didn't mean that," Blanchette said with no apology in his tone. "But his wallet is gone. It's the only thing that is, too."

Cleo slid her glance from the detectives and studied the wall.

"I don't think he was killed for his wallet," she said.

"But we all know that even two hundred or so is pretty attractive around here," Shade said.

"You mean that's the price of murder here, amongst us degenerates of Pan Fry? That *is* what you mean?"

"Or Frogtown," Shade said. "Or a lot of other places with prettier names."

Cleo lifted her head and paused, then made a decision. She reached into her black leather handbag on the couch beside her. Her hand came out clutching a beige wallet.

"It was in his pocket," she said, and handed it to Shade.

"Mrs. Rankin," Shade said. "Did you tamper with anything else over there? It's important to know." Crimes were tough enough, Shade thought, without misdirections created by family members of the victim. "It would've been better if you'd left it there."

Blanchette stood next to Shade as they examined the wallet.

"Empty," Blanchette said. "The friend who nailed him was a triple threat—friend, killer, and thief."

"No," Cleo said. "Here." She pulled a wad of cash from her purse and extended it to Shade. "I took the money out of the wallet."

"Why did you do that?"

Cleo's face became taut, then bitter. "I didn't want the first police on the spot to have a big scuffle over who gets it, that's why!"

"Hunh," Shade grunted. He knew there were thieves in uniform, cops who picked up a few watches at suicide scenes, and a bottle or two of liquor that seemed to be handy. He'd seen it happen once, and that cop wouldn't be doing it again. "That was the first thing that occurred to you when you saw your man smeared on the floor?"

Cleo flinched. She picked a cigarette from the pack on the coffee table, and lit it with a heavy silver lighter. "Alvin was successful and I've always been thankful for that. You don't know how thankful. But because of his work we never left Pan Fry. And I've never forgotten that I grew up here, know what I mean?"

"Yes," Shade said. "I think maybe I do."

"When I was a girl we lived over here about four blocks, with a patch of mud for a yard and three families in the house. One day I was helping my grandmother make a mulberry cobbler. Her heart gave up while she was carrying the cobbler to the oven. She dropped, the cobbler dropped, and I went screaming for help. I was fifteen," she said with a rueful laugh. "Old enough to know better. But I didn't. Finally two policemen came. I still remember one of them named Burris. Ugly redhead, you know, with freckles like a disease. Well, they stood over grandmother and looked down at her awhile, then said, 'Auntie Sally, she ain't gonna finish that cobbler.' They started looking around the room. It was amazing that I was the only one home that day, and they walked around the house until they came to a big old carved clock we had. It'd been in the family for years. 'Go down to Lehman's Store and call the dinge ambulance,' Burris said. And I did, like that might help her somehow. When I got back the police were gone, grandmother was still laying where I'd left her, and there was a big empty spot where the clock used to be."

There was silence, then Blanchette shuffled his feet and raised himself from against the wall where he'd slouched.

"What a sad story," he said. "Where're the Kleenex?"

"See?" Cleo said, pointing at Blanchette. "I probably saved the peace by hiding that cash. He'd pocket it in a minute."

After hooking his thumbs in his belt loops, Blanchette rocked back on his heels and grimaced.

"It'd be my job to collect evidence," he said. "I think it's page 201, or in there. That's the manual, and I live by the book. Anybody can see that."

Cleo stood and smoothed her skirt. She walked to the door and held it open.

Shade stuffed the cash into the wallet, then followed her to the door.

"I really have nothing more to say," Cleo told them.

"Sorry for your tragedy, there," Blanchette said as he passed her and stepped out onto the lawn.

Blue and red lights twirled in the night, and white uniforms were moving a sheet-covered litter from out of the house across the street. Many voices filled the air, some terse, some entertained, and some angry. A crowd had gathered, but it was largely silent, listening to the officials on the scene.

"Get some rest," Shade said.

"You just do your job."

"You don't even have to tell us that, lady," Blanchette snapped.

"Hey," Cleo said. She held her hand out, palm up. "The cash, please."

Shade stroked his hair, and shook his head very slowly.

"You're not going to believe this," he said. "But it's evidence now."

Cleo stiffened and withdrew her hand.

"You are *so* right," she said.

The two detectives studied one another for a moment, then Blan-chette shrugged. Shade turned around and handed the wallet to Cleo.

"I don't have to do this," he said. "But I am."

Cleo accepted the wallet, then backed inside the doorway.

"You got some guilt," she said. "That's all it is."

Then she firmly swung the door closed.

3

SHADE AND Blanchette drove through the streets of Pan Fry, past small wooden homes that wobbled from the century or more of hard living that they'd seen, past three-story group housing where half the apartments had windows rotting out and the other half had neatly painted window boxes full of red and yellow flowers. Occasionally there was a minor leap upscale, and there would be a prim, crisply clean, color-coordinated house, with a carport and a chain-link fence.

"How," Shade said. "I've got to ask you this. Just what is the edge in rudeness? What advantage do you think it gives you?"

After an amused and amiable grunt, Blanchette said, "I could give a good reason. I know one. I mean, I could say it's because that stirs people up, makes them blurt things that make my job easier. I could tell you that one."

"But you won't."

"Not to you, here in the dark and all alone. I mean, the truth is, people bug the shit out of me half the time. Their bullshit bores me. I don't mind a little bullshit but, you know, you ought to astonish me with it, not nod me off." Blanchette looked at Shade and winked. "You know that. The ones that really get me are the ones who say, 'Society made me do it,'" Blanchette mimicked. "'I didn't have a bicycle when I was eight, Your Honor, so naturally I can't be blamed for hammerin' nails through the nun's head and rapin' the priest when I was twenty.' Shit, man, I grew up on dirt, and now I work for more of it."

"So nobody else can complain?"

"They can complain all they want, but I don't care."

"You have no sympathy for yourself," Shade said.

"I guess I'd need more college to see the smartness in that silliness, partner."

The street lights became brighter when they'd passed out of Pan Fry. Saint Bruno, with a population of two hundred thousand, was a city of many neighborhoods, Frogtown and Pan Fry being the largest and most fabled, and great numbing stretches of anonymous, bland, and nearly affluent subdivisions.

At Clay Street Blanchette turned east with rubber-squealing confidence and stomped the gas pedal since traffic was light. Pio's Italian Garden was still open, the red neon pizza in the window flashing an all-night invitation. Blanchette found his memories of repasts taken there to be varied but sufficient, and he suddenly wheeled into the parking lot.

He looked at Shade and said, "A man's got to eat. Hungry?"

"For chrissake no, man."

Blanchette climbed from the car, then leaned in the door.

"Tragedy saps your energy, Rene. Does mine anyhow. Think I'll grab a meatball grinder."

"You're a real man, How."

Blanchette nodded in agreement, then closed the door and went into Pio's.

For reasons that Shade found to be too tangled to articulate and too elusive to grasp, he liked How Blanchette. That put him in a very small club. But he'd known Blanchette too long, their Frogtown pasts were too interwoven for him not to forgive him, even for the unforgivable.

How had started life in Frogtown, about three alleys north of the Shades, as Arthur Blanchette. His father, the eccentric and locally cherished Leigh Blanchette, had provided material for exuberant, arm-spreading barroom tales, and closely huddled, snide, post-mass anecdotes that were recounted by several generations of Frogtowners, while sticking his son with a nickname that would become both his burden and his distinction.

When How was fifteen and still known as Arthur, the Dunne family, who lived behind them, had given their sons bows and arrows as birthday presents. Soon they had an informal archery range, sending arrows flying toward the bank of dirt that formed the boundary between the Dunne and Blanchette backyards. Pappy Dunne was an Irishman with fantasies of personal talent, enormous tabs at neighborhood taverns, and a job at Jerry's Seat Covers. He wanted his children to be better than he was, better at all things, so one evening after seriously exercising his elbow with several mugs of brew, he decided to show them the proper form of archery. He pulled an arrow back, and aimed it with bold innovation by timing his staggers, then letting it fly at the zenith of his lurch. The fateful arrow cleared the dirt mound by several feet, glided past the trees in the adjacent yard, and crashed through the window of the Blanchettes' TV room.

History would never get it straight, for it was an incident clouded with possibilities from the beginning. But Leigh Blanchette did come slowly, almost furtively, into the backyard with the catalyst arrow in his hand. He gave it back to the concerned Pappy Dunne, then reclined on the dirt. It had given him quite a start, he explained, that arrow tearing through the window toward his heart. Handball is all that saved him, he reported. It gave him the reflexes to twist just that necessary bit to the side and allow the razor-tipped vessel of death to pass. Pappy Dunne was drunk but comfortable in that state and mentioned that it was just a blunt-ended kid's arrow that might KO a bird if it caught it just right, but was no real threat to your average accidental target. "Gunsmoke," Pere Blanchette responded. Could it be more than coincidence that he was watching "Gunsmoke" at the exact time when an arrow, a danger that had never before occurred to him, came at him from ambush? That's not on on Tuesdays, Pappy Dunne said. No one was listening.

Within a week Pere Blanchette would explain that he had been mystically chosen by the wily spirits of warriors past and rained upon by arrows of such number and deadly force that all he could do was cross himself in wonder that he had survived. And the really inspirational thing was, he said, that he'd been watching television and it was just at the point where Tom Jeffords and Cochise shake hands in *Broken Arrow* when atavistic combat interceded in his life. Many bottles of red wine were garnered through the elaboration of his tale, and within a month Pere Blanchette had begun to haunt secondhand shops and the Goodwill, searching for Navajo rugs and plaster Indians.

As Shade could well recall, for he and his brothers, Tip and Francois, had been as guilty as any, Arthur Blanchette began to be greeted on the street by upraised palms and grunts of "How." He was portly even then, and his face would redden while his hands clenched. It was well known that if Arthur got you down and dropped the bomb of his weight upon you it would mean victory for him, but it was equally well known that any but the most feeble of leg could outdistance him, and the more talented local hand-on-meat percussionists could do snappy Buddy Rich drumrolls about his head and shoulders before his seeking fist could hit anything solid. So he could not stop the advent of the new name.

Soon he was known only as How, his real name filed away with his lackluster childhood. Eventually he grew to accept his sobriquet after he found out that most great athletes became famous by a name other than the one they were born under. Even presidents were like that, and now so was he.

Shade sat in the dark car, watching headlights glare by on Clay Street, chuckling as he remembered minor histories.

Blanchette returned with a grinder in white wax paper, the red sauce dripping down his overaggressive fingers. He slid behind the steering wheel, then had to retrieve a meatball that he'd popped loose. He found it under the seat and slipped it back into the bun.

"If you didn't wring it like it was a chicken's neck it wouldn't goo all over you, How."

Blanchette bit into the grinder, a large, passionate bite, and chewed it with his mouth writhing in pleasureful smacks.

"Then I might drop it," he said.

"You dropped it anyway."

"Hey, man—I paid for it."

Shade grunted. "That's the crucial fact," he said.

After taking another bite that was a meal in itself, Blanchette nodded.

"I always thought so," he said.

At the corner near the station Shade hopped out of the car and walked while Blanchette pulled around to the parking lot. There were several cars parked illegally in front of the station and a gaggle of murmuring forms were flocked around the main entrance. Shade bounced his fist off the hood of a gray sedan and gestured to the man inside.

"Park it somewhere else," Shade said.

The man inside yawned at Shade, then flipped his press badge at him.

"I'm from the *Daily Banner,*" he said, as if the words were armor.

Shade objected to his tone.

"They pay your tickets for you? Or are you too rich to care?"

"I'm here on a story, officer. You're a detective, right?"

Shade walked to the driver's window and leaned down. He thumped his fist against the car door and wondered why he had chosen this car to enforce the rules on.

"Mister," Shade said. "I'd hate to have to ticket a conduit to the people, but you might make me do it. See, I don't like being a prick, there, friend." A jab of a smile crossed Shade's face. "But it's my job."

The reporter nodded with resignation.

"We could go on with this dialogue for quite a while, couldn't we?"

"And then I'd ticket you."

"I get it," said the reporter, then turned the key in the ignition.

Shade started up the steps to the station.

There was a collection of newsmen, gore seekers, and minor officials gathered on the steps. A coolly appraising ballgame crowd, their hands jerked to swat the bugs that rendezvoused below the archaic globes of light mounted on either side of the entrance, redundant with hand-painted POLICE. The word of the murder was spreading fast and more people were arriving to loiter on the smooth stone steps that led up to the white rock building.

At the door a hangdog college boy reporter named Voigt, with a cowlick and too many Izod shirts, began to close in on Shade.

"Rene," Voigt said, sidling up with a hand-slapping attempt at familiarity. Then, "Detective Shade, I mean. Any comment on the Rankin murder?"

Shade slowed down, rubbing his hair, and shook his head.

"Who's the other guy from the *Banner*?" he asked, then nodded toward the street.

"What other guy?"

"The guy I just made move his car. Salt-and-pepper hair, skin like wilted lettuce."

Voigt grimaced with understanding.

"Braverman! Damn!" Voigt threw his notepad to the ground. As Shade walked on he heard Voigt say, "I'm fine for covering kids who spray-paint bridges, or old ladies who smack muggers with umbrellas, but when a *good* story comes along..."

In the entrails of the building, on a floor waxed to approximate ice, near a door marked MEN that was propped open by a wastebasket that dribbled tan wads of paper, Shade found himself feeling strangely dumb. He was beginning to absorb the implications of the murder of Alvin Rankin. There would be gentle prods from the mount on this case. Spurs to the butt, heat and leverage, necessary doors overtly slammed.

When he passed the duty desk Shade mumbled an unfocused glob of words to the man who occupied it. He was entering the battered green door of the squad room when his name was called.

"What?" he asked the duty officer.

"Blanchette with you?"

"My man is parking the car," Shade said, then started through the swinging green door.

"Hey, Shade. Hold it. The two of you are supposed to go directly to Mayor Crawford's place. Captain said to send you right over—no coffee, no squats in the library. Straight over."

"Did he tell you to call me Shade, too?"

"What? What's with you?"

Something in the man's tone had sounded like a hidden insult, but now Shade felt petty.

"Nothin'," he said. He looked down the long, glazed hall and smiled sardonically. "It's just that some aspects of my adult life disappoint the 'eternal boy' in me."

"Hunh," said the duty officer. "And here I was just thinkin' you were an asshole."

"Now that," Shade said as he stepped down the hall, "is another of the 'eternal boy's' major concerns, if you can believe it."

The officer sat down and swung his feet to the desktop.

"I probably could," he said, "but I think I'll pass."

Blanchette leaned on Shade's arm, a pantomime of crumbling health, and swatted at his thighs in a hit-and-run massage.

"Just left it," he wheezed. "Parked it by the pole, there, you know. The pole in the corner of the lot. I think it's the quarter-mile mark or something. Couldn't Bonehead have radioed?"

Shade pulled from beneath Blanchette's weight.

"They could've."

"We need a union, you ask me. The man thinks he can dispense with technology out of callous disregard for our health. Unions make 'em pay extra, they want to do that."

This time Shade insisted on driving. The streets had evolved through the nighttime cycle, from passageways to minor entertainments and basic sins, rampant with sad revelers and charades of Dubble Bubble bliss, into the emptiness of post-party, the asphalt tickled only by taxis, patrol cars, thieves, and swing-shift nurses. But now the people who gave the bulge to the city's withering bicep had begun to commute with their hands rubbing at the spot behind their eyeballs while splashing a Thermos of scalding joe toward the seat where the cup sat, heading for

McDonnell-Douglas, the Salter-Winn Shoe Factory, the dairy, and, again, the hospital. Daylight was only a vague promise in the east, and night had girded itself for a final stand before it welcomed defeat.

Shade picked his way through the drowsy traffic toward Hawthorne Hills, a stretch of mounds that pimpled the southern edge of town, giving refuge to most of the monied and many of the elected of Saint Bruno.

A large white house lounged on a hill like a favorite chair on an afterdeck, one leglike section curled over a ribbon of creek and the other leg crooked around a swath of oaks. Shade pulled into the drive.

Captain Bauer had parked next to the tennis court. Shade parked next to him, and he and Blanchette started toward the door.

He knew that Mayor Crawford had done many things before he entered politics, but having been smart enough to be born rich beyond fear seemed like the experience most relevant to his subsequent career.

Their knock was answered by the mayor. He was in slacks and a polo shirt with a cherry half-robe loosely belted. Fit and silver-haired, he looked like the aging stud of a prime-time soap.

"Come in, officers," he said. He was wearing his job-description grief, his solemnity working overtime. "How is Alvin's family?"

"They're taken care of," Shade said.

"They must be in shock," Crawford murmured with a shake of his head.

"No sir," Blanchette said. "The woman, Rankin, Cleto or whatever, is standin' up solid."

Crawford looked at Blanchette dully.

"Her name is Cleo," he said. "And she must certainly be shocked. You may not be, but I am as well."

"What would shock How," Shade said, "would turn thousands gray."

"I see," Crawford said. "How Blanchette, hunh. Leigh's boy—am I right?"

"Yes, sir. Before I got to be two hundred pounds of short-fused earthquake, I was Leigh's boy."

Crawford laughed, then rubbed his mouth with his hand.

"Must be getting a cold," he said. "I remember Leigh. Used to hear about him down at St. Peter's, about every third mass."

Blanchette grimaced, then put his hands in his pockets.

"I'm sure you did, sir."

"He had, well, sort of an interesting mind, your father."

"I really don't want to hear about it."

Crawford's hackles did not even rise, the self-restraint of the indigenous lord confronted by a sulky serf. He smiled indulgently.

"Of course, Blanchette," he said softly, "I can well imagine that you wouldn't want to share such fond memories of your own dear father."

After wincing, Blanchette looked away, toward the captain.

"I'm thinkin' somebody ought to be monitorin' the radio, there, Captain."

"Sure," Bauer said. He waved from where he sat, surrounded by the regal brocade of a chair that could sleep two in a pinch. "That might be wise."

"I'm sure of it," Blanchette said.

As he went out the door, Crawford said, "My pleasure."

When the door closed Shade said, "He's a good man."

"Damn near two of them is what I say," Bauer cut in.

"Haw, haw."

Shade looked about the room, trying to guess how many basketballs he could swap one of the ashtrays for. He wondered why he was there. No one seemed to want to ask him much.

"Shade," Bauer was saying. "This is Detective Rene Shade."

"Another familiar name," Crawford said.

"I don't think we've met."

"I don't recall it either." Crawford poured two cups of coffee from a silver service that occupied a shelf above the piano. He handed a cup to Shade. "Black?"

"That's fine."

"I have to sleep soon," Bauer said as he stared out the window at nothing.

When Shade had seated himself at the piano bench, disdaining the chairs that he did not feel qualified to touch his butt to with sufficient appreciation, Crawford leaned toward him.

"It's a terrible thing that has happened to Alvin, poor man. It's not as uncommon an occurrence as we'd all like it to be, I know," Crawford started, then waved his hand. "What am I saying? You know about that better than I, I'm sure." The involuntary spasms of the sorrowful gaze, the sympathetic condolence of the flimsy accolade, all were the memorized lines of a political actor. Mayor Crawford slipped into each with the ease of a pragmatic Olivier. "These burglars nowadays, Shade — what do you think, are they mostly junkies?"

"There are more burglars who are burglars than burglars who are junkies."

"That sounds very informed. It doesn't matter, I don't suppose. Some river-rat Frogtowner sees an apple pie and a Ming vase in somebody's window and decides he will by God kill for a pastry that size." Crawford looked at Bauer, who squirmed, then chortled professionally. "But this, this is one burglar I want caught in a hurry. And it wouldn't break my heart if it was before he sliced the pie and spooned the vanilla on top. Read me?"

An uncomfortable weight of recognition hit Shade.

"I don't think this was a burglary. I think it was murder, straight up and simple."

"What do you think, Captain Bauer?"

Bauer cocked his head and shrugged.

"It could've been a burglar and Rankin surprised him."

"Not from the evidence," Shade said.

"But it happens all the time, does it not?"

"Sure it does," Bauer said.

"No," Shade said. He leaned forward with his elbows on his knees. "Most murdered people get that way on purpose, not as some freak accident. I'm pretty sure it's no Russian roulette sort of thing either, where you put a pistol to the *back* of your head and squeeze off *two* rounds. Nothing was taken from Rankin's house, and he was whacked while peeking at the tube with someone. Most people, when they surprise a burglar, don't ask what channel they want to watch."

Crawford caught Bauer's eye and jerked a thumbs-up toward Shade.

"Good man, Captain," he said, then turned back to Shade. "So you think Alvin Rankin was killed by someone close to him?"

"Yes, sir."

"And since he was a city councilman, maybe it all has something to do with that."

"Seems possible."

"Maybe we could start a little parade, eh, Shade?" When a response was slow in coming the mayor began to stalk about the room, lightly fingering various fine knick-knacks, gesticulating silently. "Sure, we could lead the media and the hearts and minds of all of Saint Bruno on an entertaining little trip through the local loony bin we call politics. That way we could get some bold block type asking who all is involved in the assassination of the black heir apparent. Wouldn't that just be great?"

"It'd be the first parade I ever led, Mayor. Not my line."

Captain Bauer wagged a finger at Shade.

"You know what you sound like? You sound like you miss walkin' a beat, is what you sound like. We still have foot patrol way out at the Mall."

Crawford held his hands in front of himself, a calming gesture.

"No need for that," he said. "We can rise above that."

Crawford walked to the coffee service and poured himself another cup. He did not fill the cup, but gracefully streamed three-quarters of a full load into the thin white receptacle, reducing the risk of graceless spillage.

"I remember it now," Crawford said with an unconvincing snap of his fingers. "Frank Shade, over in the D.A.'s office—you two are related, aren't you?"

"Francois is my brother."

"That explains it. You're the fighter."

"Ex."

"Just so," Crawford said. "How could I forget—you cost me a hundred dollars once."

"Hunh? I don't recall that."

"When you fought that stringbean black out at the Armory, the one who hit like King Kong."

"Foster Broome."

"That's right. Foster Broome, from Trenton or Los Angeles, or somewhere like that."

Shade's estimation of the mayor's shrewdness was in danger of being revised by this sporting revelation. Was he fool enough to have bet him seriously, or just to show faith in a hometown boy?

Shade smiled.

"That's nice, Mayor. Not many backed me outside of Frogtown. And it was pride, not calculation, that had them behind me."

"Oh, I don't want to mislead you, Shade. I'm no knucklehead. I dropped a hundred betting you wouldn't last past the third, and you stumbled your way into, what was it, the fifth?"

"The seventh."

"Whatever. Broome was starting to slip." The mayor smirked as if his contempt was, for people like Shade, an attainment of merit. "You must've been pretty sad yourself, getting your big chance and only lasting seven rounds."

"Not really. It's six and a half rounds longer than most men could've lasted."

"I suppose that's true. It sounds right. But then most men aren't supposed to be professionals at that sort of thing, are they?"

"No, sir," Shade said. He stood and placed the coffee cup on the bench beside him. "But they all act like they *could be* if they just had the spare time, and the guts."

"And, of course, the neurotic need."

"Starting to sound a lot like politics, isn't it, sir?"

"What's the matter, Shade—don't you like politicians?"

"Sure I do. I ever get a mongrel that craps in the kitchen and won't fetch I'm going to name him Politician."

Captain Bauer stood with some effort, exhaling loudly, looking worried.

"I'm goin' to step in right here, gents, and call time."

Crawford raised a hand to halt him.

"Karl, when your assistance is required it will be requested." Crawford sat and raised his cup, his dark eyes above the rim holding steady on Shade. When the cup was returned to the saucer balanced on his knee, he said, "You're a half-assed detective and I'm mayor. We get into a public pissing contest, who do you think the judges will favor?"

"Whoever got them appointed might get a few breaks."

"Oh, come on, what's the big deal?" Bauer said. "So you don't see eye to eye immediately, so what? We can work this out." The big man pointed a thick finger at his subordinate. "Shade, save your salty tongue for family gatherings, hear me? And burglary is certainly a possibility to explain this, so what's it hurt to follow it?"

"Just the headlines."

"Is that so bad?" Crawford asked, suddenly smiling.

Shade, who knew a sinking boat when he was on it, kept silent.

"Mayor," Bauer went on, "Shade and Blanchette will do their jobs. When there's something solid we'll have to go with it, but for now this angle is as promising as any."

"Okay, okay," Crawford said as his finger distractedly picked at lint on his robe. "My only concern is to avoid a lot of crazy speculation on who might or might not've had cause to be a party to Alvin's murder. The I'll-pull-on-my-asshole-and-print-what-comes-out kind of rumor-mongering guesswork can tear a town apart. It can spawn a multitude of head-high dark clouds for the innocent to walk under, if you know what I mean. That would be vicious and unnecessary."

Shade watched Crawford's face, interpreting facial fluctuations, eyebrow histrionics, and hand signals for any accidental tip-off of sincerity, but found none. He was neither surprised nor terribly disappointed that the mayor's first concern was for his own welfare. That was understandable, even reassuring, for it was easier to deal with a venial professionalism that wore the traditional price tags of power, wealth, and position than with some sincere, but combustible, altruism that sought only total victory or martyrdom.

"Why don't I just get on with it, then," Shade said.

"Fine idea," Bauer said. "First rate." He floated one meaty hand down to Crawford's shoulder and patted him sympathetically. "He's very good at street stuff, Gene. Really. We get a call that some Frogtown free-lancer has hit such-and-such a liquor store and by the time a squad car circles the block, Shade here has divined the perp's route and is sittin' on his stoop waitin' for him."

Crawford warped his mouth into a left-handed smile and raised his chin.

"A suspicious skill for a cop," he said.

"But damn handy," Shade replied. "Sometimes suspicious, but always damn handy."

"This is the truth," Captain Bauer said with a bob of his head.

The door beckoned from an attractive proximity, and Shade, following two curt nods, strode to it and out. He stepped onto an early morning lawn, the grass slicked back with dew, the air thick with natural pomade. He slid on the side of the terraced lawn, breathing deeply, his feet acting as skis on the wet slope to the driveway. He kept his balance all the way down, then leaned on the car hood at the bottom.

Blanchette sat watching him but did not gesture.

Shade found himself wondering if he wouldn't be happier as a Catfish Bar regular, a neighborhood survivor with his own stool and a drink named after him, one who could meet the people he'd known for a lifetime without alien suspicions coming between them. Would his father come by more often, with a fifth of Old Bushmills and his Balabushka cue in the stiff leather case, inviting him along on debilitating but lively weekend romps, if he had not chosen sides?

Blanchette leaned his head out of the car window.

"Come on, Rene. Shake a leg, there, huh?"

When Shade was seated on the passenger's side he said, "How, did you ever wonder if maybe, just maybe, we weren't soldiers for the wrong set of lords?"

The full, stolid face of Blanchette shook, and his lower lip hid the upper.

"No," he said. "Because we're Frogtowners and we know better. We ought to anyhow."

"Glad to hear it."

"I mean, we didn't really have what it took for that other life, you know? Or we'd be there."

"I hope that's not the only reason."

"Plus, plus we know, from knee-high on up, that all the assholes, *all* the assholes don't wear blue."

Shade grimaced, and nodded.

"Lest we forget," Shade said. "We should write that down."

4

THE SPITEFUL heat of a summer turned sullen reached Voltaire Street early. Sun-faded blinds flapped up on dusty front windows as "Closed" signs were flipped and brown-bag lunches were stashed beneath countertops by optimists seeking coolness for their tuna fish. Delivery men, customers, and owners had gotten the message that the bad sun sent out and slowed to lessen the punishment that any hint of speed would draw. Summer was the mean season along the river, the air thick as syrup, and the sky a lowdown fog that held in the torture.

One floor above Voltaire, Jewel Cobb sat on the couch back, peering out the window. His hands were scratching beneath opposite pits, fingering the bumps that an odd rash had raised. Down home he'd've figured it to be poison oak, but up here he hadn't a clue. One more thing not to like about cities, Jewel thought. Everything came at you in disguise in this human stew; people wore suits with ties and drove cars with huge stereos but they weren't really rich; women wore shorts where the cloth never showed till it was above the swell of the ass, with little tit socks called tubetops on, but they wouldn't go into the alley with a fella even if he showed 'em a wallet stuffed with cabbage. The only straight-up thing about cities was they looked unfriendly, and they were.

Clothes were an affectation in such weather, so Jewel pranced about the room uncovered. Suze still slept, her head beneath two pillows, snoring in the cave she always dug for her eyes.

Jewel drank a cup of coffee and stood before the mirror mounted on the bedroom door. The reflection was not true, he noticed shrewdly. He was thicker than this looking glass would let on. Bulgier and tighter, much prettier around the face.

His shotgun leaned against the other end of the couch and Jewel whisked it up. It was a twelve-gauge pump with a midget barrel and a chopped stock. Duncan had given it to him the night before when he dropped him off.

Me an' this, we're gonna *do it* today, Jewel thought. He faced the mirror again. Wish I had a camera, one of those sixty-second brands. He spread his legs, then bent forward slightly to flex his thighs, sucked tight on his gut, and gripped the shotgun in a squeeze that ballooned his biceps.

It'd be a damn *pleasure* to get killed by that guy there in the mirror. That is, compared to *some* who you could get shot by. Damn straight.

But, Jewel reflected as he lay the shotgun on the dressertop, niggers were sly and crafty, with fancy pistols in their belts and razor blades in the tips of their sneakers. Have to be careful. Watch 'em close.

But no sweat, cuz.

Suze slept in an old red football jersey with the sleeves cut out. Her skin was so pale that Jewel found merely looking at it to be nasty. It was like she never went outside, the sun never caught her at her work, 'cause her work was all in pillowed rooms with the curtains drawn. She was a country girl with just one real talent, but it was the one that travels well and is appreciated around the world.

The bed shifted as Jewel sat on the edge. Suze's body was curled like a hook, and he began to lightly float his fingers around the place where the worm would go. With his other hand he stroked her rump.

She swatted at him, then turned over.

He tried again.

The pillows flew from Suze's face. She raised her upper body and rested on her elbows, blinking at him.

"I am tryin' to sleep, Jewel."

"I was just gonna wake you up sweet, is all."

"What's sweet is sleep."

"There's sweet and there's *sweet*," Jewel said. "Anyhow, I'll be busy later. Won't be home."

He began to force his fingertips into her, but it was like stretching rubber and he wasn't sure he was on the right trail. She lifted his hand.

"That hurts."

Jewel grew sheepish, then a little bit angry that she was making him feel bad for going after his own girl. That's supposed to be settled, that you get *that* when you want it.

"We never done nothin' last night," he said.

"You were too drunk."

"And yesterday was too hot."

Suze rubbed her eyes and yawned, then fell back on the bed.

"Oh, baby," she said. "Your hair is a mess."

"I can't find my comb—you got it?"

"Come here, baby," she said. She took his head into her arms. He leaned into her embrace.

Then he found himself remembering Duncan's instructions.

Now listen to me. Wait at the mouth of the alley with the shotgun in the trash cans there, hear me, cuz? Then all you gotta do is this, and it's not much.

Then he remembered Suze and bent to her neck.

"You a natural rooster, ain't you, baby? You see that sun and you got to rise with it, don't you, lover?"

Now he's a big buck with a crippled right foot, so he'll be limpin' when you see him.

"Sure. The crack of dawn is askin' for it in my book."

Somehow Jewel's body was not following his mind's command and things were not happening right.

"I know what you want," Suze said. She sat all the way up and pushed him over, then crouched to him and took him in her mouth.

This cat dresses nice, he really does, with big red ties and diamond clips, and he drives a maroon LTD with all kind of Afro gadgetry hangin' off it. Can't miss him. He owns the theater there, and he shows up at five. Every day.

"Baby?"

Jewel started, then looked down at Suze.

"Baby," she said. "What's the matter?"

"Nothin'."

"I know better. This ain't like you."

She giggled.

He won't know you. None of them will know you. You pull the shotgun when he gets out of the car. He probably won't even look at you. And if he does, he never saw you before.

"I think I'll go get me some eats," Jewel said, then pushed up from the bed.

"What? What?" Suze's mouth dropped and her face scrunched unpleasantly. "Not now. Not now you don't, buster."

"Shut your face."

"It ain't right," she said. "I was sleepin'. Before you started on me I was sleepin'. Now I'm started I ain't goin' to be able to sleep." Suze swung out of bed and followed Jewel while he rounded up his clothes. "You ain't goin' nowhere under these circumstances."

He'll walk right past the alley and you'll be hidden pretty good. The blast will shake people up. They'll be runnin' every which way, so you step up close and spread his head out real good. We got to be sure.

"I'm not in the mood," Jewel said. "I got to be in more of a mood."

"Jew-el! For God's sake—I was sleepin'."

"So go back to sleep! It's all you got to do anyhow."

"Well," Suze said, then collapsed her shoulders in surrender. "I mean, praise the Lord, Jew-el."

She grabbed her clothes off the bedpost and went to the bathroom, slamming the door as a final comment.

Immediately admitting that he was no hungrier for food than he'd been for Suze, Jewel dropped his shirt and jeans back to the floor and slumped onto the couch. He pulled his guitar out from beneath the high-legged couch and began to strum an approximate rendition of "Mama Tried." As he played he could see the sidewalk across the street, a sidewalk clotted with strangers doing business, a street he didn't like. Creepy fuckin' Frogs, anyhow.

It's a piece of cake, if you keep cool.

Jewel jerked upright, then flipped the guitar across the room, snapping the E string on the dresser edge. He put his head in his hands and growled.

And you'll keep cool, right, cuz?

5

Pete Ledoux sat on the hood of his black Pinto in the shadows of the line of trees that surrounded the graveled parking lot of the Catfish Bar, using his keys to chisel at splatters of guano deposited on his car by a rare bird that shit cement and seemed to follow him around. Occasionally he looked across the lot, foul with white dust and heat shimmers, toward Lafitte Street. He was waiting for Steve Roque, and that meant that he could not become impatient and leave. Roque had said wait, and Ledoux had no choice but to do so.

The sidewalk on this stretch of Lafitte, even before noon, was rich with rod-and-reel luggers in rubber boots sneaking toward a favorite slough where a dry stump overlooked a bullhead hole; double-wide women with surplus neck who squeezed grocery bags to their chests; and diddy-bop strutters in Foster Grants who acknowledged one another with terse chin gestures. Ledoux watched as if Frogtown, the version of it that he'd always known, was on the verge of disappearing. The area had not been totally French since Lewis and Clark had partied down here prior to their famous trip, and even when Ledoux had been born the Frogs had been equaled in number by rogue Germans, ambitious Irish, and hillbilly trash. It was this new influx of wetbacks that troubled him. Those people stank the streets up with peppery smells and burned beans, and they didn't understand who was boss. If native Frogtowners didn't snap out of their soft slumber they'd wake soon to find they lived on Pancho Villa Boulevard. He was sure of that.

When Roque arrived it was on foot. He stood at the corner of the bar building and raised a hand toward Ledoux. Ledoux crossed the parking lot and joined him beneath the big sign with a blue catfish on it that swung above the door.

A bouncy kid was swaggering down the walk. He was summer brown and wore a coffee-stained dago T-shirt, dress slacks, and slick shoes with the de rigueur horseshoe taps that sparked as he walked, as if his strut were a blade and the street a perpetual whetstone. When he was even with the two men he picked Ledoux to make eye contact with.

Ledoux returned the gaze, superior and cool.

The kid shrugged and looked away, then glared back.

"Hey, punk," Ledoux said sharply, "I don't want to be your friend. Keep walkin'."

"Fuck you," the kid said, then looked over his shoulder.

Ledoux leaned toward him and the kid flashed a couple of running steps, then slowed to a walk when he saw he wasn't being seriously chased.

"I don't think I can put up with it," Ledoux said.

"Shouldn't have to," Roque said. "That's my opinion."

Steve Roque was built in the style of the local French: about five-ten, with a thick-boned frame, filled out by two hundred pounds of unpretentious, but useful, bulk. So many Frogtowners were of this body type that it was referred to as "Froggy." But Roque sidestepped stereotyping by being bald, with a long gray rough of hair on the sides. He wore a black Ban-Lon shirt, white slacks, and white shoes.

Roque jerked his thumb at the door.

"I heard there's a cool spot in this town; could be it's in here."

Froggy Russ Poncelet, the day bartender, a friend to many and enemy to none, was busy behind the bar dropping cans of beer into the floor coolers. He looked up as Roque and Ledoux entered.

"Tip's in back," he said.

"Hard worker, that Tip," Roque replied.

"How do you like this heat?" Poncelet asked.

"Not much. It's yours for a cheeseburger."

They took a table in the back, far removed from the other custom-ers. The Catfish drew a decent lunch business but it was still too early for the legitimately hungry to appear, so the few tables of customers were made up of unemployed, but entrepreneurial, young men, as well as the diurnal conventions of phlegmatic tipplers.

Roque peeled a thin cigar and lit it. As he inhaled, he looked over the room and received waves from two of the tables. Not familiar waves, but respectful acknowledgments of his presence. He nodded back.

Less relaxed than Roque, Ledoux spent considerably more time inspecting the clientele before hunching forward and saying, "I saw the papers this morning. Man, are they confused."

"Of course they are," Roque said. "What'd you expect?" His brown eyes were not cold, but warm with malice and bright with confidence. "They might unravel it, but not in time to change much. That is, if *you* can hold *your* end up."

Poncelet approached the table, drying his hands on the untucked portion of his white T-shirt.

"What'll it be, fellas? Something to drink, or you want some chow?"

"How about air conditioning?" Roque asked. To emphasize his request he scraped a finger across his forehead, then flicked sweat to the floor.

"We don't carry it," Poncelet said.

"How much is Tippy kickin' to the building inspector, huh? 'Cause this is unsafe heat."

"Is that supposed to be in the nature of *news* to me?"

Roque grunted.

"No, I guess not. You hungry?" he asked Ledoux.

"Nah. I'll just have a Stag with a glass."

"Merci," Poncelet said. "And you, Steve?"

"I want to eat," Roque said. "I'll have a tall glass of ice water and some chicken stew."

"Coq au vin, you mean."

"Right. Chicken stew with a sneer. You sound like my grandmother."

"Look like her, too," Poncelet said, then returned to the bar.

"He's a smart-ass," Roque said.

"But a likable one."

"Most of them are—up to a point."

The men sat in silence until Poncelet returned with their orders, then left them.

"So—Crane had it in him, hunh," Ledoux said. "I wasn't sure. I didn't think he would for sure."

"Well, he did," Roque said. "Took some convincin'. Had to mention Tony Duquette and Ding-Ding Stengel a couple of times. Had to remind him about Curly Boone, and how his house burned down around his ears that time when *he* couldn't pay up. And he owed me less than *you* do, I said to Crane."

"And Teejay Crane's a nigger, too. Boone at least was white."

Roque grunted, then shook his head.

"That doesn't mean a thing." Roque spooned a piece of chicken from the bowl, then took it in his fingers and sucked the meat from the bone. "Payin' what you owe is all that counts."

Ledoux's eyes narrowed as he looked away. It couldn't be true, what Roque said, about black or white not making a difference.

"Why'd you bring up Duquette and Stengel? Ain't I takin' care of business good enough for you?"

"Sure you are. I think. You keep tellin' me you are, anyhow. But no sense in mentionin' a guy like *you* to Crane, who was nervous and no idiot, you know. I think he could see how he'd be extra weight once he'd done the big dance with Rankin." Roque nodded, then sipped some ice water. "I think he'd done this sort of thing once before."

After draining half a glass of Stag Ledoux began to stroke his chin reflectively.

"It's nice," he said. "The way it fits together is nice. Crane thinks his dirty movie racket, there, is solvent again, and he don't have to worry no more about his kids and stuff. That was ruinin' his days, I'll betcha, wonderin' what closet was goin' to spring open full of Frogs with bad intentions."

"I think maybe you're right," Roque said. "He knew he was in a spot. If Rankin hadn't've started thinkin' he could be cute with me like he did, Crane would've tried to swim to New Orleans some time back. Me, though, I always plan for the future."

Ledoux, flush with the pleasures of conspiracy, began to smile serenely.

"You know, if Sundown Phillips figures out his main man got whacked by Crane, why Crane would die bad, mon ami. A lot worse than we're goin' do to him."

Roque laughed, a steel-on-cement rumble.

"Must be goin' to parochial school that made us so thoughtful."

"I always went to public."

"Well, me too. After the third grade."

The bowl of stew was not empty but Roque shoved it to the middle of the table. Ledoux, with a beer growling on an empty stomach, began to appraise an onion quarter and a piece of chicken that were left over.

"Yeah," Roque said, "if Rankin hadn't've gotten the not-so-bright idea that his committee, there, the Bids Committee, could throw us over for his own people, Phillips Construction, why, a whole lot of peace never would've got disturbed."

"It always happens. A guy needs you, so you help him, then he doesn't need you so much anymore, mon ami, 'cause you've been *so* much help, and then it's out to the shithouse with you." Ledoux shook his head at the disappointing nature of human intercourse. "You were makin' each other rich, but he wanted more — am I right?"

"Well, there's another thing here." Roque lifted his powerful shoulders and turned his hands out. "One — I really want to be the man who builds the Music Center. It's none of your business why, but I do. Leave it at that. Two — I think Phillips would've done less for him over the long run anyhow, but he didn't want to see that."

"You got a point there," Ledoux said, then unleashed his hand and let it snatch up the onion quarter and chicken part.

Roque's hand sprang forward and grabbed Ledoux by the wrist.

"Put that back!" he said.

"What?"

"Put it back! You deaf or something?"

Roque shook Ledoux's preying hand until the food splashed back in the bowl.

Ledoux wiped his released hand on a napkin.

"What's the fuckin' deal?" he asked.

"You don't take my food, that's what. That's *my* food. If I wanted you to take it I'd tell you to take it."

"You were done."

Roque leaned forward, scooting the table in on Ledoux.

"You hungry, Pete? You said you weren't hungry, but if you are I'll get you a bowl of stew and you can eat it with your own spoon and everything."

After a sip of beer Ledoux shook his head.

"Ever since I was a kid," Roque said, "I haven't liked that. People nibbling at *my* food, I don't like it."

"It was just goin' to be wasted. I didn't see the point in wastin' it when I'm just a little bit hungry."

"If I want to waste it, then I waste it. It's mine."

"Forget it," Ledoux said. He didn't know where to look, what to put his eyes on. He finished his beer and stood. "I better go get this pecker-wood and his cousin in gear for us."

"Don't go away mad, Pete. If you're hungry—eat. I'll buy."

"I'm not fuckin' hungry!"

As Ledoux stared at Roque's hard face he heard steps coming up from behind. He felt a hand clap him on the back.

"How's it goin', Pete?" Tip Shade asked.

"Okay."

"Hemorrhoids botherin' you, or are you on your way out?"

Tip sat down at the table and nodded at Roque.

"He's decidin' whether or not to eat," Roque said.

"No I ain't." Ledoux wiggled a hand in front of his zipper. "I'm goin' to go shed a tear for Ireland, that's what. Then I got business."

"Good enough," Roque said.

"What's this about pissin' on Ireland?" asked Thomas Patrick Shade, a tricultural man with dangerous pride in the two homelands he'd never seen.

"It's just an expression," Ledoux said. Nods of agreement appeared all around and Ledoux smiled. "Besides—who you think you're kiddin'—you're a Frog."

"When I want to be, I am," Tip said. "Every March I'm Irish."

Ledoux walked away, and as he sighted in on the john he heard Tip ask: "Say, what about old Alvin Rankin, there, Steve. That'll shake Pan Fry up, won't it?"

"I would guess it would," Roque said. "But as long as they only kill each other, who can gripe? Not you, not me. That's what I got to ask—who's goin' to be upset?"

6

In the heart of Frogtown, or Old French Town, as the historical markers labeled it, the streets were burnt-orange cobblestone, and brick row houses were built so that the front doors opened onto traffic instead of sidewalks. There were handmade signs for Pierre's Shoes, Secondhand and New, Jacqueline's Herbs and Spices, and at the corner of the line of row houses on Lafitte and Perry, Ma Blanqui's Pool House.

The downstairs of the house had two pool tables in what had once been the parlor and one in the former dining room. In the rear was a small kitchen, a bedroom, and a large closet without a door on it. Monique Blanqui Shade sat in the closet on a high stool from which she kept an eye on the tables. A large Dr Pepper cooler served as a counter and gave her storage space for the extras she sold.

The upstairs was a separate apartment although the door that connected it to the downstairs had no lock on it. That had never been a problem, for Rene Shade lived in the upper half. He lived there partly because he believed, despite considerable contrary evidence, that his mother might need his protection in this neighborhood, but primarily because it was cheap.

On the morning following his meeting with Mayor Crawford, Shade woke sometime before noon but could not pull himself from bed. The apartment was dark and he looked around the room, his familiarity with its accoutrements causing him to overlook the fistful of trophies on a bookcase, the Brueghel reproductions on the wall, and the clothing strewn across the floor. He found himself staring at a cooing pigeon on the window ledge, a ledge well used by pigeons; a pigeon he could not hush by voice command alone. He considered throwing something that would rattle the window and panic the bird, then passed on such a serious test of his aim so early in the day.

He pulled a pillow over his eyes and tried to sleep.

Sometime later, caught in the lucid but immobile state where the subconscious rambles and the conscious listens, Shade became aware of wet blossoms sprouting from his body. The damp tulips unfolded on his neck, his belly, and then on ground where sweet blossoms live dangerously. His hand began to follow the pattern of moist horticulture and finally grasped a bud just planted but beginning to spread.

"Got me," a voice like a blue saxophone said.

Slowly Shade sat up, a few strands of Nicole Webb's hair wound between his fingers.

"What round is it?" he said.

Nicole draped her arms around his neck.

"The first," she said. "And you're winning."

"Just a minute," Shade said. He rolled out of bed and clumsily walked to the bathroom. He bent over the sink to splash water on his face, then crouched to the faucet and irrigated the potato field that his mouth had become.

Nicole, a rare good fortune for a post-twenties single man in that she was mature but not cautious, and confident but not aloof, leaned against the doorjamb.

"You're not wearing the underwear I bought you," she said. "You must not like it."

Shade rubbed his face with a towel.

"See a beach?" he asked. "Where's the sand?"

"They're bikini briefs," Nicole said. "That just means sexy underwear."

"I thought naked was sexy."

"Well, it is. But sexy comes in stages."

Nicole wore cutoff jeans, with stylish unravelings that formed slits along the seams, and a black T-shirt that advertised Sister Kettle's Cafe. The benefits of racquetball and modest weight training gave her arms a fetching versatility of attitude. Black hair, with traces of red when in sunny silhouette, was tucked in a bun. Her waist was thin, her breasts indisputably there, although not garish, all set atop a length of leg that was extravagant and winning.

Shade tossed the towel into the tub, then put his arm around Nicole, and whispered, "I have something to show you."

They started toward the bed, the tangling energies of their affections making for awkward strides.

"I hope it's something I've seen before," Nicole said.

As the sun began to ruin the day with heat, Nicole traced her fingers over Shade's variety of acquired imperfections. There were tiny pale nicks above both eyes, evidence of his former livelihood, and a long gash beneath his chin, put there by the dangerous mix of a too-large bicycle, a small boy, and a hill of challenging steepness. Behind his left shoulder there was a puckered horseshoe, hung there by the doting mother of a busted drug dealer and the avenging end of a broken ketchup bottle.

Shade looked up at Nicole, then rolled over.

"How'd you get in here, anyway?" he asked.

"I came through from downstairs."

"Hunh." Shade stood and began to gather his clothes. "Ma let you up, or did you sneak?"

"We had a cup of coffee, then I came up."

"She never lets anybody come up those stairs. You start up those stairs, usually she hits you."

"She likes me," Nicole said with a grin. "And I don't have a key to the other door."

In his pants now, Shade walked to the refrigerator and pulled out a can of juice. He popped the top, drank, then wiped his mouth.

"That ought to tell you something," he said.

"What ought to tell me something?"

"That you don't have a key."

Groaning, Nicole twisted away from Shade and smirked at the opposite wall.

Shade went on: "You don't have a key because I've never given you one. You didn't call or anything before you came over, you just showed up. That's why I don't give out keys."

"Ho, ho," Nicole said. She slid into her shorts, then turned her T-shirt right side out, hunching away from Shade. "I've been presumptuous. There are crowds clamoring for your house key, and I circumvent your rationing plan by coming in the door that doesn't lock."

"You don't have the right to just come in anytime you want, Nicole."

Nicole pulled her shirt on, then cocked her head and smiled sarcastically.

"Your privacy wasn't so precious an hour ago. You could've sent me packing right at the start."

Bent over to tie his shoes, Shade said, "I guess I was still groggy."

Nicole laughed, though it wasn't the sweetest laugh in her repertoire.

"You could've told me before you fucked me."

"Before *I* fucked *you?* You mean before *we* fucked, don't you?"

"That's a pretty modern concept for you, Rene."

Shade's face drained of personality, and a dull commonness became his expression.

"Yeah," he said. "I can also use a telephone, plug in a toaster, identify airplanes—stuff like that."

As she wagged her head, and dazedly smiled at this intrusion of romantic debate, Nicole searched the floor for the panties that had been furiously abandoned earlier, when privacy had been a secondary desire.

In the small kitchen, Shade turned the fire on beneath a kettle of water, then put a filter in the coffee pot and scooped in a pile of Yuban. He set two cups on the counter, then turned to Nicole.

"This is crazy," he said. "I don't even mind, really. I don't know why I barked at you. A hard-learned habit, I guess."

Spotting the wad of her red panties on the top shelf of the bookcase, Nicole did not respond.

"You want a key?" Shade asked. "You want a key, you should have a key. I'm not pokin' anybody else, anyway."

"Poking?" Nicole said, the panties now in her hand. "Is that what you're doing? You're *poking* me? Is that what you tell people?"

"Ah, shit," Shade said. He concentrated on watching the kettle not boil. "It's just an expression. A bad one, maybe."

"*Maybe?*"

Nicole rolled the panties tight, then squeezed them into the watch-pocket of her cutoffs. She walked to the back door and opened it. The river roiled just beyond the railroad tracks and formed the background for her dramatic pose in the doorway.

"You have some things to think about," she said. "Me, too."

"You want a key, you can have a key."

"Rene," she said, a sonorous rebuke in her intonation. "That's not it. This is *not* about a key."

"Oh, I see," Shade said. He raised the now boiling water and poured it into the steeping chamber of the coffee pot.

"I'll get a copy knocked off over at the hardware store and leave it in your mailbox for you."

Nicole shrugged, looked down, then up.

"If you really want to," she said.

"I do."

She eased inside then, and pulled the door closed behind her.

"Today?"

7

JEWEL COBB had long conjured scenarios of murder during his nighttime fantasies, but when he was finally prepared to make the big step up in his midnight world, he found himself in a premature nocturne, the sun still walking its watchful beat, and the sidewalks becoming hectic as five o'clock neared.

He dripped potato chips as he slouched in the front of an alley between three stories of soot-bricked warehouse and two stories of Teejay Crane's retrospectively opulent theater, his hand on a string between a Kitty Clover bag and the vicinity of his mouth. There were glass chunks on the asphalt and he pushed at them with his boots until they crunched and gave way. A quart of Falstaff beer in a paper bag sat near his feet, and he occasionally crouched to it for a swig.

The shotgun was in the second of four trash cans outside the fire exit of the theater. He'd brought it in a grocery sack, the piece broken into two components, both the barrel and the stock shortened by a hacksaw. He'd huddled over the trash can like a retching drunk while he reassembled the shotgun, loaded it, then eased it along the edge of the garbage, careful not to clog the barrel, stock up for easy grabbing.

The instructions Duncan and Ledoux had given him played over and over in his mind. In the alley, wait, whack him, head shot, drop the piece and walk down Seventh Street, turn left, and escape will be waiting there in a car. Jewel had it all memorized but that failed to plump up his confidence.

The chips were all gone. He kicked at the empty bag, then squatted to the Falstaff.

He was within twenty feet of Seventh Street but no one paid much attention to him. He blended into the surroundings, just another down-and-outer, although younger than most, and somewhat of a pacesetter sartorially. Whenever there was accidental eye contact he dropped his head and began to rock it on his neck as if shaking off one of those famous drinking companions who are mammoth and pink but very rarely seen by more than one drunken witness.

He was telling time by the clock in the window of Shevlin's Fair Deal Pawnshop and Rentals across the street. Crane was said to be as predictable as misery and Jewel could see that he was due in five minutes.

All he could do was wait, and watch. He did not like the area. It was like all the cracked-shingle scruffy houses he'd ever lived in, but pushed all together in one spot, then stacked up to make a city.

The marquee of the theater announced that *Candy and the Eighth Dwarf* was "Now Playing." Jewel wondered what it was that cities put over on folks that made them want to spend money to watch strangers have real good times.

At almost straight-up five a wino with a bald head laced by what looked like scuff marks, and with fermenting clothes and white gloves, pulled out of the ambling herd on Seventh and into the alley. He carried a large grocery bag that clearly contained a gallon-sized bottle.

Jewel looked down as the wino passed, his nose wrinkling in disgust. He looked up in time to see his visitor approach the trash cans.

"Get out of there," Jewel said evenly, then sprang to his feet. "Hey, you! Get out of there!"

The wino looked at him with sleepy eyes.

"Grub your chow somewhere else," Jewel said. "Go find your own trash cans."

"But these *are* mine," the wino said in the tone of a shy boy being picked on by his teacher. "They been mine ever since Wally the Hog left. That made 'em mine. Let's see, that would be when the men went up and tracked mud on the moon. Around then. They got money for doin' it, I'd bet. It was the cleanest place in the world before they went and did that."

After glancing out to the street and not seeing Teejay Crane's maroon LTD, Jewel said, "It might still be. That's quite a while back anyhow."

"Wally the Hog had 'em longer, but he died. He never left, like I said. He died."

"I'll give 'em back to you tomorrow."

"I don't know nothin' about it, you see. My last cough drop says it was his heart. All them butts he was always pickin' up." The wino pinched two gloved fingers to his throat and gobbled, then began walking in reverse. "He thought it was just his good luck to find 'em, and it was, too, till they killed him." He stopped and squinted at Jewel. "I heard he smoked a halfie after a Chinaman tossed it — now you *know* that *can't* be good for you."

Jewel glanced down the alley, then back to the street.

"I warned him more times than I've shit," the wino testified.

"Sure," Jewel said. "I been knowin' better than that my whole life."

"Well," the wino said with a nod, "told the police 'bout it, too."

"You what?" Jewel said. He advanced on the wino, jerked him by the shoulders and spun him about, then booted his ass. "Why you old snitch — get the fuck out of here."

The wino, after an initial burst of rapid steps, settled into a measured wobble, his immediate future hugged protectively to his chest, not even glancing back over his shoulder with concern.

Somewhat irritated by his inability to provoke paralyzing fear, even in bums with spoonable brains, Jewel watched until the wino was fifty feet down the alley. He'd seen a movie once where it turned out even Comanches wouldn't tweak the noses of unknown fates by spearing outright crazies. He got the point of it, now, and it didn't have anything at all to do with having sung too many old Baptist hymns.

Jewel moved forward and began to hover on the edge of the sidewalk. The masquerade of being an aimless bum he only occasionally remembered. His eyes searched every passing car and he tensed up at the sight of every large black man who was better dressed than he was. He should've asked more questions, he saw that now. *He's a big buck who dresses nice.* A multitude of victims filled the sidewalks. Show me a big buck who *don't* dress nice, hunh? If I see one I'll shoot him, 'cause he's gotta be in with the laws.

The minutes crawled by like daddy time had been kneecapped. The clock in Shevlin's window now read nine after five.

Jewel began to pace. He kept looking back to the second trash can where just a sliver of the stock showed above the garbage. Maybe two times a year the sucker's late, and this had to be one of them. A horrible thought struck Jewel: maybe he got a ride, maybe the maroon LTD got a flat and he got a ride and I won't have no way of knowin' him. Or maybe he'd fix it himself. Maybe he's the kind of sensible nigger who'd put his hundred-dollar shoes on the floorboards and his coat on the front seat and bend down to fix the flat himself, barefoot.

Jesus.

And Cuz and the Frog might not understand the situation and leave or something.

An argument began to echo down the narrow-bricked, litter-decorated alley. Jewel turned around and saw the wino of his acquaintance being the reluctant dancer in a three-person variation of the Seventh Street Waltz. Slurred curses dribbled through the air, and the wino curled over his bottle while two erect hoofers took turns kicking his back.

What a bunch of noisy bums, Jewel thought. How can people live that way?

One of the team-oriented bums said something to the prone, stingy brother of the grape. It had to do with sharing, just like the rest of us, just like last night when I had the good day.

"Pint!" the wino screamed as he curled more tightly around his gallon of red. "Pints are silly!"

The chastening two-step began again and for the briefest of seconds Jewel thought about going down there and putting a stop to it. But it's just their ways, he thought, and anyway they'll end up slobberin' all over each other with dumb smiles on their faces once he's had enough boots to the spine. Besides, this is America—that means you can get however much you can grab, but keepin' it's your own damn problem.

So accustomed to disappointment did Jewel's eye for color become that when the maroon LTD passed in front of him he did not recognize it until the car was halfway down the block. He jerked around and looked at the trash can, then stepped out onto the sidewalk to watch the car park.

The car pulled to the curb on the theater side of the street, about fifty parking spaces down, nearly half a block away.

The driver's door didn't open.

Jewel checked the clock and saw that he was nearly twenty minutes late, and still Crane had not emerged from the long-anticipated maroon background.

What's he doin' in there, anyway?

Jewel's foot nudged the empty Falstaff bottle, then he looked down and kicked at it. A glancing blow pushed the brown-bagged bottle onto its side where it pinwheeled, then came to rest in a divot in the asphalt.

When he looked up his stomach flopped like a prizewinning bass, and his hands felt weak. Teejay Crane was on the sidewalk, limping right into Jewel's showdown midnight.

Jewel scooted to the trash can, second one in, and lifted his crime partner, then flicked the safety off. He felt as though he were floating back to the sidewalk. He leaned against the wall of the theater, using his body to shield the shotgun.

When Crane was twenty car lengths away a dark-skinned woman in blue sneakers and a shawl with leopard spots on it said something to him and he stopped.

He couldn't hear what they said, but Jewel saw that what he'd been told was true. Crane was *big*, and dressed real nice, with a red velvet pimp jacket on that looked like it would've took a three-day convention of railroad men to pay for. Fuckin' pimps.

Crane kept smiling at the woman and saying things that caused both their torsos to shudder and their mouths to stretch.

Come on, man, Jewel thought as he tapped the sawed-off against the back of his leg. Give her the brush, huh? She ain't so such a much.

Crane did not move, but stood there working on the feline-clad woman as if he wanted election and she were a crowd. His hands went up, then out, and sometimes they patted her on the shoulder. Her leopard leaped as she squealed happily, her knees buckling, then springing her back to full height.

Time was changing things. Jewel didn't know how long Cuz and the Frog would wait but quittin' time was long overdue. He thought about going down the sidewalk and taking Crane off right there. He knew that it was strictly uh-uh to do that, but circumstances weren't dovetailing with his plans.

He continued to watch, and wait, then a trembling urge for the spectacular propelled him onto the sidewalk toward Crane. He swaggered straight down the middle of the sidewalk, being cagey with the shotgun at first, then, surrendering to the flamboyance that he had long coveted, he raised it in his right hand and began to point it as if it were a pistol.

Loafers became ambulant, even speedy, as Jewel approached, and an army of snazzily dressed strangers got out of his path. Several gasped and invoked the deity, while a shrewd etiquette caused others to look away.

When Jewel had closed to within a Cadillac of Crane, the woman put her hand to her mouth and stutter-stepped backward.

"Oh, Mr. Crane," she said. "What's this?"

The barrel of the shotgun, shortened to provide a wider shot pattern and nastier look, was trained on the slightly gray head of Teejay Crane.

Crane followed the woman backward, as if the shotgun were aimed at him by accident and if he moved it would sight on something else. But when he moved the muzzle followed, and suddenly his heavy shoulders slumped. He looked at his feet and raised his hands as though the brilliant whiteness of his palms would save him.

"I ain't even surprised," Crane said dully. "I guess I knew it."

When Jewel stepped forward Crane decided to pop-quiz fate, and tried to limp away more cunningly than buckshot could follow, but when he made his first zig he was ripped high in the shoulder by the opening blast. He crumpled in a spin, once more facing Jewel.

Jewel had not really heard the shot, but he'd sort of felt it jangling up his arm. He pumped another shell into the chamber. There was blood on the sidewalk, and a little fountain of it sprayed from Crane. People disappeared from the street. He looked down at Crane, whose eyes had narrowed, his lips tightening with disappointment, as if some small thing had displeased him.

With the next shot Jewel turned the man's forehead inside out. He quickly whirled in a tight-pivoting circle.

"I ain't kiddin'!" he shrieked. He could hear his voice, the echo of it seeming to linger. Or maybe he had repeated his cry.

With the muzzle pointed down he started toward the corner of Benton Street, but several men began to move in a storefront there and one of them held his hands inside his jacket.

"No, you don't," Jewel said, backing up. "I can't believe that."

He looked up the street and down, then spun once more, dropped the shotgun, and started to run back the way he'd come. At first it was a calculated jog, his path clear as his dreams, but then he overshot the alley. He wanted to turn around because that alley was the only other way to the escape car. But people were already standing up from between parked cars and someone shouted encouragement for him to be killed.

Then he started running with nothing held back, entering blocks he'd never seen before. Blocks full of people who he was certain would not like him even if they'd known him from the cradle.

Jewel's brain began to ricochet off vague sayings and childish knowledge.

Some Indians can run a hundred miles a day. In the desert, with meat hung from their belts.

The new sidewalks of people did not part for him and he shoved his way through without articulate comment. He was lost, and running was becoming harder. His breathing was ragged and his feet did not land where he aimed them. His legs felt full of rips.

A man can outrun a horse for the first forty yards. That's proven. The first forty yards belong to the man, but what about after that? Please! What about it?

Oh, please?

8

PETE LEDOUX, a man with a vast experience of ugliness, sat behind the steering wheel of a yellow VW bug and watched people pour toward Seventh Street like a fistful of BBs down a funnel. He knew that that meant it had happened, but enough time had passed that fright had eased and curiosity taken over. Sirens already sounded their luring wail.

Ledoux turned to Duncan Cobb who sat in the back seat.

"Keep the piece hidden," he said. "Something fucked up."

The pressures of the day were reflected by the bellicose sag of Duncan's pale, fleshy face.

"That would be Jewel," he said of his cousin. "If it's fucked up, it must be Jewel."

"He might be the one who fucked up, but we're the ones with a problem."

Ledoux started the car, grimacing at the low-rent rattle of the engine.

"Couldn't you've gotten anything else?" he asked as he pulled into traffic. "I mean, really."

"You wanted something that wouldn't be too hot," Duncan said. "The owner of this car is on vacation for five days."

"How can you know that?"

"'Cause he's a friend of mine."

"You stole it from your friend?"

"Hey, it's safe, Pete. It's safe, and safe is what you wanted."

"Okay," Ledoux said with a shrug. "But I *never* go on vacation, *buddy.*"

The traffic on Benton Street was slow and civilized until it got to Seventh Street, but there many drivers stared at the fattening crowd, then pulled to the curb when the fear that they were missing a gruesome event of historical importance became too strong.

The yellow bug made a U-turn at Seventh, then cruised back down Benton.

"He ain't goin' to make it," Ledoux said. "Would he shoot it out, do you think? Or lay down and wait to be popped?"

"Maybe Crane got *him* first." Duncan began to rub at his thick neck, then exercised his head until his neck crackled. "I don't know what he'd do. How could I know? If he ran, he doesn't know his way around. If he runs he'll get lost."

"He gets caught, we're the ones who're lost. We got to find the dumb peckerwood."

"We'll find him."

After a meaningful glance over his shoulder, Ledoux said, "We better. He was your gimmick, mon ami."

"You don't need to tell me that, man."

"I just want to keep it straight. I got a good head for rememberin' who fucked up."

"That's called survival."

"You ain't tellin' me a thing, mon ami."

They cruised the neighborhood, and squeezed down alleys, searching for Jewel with no luck. Ledoux called it off, and decided to go on with things.

He drove through town, passing the thin, hungry-looking houses, the vulgarly named taverns, and weed-filled lots that were the south side's counterpart to the north side's Frogtown. It had not always been wise for Frogtowners to sightsee in this district, but over the years Ledoux had managed to learn his way around in it. As in all of the old parts of town, the river was the dominant feature here, and if you kept it in sight you could not become seriously doubtful of your whereabouts.

"I thought we had it all dicked out so smooth," Ledoux said, then looked at Duncan in the rearview mirror.

Duncan did not reply.

"Mon Dieu," Ledoux said and pulled to the side of the road. "Get in the front seat, huh? It looks sort of odd, you sittin' back there when the front seat is empty."

"Sure."

When Duncan had shifted his bulk from back to front, Ledoux headed out of town on South River Road.

The edge of town was the point at which houses became more rare, but larger and newer, with lawns kept cleaner than a Presbyterian retreat and long sleek driveways that acknowledged the street only by affecting wrought-iron gates with cherub locks. Ledoux drove past these upscale snubs until River Road crossed the railroad tracks and became a white rock lane.

The lane curved and dipped deep into the lush tangle of trees, weeds, and mud that bordered the river. The VW bounced through weeds that were double its height and around trees that were nearly as thick. Ledoux stalled twice in red-mud gullies but managed to climb out both times.

Soon they came upon Ledoux's black Pinto parked in a small clearing just back of a river bluff. Ledoux slowed enough to look over the car, then, having seen that it had not been tampered with, he drove on. A couple of football fields further on he stopped beneath the remains of a railroad bridge. The breeze bounced off of the black skeletal shape in haunting musical phrases.

He parked near the edge of the bluff, overlooking the wide expanse of strong-flowing rank water. Swirls and eddies marked the treacherous spots in the flow.

Duncan walked to look down the steep bluff, leaning carefully at the edge.

"Is it deep enough here?" he asked.

"It's been dredged," Ledoux said with certainty. "I know this river good. You could drop the Arch in there and just have enough stickin' up to dive off of."

"Hunh." Duncan had the pistol in the front of his waistband. He tapped at it with his fingernails. Offshore and thirty yards downstream there was a large sandbar that seemed handy, but remote. "Should I toss this piece over there, Pete? Or keep it?" He held the pistol up. "That'd be a good place to dump it."

Ledoux had been looking through the car for anything that might have been accidentally dropped. He didn't find anything.

"Did you use it?"

"You know I didn't."

"Then why toss it? That's a Browning Hi-Power. It's got fourteen shots and no serial number. I can't get that many of 'em, peckerwood."

Duncan's face tightened and his slouch straightened indignantly.

"Hey, man, I'm workin' for you and all, but you should know this: pricks don't make friends."

A well-practiced snort of derision honked from Ledoux.

"I don't want friends, you silly shit. Friends—hah! Friends are the ones shoot you twice in the back of the head. Friends snitch you out for the long stretches. Up the joint, you see a guy doin' life you can figure he had one too many friends."

Duncan smirked.

"Let me see. I reckon that's supposed to rattle me, huh? Supposed to sound hardcase and brilliant or something, ain't it?"

"That's what you think, but you don't know, do you?"

After a short smile-and-stare-off between the two men Ledoux returned to the car. He released the parking brake and moved the gearshift to neutral.

"We got to walk back to my car," Ledoux said. "I like to get exercise over with as soon as possible. Let's sink this hunk of junk."

The men walked to the rear of the car so they could shove in unison.

"Maybe we should wait," Duncan said. "You know, until we can put Jewel in there like we wanted."

"Uh-uh," Ledoux said. "That plan is out the window. Just do what I say."

The men leaned into the car and pushed. Once the car started rolling it was easy. The yellow VW staggered over the slick mudbank and slid sideways into the river.

They stood on the bluff and watched. Brown waves lapped at the car doors and the bug began to shake.

"If Jewel was in there we'd be done and home clean," Duncan said sadly.

"Yeah. Only *he* ain't and *we* ain't."

The VW now picked up speed downstream, not sinking, but bobbing like a gargantuan cork.

"Oh, shit!" Ledoux said. "Those fuckin' things don't sink. Lucky damn thing we didn't get the punk. He'd be propped up in there grinnin' at fishermen and skinny-dippers all the way to Baton Rouge."

"Nah," Duncan said. "They sink. I think they sink. But slow."

"It better."

"Maybe I should shoot it, you know. Help it sink."

"Not now."

The car submerged slowly as it drifted with the current. When only the roof and part of the rear window were above water the car nudged into the sandbar and stuck.

"I could blast the windows out if you want."

"No. It beat us. Let it go."

Ledoux stared at the uncooperative vehicle for another moment, then turned and stomped down the lane toward his own car. His face was pursed in serious thought and his feet sank in the mud of the lane.

"Tell me," he said, "has the moon been actin' odd lately, or anything like that?"

"I couldn't say."

"I mean, have you noticed?"

"Can't say that I have," Duncan replied, humoring the older man.

"But you wouldn't anyway, would you? You wouldn't know odd if you saw it."

"I think I might, yeah. If it was real odd."

Ledoux snorted, then sped up.

"Real odd makes the newspapers, peckerwood. For God's sake—it's the *minor* odds you got to train yourself to spot. I learned that the hard way."

"Not well enough, though," Duncan said with a laugh.

"That," Ledoux said, "will have to be proved."

9

EARLIER IN the afternoon Shade had been directed to Captain Bauer's office. He knocked on the thick maple, windowless door, then let himself in. The captain was standing in front of the far office window, his hands hanging limply at his sides. Mayor Crawford, dressed in black funereal garb of Italian cut and gemstone worth, sat on the settee with his legs crossed and his hands clasped over the dominant knee.

The cloud of contentment that Nicole's visit had left Shade on evaporated abruptly.

The mayor nodded toward a young dark man of stovepipe build in a three-piece blue pinstripe suit, with a yellow hankie flourish in the breast pocket.

"I don't believe you two need an introduction," he said.

"No, I think not," Shade said, sensing a skillful squeeze play beginning to develop. "How's tricks, Francois?" he said to his younger brother.

"Unsuccessful," Francois replied. "That's why I concentrate on just being good."

The captain turned to look at him, grimaced, then swiveled back to the apparently mesmerizing view outside the window.

The mayor caught Shade's eye and smiled.

"Your brother has caught the Rankin case—isn't that cozy? We like to see good coordination between the police and the D.A.'s office."

"Yes, Mayor," Francois said, hunching forward into the power mode squat. "That's crucial to winning cases."

"Uh, yes," said the mayor with a peaked smile. "Of course." He stood then and walked to the door. "Frank—if I may call you Frank?"

"Please do."

"—has been briefed on the case. You two do whatever it is you do. Share info, or whatever."

"What info?" Shade asked.

"Look, Shade," Mayor Crawford said, "we have files and more files on a cornucopia of burglars, I'm sure. How about starting with *that* information?"

When the mayor had gone, Captain Bauer excused himself with an embarrassed grunt, and left the brothers alone in his office.

Francois stood, smiled nervously, then strode to the massive desk and perched on the edge of it. He ran a long-fingered hand across his thirty-dollar haircut.

"Look," he said. "This is business, blood."

Shade nodded slowly.

"I'm a hundred percent ears."

"Well, what it is is there's beaucoup pitfalls surrounding this case, Rene. I mean, a dude could make one little bitty step wrong here, but it could turn out to be the giantest step he ever took—right or wrong."

Shade looked away, feeling the blood rise in his face. In front of other lawyers or businessmen or women in Parisian attire, Francois spoke in the official tongue of the upwardly mobile—articulate, guardedly precise, and devoid of any personal flair—but with his own brother he felt obliged to revert to the patois of Lafitte Street and childhood. It was as if he was not certain that Shade could understand anything else.

"Righteous," Shade said. "Everything's wired, and that's on the maximum square, blood."

Francois had a longer face than his brother, with sharper, more Gallic features, and his eyes were hazel rather than blue, but there was equal belligerence in the lines of their jaws. He cocked one thick eyebrow at his brother's response.

"Been going to night school, eh, Rene?"

"Don't do that," Shade snapped. He had not finished college, had in fact only acted as if he intended to for one year, and Francois often intimated that this lack of letter-grade accreditation was a huge gulf between them. This regularly pissed Shade off, and he found that, for some reason, with a mysterious link to logic, blood relatives could spark his temper more surely and fiercely than any other members of the planet. "This is business, I thought. We can dozen it out some other time."

Francois hoisted his chin in silent agreement.

"Okay," he said. "Now, as I have it, Rankin surprised an intruder and was killed by the undoubtedly terrified individual. Perhaps because Rankin could identify him."

"Jesus shit," Shade said. He found himself walking to the same window the captain had been drawn to. "You're supposed to ride herd on me. They put my little fuckin' brother on me to make sure I only uncover the *right* dirt. I saw it comin', soon as I opened that door."

"Come on," Francois barked. "Look, I'm just here to coordinate things. You know, a lot of people are nervous about this case. Some nasty misunderstandings could come out of this if it's played to the crowd, man. You know that. So we need to straighten it out quickly." He then pushed up from the desk and faced his shorter brother. "Besides, I'm only a year younger."

"You haven't really been younger for a long time."

A smile spread Francois's thick lips.

"I know," he said.

A sort of fond sadness meandered through Shade. It was partly because he loved his brother and knew him perfectly, partly because he did not know him at all. The unlighted chamber where one's true and most secret longings and convictions are housed has a door that is impressively sealed. The more you turn the knob and peek through the keyhole, the more you have to guess, and the less you know.

"You sound proud to be older than you should be," Shade said.

"Oh," Francois breathed theatrically, "being young is an overrated sidetrack." He shrugged his shoulders like a wink. "I'm more impressed by the mainline of things."

"You're willing enough to pay the price of riding it."

"You pay the price, big bro, whether you ride *it* or *it* rides you. Let's be our ages, huh?"

There had been a time, not too long ago, when Francois had been energetic in his defense of the stepped-on multitudes, passionate in his pleas for those mendicants before the bar, those old neighborhood losers whose humanity he would not deny. He'd had a threat in his stance toward the system that had not always been kind to those close to him, and a mind quick to become belligerent in his quest of justice for the smallfry. Justice. But over the last few years something had changed, an unexpected metamorphosis brought on by the passing of days. Marriage to a Hawthorne Hills lady; turning thirty; a series of educational connivings with triple-last-named deal cutters who groveled profitably, and only into golden cups; and consequent greenbacks. He still sought justice, but more and more, justice had become a pseudonym, an alias, for Francois Shade, late of Lafitte Street, but lately of Wyndham Lane.

"Okay," Shade said. "Let's us *do* talk some turkey. What's in this for you, ol' brother o' mine?"

Their eyes met and there was no shame or fear in either face.

"It's my job. For now." Francois made an excusing gesture with his hands. "This thing could have interesting ripples for years. Alvin Rankin was black, you know."

"I think I made a mental note of that, yes."

"Well, he was a good man. A good Democrat. It wouldn't be the worst thing for me to be the man who prosecuted on this. But that depends on whom I'm prosecuting, too."

"Ah. So if you can cook it up in a way that the party's skirts are entirely clean you might make city councilman, or something."

"Well, yes. But that's just the crudest bit of it. As far as cities are concerned, Rene, if you want to be elected in the next thirty years, you better have good rapport with blacks and Latins. A lot of whites aren't ready to understand that, but they're going to the hard way if they don't get with it."

"And this helps you there."

"It could. It's not a career maker, but, yes, it could help. I mean, any white pol who wants to be mayor and stay mayor had best take wide steps away from those old amusing Irish sorts of ways. It's quaint, but it won't play much longer."

"Well, thanks," Shade said. "That's fairly blunt."

Both men smiled, and Shade felt tickled by the vibrations of some strange, submerged pride, for he'd just been tipped by a knowing tout who had the extra grace of kinship. There was a kind of backroom pleasure in it, and he could see how a man could be captivated by the process of success.

"That's as blunt as it's going to get, too," Francois said. "And all this has put me in mind of our rather motley family constellation. To wit: how's Tip?"

"Nasty as always."

"That's reassuring. People keep mentioning him to me, you know. I wish he'd change his name."

Shade laughed.

"I have an idée fixe that *he* feels ditto about us."

"Hunh, I guess it can't be helped."

"Not much."

The brothers then got down, down to business. Shade soon found himself adrift, floating on a mirage of family interests, brotherly love, and sheer admiration of drive. He ended up agreeing to follow the burglary hope for one full day, so long as nothing solid developed along other avenues.

When they parted Francois said, "Think of the long run."

"I try to," Shade said. "I really do. But I can't quite feature it."

10

Lester Moeller, an unambitious ham-and-egger of a thief, with an eye for the backdoor possibilities but with such a spineless style of loose-change larceny that he seemed able only to lift enough to break even, shook his shaggy-haired head and raised his arms in a gesture of innocence.

"Really," he said in his sissy tone, looking first at Shade, then How Blanchette, "I mean, I ain't hardly been out of the house, let alone Pan Fry."

"Of course. Why would anyone want to leave this here castle?" asked Blanchette, his sweeping hand wave drawing attention to the hamburger wrappers on the floor, the shaky table nailed to the wall, and the windows that were gray-taped into their frames.

"All right," Lester said with an agreeing bob of his head. "I gotta leave to pee, sure. I'm not the sort who'll use the sink. And to pooh. The john here, it don't flush."

"Maybe you should get you one that does," Shade suggested. "Next time you go out, I mean."

Lester shook his head. He was young but he had come to know himself.

"I wouldn't have the exper-tise," he said. "That ain't shopliftin', you know. You gotta know how to go about it. I can unplug electric sockets, but I don't know shit about plumbing."

"That's a shame," Shade said.

"Anyway, how would you stiff-leg a toilet down the street? A fella has to think about things like that, you know."

Years earlier, when Shade had still been slinging leather for a living, he'd come out of Brouilliard's Gym into the dirt alley parking lot in back and caught young Lester trying to liberate the contents of the glove compartment of his Nova. Shade, having never found much pleasure in battering obvious inferiors, refrained from striking Lester. He put an elbow around the bird-bone neck of the eighteen-year-old, then used his free hand to unbuckle his trousers. Then he shoved him down and pantsed him. As the fledgling thief scrambled in the sunlight for the cover of a nearby fire hydrant, Shade said, "I'll leave them in the mystery section of the library for you." When he drove away, Lester was kneeling behind the hydrant in a fitting pose.

"You have some serious defects as a thief, Lester."

"Well," Lester replied with a shrug of his thin, soft shoulders, "I'm not *too* good at anything."

Blanchette laughed.

"Your rap sheet'll back you up on that."

"At least I try," Lester said sullenly. "I could be on welfare, prob'ly."

Shade stood and unbuttoned another button of his shirt. His clothes felt like fresh paint, and sweat was beading on his forehead. He looked at Blanchette, who was amazingly still in his slenderizing trench coat. Was vanity more powerful than heat? he wondered.

"Well, shit, Lester," Shade said. "You're not tellin' me anything I want to hear. What's the point of us bein' friends if you can't tell me what I want to hear?"

"Come on, don't tease me," Lester said. "You don't like me. We never was friends." He raised his round brown eyes and looked Shade square in the face. "Nobody likes me and I always been knowin' that, so cut the mean shit."

"If you hear anything, though."

"Right. But nobody I know does much over in Pan Fry, man. They catch us over there, man, they got some stick-and-ball games they play with you. Guess who's the ball?"

"I'm convinced," Shade said. "You sold me. But don't let me find out you're lyin'."

It was Lester's turn to laugh.

"I guess you'd bust me then, huh? Send me to some terrible place."

Shade and Blanchette joined in on the chuckle as well, for Lester was of the self-mutated breed that was at least as happy locked up as free. Slamming steel doors were home cooking, mama's milk and cookies, to him.

"Uh-uh, you'd like that too much," Shade said. "Next time we pop you we're goin' to pass the hat, take up a collection, and send you to vocational-technical so you can learn just enough about power tools to kill your fool self."

"I've lived through worse," Lester said as he followed the detectives to the door.

Once outside on the lean, hard-bricked street, Shade and Blanchette paused to decide what pointless visit to make next.

"It's almost four," Blanchette said. "We're losin' the day. None of these twerps is goin' to break into a councilman's house, then get confused about what they're there for, and decide to whack a guy for free, you know. Since they're already there."

"You know that and I know that, but nobody else gives a fuck."

Blanchette held his trench coat open and fanned himself with the flaps. In the following silence he walked to a parked car and sat on the hood. His short legs dangled over the fender and he scrutinized the goo-coated sidewalk as if it were a mirror. He humphed from time to time and sweat ran down his face like cracks in a porcelain Buddha.

"I just don't like it," Shade said. "If we don't do what we know we should someone else is goin' to get it."

"It won't be our fault."

"Nothing's our fault."

"Should have that on our badges, you ask me."

"Everything's our fault."

"Oh, boy. Don't start with that schoolboy bullshit again, Rene. Today ain't the day for it."

The sun rebounded off nearby windows, and heat rose from the concrete walk, giving agony extra angles to work.

"Sundown Phillips," Shade said.

Blanchette pursed his lips, then began to nod.

"That's true," he said. "If anybody knows what's happenin' in Pan Fry, he's it."

"Yeah. What say let's be sociable and go visiting, huh?"

"Okay, partner," Blanchette said in a strangely soft tone. "I was wonderin' how long we were goin' to humor that cashmere brother of yours. I was goin' to lose faith if it was more than another ten minutes, to tell you the truth."

Nodding, Shade said, "You and me both."

In the aspiring self-mythology of Saint Bruno, a town that liked to refer to itself as a baby Chicago, there were grapevine Roykos and street-corner Sandburgs who found odd connections between the Windy City on the Lake and the Wheezing Town on the River.

The pecking order of the homegrown juice merchants and trigger jerkers, green-felt Caesars, and snow-shoveling cowboys was likened to a vivid Chicago of the memory. And in this urban simile, if Auguste Beaurain, a force so devious, potent, and dangerous that he'd never even been hooked for a parking ticket, was a scaled-down Capone, and Steve Roque an irritating Spike O'Donnell, then surely Sundown Phillips of Pan Fry was perfectly Bugs Moran.

The detectives pulled into the graveled space in front of the wood-frame house that served as an office for Phillips Construction. There were two green pickup trucks and a motorcycle parked outside. A large dog with long strands of mud for hair, and a disturbingly narrow head, relaxed on the porch.

The dog rose as the detectives approached and Shade dropped a hand to scratch around where the ears should be. The dog sighed, then lay back down and Shade opened the door.

There was a small front room with a somber gang of gray filing cabinets spread around against the walls, and a receptionist's desk that was unattended.

The detectives stepped into the middle of the room and stopped. There was a picture of Martin Luther King on one wall, high up and centered, with signed photos of Satchel Paige, Itzhak Perlman, and Tina Turner on display beneath.

Shade stepped over to a white door in the corner of the room and knocked.

After a long pause the door drawled open to reveal a table circled by curious faces. A thin, butterscotch man with a Vandyke beard and a taste for clothes that were tropical in theme blocked Shade's entrance.

"This is business hours," the man said. "You got business?"

At the table in the background one of the curious faces suddenly became less so, and shoved away from the table, then stood. From top-knot to toe there was a length of body that could've maintained a decent rushing average by consistently collapsing forward. Sundown Phillips was a grade or two above large, with a leonine process of hair, and dark skin.

As he approached the door he began to smile.

"Well, well, if it's not Tomatuh Can Shade," he said with a roll of his eyes. "The Con-tend-uh!"

Shade made the Vandyke beard as Powers Jones, an occasional car-penter and full-time suspect, who worked for Phillips. He couldn't see the other faces well enough to identify them.

Sundown filled the doorway and blocked his view. His smile was as friendly as a holding cell. He backed Shade up, stepped into the main room, and pulled the white door closed.

"What's this?" Blanchette asked, leaning forward conspiratorially. "A little early in the day for a Tupperware party, ain't it?"

Sundown responded by looking down on Blanchette with an amused curl to his lips.

"See the sign outside?" Sundown asked. "This *is* a business."

"Look, Phillips," Shade said. "I want to ask you a few things."

"About what?"

"About yourself."

"Why, how nice," Sundown said. "Six-seven, two seventy, black nappy over brown, a long jagged liverish-looking one under the left armpit, and, well, like a donkey. I believe that covers the vitals."

Blanchette, who stood nose to nipple on Sundown, said, "Most people don't like wiseasses."

"Is that so? I'd like to see the dem-o-graphic breakdown on that poll."

There were certain situations in which Blanchette was of little use. Shade quickly assessed this to be one of them and asked How to wait in the car. Blanchette, however, was in need of his self-image as a ruggedly chubby, knockaround cop who had yet to encounter humanity in dimensions that could back him down.

"Okay," he said. "All right. But if it don't work your way, Shade, then it'll be time for mine."

As the door clinked shut behind Blanchette, Sundown sat on the receptionist's desk. He opened a button on his yellow summer cotton shirt, and buffed his boot tips on the back of his slacks.

"What is it, Shade?"

"That meeting in there," Shade flicked his head toward the white door, "it's about Rankin, right? You guys already carvin' up the leftovers or what?"

"Man, you got a lot of nerve, you know that? Why the fuck shouldn't we be talkin' about Alvin? We all knew him, you see. He was our man, and on the upswing, too. You think of anything more important that's gone down lately?"

"I was wonderin' if you might know who remodeled his head, or anything like that."

Sundown held his arms out, then quickly glanced down the length of both limbs.

"I don't see any feathers," he said. "And my voice ain't turned into no coo-coo sort of thing." He dropped his enormous arms back to his sides. "So what makes you think I got any statements to make?"

"I don't know. Some people feel grief, you know, Phillips, when someone they care about gets whacked."

"Grief? Grief gets action in my world, honey, not any of them fuckin' useless tears and God-hollers and such shit."

The white door opened and Powers Jones stuck his head out.

"Are we waitin' or what?" he asked.

"Or what," Sundown said. He paced about the room, then checked his watch. "It's Rochelle time, anyhow." He pointed at Jones. "Just sit tight." His long legs two-stepped to the door. "You want to talk to me, Shade, then you follow along. Otherwise, au revoir, tadpole."

They went outside and Shade gestured to Blanchette to stay put. The two men did not speak as they traveled down the sidewalk, a sidewalk that disappeared at times, and then reappeared, roller-coasted by the roots of timeless trees that would not be diverted by mere concrete.

"I got to pick up my daughter," Sundown said. "I don't like her walkin' around alone out here. You know. She takes piano after school. She's goin' to be a Keith Jarrett someday, only prettier."

"Hey, hey, hey."

This was the same man, Shade reflected, who'd played high school football like a Greek god with a score to settle, a personal vendetta that encompassed all who would dare suit up against him. He was famous for his grudge clobberings of opponents he decided he liked least, whether they carried the ball or stood on the sidelines. His style kept many an anemic offensive drive alive with penalties, but he also stopped plenty with bone-fracturing hits. He'd had the speed of a tailback, despite his size, but the dementia of his play caused even Wishbone coaches to shy away from him. The word on the street was that he ran his new enterprises of loan-sharking, gambling, and miscellaneous larceny with the same brutal logic.

Despite an odd respect for the talented evilness of the man, Shade wanted to be the guy who dropped the flag on him for a long penalty.

Several young boys in rags wheeled spider bikes from out of alleys and began to flit around the men. The boys popped wheelies that landed very near the men, then exercised their audacity by requesting quarters to stop. "I could scuff your shoes for nothin'," they said, "but when a quarter's in my hand I miss them clean." When it became clear that no protection money would be forthcoming the pint-sized entre-preneurs drifted back into the familiar alleys they'd come out of.

"Trash," Sundown said. "They can't help it. They'll never know Bartók from Bootsy's Rubber Band."

"Right," Shade said with a nod. "There's plenty to be sad about in this life."

The school was of Depression-era vintage, with the high craftsman-ship and charming fine points that grateful artisans had willingly, and cheaply, rendered. The bricks were darkened by generations of soot and smoke, but the character of the James Audubon School was still formidable.

"Maybe you could peddle some dope to the kids while we're here," Shade said.

"Hah," Sundown snorted. "You're out of touch, honey. It's the teachers who want dope now. They need it more."

"I see. So you're an asset to public education?"

"I *do* have that civic sense, yes."

The basketball courts and baseball diamond behind the school were surrounded by a high fence and gates that were heavily padlocked after hours, but democracy had asserted itself and several low passageways had been slashed through the chain links. At this hour the gates were just being locked, and a small, pretty berry of a girl in a yellow dress with red knee socks and a sheaf of sheet music in her hands stood wait-ing on the sidewalk.

This was turning out to be as much a waste as Lester, Shade thought. So Phillips's people were stunned, but not beyond alertness for gain. Who was?

"Rochelle," Sundown called.

The young girl started toward him. A true smile crossed her face and she started to skip to her father, but then she reclaimed her dignity and slid back into a more stately stride.

Sundown leaned to her face and kissed her cheek.

This, Shade thought, is the same man who the most secret of secret whispers said had knotted two St. Louis Syrians together by their arms, then sent them bobbing for rocks in a remote slough.

"We listened to Chopin today, Dad," Rochelle said brightly. "But we practiced 'Yankee Doodle Dandy.'"

"Look," Shade said. "This is heartwarming and all, but I need to know a few things."

"Correction. A lot of things."

"That's trite. No score. Now we can talk here like citizens, or on Second Street like what we are. Suit yourself."

"Come on," Sundown said. "I don't know what it's all about. If I did you think I'd be sittin' around my office *talkin'*?"

"Is that all you're doin'?"

A car horn began to honk, and Shade turned to see Blanchette squealing up the street in the city-issue Chevy. When the car was abreast of Shade it stopped, and Blanchette called out, "Come on! There's something on Seventh Street, and it's ours."

Without a word Shade jumped into the car, grateful for action, eager for a problem he could wrap his hands around.

11

EVENTUALLY HE recognized the river. He'd been running near it for many minutes before he realized that the great, flat, flowing noodle of murk was a signpost back to the apartment. But was he going the right way?

Jewel tried to judge directions. Was that east? Or south? No handy mossed trees to clear things up, so it's all a toss-up. His face was scarlet in the cheeks, with webs of sweat running down his body. The blond pompadour that he usually doted on had now warped into fashions of desperate design.

No, that's the sun. It is. That's the sun!

Ooh, that man's head was bad frayed but maybe he never did die.

But this way, this way is home. That's the sun!

Although his lungs were clawing at his heart, he began to run once more. He followed the railroad tracks that paralleled the river. The woods were thick between the tracks and the water, but there were cracked-glass warehouses full of lunch-bucket men, and coal bins with roofs and lattice-planked walls on the other side. Too many people here. Some of them turned their faces on him. They looked strange.

Wads of paper were punched by the breeze and rattled like screams along the tracks. Occasionally suspicious heads popped up on the brush side and studied him before disappearing once more. Everywhere was now really a passing strange place.

They hate me. They talk. They hate me and they talk.

And I did do it.

His feet sank in the gravel between ties, sounding like a sprout of chains that he was going to have to get used to dragging.

When the heartscratch of exhaustion was becoming too much, he rounded a bend. He saw the tarnished copper dome of a church with a cross aged black atop it.

That's it.

Frayed head and shells talk hate me all over.

That's it! That's home up there!

Pete Ledoux stepped carefully down the slabwood stairs to the basement, dipping his head at the overhang. Even the clearest of plans can be warped by events into a bog of confusion, he'd found out this day, and now he wanted to pass the buck to Steve Roque.

Mrs. Roque, a knowing and pleasingly plump woman in jeans and jewelry, had shown him to the basement door. In the musty basement with green-painted cement walls, he located his boss in gym shorts and T-shirt, exercising to keep some order behind the treacherous expansion of his gut. He explained the new situation as Roque did sit-ups.

At the completion of one hundred sit-ups, Roque stood. Ledoux had ended his canted recitation of the day and sat on an old chair, silently waiting.

Roque raked his fingers through his moist gray hair, then picked up dumbbells and began to do curls.

"What a fuckup," he said between clenched teeth, at about the fifteenth curl.

"You're awful strong, Steve," Ledoux said, when he realized those were eighty-pound weights.

"Rheumatic fever," Roque said. "I lost most of my hair at sixteen. And ever since I turned bald, I got serious about muscles."

"Well, I don't know — you look sort of good bald."

"That's 'cause you've never seen me with hair." Roque laid the dumbbells down. "*I've* never seen me with hair, either, really. Not as a man."

"Some women like bald guys," Ledoux said, nodding at his own perceptions. "Even if they wasn't barkers themselves, and could have a guy with hair, why they'd rather take a bald one. I've seen it happen."

"Listen, fuckup," Roque said crisply. "Don't pull that soft-con shit with me, hear?" Roque toweled sweat from his face and neck. "I mean, that's a real boost to my confidence and all, Pete, but I was wonderin' how much pussy you figure me to cop up in the joint?"

Roque tossed the towel to the floor and stared at Ledoux, who looked away.

"Maybe, though," Roque went on, "you think I could be real happy over at the pen, now, in Jeff City, since I got lucky and went bald during high school, but bald is in now? I won't have to be the lonely guy on the cell block, this time. Lots of ivory-assed canteen turnouts'll be wantin' to oil down my special bald head, you figure?"

Ledoux studied his feet with an embarrassed slump to his body.

"Now, you're startin' to talk negative, Steve. Nobody has us on this, mon ami."

"The kid has you. You have me. Is that nothin'?" Roque stood spread-legged and tapped his belly. "It's like one coil of the noose leads to another."

"Well, you're right. The kid's a problem."

"The kid's a problem to you, fuckup." Roque stripped his soggy shirt off and hurled it toward the washer and dryer in the far corner. "You're a problem to me."

With his chin cupped in one hand and the other fanning the clammy air, Ledoux said, "I don't see where *I'm* a problem. To nobody."

"As long as the kid's a problem—you're a problem."

"That kid's goin' to die."

"Sure he is," Roque said. "But you stay away from him. You already fucked it up pretty good and now we can't go near him. He's too hot for us."

"Maybe I could have his cousin whack him. Diddle his girl once or twice, then whack him in the head." Ledoux hopefully wagged his eyebrows, and inclined his head toward Roque. "Now you might peddle that as your basic crime of passion, if the cousin's dick's still wet, you know. It could work."

"No. You're very clever at dumb shit, fuckup, but I think I'll nix that plot."

Roque stood under the lone light bulb and did side-to-side cool-down stretches. There were purple gouges in the small of his back, and several thin crisscross scars on his chest.

"Where'd you get those bites taken out of your back?"

"Frozen Chosen. That was Korea. Mortar shower."

"Ah. That's kind of neat, really. They didn't take me."

"Bad heart or something?"

"Nah. I'm a crook from the cradle. They don't want crooks who admit it. You should've told them."

"Yeah. But actually I wasn't much of a crook yet, at the time."

"The war grew you up, eh, mon ami?"

"Something did."

"You got to follow your talent," Ledoux said. "That's no sin." He gestured at Roque's hairy chest. "Those slits on your titties, there— those from the same mortar?"

"Uh-uh. That's razor blades, from the neighborhood. I had a point, but I should've kept quiet about it."

When he'd finished his stretches Roque sat down on the weight bench. His expression was smooth, nicely calmed by the workout, late-coming sweat dripping from his nose.

"I'm going to tell you what to do, dipshit. Then you'll do it."

"You know I will. If it can be done."

"I never mistook you for Superman, take my word. This is something you can handle. We can't go to the kid, now, and peg him in the neighborhood. Everybody knows us down there. So what you're going to do is, you're going to call Sundown Phillips and you're going to tip our peckerwood shooter in to them. Say it's because you don't want no misunderstandings, just because the kid's workin' out of Frogtown."

"But why would I do that?"

"You dumb-ass. You don't even make me laugh, you know that?

Use your fuckin' noodle, will you? You say something like you've been told this kid did it, robbery or something, and you're giving him up for peace, that's all."

"They'll go in and kill him."

"No shit? Have I told you how dumb I think you are lately? I mean, no shit, Pete—if we're lucky they'll kill him."

Ledoux stood, his legs not quite steady, and nodded toward his boss.

"You're the man," he said. "I'll go do it. But I got to say I don't like tellin' niggers they can come into Frogtown, you know, and shoot a white man."

"Grow up, Pete. Get the niggers out of your nightmares and grow up. It's business."

"I hear you talkin', but I don't like it, lettin' 'em come in down here on their own and kill a white man. It could start a trend. I don't like it. But I'll do it 'cause you say to do it." He faced away from Roque. "Nothin' else could make me."

Roque lay back on the workout bench and shaded his eyes with his hands.

"So long, Pete," he said. "It's time to cut fresh bait and fish deep. Don't fall in."

The inside of his car was still baking hot, and everything liquid in him seemed to be dripping down his neck. Ledoux drove along the cobblestone street where cars were jammed to the curb, and kids played fuzzball between passing vehicles. This was it: aged brick row houses; idly athletic punks; twelve-year-old cars; and ancient litter. Home. Ledoux had protected this ground many times in his life, stretching all the way back to when he was ten, and the south-side Germans had come in three quick cars to seek revenge for some slight to their vanity that was now long forgotten. He'd broken his wrist that day when knocked on top of it by a grim-faced Dutch Boy who was at least fifteen, twice his size, and no fan of fair play. There had been many such days, and nights, run consecutively to make a life.

And now he was inviting Pan Fry to forget old scores and come on down and waste a white man. Or two, or three. Aw, things change so much.

But better it be him than me. That never changed.

Someday he would have it worked out so no man could treat him like Roque did. That was a life plan. But business came first.

At a pay phone outside Langlois's Package Liquor Store, he pulled over. The hinges creaked as he shoved his way into the booth. The walls were mightily embellished with liquored taunts and slurs and several sloppily scrawled but robustly recommended phone numbers. He thought about how he had spoken to Teejay Crane a week or ten days earlier.

"Look," Ledoux had said as they huddled in the lobby of Crane's theater, "Roque has got you. I don't know your excuse for why he's got you, man, but he's got you by the nads."

Teejay Crane's nose was tapered at the bridge and bellbottomed at the base. "A brother man sold me out," he said. "That's all that gives Steve a complaint with me."

"I don't think that's it," Ledoux said. "I think it's that you owe him money you ain't paid. Steve's one of these sensitive guys, you know. He don't like gettin' fucked over."

"Who does?"

"You, I guess," Ledoux said. "You go into hock to rev up a little coke and a live pussy show here, in this joint, only Sundown whatch-amajigaboo don't like you free-lancing. He's down on your independence. In fact, that's why you're gettin' shylocked by Roque. But then you get popped by the cops who seem to know exactly what you're up to and in what room. And now you tell me you ain't sure you want to square things up." Ledoux wagged a finger in Crane's face. "That to me sounds like a guy who sort of *likes* gettin' fucked over."

Crane leaned against the stair banister to rest his lame right leg. There were salty patches in his black hair and he didn't look as though he'd slept too well lately.

"I needed the green to grease things," he said. "Sundown, he's one stingy nigger. He wouldn't allow me to start out on my own. Like, you know, my little bit of action might keep one or two pennies from rollin' into his own big pocket. So I had to grease things on my own, all the way up to Alvin Rankin."

"You think."

"I know. I know 'cause Alvin called me and gave me about two breaths of warning that I was gettin' raided. Said he couldn't help me. Said he had bigger fish to fry." Crane sighed and shook his head. "To my mind that man is just another snake. Give him your votes and he forgets where he got them. He could've stood up for me, but Sundown leaned on him to let me go down. I know that's how it was."

"Yeah," Ledoux said, "it's like, I sympathize with you, Crane. You're givin' my heart a nosebleed, no question about it. But if you want *me* off your case you got to get straight with us. Especially Steve. He'd rather waste a welsher than eat apple pie, if you know what I mean."

"I understand that," Crane said. "But try to see it from my side."

"What I see from your side is a guy who's in trouble and won't try to get out of it. Rankin robbed you, you asshole."

Crane reared up his head at this.

"Yeah," Ledoux said, "asshole. I said it. You're an asshole. The man robbed you to keep you a peon and you'd still rather die than get even with him. I mean, you know you're goin' to die, don't you? If you don't get Rankin for us."

"I've had that suspicion."

"It's a fact."

Crane stood erect and walked to the door. "I'll talk to Steve," he said. "I know I'm in a spot."

"Your whole fuckin' family is."

But Crane was out of the spot now, Ledoux thought grimly as he dumped the coins into the telephone slot and dialed the number, feeling worse than he had all day.

On the third ring the phone was answered.

"Phillips Construction. Powers Jones talkin'."

"I want to talk to Phillips."

"Ain't here. Who is this?"

"Nobody."

"This Pete Ledoux, ain't it?"

"So?"

"You got somethin' to say, say it."

There was a long pause, a pause long enough for several decades to be overruled.

"Yeah. I got somethin' to say. You be sure and tell it to Phillips. What it is, is this..."

12

THE CROWD was pressing forward, butting against the police cordon of three black-and-whites, their expressions a fusion of the horrified and the entertained. They gawked loose-jawed at the body of Teejay Crane, unified in their fondness for the misery of strangers.

At 5:46 Detectives Shade and Blanchette arrived on the scene. They approached a knot of officers in uniform and shirt-sleeved detectives who stood around the body. A departing patrolman grabbed Shade by the arm.

"Jesus, it's a mess," the young patrolman said.

"Never seen brains before?" Blanchette asked.

"Not in so many different places."

Detective Tom Gutermuth, a liver-spotted, mellow, robbery detail man, who'd happened on the scene first, told Shade that there was not, in fact, much to tell. Blond kid with Elvis ambitions, waving a sawed-off, point-blank, two shots. The weapon has been found and black-and-whites are cruising for the shooter. The victim was the owner-operator of the Olde Sussex Theater, and there were witnesses.

"A porno prince," Blanchette said.

"Right," Shade said. "We should pull in everybody we see in stained raincoats, I reckon."

"And shitpaper stuck to their shoes."

There seemed to be no benefit in standing around scrutinizing the corpse, so Shade decided to do what he thought he was best at: trail a danger through the hard streets and volatile alleys of Saint Bruno. Something, at least, might be turned up through action that contemplation would let slip away.

Blanchette stayed at the scene, and Shade set off alone, on foot.

The blond shooter had definitely made an impression. His passing had been memorable and Shade had no difficulty following his route from the Olde Sussex to Second Street. Shade would tap on windows and ask loiterers if they'd seen a panicked whitebread with lunacy in his eyes. Although the area was a mix in terms of race, the ambiance was black. The thumping bass backbeats that echoed from nearby sound systems were of sepia artistry, and the voices, even those of the honkoid denizens, rapped black. They always remembered the blond but rarely spoke, only pointed "that way," toward the river.

Shade began to trot down the streets, knowing that he was most of an hour behind. The retail businesses had closed as a rule, and only taverns, the Woolworths, and video arcades were open. He paused to ask questions in the arcades, thus giving every would-be wiseass and nascent tough guy the chance to define himself by his response. Adolescent drollery and derivative insolence. Shade didn't have the time for it, so he turned toward the river and began to lope.

He was winding back toward the edge of Frogtown. The blond seemed to have been set on a course to the river and once there he could only go south, or north to Frogtown. Instinct and long experience prompted Shade to follow the northern chance.

Rousseau Street flanked the river. It was a street of warehouses, flophouses, and Jesus missions, peopled by winos, the perpetually hard of luck, and one or two who were roughly saints. Coal bins lined the tracks, providing a haven for those rambling men who couldn't spare the buck for a flop and refused to perjure themselves on the God issue for the payoff bowl of soup and green-blanketed bunk. Urban Darwinism was at work in the grim light of this place, and the mean got over with their no-limit rage, while the weak went under, silently.

Shade approached a quartet of men who were joined in a medley of petty frustrations and narcissistic defeats. Two of the men were gray, with features matted by time, and the others were working toward the same transformation.

"A blond came by here," Shade said. "He was running, probably. See him?"

"I ain't seen nobody I *wanted* to see since Glenn Miller died," one of the grayed men said.

"Blond, huh?" said one of the less grayed men. "Blond. My friend Terry is blond. Sort of dishwater blond. I like him, he likes me. But he lives in Memphis, you know. That's not here."

"Right," Shade said. He turned to the youngest-looking member of the group. "You see the kid I'm talkin' about?"

The man shook his head.

"I never do," he said. "That's a credo, you."

"I knew it was," Shade said, and loped on.

Further along the worn-down street, Shade, remembering the mornings of his youth when a sport involving rocks and taunts had been made of the passed-out losers who slept in the woods near the river, thought about searching those woods. He stopped in front of the Holy Order of Man, a Catholic snooze joint, and decided that it would take too many searchers to do it right.

He heard something knocking and turned to see a man with purple thumbprints beneath his eyes motioning to him from the doorway of the Holy Order.

"You're the law," the man said, raspily. His skin had the pallor of sickness, or asceticism, and his head had been recently shaved. "You're standin' around with your thumb up your ass, and I'm sayin' to myself, 'That man is with the law.'" The man scraped a kitchen match along the windowsill and lit a smoke. "Am I right?"

"How'd you know?" Shade asked, although an ability to spot cops was not, in his experience, a particularly rare skill.

"I'm a lay brother," the man said, displaying his yellow teeth. "But there was a time I'd get in your upstairs window and get out again with your RCA TV and your stash of Trojans while you're takin' a two-beer leak. Then one time some citizen didn't nail his gutter in exactly solid and I fell." He blew smoke and nodded. "I was caught, but I woke up knowin' Our Lord real well."

"Mysterious ways."

"Cheap nails."

"I'm lookin' for somebody."

"No joke?"

"Blond kid, on the run."

"Did he do bad things?"

"Yes," Shade said. "He did bad."

"Well, I'm sure Our Lord still loves him."

"Our Lord should've stopped him."

The man inhaled like a whistle, then shrugged and exhaled a serpent of smoke.

"The Lord's not that possessive," he said. "That's a good thing about the love of Our Lord, you know. He's not at all what you'd call *clingy*, but keeps pretty cool about the whole affair."

"Uh-huh," Shade grunted. "I've noticed that."

"But I'm a new man these days. I'll even tell *you* something. I saw the sinner ye seek."

"Which way did he go?"

The man pointed north along the tracks.

"Yonder. He'd seen the Devil. It was in his eyes and he was stumblin'." The man looked Shade in the eye and nodded. "I never much helped the law before, and you know what? It don't make me feel any better, copper."

"Keep doin' it till you get off parole, though, won't you?"

Shade set off at a fast pace. It was only a few more blocks to Frogtown and he covered that ground quickly. A few times he passed people who sensed his quarry, stopped, and pointed north, north to the neighborhood he'd spent his whole life in. A splotch of houses and memories, failures and rancid conquests, a small scoop of earth that he knew more deeply than he knew his own father.

It had certainly given him more guidance.

13

POWERS JONES, the butterscotch shooter whose clothes had a floral, South Seas theme, moved down Voltaire Street like a stealthy hurricane. He paused at the Chalk & Stroke. The door was propped open in the hopes of attracting a breeze, but drew only flies. Powers stood in the doorway and scanned the crowd. It was the sort of poolroom that required air you could shake hands with before you breathed it, and husky smoke made it so. There was nothing there to interest him, so Powers Jones walked on.

A Ford station wagon was keeping pace with the tropical stranger, but stayed several yards behind him. He motioned to it from time to time, and shook his head. Finally Powers halted across the street from a crotchety hair salon and looked above it to a ramshackle window where a lamp shone in the dusk. He signaled to the Ford to park down the block a few car lengths, then walked to it.

He opened the rear door and ducked into the seat. There were two young black men in the front. Powers rested his elbows on the seat back and scooted forward.

"This the place," he said. "Farm boy's crib. Time to earn your beans."

The driver checked the street with a stiff-necked swivel, so cool he was almost paralyzed. The other accomplice, clearly a freshman on the mayhem squad, was openly nervous.

"I just watch the door," he said. "I've did that before."

Powers Jones lit a Salem and leaned back in the seat.

"I'll be doin' what has to be," he said. "So hang loose, Thomas. We can't move till we sure the cracker there, anyhow."

"The light's on," Thomas said.

"Yeah, well, it could be to keep thieves back, you know. We wait till we certain he's in there."

"When will that be?"

"Huh, huh," Powers chuckled. "It'll be when that fool cracker start hangin' his nose out the window. And he will, if he there, 'cause he real jittery, and he got to be devastatin' dumb. Huh, huh." Powers Jones propped his feet on the front seat so that they dangled between the two trainees. "He so silly *everybody* want him dead."

Suze leaned against the bathroom door and knocked again. She was wearing her blue two-piece swimsuit with the white polka dots that were juggled when she walked. She bent down to the doorknob as if it were an intercom.

"Come on, baby," she said. "Come out of there. It's your special favorite—fish sticks and fried okra." There was no response. "Are you sick? You looked sick. Don't eat in these cafes around here. I see 'em feedin' cats at night, but their faces don't really look that kind. Eat what comes in a bag. That's sanitary."

He'd come in half an hour earlier with hair twisted into a nest, his face blood-red wherever it wasn't deathly pale, and his clothes all wet. The first thing he'd done was get his pistol from the dresser. Suze asked him what was up. He'd smiled then in a way that made her chest feel bubbly. "Oh, just gonna see somethin', is all." He'd been in the bathroom and silent ever since.

"Look, Jewel—should I throw it out, or what? It won't stay crisp, you know."

The lock scraped and the door opened. Jewel's hair was combed, and his face had been washed, but his eyes were twitching.

"Now there's my baby," Suze said, and threw her arms around his neck. She leaned into him lustily and rubbed her breasts to his chest.

Her right leg slid into the inviting gap left by the spread of his, and she forced a bumping of groins. "Mmmm."

"I didn't eat no cat," he said stiffly. "That's awful."

"Good. That's good. I cooked you your special favorite." Suze began to slither encouragingly against his sensitive regions, then hung a finger in her mouth and tried to look smoldering. "Baby, you started me off this mornin' with a certain sort of ideas. I've had 'em all day long. That made your sweet magnolia get, you know, a little damp."

Jewel rested his hand on the pistol in his belt, then eased Suze away.

"I'm not sick."

A sweet giggle came from Suze.

"To be honest, I patted it dry with my fingers 'cause I didn't know *when* you'd get here." She pushed herself up close to him and turned her face up to his. "Twice. And I was startin' to look at the ketchup bottle funny, too." She laughed.

"I don't think I can eat," Jewel said. He turned away. "There's things in this world that is really gonna shock you, girl."

"Aw, Jewel," Suze whined and walked to the couch. "What is it with you, anyhow?" She flopped onto the couch, knowing that her plans for the evening were off. "What's the matter?"

"Men business."

"You meet you some gal who's got a car or somethin'?"

"I told you, girl, men business."

"Well now, that don't tell me just a whole hell of a lot, does it? I mean, you been playin' baseball or shootin' rabbits, or what?"

Jewel walked to the window and stuck his head between the curtains. There was still light to the day and there were plenty of people on the street, but none who meant anything to him. He went back to the couch and sat on the thick padded arm.

"Did you steal somethin', baby?"

"Don't ask."

"You've done that before and not got caught. Don't get worried up about it. There's lots more thieves up here than back home. They won't even think of you around here."

Jewel pulled the pistol from his belt and set it on the couch beside him. He saw his guitar with the snapped E string still on the floor where it had dropped after he flung it away that morning. While staring at it he drifted into thought, one finger motionless at the side of his nose.

"Jew-el, tell me what's goin' on."

He blinked several times.

"We're not married," he said finally. "They could make you tell on me."

"But I wouldn't. I never would do that."

"Oh, yeah," Jewel said, then stood. "Sure." He began to pace, then suddenly stopped. "Do you know somethin' you shouldn't? What do you know?"

An unexpected boom resounded from the apartment door, then another, and the door drunkenly wobbled open. And a bouquet of flowers with a man inside it stepped through pointing a long-stemmed pistol.

Jewel ran toward the rear of the apartment. There was a window in the back with smoked glass that he'd never been able to lift, and he didn't know what it opened onto, but finely tuned fear instantly propelled him toward it.

"Don't talk," Powers Jones announced, then took a wild shot at Jewel in the shadows.

Squealing, Suze rolled onto her back on the couch, covering the pistol, and curled into a baby-nap ball, her scant costume flexed taut.

Powers pointed the pistol at her.

"Oh, yes," he said, then followed Jewel.

Thomas stepped inside the door, a silver automatic in his hand. His feet kept moving as if he were stamping out a grass fire, and the pistol aimed at everything at least once.

The damn window naturally wouldn't open, as Jewel had suspected that it wouldn't, even with life on the line, and all he could find nearby was a frying pan with a layer of pork grease thickened in it. He picked it up by the wooden handle and began to beat at the window, pig essence and glass chips splattering up his arms and chest.

"He's got to have a gun!" Thomas yelled. "Watch it!"

Slowly, Powers Jones edged along the wall of the dim hallway, waiting for the split-second meeting that would end this thing and raise his asking price in the future.

The frying pan thumped and glass could be heard tinkling down.

The pistol was a dull ache in the small of Suze's back, then her hand found it and some basic instinct for combat took over. The flowery spade was most definitely the more dangerous, this took her but a blink to decide, and she rolled off the couch, knowing that life was a miracle, lobbing bullets toward the handiest danger.

The bullets whacked the walls of the hallway and grooved gashes in the ceiling, dropping a fine drywall mist.

"She's shootin'!" Thomas yelled now. "Get her!"

Powers Jones was suddenly flat on his heaving belly in the dark hallway of a redneck nigger-killer's hovel, with a lame for a partner and a white-trash mama trying to snuff him by sheer luck.

"Give me some help!" he hollered. "God damn, Thomas, she right by you!" There was no answer. "Thomas!"

The bathroom door had a lock on it, as every secret lipsticker knew, and locks kept people out. Suze made an acrobatic leap into the john, and slammed the door shut, then twisted the lock. She faced the door and sank in the corner between the tub and the toilet, her legs splayed out, the pistol on her lap.

Powers Jones raised himself to his knees and paused.

The window looked out over the rear room of the downstairs hair salon and an alley. There were jigsaw scales of glass still in the panes, but Jewel hurled himself through, then fell the six feet to the roof below. He was ripped on both sides but the cuts didn't hurt, not like the jolt of landing did.

Abandoning stealth and cool, Powers Jones sprinted to the rear window and leaned out of it. He snapped two shots at Jewel, then watched as he rolled off the roof and out of sight. A woman with blue hair had been standing in the alley, patting her new do as she inspected herself in a compact mirror. Her mouth was now a grimace and she stared at the window.

"You get out of here!" she barked.

Powers met her gaze, then lazily shook his head.

"Forget you," he said.

He started toward the apartment entrance. Thomas had now come into the room and was waving his pistol at the bathroom door.

"In there," he said. "She's in there."

Adopting his most withering look, Powers Jones glared into the younger man's face, then stepped quickly past him and out the door.

"Hey, wait, man," Thomas said. "I watched the door, didn't I?"

He looked from john to exit, indecisive, then blasted three rounds into the john. The wood splintered, something thick shattered, and there was a sharp shriek, then a moan. Thomas backed out of the apartment lest the wounded fox come back tough, his pistol at the ready. At the door he turned and saw that he was being left behind, shuddered, then ran.

14

IT MUST be voodoo, Jewel thought. Some brand of voodoo that's connected by the clouds, or city pigeons, maybe. Some nigger magic is at work, that's certain—how else could they find me so quick?

Jewel moved down the alley in an original gait that had the stealth of a chorus line and the speed of a paranoid diva. Run, drop to the ground, look for cover, stare toward the rooftops, then spring up and run some more.

His sides did not hurt, really, but sometimes there was a pesky stinging. He put his hands over the cuts, one on each love handle, and tried to stop the bleeding. But for something that didn't really hurt, those cuts bled a lot.

Night was beginning to lower a protective veil of darkness, but Jewel's passage was not secret. The sidewalk was skittering with people who'd had a lifetime of experience in looking the other way while still noticing the shoe style and wallet potential of those they'd never seen before, officer. Honest.

Jewel was aware of everyone. His hands at his sides had droplets of blood bulging on the fingertips, and he looked down to watch them plop to the concrete. The trajectory of his vein-dribbles bombing the sidewalk occasionally caused him to stop. He stood still with hopelessness as the weight of the droplets built, then gently swayed his body to aim the blood at cracks, cigar stubs, or shards of glass.

There was altogether too much strangeness afoot in this place. People went around you, heads turned the other way, but they knew you were running. Look up and they're watching. Fall down and they'll close in. They're that way. You can tell.

When Jewel had gone three streets east and the bombardiering of his own blood was less diverting, he leaned against a phone booth to rest. He was trying to think, but he'd grown shy about reaching conclusions. His own thoughts seemed clumsy and weak, and ever having believed them to be snappy and strong had been his big mistake. He thought that now, and suspicion of his own brain was paralyzing him. He thumped at his head with bloodied hands, wondering whose side his mind was on, anyway!

Jewel pulled his hand away from the glass phone booth and saw that he'd left a palm print of blood. He raised his elbow and smeared the print, then was stunned to stillness when a lurking idea jumped his consciousness. It was the only thing to do that he'd come up with, and when his hand searched his pockets he found that he had some change. The phone book had not been ripped out of the booth, and this, too, seemed like a good omen.

Jewel found the number and dialed with shaky fingers.

On the sixth ring the phone was answered by a woman with a big-city tone.

"Kelly's Pool Hall, Kelly speakin'."

"What? Where is this?"

"Who you lookin' for, Bub?"

Jewel's free hand was disciplining his head by jerking at the hair.

"I got the number from the book! I'm tryin' to find Pete."

"Pete? Pete the snooker player? Sure, he's usually here, but not right now."

"Do you know where he lives?"

The woman's laughter made Jewel yearn for rural crossroads with small stores, polite women, and good-natured sheriffs who winked on Saturday nights.

"You moron," she said, finally. "He lives here."

"I dialed this number."

"Is this Cobb?"

Oh, no, Jewel thought.

"Why do you want to know?"

"'Cause Pete the snooker player is lookin' for you, asshole. That's why." The woman paused, then made her voice solicitous. "Where're you from, anyway, Cobb?"

The sudden friendliness of her tone prodded Jewel toward nostalgia.

"A sweet little place called Willow Creek."

"Is that right? Well, there sure must be a lot of dumb motherfuckers come from around there, judgin' by you."

"Geez, lady," Jewel said in a pained voice. "What is it, anyhow? You don't even know me—why you gotta be so mean? I might be the spittin' image of your favorite uncle, you know?"

"Poor lambikins," she said. "I'm Peggy, Pete's woman, and I ain't friendly to nobody that's friendly with him."

"Oh. I'm not his friend, I'm just tryin' to find him, is all."

"Try the Catfish."

"The what?"

"The Catfish Bar. It's on Lafitte Street, by the river. He'll be there elbow-buffin' the rail, unless I'm wrong, which ain't likely."

The phone clicked in Jewel's ear but he still said thank you before hanging his end up.

15

NEAR THE corner of Lafitte and Clay streets, Shade saw a small, murky man whom he recognized as Claude Lyons. Lyons was sitting on the hood of a dented Toyota parked in front of a white stone tenement stoop, drinking from a plastic quart of Tab.

Shade sat next to him, with his arms folded.

"How's it goin', Claude?"

Lyons raised his blunt face and almost smiled. His hair was dense brown and spongy, his body short and broad.

"Hey, Rene. You makin' what you call a canvass of the neighborhood, huh? I thought you'd come up in the world."

Shade nodded even though he didn't quite get it.

"Is she dead?" Lyons asked.

"Who?"

After a swig of sugar-free, Lyons glumly faced Shade.

"It was the coons, I heard. I thought that shit had died down. If she's dead, that is. You tell me."

"What're you talking about, Claude?"

"The girl over on Voltaire that the coons shot." Lyons rested a hand on Shade's arm and leaned toward him. "You can tell me—is it true she was preg-o?"

"Where was this?"

"Just down Voltaire, man. You been gone fishin', or what? Little while ago a busload of coons come down and murdered a pregnant girl over there. Shot her through the baby's head, killed 'em both."

"Are you sure of this?"

"I heard it from Leo at the grocery."

"I better get over there."

"No kiddin', man," Lyons said. "And believe you me, Rene—ain't nobody happy about this shit comin' round again. I thought we'd settled it."

Shade walked quickly toward Voltaire Street, his senses pitched for weirdness, for clearly ominous coincidences were occurring. There was more shooting going on in a shorter span of time than Saint Bruno had tolerated since Auguste Beaurain had swept Frogtown clean of conspiratorial St. Louis dagos back in 1967. And *that* combat had had a mutant sense of civic pride about it that the present carnage lacked entirely.

The bored sweaters from the Chalk & Stroke were still on the sidewalk assessing the merits of the action across the street. They stood there in somber clots, the slack-lipped recorders of neighborhood legend, absorbing it all for improved retellings, countless. Shade walked through them and heard several angry voices speak of revenge.

Two uniformed cops were at the narrow door that led upstairs from between Connie's Hair Salon and the Olde Frenchtown Antique Shop.

As Shade approached, How Blanchette came down the stairs. He began to shake his head when he saw Shade. He held his meaty hands to the sky.

"Shade, I been lookin' for you. Baby, somethin' is goin' on, and, like, we don't know what it is."

"What happened here? Guy over on Lafitte stopped me and said a woman got wasted over here."

"Nah," Blanchette said.

"By blacks."

"That part is makin' the rounds accurate. But the girl, a little spotted panty-type farm girl, with tits like your head, she's not gonna die. Blood all over her, but she's not really hurt that bad."

Shade pointed upstairs.

"Anything to see?"

"Blood. A guitar. Some cold fish sticks."

"Hunh."

"The girl, you want to know who she is?"

"Tell me who she is, How."

"Okay. Name's Susan Magruder. She's better known as the old lady of a plowboy hard-ass named Jewel Cobb." Blanchette chuckled. "Now, from the name you might figure him for an Afro-Sheen sort of guy, but you'd be wrong. Actually he's about twenty, with—and I think you'll find this interestin'—no visible means of support and a glob of blond hair that he piles up like a sort of Casper the Ghost Elvis."

It was no surprise.

"I had a feeling it might be a guy like that."

"Two or three black hoods come in here," Blanchette said, "and old blondie does a bellywhopper out the back window. He leaves Miss Tits to the dinges, and she hides herself in the john. Only one of the hoods seems to have heard of that trick, you know, and sends her a couple of goodwill messages through the door. Poor thing got some splinters driven into her shoulders, and a bullet chipped off a piece of thigh." Blanchette nodded at a blue-haired woman who was sitting in a police car. "She saw the white guy come out the back window and one of the guys who was tryin' to shoot him. She's sort of outraged, you know. An old-time neighborhood lady, you see, doesn't think it's right, smokes comin' down here to kill a white guy, even a stranger."

Although night was now nearly full-fledged, the heat of the day was lingering, hairlines dripped down faces, tempers went on the prowl, and relief was driving a hard bargain.

Shade spent several minutes talking to Mrs. Prouxl, the blue-haired lady. She told him that she'd just come out of the hair salon where not Connie but her assistant, Hank, had given her a new do that tended to draw an admirer's gaze up to her eyes, which were her best features, or at least so she'd always been convincingly told, when this blond, a boy, really, flew like a brick out of the second-story window and an eyelash later one of our equals under the law stuck his burrhead out the same window and tried to kill him for no reason. How could there be a reason for that? The white boy seemed to be bleeding, too, although from a bullet or what she couldn't say, and the whole ordeal just made her glad she was closin' in on gettin' called home, because in her day it just never could've happened, and if that was what modern life was going to be like, she'd rather switch channels in a very big way.

Shade thanked her so profusely that he felt just a little bit ashamed. He then rejoined Blanchette.

"It doesn't make any sense yet," Shade said. "But it's startin' to add up."

"Uh-huh." Blanchette sucked on his lips thoughtfully. "Crane and this Cobb kid hooks up easy. Now, is all this hooked to Alvin Rankin, too?"

"What do you think?"

"I think yes."

"Me, too." Shade watched as Mrs. Prouxl walked away, being queried by a couple of the spectators from across the street. She held her purse to her navel and didn't turn her head to her questioners.

"Grandma gave me some ideas. I'm going to check the alley."

"We already did that."

"I'll do it again. Make sure."

"Whatever makes you happy. Should I wait on you?"

"No."

The alley was a pothole with a few shovels of gravel thrown on it, and situated as it was, to the rear of ramshackle Voltaire Street, it offered a wonderful view of nothing wonderful. The garbage bins behind the hair salon smelled of permanent solution and a broken vial of eau de something or other unlikely.

The shattered window that Jewel had squirreled through was illuminated by a naked bulb in the apartment. Shade could see the jagged frame of glass that he would have had to slice himself on. The drop to the alley was not deadly, but the kid could easily be hurt by it.

He followed the alley to its southern exit, then turned left and crouched beneath the well-lit window of a doughnut shop and inspected the sidewalk. Still in a crouch he duck-walked in the pastry-bullied air, drawing a few interested glances from passersby. Then he saw what he sought. He dabbed a finger into the moist evidence and raised it to the light. Blood.

The trail of claret, although indistinct and occasional, could be followed with only minor hesitations. Shade hung with it across streets and around chancy corners, until he came to a telephone booth with a bloody payoff smeared at chest height. He looked in the booth but found only a closed phone book and extra flecks of blood. He knew that if the seepage did not stop soon Jewel Cobb must weaken. Of course the kid could find a taxi or a friend and disappear, Shade thought, but for now this trail was all there was to go on.

One block later good luck ran out and the trail disappeared. It was at the corner of Rousseau and Clay, but catty-cornered to Lafitte and an alley. The kid could've gone any of a dozen directions from here, and with no telltale drips it was impossible to follow.

Shade leaned against a lamppole and took what he had planned to be a healthy suck of night air, but turned out to be a greedy toke of stench. The weather was condensing the river, rotting it in its own broth. Shade made a face, then sniffed his shirt and made the same face again, only better.

The Catfish Bar was only a block away on Lafitte, and Shade, having decided that his sleuthery would be enhanced by the input of a couple of tall cool ones, figured the Cobb kid might've gone that refreshing direction as well as any other.

He passed his mother's poolroom and his own apartment. He halted to look in the window and saw that the tables were being put to good use and his mother was sitting on her stool smoking a long black cigarette. This had been home for most of memory but not all of it. The Shades had once lived in a house two streets up, with a dog-run yard and a cement basement, until the early morning Daddy John X. had laid the soul-search conclusion on Mama that his true self, his *real* true self, was a river-rambling man who frankly knew more than one doll and even more than one was no good if the mix was not kept sassy. So he wasn't leaving over no other woman but because of *women* who are an animal fact, so don't think shitty of him 'cause what he's got honestly is a problem that he ought to work out on his own, don't you see.

But he *will* send money, sure, whenever that smile-yellow nine ball staggers in on the break. That had been twenty years before, and on the evidence, modern nine balls must have been glued to the felt.

Shade stood looking in the window for a moment more, then walked on.

When he entered the Catfish he thought his brother might give him a hard time. He was prepared for tension. He sat himself on a stool until Tip noticed him. There was a second of deadpan hesitation, then Tip smiled.

"Hey, Rene, how you doin'?"

"Hot," Shade said. He looked at his brother's broad, tough-guy face and saw friendliness. Odd. For even when Tip was full of joy he tended to scowl, and now he was doing a thick-necked, pockfaced parody of the Mona Lisa. "This town has busted loose."

"Yeah," Tip agreed. "I been hearin' about it." He shrugged. "It's time, I guess. Things have to go crazy every few years, you know, just so somebody can step in and put it all back in line."

"The bartender's view of life," Shade said. "Give me a draw."

As Tip went to get the beer, Shade turned to face the room. There was a total absence of blonds, let alone one who impersonated Elvis. In the corner there was a table of shot-and-beer locals who'd gotten news-caster haircuts and put on suits that were already smirkingly behind the tide of fashion, talking loudly about having to settle down and get *real* jobs, and ordering practice martinis. They laughed so much it was obvious that real jobs were not threateningly close at hand.

Bonne chance in the executive suite, Shade thought. But keep your shovels scraped, boys, and don't lose those double-thick leather work gloves.

Tip sat the beer in front of Shade. He turned and drank heartily. He could not afford to waste time, but the beer was uplifting and no sense being tight-assed about a brew or two.

"Hungry, li'l blood?"

"Not really," Shade said. "I could eat a sandwich."

"No problem."

Tip went through a swinging door into the kitchen as Shade watched. Again he found himself bemused by the apologetic attitude of big Tip.

When Tip came back out of the kitchen he turned and watched the door close before carrying the sandwich to Shade.

"Plenty of horseradish on it," he said. There was an uncertain tightness about his face. "The way you like it."

"Merci."

Tip glanced toward the kitchen door. Shade caught the glance and he thought nothing of it, but immediately it happened again and his spine sort of itched and his shoulders felt heavy.

"Expecting somebody?" he asked.

"Hunh? Oh, shit no. I was thinkin' maybe I should knock a hole in the wall there, so's you could watch the cook."

"Sure."

Mike Rondeau, a tall drink of a man sloshed into a squat glass, with a belt that could double as a lasso and a volume of ambitious lies that he called his life, came in the door and laughed.

"The Shade brothers," he said. "I had a feelin' I'd bump into you."

"This is where I work," Tip said. "Does that make you a prophet, that you found me here?"

"Oh, ho," Rondeau said to Shade, "you can always count on *him* for bad temper."

"Usually," Shade replied, then thought, yes, usually.

"What'll you have, Slim?" Tip asked.

"Do you have any carrot juice, perhaps?" the solemn-faced Rondeau asked.

"Sure, but not fresh. We have frozen."

"Ah," said Rondeau. "In that case make it a double rye with a beer back." He turned to Shade, winked, then ran a hand across his thin patch of white hair. "Have to nurse the old timekeeper."

"Yeah," Shade said. "I heard you had a heart attack."

"Just a little four-rounder on the backside of the heart. I got the decision."

Knowing that Rondeau was self-employed as a plumber–gambler–widow–lover, Shade said, "Must make business tough."

"I don't walk as fast, that's all. But when you win you can stroll, and when you lose—what's the hurry?"

Tip sat the drinks down and collected the money.

Shade caught Tip eyeballing the kitchen door again.

After a sip of rye and a follow-up of beer, Rondeau said, "Saw you boyses' daddy down in Cairo a week ago. Went down there to play some stud with a beaner philanthropist called Baroja who never showed. Ended up in a six-table joint by the river watchin' Little Egyptians shoot nine ball for quarters when in walks old John X. himself. My favorite man. Had a coat on that was green and glistened like he'd hooked it up off the bottom of the river and cut the gills out for arm-holes. Flashy, you know, in a way only a shithouse Mick could think was flashy."

Tip and Shade looked at each other, then turned away. Both felt dumped by their father, and despite the years alone, neither wanted to be.

"I'll have another," Rondeau said, rapping his empty glass. "He paid for my trip, plus some wingding dough. He got into a little nine-ball action with a fella called Dickie Venice, who's from New York and hasn't got any eyelids. His eyes're always open and you wonder why they don't dry out and crack but they don't. Looks like a cue-ball gold-fish, this Venice fella does, but with a silky stroke, you know. Really smooth. I hung back and laid off of John X. at nine ball, then backed him to the limit when they switched to one-pocket. Got to be a fool not to bet him in one-pocket."

Tip slid the fresh drinks to him.

"He mention comin' up to see us?" He and Shade were both a bit weak when it came to John X., and wished they weren't because then they could show the old man their backs forever, but he was a hard man to do that to. "He say anything about us?"

"Let me think," Rondeau said. He raised his drink and took a bird-beak dip into it. "No, not really," he said in a soft tone. "See, he had some dates with him." He looked at the brothers, who both looked elsewhere. "Probably didn't seem like the time for family chat, you know. Couple of escaped wives on his arms, he wouldn't talk about birthdays and graduations, most likely."

"Escaped wives," Shade said. "He's good at escaping wives."

"He's still married to our mother," Tip said. "The prick. He should at least ask about her, don't you think? In between games when the balls are bein' racked, he could maybe ask, 'How's Monique doin' these days?' or somethin'."

"That's a sweet sentiment," Rondeau said. "But it's askin' a lot of the guy, under the circumstances."

There was a momentary silence, then the kitchen door swung open and a man with fingers of gray running through his brown hair came out. He walked briskly to a table where a lone beer had been left.

Shade knew he knew the man, but the name was not coming to him. Tip patted his arm.

"How about another one?"

"I might could drink another."

It's Ledoux, Shade thought. He watched the man drink his beer. Yeah, Ledoux, Pat or Paul or Pete. A character, too, with several priors.

The table of double-breasted unemployed who'd been drinking martinis to acclimate themselves to higher-life beverages, but who still had that underbelly pride, which fears selling out, were herding on stiff Florsheims toward the door, their voices raised in lopsided harmony.

There was a twitch beneath Tip's eye, Shade noticed, and he seemed to be reining hard on his head to keep from looking at Ledoux.

As Shade hoisted his brew he felt Ledoux walk behind him. He watched Tip. Tip's eyes rose for the length of a wink, then lowered like a phantom nod. Shade turned to watch Ledoux go out the door.

The itch was back in Shade's spine, along with the heaviness of shoulder and shot-in-the-dark suspicions. After another contemplative sip of beer he scooted off the stool and went toward the kitchen.

"What?" Tip asked. "Hey, man!"

Shade pushed the door open. The grill was off and a kettle of stew steamed on the range. The floor was wet with fresh mopping and the backdoor was open to the screen. Russ Poncelet, looking institutional in his all-white ensemble, was rubbing a rag along the sides of the steel cooler.

Shade stepped into the room, looking for anything solid to confirm his suspicions.

Tip leaned in the doorway.

"What're you doin'?"

"Just lookin'."

There was nothing strongly out of place in the room.

"Can't get us on cleanliness," Poncelet said. "I just gave it a washing down. You could eat off the floor safer than usin' your fingers. Pine-Sol."

Shade felt ridiculous but not ashamed, and spun on his heels. He pushed past Tip.

"You're a pain in the fuckin' ass," Tip said as Shade went to the exit. "You're a punchy fuckin' weirdo sometimes, you know that? You should've ducked once in a while."

Outside in the pungent night, Shade sprinted around the corner to the parking lot. The white dust shone in the moonlight and small scudding wisps of it lingered in the air.

He's gone, Shade thought. Maybe it was just as well, for what had he really planned to do? Say, "Man, you make my spine itch, what is it," or what? It could've been silly.

But he didn't really think so.

16

Saint Joseph's Hospital served the maimed and mauled on the B side of the city. Pan Fry, Frogtown, and the south side kept the emergency room relevant and made it a frequent meeting place.

The room itself looked like a bowling alley that had missed a payment on its lanes. Lots of faded plastic chairs in muted colors, flaking green paint on the walls, with only one bright light and that directly above the nurse's desk.

When Shade entered, a young tattooed man with skin taut as rice paper, a showy flattop, and an incredible amount of patience was standing at the desk holding a Baggie up.

"It's my thumb, lady. It flew past the toolbox but I found it. I don't know how long it'll keep."

Shade saw that one of the man's hands was knotted by a sky-blue towel that had recently become two-toned.

"It hurts like hell, lady."

"You're not goin' to die," the nurse said. "That means you have to wait."

"Lady, my thumb gets room temperature, I'm fucked. Damn, it hurts!"

Shade walked on, cutting through the building to the main desk on the far side. Once there, he was given the room number and got on the elevator. He got off on the fourth floor. It was getting late in the shift, and the nurses' uniforms had lost their crispness. The floors were waxed to brightness and the air conditioning was chilling.

There was a uniformed officer in front of room 446. Shade showed him his shield and was admitted to the room.

Suze was awake, propped up in bed. There were bandages on her shoulder, neck, and thigh. Her skin was pale as steam, and her hair was matted into a straggly clump.

"I'm Detective Shade, Miss Magruder. We need to talk."

"Well," she said, her voice made meek by painkillers, "I already talked to the fat guy."

"This is different."

Suze looked at Shade appraisingly, then sat up straighter in bed.

"Okey-dokey. But keep the fat guy away, will you?"

"I'll try to. Why do you think this happened?"

"Is Jewel okay? Have you found him?"

"No."

"He's dead, ain't he?"

"We don't know that. I don't believe he is."

"He will be."

"You're sure they wanted to kill him? Not just scare him?"

Suze's eyes widened.

"Oh, no," she said, shaking her head. "These was *real* sincere people. They're gonna kill him."

"What's Jewel's business up here? You and him, you're not from around here."

"No. No we ain't from nowhere's around here." She spoke in a resigned tone. "We come up here for the better opportunities. Jewel's got a cousin out in one of these buildings around here."

"Is that right. What's his cousin's name?"

"Duncan."

"Duncan Cobb?"

"Sure. That family is considered trash in other places just 'cause they're rowdy."

Shade sat at the foot of the bed and smiled.

"They get blamed for a lot of things?"

"Just about everything short of weather. They usually did it, too, but you can't just *know* they done it, you have to *prove* it on 'em. So they don't stop. Real rowdy folks."

"Look, I have a better chance of helping Jewel if I know what he's involved in. What is he into?"

"Look, mister, I can't say. Jewel, he never told me anything I wanted to know." She was beginning to quaver but not out of control. "He's not that sweet of a guy but I love him in that bulldog way, you know. Pup nips you, you still feed it. We had some fun, me and him. We used to smoke a joint and drink some beer—romp around the woods and stuff. Get naked in a pond when the days are that way. We might find a lost shoat once in a while and gig it with a spit over our campfire—but, shoot. That's just livin'. Only Jewel said you have to get serious sometime. I reckon he did, too."

"It looks like it," Shade said. "Could you recognize the men who shot you?"

"I already told the fat guy that I couldn't. I hardly even saw 'em. Alls I know is, they come in like the real thing, mister. There wasn't nothin' TV about it."

After thanking Suze, and wishing her well, Shade left the hospital intent upon checking out this rowdy relative, Duncan Cobb.

It was four hot blocks to his own apartment. The light was still on downstairs and he could see that there was some straight pool education going on. He went up the back stairs to his apartment.

He opened his refrigerator and found a frigid can of Stag beer buried behind the wheat germ jar. He plopped on the couch and opened the brew, then reached for the telephone. He called How Blanchette at the station.

"Blanchette."

"This is Shade. I followed this Cobb kid but I couldn't find him. He's got a cousin, though, and we ought to check him out, I think."

"I know," Blanchette said. "Duncan Cobb, twenty-nine, five-nine, one eighty. Two priors, both misdemeanors. Busted for assault seven years ago, and he got popped with fightin' spurs at a raided cockfight about three months ago. Paid a fine."

"Doesn't sound like a desperado, exactly."

"No, but he works for Micheaux Construction—find that interestin'?"

"Steve Roque."

"Yes. And Pete Ledoux."

"Pete Ledoux," Shade said, verging on a revelatory quake. "I tell you what, I just saw Ledoux. I lost the kid but ran into Ledoux at the Catfish."

"Ledoux's one of those swampfrogs, lives out on Tecumseh Road, there, just before you sink into the Marais du Croche. Someone should go visitin', I think."

"I'm going to."

"But be careful. Pete Ledoux's the sort of guy who, if he saw a Mack truck comin' in on him he'd just tuck his chin behind his shoulder and double up on his hooks, you know. Not your basic candy-ass, that guy."

"I'll be on my best behavior."

"Also," Blanchette's voice dropped to a conspiratorial whisper. "A Miss Webb called for you. Didn't leave a message, and I'm no psychiatrist, but I *do* think I know what she wants."

"Yeah, well save it for when you're alone, your guesses about what she wants."

"Just tryin' to help a buddy, buddy."

"Give me Duncan Cobb's address," Shade said. "I think I'll fire up my Nova and drop in on him, too."

"You do that. He lives at 1205 Twelfth Street," Blanchette said. "I got to go to the mayor's office and explain why his town is explodin'. I think I'll blame it on the weather."

17

THE DARK of the nighttime streets was carved by lights of many hues and varying constancies; the red from the Boy O Boy Chicken Shack was a quick flick of the wrist and the green from Johnny's Shamrock a steady stab, while the rainbow in Irving's Cleaners was a slight but constant scrape. Streetlights and porch lights helped to slice away at the blackness, but the night had heart and stood up under it all well.

Powers Jones sat in the back seat of his own red Thunderbird, for the Ford wagon had been abandoned. Benny, his too-cool-to-be-true driver, and Lewis Brown were in the front seat. Lewis had been given the start over young Thomas, who was holed up in a double-locked room trying to convince himself that the terrible shaking of his limbs was a result of his having skipped supper.

"This man the cousin," Powers said as they circled the block. "Our voice on the cops says he works for Froghead Ledoux, too. *He* the one started this."

"Don't need to hear about it," Lewis said, jabbing his chin upward. "I don't remember nothin' I never heard, you see."

Lewis was a dreadlocked thirty-year-old with a vest of pudge and ganja-inspired eyes. Despite the flab and his short stature, he did not give an impression of softness.

"Cool," Powers said. "You solid ice."

On the next circuit Benny pulled over and parked near Johnny's Shamrock.

The window of the bar was wriggling with the jocular hoistings of the hard-drinking patrons. Mugs of Guinness, Irish hats, and cigars bobbed in the haze of blue smoke and high-tenor bullshit.

"He'll be in there," Powers pointed out. "Gettin' a bag on like they always do. They got to be lit to work. Me, I get lit after."

"Mmm-hmm," Lewis agreed. "They breed 'em too gentle for the life anymore."

"That is true. Except for them Frogs."

"You right. You are right about that. Why *is* that?"

Powers stroked his beard thoughtfully.

"They too stubby for sports and too lazy to work," he said with some wistfulness. "But they need that prestige, so they *can* be rugged."

"Everybody needs that," Benny said, speaking for the first time in hours. Benny had been an assistant librarian at the Boonville Reformatory for one-to-three and had garnered some sophistication about the world. "Chinese, A-rabs, Texans—they all about the same when you come right down to it, far as that prestige thing goes."

"That so?" Powers responded. "You know, you talkin' too much, Benny. Why'n't you eat another down, huh?"

"Downs," Lewis said. "This boy on downs?"

"I can still drive," Benny said. "I ain't scared of nothin'."

"On the road? Can you drive on the road?" Lewis asked. "That's a myth, that gettin' down. Drugs are for gettin' high, man, not that down like you dead shit."

Powers thumped his fist against the seat back, forcefully redirecting the conversation.

"Hey—that's him. I seen him before around town. That is him for certain."

Duncan Cobb was standing on the sidewalk in front of the Shamrock, making rude gestures into the window and laughing Gaelically. Several fingers responded with raps on the glass, bidding him carnal farewell. He laughed, then began to walk home with a Guinness lilt in his step.

"You get up ahead of the man," Powers said to Lewis. "We can't be messin' up on this one, neither."

In his yellow shirt and white pants, with the eye-catching roll to his walk, Duncan was suicidally luminescent. He paused to light a cigarette, but since he smoked only when he was drunk he found the process taxing his coordination. As he scratched a match he heard footsteps and looked up to see one of his pet peeves blocking the sidewalk.

"You seen my mama?" Lewis asked him gruffly.

"This is Twelfth Street, bro," Duncan said. He dropped the cigarette and matches, then shifted his weight more or less into punching balance. "I ain't even polite on Twelfth Street."

Lewis backed up half a step and tried to look intrigued.

"I'm lookin' for my mama 'cause I'm in a blue funk," he said, then woefully wagged his dreadlocked head. "When I feel this a way, see, my mama, she lets me beat on her till *I* feel happy again."

"I ain't your Ubangi mama, bro."

As swift as a gnat in the eye, a pistol appeared at Duncan's side with Powers Jones backing it up. Duncan turned to face down the barrel.

"But you'll do, motherfucker," Lewis said, then professionally punted him in the balls.

The grit on the floorboards had begun to rub Duncan's face raw. There was a boot on his head and nausea in his gut. He was confused and bruised and full of wonder.

"This is uncalled for," he said, the blare of the car radio overriding his words. Someone turned the sound up and an old Jackson Five tune about young love blasted in the air.

The car careened and swayed through a mystery of streets, then came to a halt. Duncan had no idea where he was. His arms were grasped and he was rudely extracted from the car. Once outside he saw that they were in Frechette Park, going up the walkway to the Boys Club. They used the rear, unlighted entrance.

"I don't know what this is," Duncan said. "I really don't. I certainly don't. It's uncalled for. You got the wrong man."

"You ain't no man. You a shitpile with feet."

The heavy metal door was held open by a blurred figure in the shadows. Duncan was shoved inside. The blur handed a wad of keys to Powers and told him to drop them by later.

The corridor was dark but Duncan was pushed along at an unkind pace, his body moving uncertainly, awkwardly tensing for a blind collision at any moment. If he'd known his way around he might have tried running, but he didn't and knew it, and they did. He knew that, too.

Soon they came to a door. There was a blade of light coming from the bottom gap.

"Open it," Lewis said.

Duncan turned to the voice. There seemed to be three of them: the plugged-in one with the charged hair and the understanding mama; the bearded one with the gun; and one who breathed real loud.

He hesitated at the door and received a jolt in the kidney.

"Now, motherfucker!"

He opened the door and entered the bright room. There were thick quiltlike pads on the floor. Parallel bars and a pommel horse were in the center of the room.

Sitting on the horse was a smorgasbord portion of bad, bad luck, eyeballing him.

The no-blarney menace stood and clasped his hands politely.

"My name is Sundown Phillips—you've heard of me?"

"Well," Duncan said, "I think maybe I have. This is, this is uncalled for, man."

"We'll see." Sundown motioned to a chair near the horse. "Have yourself a rest."

Duncan sat and looked up at his host who sort of thunderclouded over him.

"I been around the block many a time, Mr. Cobb, and I've gained a certain *regard* from the people on the street."

"I've heard that," Duncan said. "I've heard folks, many people, say things of you, you know, man, with a high regard. High regard."

Sundown flared his lips and beamed toothily.

"That's nice. I like to hear that. I know lots of folks consider me to be kind of sinister, but I just think I been lucky."

Duncan agreed.

"I never knew nothin' bad about you, man."

After a smiley pause Sundown hunkered down to Duncan's level. He nodded and put a fracas-gnarled hand on Duncan's knee. He then wagged a finger in his face.

"There's a lot of things goin' on here," Sundown said, the smooth con disappearing from his voice and a tone that suggested razor fights and happiness *about* razor fights replacing it. "And you could fill me in on it."

"What? What do you mean?"

"Like your blood, Jewel, who been goin' around town dealin' out brothers."

"Oh."

Benny, who'd been doing a circular nod-walk inspecting things, suddenly began to kick at a locked door. His red platform shoes went skidding across the buffed floor, but he kept up the attack with a naked heel. The booms rattled in the room but the door stood firm.

Powers moved toward him.

"Benny, what the fuck you doin'?"

Benny turned, a look of stoned perseverance on his face. His speech was slow.

"That's where they keep the Ping-Pong balls," he said. "You got to post a quarter bond to use one. Every time. I always wanted to bust in there. This my chance."

With a look of nervous consternation on his face, Lewis said, "I ain't ever workin' with that boy again. Make sure he forgets all about me, hear?"

"Benny, go outside," Sundown said evenly. He watched Benny leave, then patted Duncan's knee and wagged the finger again. "I think you can tell me just about all I want to know, Cobb. And, just for fun"—he smiled widely—"let's us *pretend* that your *life* depends on it."

A look of timid shrewdness came into Duncan's eyes, as if he knew in advance that his lies would be inadequate, but he had to take the chance of telling them. He looked from face to face in the room and found little comfort in the various expressions.

"I don't know what you mean, man. I really don't."

Sundown curled his lips, sighed, then nodded sadly.

"Lewis—show him what I mean."

Lewis Brown, a man who found a personal music in the moans of others, stepped up to Duncan.

"I want you to know," he said softly, "that I *like* your attitude. I really do. But I *am* gonna have *fun* changin' it."

When Duncan could focus again he realized that he was hanging upside down, his wrists and ankles lashed to the parallel bars. His teeth felt mushy and his arms felt ingrown. There was a new arrangement with his eyes, one opened and one wouldn't.

His whole life seemed like a cramp now.

"He's back," Powers said. "The eye on the fresh side of his head fluttered up."

Sundown crouched toward Duncan's loyal eye. His face was stern and not bored.

"It ain't goin' to get better," he said. There was a dull aloofness to Duncan's arms, and extra knobs at his shoulders where bones had been freed from sockets. Purple and blue welts swathed his face, leaving just the one eye bare.

"Ohh," he groaned. "Ohh, Jesus. I'm not. I'm not Jewel. Man! Ohh!"

Sundown raised one loglike leg and rested his toe in the soft space between shoulder and arm.

"Man, I know you're in it with him," Sundown said. "And must be Pete Ledoux is in it, too. And Ledoux, he don't do *too much* without Steve Roque givin' the okay on it." He prodded with his toe and the interviewee writhed. "You just meat to them, Cobb. I like you. And I'm the only man can help you right now."

"Ohh, I just don't know, man!"

After a reflective pause, Sundown leaned his full weight behind his probing foot, and there was a brief, high-note scream, then blackout silence.

★   ★   ★

On his next return to this world, Duncan Cobb, oldest son, faithless cousin, cautious lover, and pal of killers, awoke infused with the lucidity born of no escape, and a mortal dose of honesty.

He spoke in spasms, his body swaying in its moor, his voice leached of emphasis. All recollections were becoming equal.

"Music Center," he said. "The nigger who was elected—he was a businessman. Ohh."

"Alvin Rankin?"

"Him. Oh, him. He did business. He shopped around. We bought the Music Center job. Thousands, maybe. Thousands in it."

"No, you wrong," Sundown said. "*I* got the Music Center."

"He shopped it twice. Ahh. We done deals with him before you. Cut us out when the bread gets, ahh, long."

"Who the fuck hit him?"

"Ohh." A gurgling sound like an afterlife chuckle came from Duncan's throat. "Guh, guh. Crane. Your boy. Crane."

"No."

"Guh, guh. Ohh. Had him by the nuts. Juice was eatin' him up. Way in the hole to us. Had kids, too. Ahh. Way. Way in the hole."

"The hit squared him up, huh?"

"Guh, guh, guh."

Sundown rested on the pommel horse, a stunned sag to his posture.

"Alvin died over this? I would've stepped out to keep him from bein' whacked over this, for God's sake. It ain't worth it. I could've straightened it out later."

"Oh."

"Steve Roque is behind this."

Sundown turned to Powers and Lewis, who'd pulled the bottom bench of the bleachers out and were squatting there, elbows on knees, chins in hands. His brows clenched into a serious V and his fists balled.

"There some nefarious deeds goin' on," he said. He saw the chopfallen look on his associates' faces. "That means dark and shitty stuff."

"We equal to it," Powers Jones said, jumping up. "They get it started, but we *more* than equal to it."

"Of course," Sundown said, dryly. "You've proved that."

Lewis gestured at the dangling Duncan.

"What about this boy?"

Slowly Sundown turned his gaze on his reluctant oracle. Duncan wiggled his body so that he could see, with his one now-wide open eye, Sundown's face.

"Well, we got to do the right thing by this boy," Sundown said. "The *right* thing."

Duncan's neck relaxed and his head flopped back gratefully.

"Uh-huh," Lewis said. "Naturally we'll do the right thing by him."

"Then after that," Powers interjected, "should we dump him in the river?"

Sundown raised his arms and shrugged.

"What else? Carp got to eat, too."

Now comprehension made Duncan rigid, and he let his important eye flap shut, choosing not to view the most glamorous occurrence, the straight-razor finale, to this his gaudy, but already forgotten, life.

18

THE DOCK was all in darkness, even the full moon's rays being blocked by the high loom of nearby trees. Jewel Cobb lay on his back staring up, listening to the night sounds of the river and the Marais du Croche beyond. Owls hooted, and the river sidled up to the dock with wet whispers. Something snapped a branch on the other side and the sharp note of the crack wafted across the water. He sat up.

He'd been waiting for most of an hour. It had taken him fifteen minutes to sneak there from the kitchen of the Catfish. Ledoux had inspected the cuts on his side and said, "You cut bad, mon ami. Get up to my place and we'll take care of you. Watch out for niggers."

All Jewel could think of as he slinked along the dirt lane that led upriver was "buenas noches" and "hasta luego," for he was of the opinion that it was Mexico for him. But he didn't speak Mex. He could get patched up, though, then smuggle on downriver to some place with an airport and get to greaseball country where the laws were silly and you just paid off for anything you done like it was a traffic ticket. Yup, that'd be the place to cool out.

There was a splash nearby, a warning splash, a splash of something that might be big enough to come up on land with its mouth open. Jewel looked to where the sound had come from but couldn't see anything.

The bandages on his sides were coming loose. The big pock-faced guy in the kitchen had been nervous, in a hurry, and Ledoux hadn't really taped him up good. It wasn't that much pain, or blood, anymore, but it'd still be better if Pete showed up, 'cause he was getting dog tired. He could relax, just get in the boat and relax, once Pete came home and took charge.

That'd be the ticket.

Yeah.

When Pete Ledoux entered his house he saw a cigarette glowing near the window.

"Peggy?" he said.

"Where's the car?" she asked.

"Down the road. My boy get here?"

"I told him to wait on the dock. He's a puppy. He's just layin' there."

"Good."

"You could hear him if he walked," she said. "I'm goin' to have a beer — want one?"

"Nah." Ledoux went into the bedroom as Peggy opened a beer. When he came back out he carried a Remington 876 shotgun. "Where're my shells?"

"Am I supposed to know?" Peggy asked. She swigged half a beer and wiped her mouth with her hand. "You used some when you splattered that gar, whenever that was."

"I know the plastic ones are on top of the fridge."

"That's right," she said. She reached up and brought down a tattered box of plastic twelve-gauge shells.

"No," Ledoux said. "Keep 'em, they're for shit. Cheap-ass shells."

Peggy finished her beer and tossed the empty into the trash.

"You're *such* a man, Petey. Why the hell don't you just club the snot-nose to death?"

Ledoux shook his head.

"He's only a boy," he said. "That means energy. It could be too messy. Or he might get away."

"Use the plastic shells, then."

"I guess I have to." He waved his hand in Peggy's face. "If you kept decent house I could find the good shells. Can't find shit around here."

"Aw, Petey, honey—if I kept house you'd lose respect for me. Respect's important to a marriage."

"My gun jams with cheapshit shells I'm goin' to slap your face, 'cause it'll be your fault."

"Everything always is," Peggy said, and opened the fridge for another beer.

After a grunt of dissatisfaction, Ledoux took the plastic shells and grimly stepped out the door.

The footsteps came like drumbeats down the suspended runway to the dock.

Jewel stood up.

"Pete?"

The steps came closer.

"Pete?" Jewel trembled, then jumped back. "Hey, man! What's with the piece, huh?"

"Relax, Cobb," Ledoux said as he walked past him. "Keep your fuckin' head on straight." There was a boat with an outboard motor tied up to one of the dock pillars. Ledoux stepped into the boat, steadying himself with a hand on the pillar. He laid the shotgun on the dock. "See if I can get this sucker started."

"Uh-huh. Where're we goin'?"

"Cabin I got, over there." Ledoux pointed toward the swamp. "In a couple of days we'll go to the other side. A guy'll pick you up there. Nobody'll know."

"Can I send a message to my girl?"

"Oh, hell yes, you peckerwood idiot. Send her a message and a fuckin' map, why not, so's she can bring you some sugar cookies and another squad of niggers with guns. Hell yes."

Jewel backed off.

"It don't matter," he said.

The engine kicked over easily and rattled to life.

"Mon Dieu," Ledoux said. "Runs like a tee."

Ledoux stepped back onto the dock and picked up the shotgun. He held it loosely by the trigger guard.

"Go on and get in. Be careful you don't tip it over."

As Jewel stepped into the boat Ledoux jacked a shell into the chamber. Jewel collapsed to the boat bench.

"Sorry, kid," Ledoux said. "You gotta go."

Jewel curled up in the bottom of the boat.

"I ain't gonna tell, man! I don't know nobody *to* tell!"

Ledoux wanted a head shot. The boat was wobbling and Jewel lurched with it. He pointed between Jewel's eyes and nodded, then pulled the trigger. Click. Nothing. He pumped another shell and the ejection slot stuck open.

"Damn!" Ledoux shouted, then quickly added, "You pass, kid. Duncan said you were cool as polar bear shit, and you really are. Lotta heart, kid."

"What the fuck?"

"Just checkin' your balls, Cobb. Enormous. Really. Now I feel like we can be partners."

"Man, don't do that shit with me!"

The engine was loud. Ledoux bent to Jewel for easier dialogue.

"I gotta run back up to the house, mon ami. Get us some grub. You like corned beef, I hope. You wait, huh? Then we'll be gone."

Jewel nodded slowly, his eyes never leaving his new partner's face.

Halfway to the house Ledoux heard the pitch of the motor shift and turned to see Jewel speeding off in the boat, pushing into the night.

He dropped the shotgun and kicked at it, spinning it off the runway.

"Goddamn fucking women!" he screamed.

It's all water and none of it's safe. Home was some kind of weak-hope shit, but better 'n this. Jewel tried to steer but he didn't know where to go. He headed for the trees, thinking that land must be near them.

Gonna kill that bacon-fat Duncan and his whole limb of the family tree. That'll be my payback.

The boat was run aground within minutes, ridden up on a spit of unexpected earth in the Marais du Croche.

Jewel Cobb sat on the boat bench, still and silent, waiting a long time before getting out. He gingerly tested the earth with his foot. It seemed he could walk on it, so he did, his heels sinking with each step.

19

As RENE Shade drove north on Tecumseh his thoughts were of change, the changes on the street. In his father's day, or so he'd been winkingly told, skull cracking was a sort of larkish after-mass sport, but using a knife was considered a sign of natural girlishness. But he was Irish. Shade's grandfather Blanqui, on the other hand, had never been without his hook-bladed linoleum cutter, and frequently wheezed cheap cigar breath while practicing pulling it from his pocket and opening it in one malevolent move. By the time of Shade's own sharp-toed shiny shoe period, knives were mundane and single-action pistols a sign of mature vision. And today, today it often seemed that any fifteen-year-old worth nodding to had at least shot *at* somebody with a secret Armalite. Violence had lost the personal touch, the pride had gone out of self-preservation, and mere chickenshit possibilities of improved technology replaced it.

Shade had gone looking for Duncan Cobb but with no success. He'd checked the address they had on him and prowled the corner tavern where it seemed no one had seen him, now or ever. So Shade was heading north to Pete Ledoux's. The headlights picked up the shock of weeds that flanked the lane and the water-filled gullies in between. There were no street signs out here, but mailboxes offered an occasional clue. Soon Shade found a lane and drove down it until his path was blocked by a black Pinto.

He parked and approached the house. He could see a light on inside. When he drew closer he saw the blue flicker of a television set.

He thumped on the porch door but no one answered. He let himself in, then knocked again at the interior door.

When the door opened he flipped his badge at the shape that stood behind it. His other hand grasped the butt of his thirty-eight.

"Detective Shade. Can I come in?"

The shape turned on a light. Her blond hair framed her face like crabgrass does flagstone. There were black highlighters beneath her eyes and a can of beer in her hand.

"Can I stop you?" she asked.

"No."

"Say no more," she replied and walked away from the door.

Shade followed her into the room. The television had a fuzzy picture and newspapers from barely remembered Sundays littered the furniture and floor. An intimidating load of dirty laundry was piled in one corner, and plates with entrenched yolks sat on the table.

"Cop a squat," Peggy said. "Just shove some shit off the chair, hunh."

Shade decided to sit on top of the newspapers in a rocking chair.

"Is Pete Ledoux here?"

"Not right now."

"You're Mrs. Ledoux?"

"Roughly," she said. "You know anything about TVs?"

"Not much."

"Too bad. I'm not much of a talker when the tube's on the blink like it is. I ain't a thumbsucker but I *do* need that tube, you know?"

"Where's Ledoux?"

"Brazil."

"Oh, yeah?"

"Not really," Peggy said. She drank some beer, then rested the can on her thigh, where it left damp circles. "It's one of my lies. Not too good, is it?"

She was still an attractive woman, Shade saw, beneath that sullen veneer of bloat.

"I've heard worse and I've heard better. You are in between."

Peggy shrugged.

"I'm not even really tryin'."

"Where is he?"

Peggy stared at the television.

"Now you tell me something," she said, pointing at the static warped screen, "that picture, there—is that Ted Koppel or Johnny Carson? Which is it?"

"You stump me," Shade said. "But I'm gettin' bored with it." Curiosity about how lazy one person could be drove Shade to check the set. He noticed that the screws holding the antenna wire were loose. "Got a screwdriver?"

"I don't know where. Can I get you a beer?"

"No thanks."

Shade pulled a dime from his pocket and used it in lieu of a screwdriver. The picture cleared immediately.

"Is that better?"

Peggy was attacking a fresh beer but took the time to look at the picture.

"Somewhat," she said. "It's somewhat better. Let me see that dime."

Shade handed it to her.

"Wouldn't Cobb fix it for you?"

"Who?"

Her face was calm. She bent over the television set and scraped the dime against the panel, then dropped it in her pocket.

"That's my dime."

She backed off, sluttishly coy.

"You have the prettiest blue eyes," she said. "Why don't we wrestle for it?"

"No thanks," Shade said. "Get yourself somethin' pretty, though."

She slumped back to the couch.

"Bashful," she said.

She caught Shade looking at the pile of laundry.

"Pete won't let me touch that," she said, then nodded. "It's a scientific experiment."

"Uh-huh."

"He's an evolutionist, you know. None of that Bible blather. He thinks you leave enough dirty T-shirts in a pile, sooner or later there'll be some bubblin' and gurglin' and a rack of Arrow shirts'll come foldin' out."

"Old Pete sounds like quite a guy."

"Oh, he is. He really is. Scientific mind, that guy." She stood and closed in on Shade. "It's my weakness. I'm just a sucker for scientists."

"That sounds pretty safe."

"You know what makes a kettle of water boil?" she asked, sliding her leg between his and turning her tomatoey eyes up to him.

"Heat," he replied.

A look of viperine certainty came into her face, and her free hand dropped to his crotch.

"See," she said with a loll to her head, "you're sort of a scientist yourself."

"I thought I might qualify."

Someone began to knock on the screen door in banging combinations. Without waiting for an answer a tall man with an angry face and an overfed midsection came inside.

"Where'd your fuckin' old man go, Peg?" he asked. He looked at Shade and didn't seem impressed, then did a double take. "I know you. You used to be a boxer."

"Right."

The man snorted.

"Saw you get your clock cleaned a couple of times."

"Sure. Nobody seems to have seen the ones I won."

"Yeah, well, I seen you and you never showed me shit." He poked a finger at Peggy. "Your old man came down and took my boat. I don't like that. He didn't ask, he just took it."

"Our boatline snapped," Peggy said. She was looking at Shade. "He's tryin' to catch it before it drifts too far."

"Huh. I didn't see it float by. And I just come up here on my other boat and I seen runnin' lights *upriver* at the swamp."

Peggy's chin went south and she faced away.

Shade went to the phone on the table and began to dial.

"What in hell's goin' on?" the neighbor asked.

"Have a beer," Peggy said.

When Blanchette answered, Shade said, "It's me, How. Ledoux's in this thing. It's him. I'm at his place."

"You got him?"

"No. He's in a boat. I think Cobb is, too. They're over in the Marais du Croche. I'm going after them."

"Hey, be cool, comrade. That's a mess over there."

"You just get up here and back me up, How."

Shade dropped the phone back into the cradle, then looked out the window. He saw the running lights of a boat tied to the dock.

He approached the neighbor and flipped his badge.

"I'm goin' to need your boat. Police business."

"I don't think so," the big man said, then blocked the doorway. "Nobody's takin' my boat."

"I'm a cop."

"I don't fuckin' care if you're *six* cops, buddy. I'm Harlan Fontenot, that's *my* boat."

Shade feinted a right toward the jaw, and when the big man's hands went up he leaned into a left hook that sank deep into the mashed potatoes. The man sagged, and slumped to the floor.

Shade stepped around the man. "I just don't have the time."

He went out the door and ran down the walkway to the dock. He got into the boat and pulled away from the dock, trailing at least one killer into the swamp called the Marais du Croche.

20

The Marais du Croche was whorled with sloughs and mud rises like a gigantic fingerprint. It teased those who thought they knew it, and made a mockery of maps, as it changed with each heavy rain and was born anew with the floods of spring.

It had been years since Shade had been in the swamp. At the ducktail hairstyle and matching jackets stage of Frogtown adolescence the edges of the Crooked Swamp had provided a haven for queasy rites of passage. Chicken coops were erected there and called clubhouses, with blotched mattresses on the floor, surrounded by Stag beer cans, crushed by fresh virility, and empty mickeys of fruit-flavored vodka, dramatically pitched toward the corners. Unlikely magazine pages were taped to the walls and desperate girls acquired insurmountable local reputations there, on the mattresses, in the clean spots between the major stains. Shade had once felt that this was his turf, that he knew it well. But he knew he was a visitor to it now.

The moon was full and the sky had been dusted clean of clouds, so the half light of the bright orb was unobstructed.

Shade circled in his borrowed craft, slowly searching the inlets and ditches for the other boats. The various waters flowed and ebbed and splashed and heaved, keeping up a constant fluidic murmur. Sometimes he could hear another boat but the sound was diffused by the swamp — one moment seeming to come from the main-coiled slough, and an instant later from downriver where the huge sandbars were.

The low arch of branches forced Shade to kneel as he steered the boat down sluggish tracts of bilious water. His hair was snatched at by swamp-privet strands, and the moonlight was no longer of use in such density. The water bubbled. Stinks that had been fermenting for lifetimes rose from the alluvial depths, then farted beneath his face. It was a rare, rich, meaningful stink, and not unpleasant to his nose.

He hadn't been here in a time that was too long. He felt that now.

To have a plan in a place that defied plans so completely was to embrace delusion, so Shade went where accidents took him and stayed alert for signs.

As one branch of swamp circled into another, taking him in toward the center, then drifting him back to the fringe, Shade hefted his pistol. He hoped to save a life, but he was awake to the possibilities and prepared also to take one if things fell that way.

This boy Cobb had the ways of a punk and a loser's heart, and Shade hoped not to kill him. Things could happen so many screwy ways, and half a lifetime ago he might, but for timidity or luck, have been in the same boat. He had always known that.

This is where Shade thought his life could make a difference. He was not guided by a total love of law, but he was more for it than against it, and this, he felt, made him reasonable. And that was the summit of his aspirations.

He hadn't heard the other motor for a long time when he saw a boat jumped up on a spit of land. The rotors of its engine had dug into the mud like frantic fingernails.

He pulled up to the spit and tied his bowline to the grounded boat. The beached craft was empty. There was a string of earth that led between the trees, deeper into the swamp.

The ribbon of mud was untraceable by sight, trailing into the gloom of undergrowth and woods—a mystery after twenty yards.

He decided to follow it.

Jewel Cobb soon decided that trying to get anywhere in this swamp was sort of childish. The next step was half the time into darkness, sinkhole or ditch, the rest of the time it was mud that gave way enough to goose your heart, then solided up. He'd fallen into the water twice. His shorts seemed full of coffee grounds and his asshole felt pounded with sand. There was ancient compost between his teeth and his boots squeaked like a third-grade violinist.

For a while Jewel had broken into a demented sprint, bouncing off trees, catching his boots in willow roots, stumbling, moaning, and kicking his feet high through the ditches, and laughing, propelled by some hopeless hilarity.

These could be the very last laughs coming to him from life as he'd made it, he knew, but that didn't make them worth much more.

Soon he just sat. There was a bullfrog chorus, gone silent at his approach, which quickly sized him for a chump and began to blat amphibian blues. Their tune made him feel less alone. But he couldn't relax. He nodded to the syncopation of the gut-bucket blats and tried to breathe quietly because telltale sound carried on the water and there was water everywhere.

Duncan, lard-faced cousin Duncan. Meet him again, someday sure, kick his butt around the block and piss on the bloody spots. Uh-huh.

Snakes, Jewel sensed them everywhere on the tangled floor. Limbs and slithery roots shadowed indistinct, all over. Anything could be a cottonmouth sleeping with a poison sac waiting to squirt the end of everything into your ankle veins. These places were famous for that. Fangs.

He shook through his pack to find an unsoaked smoke, which he then lit with his lighter, dangerous motion or not. The fatigue of prolonged tension had weakened his limbs and they began to shudder. His life was all a dream now back there behind his eyes and he thought of highlights from it when he had fun or fought and won. Then some when he lost. And other times, too, when he'd been up to this or that but all of them began to have an "Oh, shit, I never should've did that" coda tacked on.

They want me dead now. Stone cold and dirt hidden.

He flipped the cigarette butt away from himself in a loop and it disappeared instantly, not even the smoke of it left in the air.

Yeah—it's like that.

★　　★　　★

Pete Ledoux had managed to unjam the shotgun, and when he'd gone back to the house Peggy had uncovered the good paper shells, which made him want to finger God or something. So much of life had come to him that way, too late, overdue, never enough of it there when it did show up.

This whole thing was fucked up beyond taking pride in now. You devise a scheme like an exotic domino loop but if the first bone tumbles sideways instead of straight it won't fall in the design you planned for. So then you made it up as you went. That meant trouble.

The Cobb kid had some kind of ridiculous gris-gris working for him, too. That couldn't've been planned for. You never know who'll have luck like that and certainly not why. Any grumbling about fairness was for kids and clergy.

Ledoux's face was pebbled with mosquito bites. Forget the Cutter's and that means every needle-nose bug in the woods spare-changes you for blood like cornerboy hustlers spotting a strung-out Kennedy trying to score on Seventh. Like you got plenty to give.

The water reflected moonlight in between trees. Ledoux cut the engine and now pulled the boat down the waterways by grabbing at the dome of branches and vines. It seemed that all the twigs had stickers and where there weren't stickers there were natural points. He could feel the blood beading on his hands.

There were things running through the trees. Scampering things that chattered and squatty bold things that he could feel looking back at him. There were rabbits that could swim out here. Flying squirrels. Bobcats that weren't too good at either feat but ended up eating plenty anyway. That seemed natural somehow.

None of this was new to him, not swampy nights or mortal chases or killing. He'd seen it all before. The sounds were not baffling nor were the sensations of the hunt. But when he did hear something that pricked his senses he knew it was a man. Then he knew the metallic click as that of a lighter being lit. Straining, it seemed that he could hear an inhalation, even the dull smoky taste, that was coming to him, too.

He was trying to scent in on the cigarette but that smoky hint was

148

hard to locate. Ledoux slid out of the boat and sank titty deep into the water. He held the shotgun level with his forehead and walked with the sluggish current at his back. That Zippo click clue seemed to have come from the peak of a mudbank that was covered by cockspur hawthorn.

Must be very careful and silent, get into range, then boom! boom! and birds and squirrels and even some unnameables will scatter like that peckerwood's head. To quieter places.

Even in daylight it was hard to tell solid ground from sinkhole in this place. Take a step wrong and you'll come up coughing shit that flushed out of St. Louis about a year ago. The surface of the water was coated with scum, branches, and greenery, looking like a path to morons. Like fool's gold, only it was earth. Fool's earth.

Ledoux walked down the slough, holding his upper body rigid, stepping stiff-legged underwater to avoid splashing. When his feet slipped he went with the slide instead of fighting it. The key to the swamp was to agree with it, accept the way it was.

As Ledoux worked his way toward the suspect mudbank he knew that this whole affair was too sloppy to come through unhurt. Bound to get caught out in a messy deal like this. He knew he could do another bit in Jeff City if he had to, not standing on his head or without taking his shoes off, but he could stand it. But he couldn't handle pulling life and that Cobb kid could whine some plea-bargain ballad that would get that done to him.

Plenty of reason to erase the boy's voice right there, even if he didn't, by now, just plain old *want* to kill him.

Everything was pale in the sky, black on the ground, gray in the night-wash that was the huge in between. Shade tried to will his eyes to adjust, to focus into X ray and show him where he was. He was as lost as any child could get but more worried by it. He looked this way and that, and saw all that could be expected. It wasn't enough.

He thought about climbing one of the hairy-barked trees that cow-licked out of sight. But it'd just be to rip his britches and see more trees and less ground. No point.

Shade had quit on trying to stay dry. Wetness was dues in a swamp, and he had paid up, first just to his knees, then a backstep misstep had put him into the thick water, flat, face up, nostril-deep. Unknown things rubbed against his skin and he had frequently walked into the ditch-spanning webs of absurdly ambitious spiders. They felt like nets breaking over his head and shoulders, sticking like spun sugar.

Leeches.

Shade's hands went inside his shirt. He ran his fingers over the tautness of his chest and belly, and found three moist clingers at his midriff. They felt like nose hockers but they'd buried their heads and wouldn't pull loose. Have to singe them out. Shade slumped. Forget them for now.

He trudged on resolutely, staying in the ditch water because once you were past dainty notions of dryness it was the clearest path to follow. The growth on the banks was an incestuous tangle of verdure. No single plant stood out, just a solid mass of related limbs and leaves and vines, all atop one another with stickers on the handholds.

The hum of everything that flowed or splashed, sang or chattered, was in constant need of deciphering. Was that a footstep? A cough? Wind? A rifle sighting in on the back of your head?

At some places the bottom went deep and Shade had to dog-paddle to the next muck promenade. He tried to keep his pistol dry but it didn't really matter.

After a while he began to hear a soft thump, a regular flat tap that seemed out of rhythm. He went toward it but couldn't see what it was until he was nearly touching it.

A johnboat adrift. That meant two people at least were out there somewhere.

Shade chinned himself on the gunwale, tilting the boat for a look inside. Nothing but a cracked paddle and an empty coffee can. He'd thought there might be an inert someone in the boat and was not entirely relieved that there wasn't.

As he released the gunwale and eased back down into the water, he found himself remembering a time that he kept hoping he would forget. It had been one of those gentle summer nights when the whole world had sweet breath, especially if you were sixteen and barely scarred, and he'd felt magically carefree, standing as he was in front of De Geere's Skelly Station because it was the closest place to home that sold red cream soda, holding a handful of bottletops that he flying-saucered across the traffic. On such a night he had believed that no one could take offense at harmless fun, even if the serrated disks had skimmed the hood of your new Impala. So he had hardly noticed the car suddenly whipping to the curb and the wad of man that jumped onto the sidewalk before the door could bounce shut behind him. The man was thirtyish with high straight shoulders and a face that said he had many scores to settle but couldn't, yet had lucked onto one that he could. As he closed gregariously on teenaged Shade, his cheeks jerked and he said, "Don't mess with me. You're goin' to learn that."

Shade was surprised witless, an incredulous smile on his face, holding his soda and the remaining tops. "What's the problem?"

"Ain't none." And a serious fist popped upside Shade's head. He saw stars and daylight and fell, then skittered on his hands and knees across the pavement. A toe caught him in the butt, hurting more than he thought it could. He came up then with the Big Boy cream soda bottle and whacked the man on the elbow, which straightened his arm, then on the ear, which downed him. Shade stood over the flat man and shook with indecision, then bent and bashed the prominent teeth out, then hit again in the empty spot, blood pulp and white chips flecking his hand.

Old lazy-eyed De Geere had come running from the limestone station, "Get on out of here!" Then, as Shade stood by dumbly, "See what you done? You done killed the man, fool! Whoever told you you was tough, you sissy? 'Cause you ought've done it to them! You just one more Frogtown idiot boy."

And for two wired, crazy days he had run for relatives, believing that it was true, he'd killed a man and life was over.

But he hadn't really, and it wasn't, but that is when it had started to change.

★   ★   ★

Not much for it but to sit it out, Jewel thought. Off to one side he could see a tree that was leafless, drowned by too much water. The tree rose all dead by itself amid the live ones, beckoning like a lean-fingered taunt from the deep-sixed beyond.

Why would one die from what the rest get fat on?

He was in contemplation of that and other big questions, like had his life turned in the fifth grade when he'd had a teacher he could tell to shove it and she'd just shrug, when he began to hear the sounds.

Somebody was coming up the little rise, not even being too quiet about it. Boots dragged in the mud and saplings were bent into grips. Loud breaths.

Running wasn't worth it anymore. After this there could be nowhere left to run. He was caught. There were men who'd been shot up to seventeen times and lived to talk about it too much, and commandos with shoe-polish faces could slit half a dozen sentry throats in a night's work. But he didn't have a blade or any real confidence that he was one of those seventeen-bullet guys.

So he sat back in the shadows and waited, wanting only to die like a man, although no one much would ever know if he did or he didn't. Not out here.

The noise was closer now, on top of the bank. He could see that it was Pete the frogfucker he never should've known.

He watched as Pete poised catlike and swiveled his eyes all around the dark spots and tangled shapes. There was nothing for it now, and Jewel's hand hoisted a chunk of rock. He stood, hoping only to bean the guy once before he was exploded across the woods like so much red sand.

"Yo, Pete," he called. "You wouldn't be lookin' for me, would you?"

Ledoux hunkered small at the jibe of the voice, his fingers tapping on the stock of the shotgun, his body swinging toward the sound.

"Hey, boy. Why'd you run out?"

Shade, immobilized by the memory of a man he'd almost killed, was shaken when he heard something a little bit clumsy going up a muddy incline straight ahead, rustling bushes. He crouched in the water and stared toward the sound. There was more of it. The mud terrace had cockspur all over it, and he distinctly heard a sharp breath. He began to slow-motion through the water, careful not to splash, sneaking up from behind.

Moonlight oozed through the trees and spotted the water now and then. In one such brief illumination Shade saw the surface wriggle with a chilling sashay two steps in front of him.

Cottonmouth.

He stood still but the snake had some interest in him and turned toward the heat of his body. The curiosity of the reptile had peril at its core, and Shade pulled no air, shyly watching the triangular head weave side to side to within inches of his face. He tried to not look edible and to remember correctly the folklore that said either snakes never bite in the water or they *only* bite when afloat. It was confused in his mind.

The snake's length was strung out in the weak current, but his head was still right there.

The sound on the mudbank became louder and regular, then there was a blast of a shotgun and a yell.

Shade cupped both hands beneath the water, then shoved a wave at the snake and dove to his right, his face submerging. When he came up he began to run toward the shot, looking for the cottonmouth that he couldn't see, reaching for his pistol which he pulled and cocked.

In the pause, Jewel heard the click of the safety being punched off. It rang out like half of a ding-dong.

"Couldn't stand the idea of corned beef, you frogfuckin' shit."

One of the myriad of shroud shadows moved and Ledoux stared at the area. He peered into the thicket, then shot, hoping for luck.

The pellets ripped through the leaves above Jewel, pattering like supercharged rain. He fell to the ground and began to crawl. His elbows squeaked in the mud. The rock was still in his hand, but useless.

Rapid splashes began to sound from the ditch down the mudbank. A pistol was fired in the air.

Jewel saw Ledoux stop, startled by the new dynamics, and thought, Duncan, Duncan has come to the aid of blood thicker than any water, even this.

Quickly another form appeared and a voice unrelated to him said, "Don't, Ledoux!"

Ledoux backed toward Jewel, going "Huh?" then suddenly fired at the man. The pellets were screened by the curtain of leaves and limbs and the man did not fall or even cry out. He fired back, and Ledoux did a headfirst backflop into the mud, the shotgun flying from his hands.

Just one bullet, Jewel thought.

He went after the body with the rock swinging his hand, knowing that he didn't know much but this was it. No mistake.

One more chance.

Shade came forward under the trees, his pistol hand trembling, his gaze centered on the man he'd just tumbled. The man was bucking convulsively and groaning a long single tone.

The shooting had the sanctity of self-defense but the gurgle of the downed man ruled out any feeling of righteousness. Shade had never shot another man and he walked cautiously, looking for the shotgun that might still figure in all of this.

A wild screaming blond came running from the dark, crouched to the ground, one hand raised above his head.

"Stop!" Shade yelled.

But the blond closed on Ledoux and began to beat at the fallen man with a frenzy of blows. Something cracked and the feral sounds from both men were raised in a sickening duet.

"Damn it, stop!"

Shade stepped quickly to the men and shoved Cobb away. He saw the rock in the boy's hand and pointed his pistol in his face.

"No more, Cobb."

Jewel breathed loudly, sitting back on his haunches, his legs spread before him.

"I got to kill him, he wants to kill me." Jewel sucked for air and jerked his words. "He wants to kill me." He looked up at Shade, his eyes glowing. "I'm a killer."

"No, it's over. It's over."

Jewel backed off and lay on the ground, sobbing for breath.

Kneeling, Shade checked Ledoux. He'd been ripped in the lower left chest, inches below the heart. Blood was leaping from the wound. Cobb's rock pummeling appeared to have been ineffective, only adding some deep bruises to his chest.

"It's bad," Ledoux said. "I know. Oh, shit this upstream life."

Shade stiffened his fingers straight, then pressed them inside the hot wound, trying to block the hole.

"Oh! Oh!"

"You try to run, Cobb, and I'll kill you."

"I guess I won't," Jewel said, his voice dreamy with weakness.

"We can't get out of here in the dark, Ledoux," Shade said. He pressed his fingers against the moist rim of the wound he'd given the man. "You'll have to hang on."

They all sat silently for a moment. Ledoux, his face warping with pain, stared up at Shade.

"I've seen you," he said.

"I'm Rene Shade. I want you to know."

"Ugh. Sure. Lafitte Street Shades. Shot by you."

"You made me."

"Oh, I remember you, mon petit homme. You ain't clean. None of you are."

Shade nodded.

"You were a punk," Ledoux said, his voice warbling, his breath flecking blood. "You stole, all of you."

"Yes."

"Oh, hell, you've shot me. *You.*"

The sounds of the swamp had come back to life, the intrusion of the shots having been forgotten. The amphibian blats and limb–rattling movements of coons and others sounded all around.

"You hurt people," Ledoux said. "Where do you get off shootin' me?"

"I never would've killed," Shade said. "Take it easy, Ledoux. You would've."

"So? Ugh, ugh. I had ambitions, so?"

"Save your strength."

Jewel Cobb was now relaxed with the final relief of having been caught. He lay on his belly, head on arms, and mumbled sleepily into the mud. Shudders made his body palpitate in the muck, and his voice would raise incoherently.

For a long time Shade had hopes that Ledoux would live, but he felt the odds get longer against that chance with each squirt through his fingers.

Once Ledoux raised his head, with an effort that shocked by its difficulty, and said, "Can I be forgiven?"

"I don't know."

Ledoux slumped back.

"Fuck it."

"Maybe."

Soon after that Shade withdrew his fingers from their pointless position and leaned against a tree trunk, weary, sick to the bone, and sad. He looked up through the trees where a bit of sky showed. Since the swamp was essentially impenetrable at night, they could not leave until morning and help arrived. He sat looking at the sky and the corpse he'd made, waiting.

Waiting.

As the night sky began to pale, carp, following some primal urge, came up to the mudbanks and began their fishy barks that sounded the coming of dawn. The weird prehistoric grunts roused Shade from a flinching slumber.

The Cobb kid was still asleep and the world was coming awake. The sun rose pink in the east and the various flows seemed somehow louder in the light.

Shade, his eyes like robin's eggs in tablespoons of blood, stood when full dawn arrived. Soon he heard them. The full throttle hum of searching boats.

He raised his pistol with a slack arm and fired the three SOS shots of one in distress, into the sinkhole tangle of the Marais du Croche.

The Coming Days

THE HEAT hung around until it was no longer mentioned as weather but only as some cosmic revenge. The big brown garbage scow of a river began to steam with malodorous ferment, and one Nelda Lomeli, who had just the week before dredged out a channel cat with whiskers that would shame a weeping willow, and that dressed out to a grand eighty-four shit-fattened pounds, returned to the same spot. She cast into the water and when she began to reel in, found that she was snagged. Then she thought that perhaps it was another monster cat, and pulled hand over hand on the thick-twine line. Whatever it was lifted off the bottom and rode with the current and she stepped into the flow to grapple with it. She did not scream when the head and shoulders appeared, for she was a longtime river woman, but she didn't want to touch it. Finally she dragged the bloated body to the lip of the sandbar, and Duncan Cobb, with a whole lot of extra mouth where his throat used to be, was found.

Alvin Rankin was now dead to the withered-wreath stage, and downtown, in the white stone City Hall, Eddie Barclay, a terra-cotta runner-up, was sworn in as his replacement. Mayor Crawford proclaimed it a continuation of Rankin's good work, and Barclay, as his first official act, gave the Music Center contract to Dineen Construction of Hawthorne Hills and was instantly free of debt.

Over where the windows had bars and shoestrings were considered to be a temptation to take the easy way out, Jewel Cobb sat awaiting trial. He knew nothing, everyone he could finger was dead, and his ignorance was so convincing and total that he had little to bargain with. So he was pleaded guilty but not special, although he knew that a jury of his peers, even selected by the random dozen, would recognize the punch line way before the end of *that* joke.

And the baffling events of summer had another daffy moment when Steve Roque carried his trash to the curbside bins but found the twist tops of the garbage bags to be undone and paused to tie them, only to be shot for it under the arm, in the side, and just above the knee by some invisibles, who remained so. He would live, but never talk, and it was considered to be injury by misadventure.

But the town went on, Saint Bruno sucked up and staggered tall, for there were regular worries more pressing—like the floods that would come as they always had, and those pushed out by the rising tide would once more be driven before it, forced to connive toward all those higher grounds...

On a Sunday of continuing punishment, Rene Shade, out for a peaceful drive, passed the Catfish Bar and saw his brother in the doorway. He pulled into the lot and let himself in. Tip was sweeping the floor, all alone.

"I've been wanting to see you," Shade said.

Tip paused with the broom in his hand, then dropped it.

"You've had plenty of time. Haven't seen you in weeks. I've been expectin' you."

"Fix me a drink."

"Why not."

When Tip went behind the bar, Shade followed. He leaned against the cooler and watched Tip lift a bottle of rum.

"I had to kill a man because you lied to me, Tip."

"Don't lay that off on me, li'l blood. That's your job. You picked it."

"Cobb was right there in your kitchen and you didn't tell me."

Tip scooted the rum along the bar.

"I didn't really know what was goin' on, man."

"You could be busted for that."

"Bullshit. It'd never stick and you know it. How's your drink?"

"I'm very angry."

"Nothin' you can do about it. Now drink your drink and get—"

Shade's right hand banged the heavy whiskey glass on his brother's jaw. The big man was stunned but managed to throw a windy left that spun him when it missed, and Shade stepped in with a pop to the mouth and a quick knee to the groin. As Tip began to slide down Shade dropped the glass, then threw an overhand right at his dodgeless brother, and knocked him cold.

He stood there over the sack of flesh that was related to him in too many ways and began to shake. Blood was flooding from his brother's mouth and his eyeballs shuddered behind their lids.

He shoved open the cooler and grabbed a handful of ice, then knelt to Tip. He cradled his head in his lap and held the ice to the torn mouth.

"You dumb bastard," he said, his eyes blinking rapidly, "I love you."

MUSCLE FOR
THE WING

"Why, a human being should be the most fabulous creature of all, which is the way the Man Upstairs intended when He put the show on the road in the first place. But what happens is, one human gets to plotting with another human and maybe another and another, and after a while they all decide to be generals. So right away they form a combine in order to get the Hungarian lock on the mooches and the suckers, and that kind of action touches off all the war jolts from here to Zanzibar. That's human endeavor for you."

—MINNESOTA FATS

1

WISHING TO avoid any risk of a snub at The Hushed Hill Country Club, the first thing Emil Jadick shoved through the door was double-barreled and loaded. He and the other two Wingmen were inappropriately attired in camouflage shirts and ski masks, but the gusto with which they flaunted their firearms squelched any snide comments from the guests seated around the poker table.

Jadick took charge of the rip-off by placing both cool barrels against the neck of a finely coiffed, silver-haired gent, and saying loudly, "Do I have your attention? We're robbin' you assholes—any objections?"

The table was a swank walnut octagon, with drink wells and stacks of the ready green on a blue felt top. The gentlemen who had assembled around it for an evening of high-stakes Hold 'Em were well dressed, well fed, and well heeled, but now their mouths hung loose and their poolside tans paled.

"Hands on the table, guys," Jadick said. "And don't any of you act one-armed." A short man with an air of compact power, Jadick moved with brisk precision and spoke calmly. He pulled back the hammers on his archaic but awesome weapon and said, "Scoop the fuckin' manna, boys."

"Check," said Dean Pugh. He and Cecil Byrne, his fellow Wingman, went slowly around the table shoving wads of cash into a gym bag that had St. Bruno High Pirates stenciled on the side.

Twelve hands were palm-down on the blue felt. Manicured fingers twitched in obvious attempts to covertly twist wedding bands and pinkie rings so that the flashy side was down.

Jadick watched the fingers and rings business until two or three had indeed been twisted into seeming insignificance, and the owners began to relax. He then said, "Get all the jewelry, too."

"Check," said Pugh, a daffy man who oddly relished the orderliness of military jargon.

Pugh and Byrne both carried darkly stylish pistols, and as they went around the table they pressed them to the ears of the players. While they raked up the money and jerked fine gems from plump fingers, Jadick scanned the room, nodding his head at how closely it resembled what he had expected. Tournament trophies and low-round medals were enclosed in a huge glass case, along with antique wooden-shafted clubs and other golfing memorabilia. A long horseshoe bar of richly hued wood halved the room and several conference tables were dotted about the other side. Just beyond the poker table, nailed at a dominating height on the wall, there were scads of stern portraits, presumably of the exclusionary but sporty founders.

"Hah!" Jadick snorted. Some long-festering desire took hold of him and he shoved the shotgun against the neck of the privileged man before him until he was rudely rubbing an upscale face against the tabletop. "I bet all of you sell city real estate to niggers and live in the 'burbs—am I right?"

One of the wide-eyed, harkening faces turned to Jadick. This man was younger than the other players, with a big bottle of Rebel Yell in front of him and an empty spot where his small heap of money had been. His hair was closely cropped and blond and his cheeks were full and flushed.

"Your accent," he said, "it ain't from around here. It's northern. That's why you don't know you're makin' a mistake, man—this is a protected game."

"Really?" Jadick said. "If this is '*protected*,' I'm goin' to get over real good down here."

Despite the low hum of air-conditioning, the victims sweated gushingly and shook with concern, for, not only were they being shorn of their gambling money, but history was staggering and order decaying before their eyes. The swinging side of the St. Bruno night world had been run as smoothly and nearly as openly as a pizza franchise for most of a decade and now these tourists from the wrong side of the road somewhere else were demonstrating the folly of such complacence. Auguste Beaurain, the wizened little genius of regional adoration, had run the upriver dagos, the downriver riffraff, the homegrown Carpenter brothers, and the out-of-state Dixie Mafia from this town and all its profitable games in such an efficient and terrifying manner that no one had truly believed he would ever again be tested this side of the pearly gates.

But here and now these strangers, too ignorant of local folklore to know how much danger they were in, were taking the test and deciding on their own grades.

"I think we should make 'em drop trou," Pugh said. He widened an eyehole in his ski mask with a finger from his gun-free hand. "These are the sort of hick sharpies who figure money belts are real nifty."

Jadick nodded and stepped back so that he had a clear shot at all concerned.

"A fine notion," he said. He raised the barrel up and down. "You heard him, dudes—stand up and strip." Jadick added scornfully, "Don't be shy."

At this coupling of humiliation with monetary loss, there were some sighs and whimpers. But all of the men stood and unbuckled their pants; then, five of the six dropped them to their ankles.

"What'd I say?" Pugh said. "There's a money belt." Pugh advanced on the man with the thick white money belt and pulled on it and it stretched like a big fish story. "What the hell?"

"Man," said the shamefaced tubby, as the released elastic snapped back, "man, it's a corset. Over the winter I got fat."

"Shit," Pugh said, then noticed that the blond man who'd earlier yammered about "protected games" had yet to bare his butt to financial scrutiny. "Say, Jim," he said harshly, "take 'em down!"

"Come on," Cecil said, "I got the dough—let's cut."

"Not 'til this guy does what I said. He's holdin' out."

The blond man's face was red and wet. Fear was wringing his features like a sink-washed sock. He was too jammed up to make a definite response: he looked from one face to another; studied his feet; blinked rapidly; then said: "This is a protected game. I'm telling you all…"

"Shut up, Gerry," the corseted man said. "If you'd been at the door like…"

Jadick rapped the shotgun barrel on the table.

"He's the guard," he said. "Get his piece."

But as that final sentence was still being uttered, the blond, with one hand holding his unbuckled trousers, slid the other hand behind his back where holsters clipped on, and began to spin away, grunting and sucking for air.

Pugh screamed, "Yeah, right!," then cut him down before his pistol cleared his shirttails, spotting his shots, tearing the man open in the belly, the thigh, one wrist and, finally, just above the left ear.

The body slumped against the wall in an acutely angled posture that nothing alive could withstand. Blood pumped up out of the wrist onto the wall, and instantly washed down in a wide smear.

"Anybody else?" Pugh asked, expecting, as a response, silence, which he received. The Jockey-shorted high rollers were immobilized by the noise, the blood, and the lingering scent of gunfire.

"Hit the door," Jadick said gruffly. He used the gun barrel to point the way. "Let's go." He was not upset that murder had been required, for, in the short run, the only run that really mattered, it might set a useful precedent. Yeah, the hicks will know that some new rough element has dropped in on their town. "I'll be right behind."

Pugh and Byrne backed through the door while Jadick acted as rear guard. He looked out of the Chinese-shaped eyeholes and saw so many of the things he'd never liked reflected in these tony, awestruck, half-dressed money-bag types that he couldn't pass up a chance at scot-free revenge.

★   ★   ★

The silver-haired man whose neck he'd used for a gun rest was at a handy remove so he hopped forward and chopped blue steel across his fine, blue-chip nose, heard the crack and quash and knew the gent would now have a common Twelfth Street beak he would be ribbed about on the nineteenth hole from here 'til the grave. With considerable satisfaction he watched the dude sink to his knees, torrents of red ruining his tasteful silk knit ensemble. He did a little swivel, flourishing that ominous piece, and all of the men went belly-down on the carpet with their hands uselessly over their heads, and Jadick, as a signature of his scorn, blasted the fancy tabletop, scattering cards and whiskey-sour glasses, a liter of Rebel Yell, a pint of Maalox, and the thoughts of all those prone below him. The blue felt was tufted and ripped and unsuitable for any more games, and Jadick, as he left, said, "The universe owes me plenty, motherfuckers, and I aim to collect!"

2

Paradise might be a setup like this, Shade thought as he swiveled on his barstool. That is, if paradise turned out to be a long, narrow tavern on the near northside of a grumpy downriver town, that attracted a primarily female clientele who packed the joint to drink and gossip, smoke and be seen but not picked up. The place never echoed with come-on lines, and unescorted males were not encouraged to hang around. Beauticians, secretaries, a lawyer or two, frazzled housewives, and sorefooted hustling gals sat on the stuffed chairs and bamboo thrones lined along the walls, their drinks on small white side tables. Many thumbed through copies of *Vogue*, *True Romance*, *Sports Illustrated*, and *People* that were left in stacks on the corners of the black bar. A sign above the pyramid of wineglasses behind the counter said, MAGGIE'S KEYHOLE, LADIES WELCOME.

Jazz from more romantic days played on a tape machine and came swinging sweetly from speakers hung below the ceiling. Feet shod in high heels and flat heels, cowgirl boots and tennies tapped the polished wood floor unconsciously but in perfect time with Sidney Bechet or Johnny Hodges, Fletcher Henderson, the Duke, the Count, the Hawk or the Prez.

Shade, one of only three males in the room, was diverted from his smiling surveillance when the bartendress, Nicole Webb, said, "See anything interesting, Rene?"

"Oh," he said beatifically, "it's *all* interesting."

"Is that so," Nicole said. "You pick the ones you like, point 'em out, and I'll be glad to make the introductions for you, there, stud."

"That's a very modern offer," Shade said as he turned to face her across the bar. "But I'm just here waiting on you, Nic."

Nicole was on the perky side of thirty and had wild, tumbling cascades of black hair that hung to her ribs and had never been quite brushed into submission. Her eyes were green and widely spaced on her thin, sharp-chinned face, giving her a vaguely vulpine expression. She was tanned and tall, with no slack on her at all. Every move she made gave an impression of cultivated energy. Though it was the baseball season she wore a red basketball tank top with blue lettering across the front that read, Maggie's Keyhole Peepers.

"Well, why don't you look at me, once in a while?" she asked.

Shade tapped his empty glass, shrugged, then said, "If you'd bend over more, I would."

Nicole pulled herself straight, arched her spine, theatrically jutted her rear, then slid a hand over her tight denimed haunch.

"Nice stuff, huh, buster?"

"You know it," Shade answered. "Private stock."

"That's odd," she said as her posture folded back to normal and she removed the empty glass. "The Culligan Man always says the same thing. You two ought to meet." She put the glass in the sink, dried her hands and pulled out a deck of cards. "One hand for the next drink, okay?"

"Deal 'em." Shade won three hands in a row and demonstrated his recent conversion to cocktails rather than neat slugs of rum by ordering a manhattan, a vodka martini, and a sidecar. "I'm on a roll, which is maybe good, or bad. My gut doesn't know yet."

As Nicole dealt the blackjack hands Maggie Gallant came in from the back room and stood behind her. Though Maggie was well into her seventies, her hair was still colored in a dark hue so vigorously youthful that only vain old dames or presidents would try to pass it off as natural. She wore, as usual, a floor-length black outfit that hid her wide beam and gnarled legs and gave her a serious presence.

She looked at the cards and said to Nicole, "Take a hit, honey."

"On seventeen, Mag?"

"Take a hit."

Nicole did so, and when the down cards were flipped found she had bested Shade's pat nineteen with a longshot three.

"Hah, hah," Maggie said, stating a laugh but not having one. "Don't try that with your own money, honey."

"My streak is ended," Shade said. "I guess I'll actually *buy* a beer now." He put a dollar on the bar and Nicole pulled a draw, then slid the mug to him. "Bois-sec," he said, raised the beer and took a swallow.

Maggie tapped one of her sharp-nailed fingers on his forearm, snagging his attention. "So, Diamond Jim," she said in her low raspy voice, "I heard you're gonna take my gal here up into the woods somewhere and make her sleep on the ground, in the mud where snakes crawl. I heard you're callin' it a vacation."

"It's a fishing trip, Maggie."

"You have to sleep on the dirt in the woods to go fishin'?"

"That's part of the experience."

Maggie shook her head and sighed with something akin to disdain.

"It figures," she said. "You cops are the cheapest fuckers I ever met. Any two-bit horse player'd at least take her to the Biloxi Beach and put her up at a Motel Six."

"Right," Shade said. "And charge it all on a stolen credit card."

"So? What kind of a cop are you who can't scare up an extra buck for vacation?"

"A more or less straight one, Mag."

"Oh, I get it," she said with raised brows, "you think that'll help you someday."

"Naw, Mag, I'm cute but not stupid." He drank some more beer and smiled. "I'll make her a bed of pine needles and feed her rainbow trout grilled fresh from the stream."

"That part sounds fine," Nicole said. "But I've gone fishing with you before and I've never seen you actually *catch* a fish."

"I will up in the Ouachitas," he said. Shade was about sixty stitches past good-looking, with pale nicks around his eyes and a high-bridged nose that had been counterpunched level lower down. His blue eyes were suggestive of heat and doggedness, and the trimness of his body indicated physical discipline. His hair was long, brown, and weeded out slightly on top. Though he had lately begun to yearn to cast a more dashing silhouette, he still dressed like a laid-off longshoreman, favoring tight, dark T-shirts and khaki slacks, no socks and white, slip-on deck shoes. "From what I read in the paper, the trout up in the Ouachitas are practically gangstomping unwary anglers."

"How exciting," Maggie said. "I think you can buy 'em tamed and frozen at Kroger's. It's not even that far of a drive."

A Johnny Hodges version of "Don't Get Around Much Anymore" was lilting from the speakers, and the miscellaneous hullabaloo of the tavern merged with the jaunty sax to make a pleasant racket. Two women sitting on a short couch near the bar seriously debated the merits of Krystle and Alexis, while another audible pair clanged empty beer pitchers and said, "*Home*-ward! *Home*-ward!"

"Aw," Shade said, "listen, up there it's another world. That's what I want on my vacation. I don't want a beach version of St. Bruno. I want another world for five days. The river up there, it's not the color of shoe leather like this one here. Huh-uh. It's clearer'n baby piss and cooler'n Duke Ellington. You drop in a six-pack and in ten minutes you got the perfect beer." He emptied his own mug of brew. "I got a pup tent, too, you know. For comfort."

Shade's conception of comfort, trotted out so baldly, caused a pause in the badinage, the two women looking on him with the same sort of worldly pity that a claim of actually preferring store-bought biscuits over those made from scratch would have drawn. Their unsmiling but tender stares masked the little voices in their heads that said, "Son, you are not to be trusted on matters of taste. But to tell you would be too sad."

For his part Shade was transported between his ears, already several hours away by car, in the middle of a brisk, chill stream of modest depth, sniffing the abundance of mountainside pines, using ancient angling cunning to con a few fillets from that old bumpkin, Mother Nature. He would watch for the eagles known to be there, in the highest parts of that rugged geography, always ready to be awed by a glimpse of the elegant floating predator, the swooping national symbol.

"Did I tell you they've got eagles up there?" he asked. When no one seemed to have heard him he said in a louder voice, "Hey, give me another beer."

Shade watched as saucy Nicole, the longest-running romance of his adult life, her arms and shoulders bare in the hoop top, went to the tap and pulled back the spigot, the movement raising her left arm, offering him a tantalizing view of her pit hair which she never shaved, a fashion touch she'd adopted at nineteen while spending a year in Trieste pretending to be a Euro-peasant. As she brought his mug toward him he watched the familiar, slight wobbling of her endearing, pert little tits, and found himself suddenly flashing on sweaty, naked scenes in a soft bed.

"When is Maggie going to let you off, Nic?"

She set the beer on a square pad in front of him.

"Oh, Carol should be here in a few minutes. At midnight. Mags'll let me leave then." She put her elbows on the bar and rested her chin in her palms, her face close to his. "Baby, you're getting a little red around the eyes."

"It's those cocktails," Shade said. "I should stick with what I know."

Near the door a clutch of white-haired gals called out, "Yoo-hoo, dearie—we need more of that sour-mash tea, please."

As Nicole headed off to wait on them she said from the side of her mouth, "Just don't drink yourself useless."

Maggie rejoined Shade, a can of diet Dr Pepper in her hands.

"I'm holdin' some dough for you," she said.

"I know."

"You want to cash it in or let it ride on something?"

"There can't be much," he said.

"Thirty-five measly dollars," Maggie said. "I wouldn't even bother to handle your chickenshit bets if I didn't like you." She sipped her soda, hardly taking enough to swallow. "Less my ten percent and you got thirty-one fifty."

"Ooh, I'm rich," Shade said in a flat tone, "but I'll risk it all."

"I *adore* you sporty cops. Who're you takin'?"

Half lit and feeling expansive behind that recent flash of carnal expectations, Shade said, "The trustee at the nut house gave me a tip, Mag. Those crazies are so wired to the unseen I'm going to take it, too. Whoever's going against the Atlanta Braves gets my nod. And let it roll like that day by day 'til I lose, or own this joint, okay?"

"Whatever you say, mon petit chou." She placed her hand over his. "But that's sort of a wild bet for you."

"Aw," Shade said, "I'm trying to build up my retirement fund."

For the next several minutes Shade kept his whistle wet and watched as Nicole marched up and down the narrow room, carrying pitchers of beer and margaritas to the needy. Finally there was a respite when everybody had a drink and she came and stood behind the bar at his end of the rail.

"Whew," she said, "it's midnight—where's Carol?"

"Wish I knew."

A second later a pair of hands slapped down on the bar.

"Hey, Nicole," the young woman said, "how you doin'?"

"All right, Wanda. How 'bout yourself?"

"Aw, the normal. Give me two sixes of Jax in a sack, will you?"

"Sure."

Shade always checked out anybody named Lulu, Candy, Dixie or Wanda, so he did a quick scan: a young gal of about the old voting age with hair of that eye-catching, burnt-red color that spelled trouble in pulp paperbacks, a short, juicy build with an abundance of feminine bounce and a feisty freckled face that dared you to make something of it.

As the sack of beer was laid out Wanda pushed a bill across the wood. When she pocketed the change she picked up the bag and said, "Be seein' you, Nic."

"Not for a while," Nicole said.

"Oh, yeah? Why is that?"

"Rene, here," Nicole said, pointing her head toward him, "is taking me on a fishing trip tomorrow. We're going to sleep outside on the dirt—like the homeless."

"That's men for you," Wanda said and favored Shade with an unfavorable glance. "They always expect *you* to sleep on whatever hard ground *they* picked out." She then turned back to Nicole and smiled. "Have as much fun as he'll let you."

After Wanda was out the door Shade asked, "Who is she?"

"Just a Frogtown girl," Nicole answered. "Tough kid. Plays on The Peepers basketball team. Rugged little heartbreaker, too—flings elbows all over and led the team in rebounds from the guard spot."

"I guess I don't know her."

"Well, her name used to be Wanda Bone, but she's married now. It's Bouvier, I think. Something like that."

"I know a couple of Bouviers," Shade said. "But not the young ones."

Nicole looked at the clock, then at the door, hoping to see Carol.

"Well, the one she married is a lot older'n her," she said. She took a sip of Shade's beer. "He's older'n you."

"Could it be Ronnie Bouvier?"

"Yeah, I think so. I think that's him."

"Ronnie's in the joint."

"Yeah, life's a bitch," Nicole said. There were other things on her mind. "If Carol doesn't show pretty quick I'm going to send you out to find her."

Well, just at that moment huffing Carol came in the back door, carrying her shoes. Nicole huddled with her briefly to hear the latest excuse, for Carol generally excelled at them, but this time she told the lame one about the dead car battery and the long dutiful walk in the midnight hour. In any case she took Nicole's place behind the bar.

After telling Maggie they'd be on the road at dawn and back next week, Shade and Nicole made it out of the bar and into the pleasant shirt-sleeve weather of a late summer night in the delta.

"So," Nicole said, "what's the plan?"

"Don't need one," Shade answered cryptically. "The rest of tonight is preordained, Miss Nastiness."

"How's that?"

"I read my horoscope this morning," Shade whispered as he pulled her close, slipping the straps of her tank top down and cupping a bared breast. "It was spelled out."

They made it to his car behind the bar and leaned against it, doing some sloppy tongue weaving there beneath a dim streetlight.

"Uh-huh," Nicole said, "I'll bite — what'd your horoscope say?"

"It said, and I think it's true, that I should follow you tonight and sex you down."

"Oh, that's all?" Nicole pulled her shirt all the way to her waist and clasped her hands above her head. "It didn't say where?"

"Baby, the stars left that up to you."

3

WANDA BONE Bouvier had that thing that makes a hound leap against his cage. It was a quality that was partly a bonus from nature and partly learned from cheesecake calendars and Tanya Tucker albums. Wanda had realized early on that her body was a taunt that sent would-be Romeos off on quests for Love Oil and ceiling mirrors and nerve. She had gone clean up to her sixteenth year, wandering school halls and pool halls, public parks and private parties, doing an earthy shimmy and sashay through them all. Though she had a deadpan gaze she had always sharply noted the weak knees and lolling tongues around her. She had found this effect to be delightful and fun until that fateful sixteenth year when she had gone with a girl friend to a roller-skating rink at dusk, and left before midnight in love forever with a fortyish gangster.

And, though this fine love had turned her around, and once or twice out, it had not turned suitors away. Her butt got pinched more than a baby's nose and even her snappy slaps back couldn't stop them. Since Ronnie had gone away to the Braxton Federal Pen she had come to feel like she was a go-go girl in strange men's dreams, for so many of them called or stopped her on the street to say they'd been thinking of her, constantly.

When Wanda parked in the drive of the drafty hulk of a house she'd been reduced to by jail widowhood, one of the more harmless of her trailing pack came across the street from the only other nearby house, and said, "I got off early, Wanda. Can I carry the sack?"

"That's okay, Leon," she said. She hoisted the sack and held it with both hands. "I'm tired tonight, but I can carry a little beer."

Leon Roe was a couple of years Wanda's elder, and he worked at a bump-and-grind place called The Rio, Rio. Roe was a combination disc jockey–emcee. The man's sad slouch kept him under six feet tall. He was thin, with brown spit curls drooling down his forehead, and he wore a black coat with narrow lapels, a white shirt and a string tie, all in accordance with the resurging style of the rockabilly bad boy.

"When are you gonna take a lunch with me?" he asked, using a phrase that was meant to demonstrate that though he was on the bottommost rung of the showbiz ladder, he knew the lingo.

"Oh, are we goin' through this again?" Wanda said. "I always reserve the right to do whatever turns me on, Leon. And takin' a lunch with you ain't it."

Leon looked down at his boots, then up at the trees that swayed gently in the murky night.

"You know," he said, "it's totally dark out here."

"Don't even think about it," Wanda said firmly. "Look, you're an okay fella but not my sort. That's all. But if you think that because it's dark out here you got any chance of doin' somethin', you just forget it."

"I think you're the most beautiful girl in Frogtown," he said.

"Yeah, you've said that before, Leon. It won't get you anywhere." Wanda started up the dirt rut to the house, the sack of brew rustling in her arms. "See you later, Leon. Don't be mad."

When she reached the front door she looked over her shoulder and saw her only neighbor going back across the street to his house. Once inside she started turning on lamps in all the rooms, a nightly exorcism of fears she kept to herself. For, living out here past the railroad bridge, beyond the comforting reach of family and streetlights, Wanda survived cheaply but nervously. Vache Bayou, an offshoot of the Marais du Croche, was less than a freethrow toss behind the house. Being alone in this remote stretch of Frogtown, a section of the city where folks who thought they were tough got plenty of chances to prove it, left her feeling vulnerable to any number of the sneaky vicissitudes.

After a hot shower Wanda took a Baggie of home grown wacky-backy from the vegetable crisper in the fridge and sat at the kitchen table to twist a few sticks while letting the warm air dry her damp body.

A few minutes later she felt dry so she lit a joint and padded into the back room and turned on the stereo. As she listened to Roseanne Cash sing of people who could just about be her, Wanda dressed. She slipped on a sky-blue camisole with a ragged hem that reached to the bottom of her ribs, then pulled on a pair of shiny white satin shorts that seemed wetted onto her ass like hot breath on a cold jewelry window.

On her way through the kitchen she grabbed a Jax and went out to the screened-in back porch that overlooked the vast gumbo known as the bayou. She had left the arm up on the stereo so the album played over and over, and as she listened she pondered the regular things, the things she'd been pondering for the twenty-two months that Ronnie Bouvier had been in stir. Tonight she mainly contemplated what he'd asked her to do; that worried her the most by far, because she was already doing it. She loved him and she would do what needed to be done, as she always had. And to think that once upon a time, really just twenty-two months ago, he had seemed in possession of the answer to every important question in her life. But now *she* was expected to take care of *him* and get him out of Braxton with his future wrapped up and waiting pretty as a gift.

Oh, it was a spring night only five years before when she'd gone roller skating, a girl with a grown-up bod and an undeniable naughty rep, only to have Ronnie Bouvier, his black hair slicked back like a singer, pull up in a blue Corvette, idling alongside her at the Dairy Maid next to the rink. The first thing he'd said to her audible over the rumble of the powerful motor, was, "Those your tits, darlin'? They look like a movie star's tits to me." And she said back to him, "Well, I never," but truly she had, and in what seemed no more than a blink this man who was actually older than her father worked a romantic smash-and-grab on her, right there next to the skating rink, big-timing her out of her hip huggers before they even left the parking lot. She had instantly understood that he was different, and that this clothes-off grunting and pumping was the sweaty way of love. Two days later she moved out of her parents' house and into a brand-new world of sit-down restaurants, late nights in roadhouse back rooms, and money. Plenty of money. Then one day Ronnie told her the news that bad luck had been circling his block his whole life long and once again it had found a parking space right outside his door. It was a little federal thing Mr. B. set him up for, he explained, and it sounded worse than it was, so don't fret.

One week before beginning his sentence they were married legal at city hall.

Wanda heard the front door open but did not rise from her chair. She stared out through the screen, into the black and noisy bayou night. Her inhalations made the joint beam in the dark, and then the music died, and over the beep of bullfrogs she heard not one person, but a few, coming through the kitchen toward her.

The clopping feet stopped and she turned to see three men, backlit by the kitchen light, staring down at her.

"Emil," she said in a tone stoned flat, "you're supposed to come alone."

"I knew that," Jadick said. He came onto the porch and sat on the wide arm of her ratty old chair. He plucked the joint from her lips and took a hit. "I wanted to come alone, pun-kin, but we got ourselves a slight problem."

"Oh, yeah?"

"Yeah. Dean, here, killed a dude at the country club."

"Tell me you're lyin'."

"It ain't no lie."

"Oh, man," Wanda said. "Oh, man."

"He had to do it, Wanda. The dude did a no-no. He went for his piece. You understand we couldn't allow that."

Wanda raised her feet to the wide windowsill, crossed them, then leaned way back in the chair and kept her eyes fixed on some unclear thing out there in the nightbog that had her mesmerized.

"I sure am glad I'm ripped," she said. "There's beer in the fridge. Help yourselves."

Later, Dean Pugh came out of the bathroom and stood in the hall, rubbing his skinny butt with both hands, and said, "I feel like I shit a hungry kitty!" After this unprovoked announcement he took a seat at the kitchen table, joining the others. "I want you to know," he said straight at Wanda, "that I hated killin' a white guy."

"Uh-huh," Wanda responded. Her eyes matched the shade of her hair now. Another half-smoked joint was dried to her lower lip and bobbed as she spoke, the cold ashes fluttering down. "I don't think they'll let you hide behind that, though. *Not legally.*"

"Well, I done hid behind a mask, lady, and it worked just fine."

Wanda had already listened to the whole dingy tale twice. The victim, "just another golfer type," was clearly dead, definitely in the processing department of Hell even now, the stolen getaway car had been left in an unpopulated part of Frogtown, and while they'd driven the clean car from there to here, the death gun had been pitched into the bayou. It hadn't seemed smart to be driving around town late at night after a robbery-murder so they would lay up here until it felt like time to leave. Probably by midday they'd cut out and get upriver to the deep swamp cabin they'd intended to stay in, and wouldn't be back until she'd cased the next job.

"Auguste's goin' to be awful mad," she said somberly. "That's a scary event, too, when *he* loses his temper."

"Fuck him," Jadick said. "Let him run all over bein' mad—that's what we want. That's what *Ronnie* wants." Jadick smoothly sucked off half a can of brew. "When us guys have got it set up and Ronnie and them other Wingmen get out, why, bein' mad at us will be a mistake."

Finally noticing the dead roach dangling from her mouth, Wanda spit it onto the tabletop.

"I don't know," she said. "I don't know about doin' any more of this if you all're goin' to waste people. That might be the wrong gimmick for around here."

"Bullshit," said Dean, hotly. Cecil, wraithlike Cecil, watched him with admiring eyes. "Listen up to me, girl. We got a schedule, a plan, a design for The Wing." He pointed at her face and his own bony visage scowled. "Now, Ronnie won't be happy if you wuss out on us, and I *guarantee* you the rest of The Wing won't be happy with Ronnie, either. And Braxton is a small place. Funny things happen with steel around there."

"I get it," she said.

"Do you?" Jadick asked.

"Yeah, Emil. It's simple and I understand you all's sort of subtraction."

This Dean Pugh character would need close watching. He was foul and lean, junk-food raised and opposed to dentistry judging by his greening teeth. His skin had a yellow tinge, beneath shitfly green eyes, and his brain was possibly odd enough to posthumously set off a bidding frenzy among scientists. He generally seemed batty as a loon, goofy as a goose on ice, immaculately weird, with no stain of normalcy on him at all.

And Cecil Byrne was his *friend*.

They could have Ronnie killed with a phone call.

"I'll get right on checkin' out the next place," she said, looking down. "It might take awhile to find."

"That's what The Wing wants to hear," Jadick said pleasantly. "Us and Ronnie and you, we're going to use this town to get even."

"Even with what?"

"Just even," he said. "That's what everybody really wants, is to get even."

"If gettin' even is so hot," Wanda said, absently rubbing a flat palm over her midriff while staring out through the porch door, "how come nobody ever stops there?"

In the wee hours she said, "I'd like it if you'd shut the bedroom door first."

"Ain't we delicate?" Jadick said, but he did close the door. A thick red candle sat before a vanity mirror, filling the room with soft, waltzing light. Emil pulled his shirt off, looking down at Wanda, who lay on her back on the bed, watching him. He checked himself out in the mirror, admiring the jailhouse sculpture he'd pumped his body into being. "I'm as strong as I look, too," he said.

"I know," she said. Last week Wanda had thrown him a fuck to seal the pact, and, though she'd done it out of a sense of duty, she'd been shocked at how badly she desired this duty. She had nimble fingers, a dirty mind, and plenty of privacy in which she'd utilized the two, but it had been a long time between injections of the real. "Your tummy is the strongest one I've ever seen in person."

Jadick smiled.

"Three hundred sit-ups a day, pun-kin. Nothin' else to do in Braxton, you know. Locked up like that, you get into fitness." Jadick had short, limp black hair, a stumpy neck, and muscles everywhere. His face was wide and flat, a common enough look back in Parma, Ohio, a bohunk, polack, et cetera section of Cleveland. "With baby oil," he said, "my body's a real slick temple."

Suddenly his face split with a wide smile.

"I got something for you," he said. "Answer me this—what's the most romantic word there is?"

Wanda stared at him dully, showing him that tough expression she generally showed the world.

"Ouch?" she said.

"Ouch?" He looked at her with his eyes narrowed. "No, no, ouch is the *second* most romantic, there, pun-kin." He reached into his pants pocket and brought out a handful of rings. "Diamonds, Wanda. *Diamond* is the number one most romantic word."

The bed was a Salvation Army bargain, a mottled pink mattress tossed on the wooden floor. Jadick sat on the edge and lifted Wanda's left hand. He held various rings up to her fingers, then pushed a nice showy one on, shoving it up next to her wedding band.

"Wanda," he said in a childish, playful tone, "will you be my valentine?"

"Valentine's is long past, Emil."

"Yeah, that's right," he said. He slid his hands between her shiny white shorts and her ass, palms up, and squeezed. "So, you wanna fuck?"

She smiled up at him and his highly defined arms and chest, and said, "I'm too worn out to scream."

Jadick pulled his hands free, then stood. He positioned himself so that he was visible in the mirror. As he undid his trousers he fixed his face into a stern but smoldering expression. He kicked his slacks off, then stood on the bed over Wanda, and put his hands on his hips and flexed here, there, and all over. She went, "Mmm," and he slowly lowered himself until he was kneeling between her legs. His hands went back to her hard round ass and as he lifted her up, he pulled the shorts apart at the seams, then raised her higher, his eyes on hers, and higher still, then licked her buttocks and ran his tongue straight up through the wetness to her belly button. He sprang forward on his knees, beneath her, and lowered her onto his cock, pushed her back flat and thrust hard once, then raised himself on stiffened arms. A bead of sweat ran down his nose as he glared at her from above, and he gruffly said, "Ouch, huh?"

The dawn came on, pink and sweet, to find Emil Jadick sitting bareassed on the back porch, having an eyeopener of beer. Somehow, being down here in chitlin country made him feel reflective. He was now at that jarring, mid-thirties turning point, that age where persistent losers often decide that the cause of their failure is not lack of talent, but scope. Yeah. That's it. Something big, something truly audacious, would cause that self-rumored talent to boil to the top and be seen.

Taking over all the night action and daylight graft of an entire redneck town—that was something big. And The Wing was the crew to do it, too. With himself in charge, why, only bad luck could mess it up.

The Wing was a white prison gang, a loose nationwide cartel of sorts that kept in touch via three-to-five jolts and visitation privileges. Though not as strong as The Aryan Brotherhood or The Brown Mafia or The Locked-Up Muslims, The Wing had dirty fingers that could pull triggers on both sides of those high federal walls. Federal prisons served as a kind of criminal headhunter's service bringing hoods and hustlers from all parts of the nation into contact, and this led to frequent yardbird seminars on how we did this in Chicago, L.A., Boston, or Louisiana, and how it will work *even better* next time now that this rap has highlighted the flaws in the gambit.

As the bayou sounds shrank from the growing light, Jadick felt strong. Dean and Cecil were in the front room, snoring in each other's arms, but ready to back any play he made. The Wing planned for him to raise the financing with Wanda's help, then in a short while, Ronnie and a dozen others would be paroled, sprung from joints across the country. They'd roll right over this Auguste Beaurain asshole. No question about it. Things would be changed then. Some members of The Wing held odd religious opinions that not only did not rule out a life of crime, but, in fact, made it seem a holy path to trod in the service of a truly deciphered Lord. None of that shit mattered to Jadick for he merely wanted to be with a strong set of movers, and if what he was up to was in any way religious, he knew that he was only on the muscle end of that theology, looking for a way to shake down the future.

"Mornin'," Wanda said. She came onto the porch carrying the rags her shiny shorts had become. She took a seat next to Jadick. "I'll make biscuits and gravy."

"Fine."

"Oh, man," she said, "I'm drippin'." She began to swab at her crotch with the shorts, her head down. "Emil, I wonder what my husband thinks about all I'm doin' for him."

"Pun-kin," Jadick said, staring out across the backwater mire. "I don't see how Ronnie could be anything but proud of you."

4

FROM THE winging city pigeon's vantage point the neighborhoods of St. Bruno looked like a fist clutching at the lifeline that was the big greasy river. There, to the south, perched on a few modest mounds, was Hawthorne Hills, a reserve for the tony, where neocolonial was the favored architecture and attitude. The next thing upriver was the south side, a downtrodden but proud throng of streets, where the architecture had been inspired by the simple square, to no one's aesthetic pleasure. There was a vast midtown to be seen from an avian perspective; the seat of government was there by day, in the center of a warehouse district, and by night it was the preferred falling-down spot for winos and otherwise addled seekers. Up the hill from the river was Frechette Park, a surprisingly well-kept sprawl of greenery, and next to it Pan Fry, the longtime black neighborhood where the housing was HUD approved and roundballs of various sizes and snowcapped schemes offered the dreamy ways to better quarters. On down the hill, sprung up from the wet land, there was Frogtown, the white-trash Paris, where the wide brown flow of rank water scented all the days, and every set of toes touched bottom.

And down below, in the formative stage of the day, on a Frogtown street of frail frame houses, Detective How Blanchette stood on the porch of one rented to Miss N. Webb, and pounded against the door.

Presently the thick, inner door cracked open and Rene Shade bent around it, just his head showing behind the screen.

"How."

"Sorry, Rene. We got business."

"Come on in."

Shade backed into the living room, a space dominated by several travel posters of America with Italian writing on them, and a huge Persian rug with a path worn diagonally across the rich intricacies. Shade wore only a black T-shirt and he collapsed groggily onto a couch and bent over to strap on his ankle holster.

"I still feel hammered," he said. "I don't know where my pants are."

Blanchette held out a pair of khaki trousers, then threw them at his partner.

"I found 'em on the porch, you pervert."

"Oh, yeah," Shade said, red-eyed and smiling. "Now I remember." He stood and stepped into the pants, then, just as he latched the buckle he said, "Hey, my vacation starts in about an hour, How."

" 'Fraid not."

" 'Fraid *so*," Shade said. "We're off to the Ouachitas to feed fish to the eagles, sleep in the mud."

How Blanchette was sandy-haired and ruggedly chubby, with an innocent moon face and a cynical manner. Porkpie hats had never gone out of style with him and he was now, as usual, in his black leather trench coat which he believed trimmed twenty pounds from his shadow. His shirt and slacks were part of a large acquisition he'd made of fire-sale plaids, and he smoked a ten-cent panatela.

"The Captain canceled it," he said. "We've got some serious business at hand."

"It can't be serious enough to keep me here when the trout are biting."

"Rene, a cop got whacked. Shot four times, he was, then dumped in front of St. Joe's emergency room."

"Who?"

"A Patrolman Gerald Bell—know him?"

"Not really. Maybe if I saw him."

"Well, I just did and he don't look like anybody anymore."

Shade rubbed his fingers on his cheeks, then pulled his hands up and straight across his hair.

"I don't want to wake her," he said. "I'll leave a note."

"Do it quick," Blanchette said, then raised his nose and elaborately sniffed the air three times. "And get in there and wash your face, too. You smell like yesterday's fish."

Blanchette drove the city-issue Chevy and Shade followed him in his own blue Nova. They went crosstown to the south side where Gerald Bell had shared a home with his father.

The small square white house was at the very dead end of Nott Street, perched just above a wide ravine. Old refrigerators, rusty tin cans, and assorted trash of varying vintages littered the ravine, making it an attractive playground to boys and disease.

Shade and Blanchette went up the gray slab steps to the side door which they knew from long experience would open directly to the kitchen. The inner door was swung back and through the screen they heard music and smelled a wonderful, simmering aroma.

Before they could knock a voice from inside said, "Uh-oh, who the hell are you guys?"

"Police, Mr. Bell," Shade said, "can we come in?"

"Gerry's not here, fellas," Ray Bell said. He walked over and stood close to the screen. He was a short old sport, with thin white hair, a messed-up nose that undoubtedly had an interesting story behind it, and a retiree's pleasant paunch. "He must have scored some poon last night. I been waiting for him to drag on in."

"That's why we're here," Blanchette said.

Bell's lower lip drooped.

"Oh," he said, and let them in. They showed him their shields and he nodded absently, then took a seat at the small kitchen table. He slapped a radio and killed the country music. A heavy black kettle steamed on the stove, and the bubbling red sauce in it filled the air with a savory scent. "Is he dead?"

"Yes, sir," Shade said.

Blanchette went over toward the sweet sauce and stood near it, then lowered his head and inhaled, his eyebrows raising with approval.

"You know," Bell said as he watched the kettle, "that sauce, why, it seems like an omen. Bad luck, I guess. You know, Ramona, the wife, she died a year ago, right about where you're standin'. Too many years of bacon I guess. That's what they say anyhow. All that grease. We was raised on the stuff, or worse. You know what was cookin'? Right, that sauce. I was cookin' up some of that sauce 'cause I wanted a ham basted slow and she come in here and said, 'Can I help?' and keeled over practically dead before I could even answer. It makes me feel like I'm to blame for not pickin' up the signs from God, 'cause today is the first time I made up a batch since then." He lowered his head and growled sadly, like a wounded thing. "Oh, fellas, there's a bottle of Rebel Yell in that cabinet, there. Be good to me."

Shade fetched the bottle and set it in front of Bell.

Bell unscrewed the lid and took a tentative sip of the bourbon, then raised it again and chugged. After lowering the bottle he wiped his mouth with the back of his hand.

"What happened to my boy?"

"Shot to death," Blanchette said. He was taste-testing the red sauce, slurping off the ladle. "Don't know where he was killed but his body was dropped off at St. Joe's. He'd been dead a couple of hours already."

"Christ almighty," Bell said. "Man, I've got to wonder who'd have the stones to do that on a cop. Don't you all wonder that?"

"He was in civvies."

"Well, sure." Bell took another drink. "He was off duty."

Shade sat at the table across from Bell. Last night's cocktail fog was slowly evaporating and he was finally beginning to feel awake.

"I didn't know your boy," he said, "but we can't have this, Mr. Bell. Nobody wants to stand for cops getting whacked out like street slime."

"I know that," Bell said. "I was raised up here, in this town, and I always have noticed this strange thing that when a St. Bruno cop gets powdered, pretty soon after that one or two or even three street studs turn up, shot dead tryin' to escape. I know the drill, Detective, and don't change it now."

Blanchette, the dripping ladle in his hand, said, "Did your kid tramp his dick across private property, stuff like that? I mean, whoever took him off made him wince a good bit first." He licked the spoon, then ran his tongue over his lips. "Could've been a pissed-off husband type."

"I resent that," Bell said. His eyes had a sad, shiny look to them. He shoved up from his chair and took the ladle away from Blanchette. "I resent that comment about my dead son 'cause he wouldn't screw no married woman. Not unless he won the tail in a Hold 'Em game, at least." He put the big spoon into the kettle and began to stir. "If it was anything that got him in a jam that's what it'd be—the gamblin'."

"Was he a big gambler?" Shade asked.

"Naw, but he kept tryin' to be." Bell reached above the stove to the spice rack and selected a bottle of ground cayenne and shook it over the sauce. "If he won today he lost tomorrow. He was searchin' for consistency but it eluded him. I would reckon he was the sort of gambler all the *real* gamblers are always glad to see at the table."

"So he was a regular loser, uh?"

"He didn't call it that." Bell was now grabbing spice tins at random, and dumping what would certainly be an original and zesty blend into the sauce. The big spoon scraped against the kettle gratingly. "No, he didn't call himself a regular loser. He said he was a fella with a system." The old man looked older, and weak and weepy. "Oh, you boys have took my legs out from under me." He turned and leaned against the counter, the ladle held at midthigh, dripping long red streaks down his legs. "I'm goin' to tell you all some stuff you'll know pretty soon anyway. Gerry, I think he owed money or something. I heard he stood shotgun at crap games and such. This is what I heard but he wouldn't answer me when I brought it up. He only said, 'We both like to eat, Pop.'" Bell noted the streaks sliding down his legs and set the ladle on the stove. "You fellas, you're local, you know how it is. It's the same as always. Most everybody around here'll bet on which is the dry side of a raindrop or what hydrant a dog'll piss on. Gamblin' has always been more or less open here."

"Look," Shade said, "we won't do anything to make your boy look bad." Shade pulled the Rebel Yell near and sniffed the whiskey, then screwed the cap back on. "What aren't you telling us, Mr. Bell?"

"Aw, I heard something else. I was at Johnny's Shamrock awhile back and some of the talk there was about Gerry."

Blanchette lifted the ladle, smelled the blindly spiced sauce, and poured it back.

"Spit it out, sport," he said. "What were they gabbin' about at The Shamrock?"

"Now you, you're a rude motherfucker, ain't you?" Bell said. He pointed a gnarled finger in Blanchette's face.

"My mother's dead," Blanchette said, smiling slightly as he generally did when called a name. "The rest of it is personality."

"I see," Bell said. "A defective." He dropped his hand back to his side. "What I heard at The Shamrock was that Gerry, Gerry, maybe, possibly, had took a little battin' practice on some Frogtowner's knee-cap." Bell raised his hands and spread them. "He's gone now, ain't he? But that's what they were sayin'."

Shade stood up from the table and passed the whiskey to the trembling, sagging man.

"They say who it was?" he asked.

"Um-hmm." Bell gulped a slug of sour mash, and sniffled. "Willie Dastillon—know him?"

"Like a dog knows fleas," Shade said. "We'll check it out. You got any relatives who can sit with you today?"

"You better believe it," Bell said. "You cops better straighten this out before we do. I was pretty tough once."

"Naw, shit," Shade said, "none of that. Have a wake, or whatever, belt out some prayers, but don't get in our way. Your boy was one of ours, mister. We'll take care of it."

"Go do it then." Bell faced the stove and the boiling sauce and shuddered, then lifted the hot kettle barehanded and slopped the whole bucket into the sink, splattering the walls and counter top. He put his quickly blistering hands beneath cold tap water and said, "I ain't eatin' today."

Grif's Grubbery was a breakfast and lunch place set under a warehouse at the city market, in midtown. There was no sign out front, but forty years of word-of-mouth had caused the steps leading down from the street to become worn and smooth. It was a cozy, triangular room, with a short counter at the apex and long, communal tables in the open area.

Shade and Blanchette sat at the counter in the poorly lighted room. Grif Rosten, the owner, leaned his lanky, knobby self over the counter at the other end where he was using his side of a three-way conversation to lecture two young teamsters on the Haymarket Riot, the Reuther brothers, and other topics they deemed musty and evinced no interest in. Grif had boxcarred into town in the thirties from the West Coast where he claimed to have known Harry Bridges, Max Baer, and oriental ways of love. Though his historical and cultural hectoring resulted in frequent offers of bus tickets back to Oakland, the food kept the diner packed.

"Well," Blanchette said, "I think it might turn out that Officer Bell was a scandal waitin' to happen. That's what it looks like to me. Hey, Grif! Grif, we're hungry down here!"

"It wasn't Willie Dastillon," Shade said as Rosten slowly came toward them. "Willie might steal a hen but he wouldn't break an egg."

Rosten had slightly more than a basic issue of nose and long thin white hair that curled up at the back of his neck. He stood behind the counter, wiping his hands on a big red bib he always wore that had Texas Chili Burn-Off stitched in a circle on the front.

"Oh," he said, "the fat guy and the pug're hungry. So they yell at me. That was a yell, wasn't it? It sounded like a shout to me. A yell, a shout."

Shade was merely a customer to Rosten, but he knew that Blanchette and Grif were, behind a façade of insults, friends. It was one of those odd couplings of disparate personalities, and he understood that they frequently went duck hunting together, split a bottle of Glenlivet, or drove to Beale Street and acted shameless.

"Rosten, we're in a hurry," Blanchette said. "I'll have the usual. Rene?"

"Tomato juice," Shade said. His tongue was furry, his mouth tasted like barroom floor grunge, and his eyes felt dry. "And some of those buttermilk biscuits with gravy."

Rosten wrote the order on a small pad.

"Hung over are you, Shade?"

"I guess."

"Uh-huh," Rosten said and raised his brows. "You ever think maybe you're brain-damaged a little bit, there, Shade? Ever wonder if maybe old Foster Broome didn't jab-and-hook some useful knowledge right out of your brain?"

"I know he did," Shade said, looking up with a red baleful gaze. "But what it was that he beat out of me was all those general rules about how young guys ain't s'posed to pound on old white-haired wiseasses just to hear 'em go 'squish.' I have to work real hard to remember that one, Grif. I'm real hazy on it. Squish is a beautiful sound. Bring me some eats, huh?"

"Hey," Rosten said as he moved toward the kitchen, "just fillin' you in on the AMA report, champ."

When Rosten was gone and the knife-and-fork hubbub of the room had made silence tiresome, Blanchette said, "Lighten up, Rene. After we eat, go home, clean up, and so forth. This thing is goin' to be a full-tilt fuckin' boogie 'til we find the perp, dig?"

"Yeah," Shade answered. "He's all right. I know he's your buddy."

"Forget that," Blanchette said. He was sucking away at a soggy cigar, his coat and hat still on. "After you get cleaned up you go see Willie. I'll head back to Second Street. Bell's partner, a guy named Thomas Mouton, is supposed to be there. You see your old pal Willie, then meet me and Mouton at the station."

"Right," Shade answered. "If I can stay awake."

"You want a black beauty, there, sleepyhead?"

"Naw," Shade said. "I don't like the way I talk behind that shit."

"Good," Blanchette said. "I don't know if I have any anyhow. Knock back some of Rosten's joe."

Shade walked over to the coffeepots and helped himself to a cup. He then returned to his stool and blew on the joe.

When Rosten brought on the chow Shade was, as always, taken slightly aback at Blanchette's "usual" breakfast. He had two pork chops seasoned with fennel and skillet-fried, thick white gravy over biscuits, three eggs beat to a sludge and cooked soft, and a butterscotch shake. It was the idea of shakes before noon that put Shade over the edge.

"You are a marvel," he said to Blanchette whose mouth was otherwise employed, prompting a grunt in response. "Most guys who eat like you would get fat or something."

"Uhnn," Blanchette responded, nodding as he wrapped up a chew. He picked up a pork chop and tore the perimeter of fat away, stacking the greasy, undesirable slivers on the side of his plate. "That's my secret," he said; then, with one big sucking chomp, he turned the chop into a bone.

"You mean not chewing?" Shade asked. "That's your secret?"

"And trimmin' the fat," Blanchette answered. "Plus, let's face it—I am a little bit stout."

"Really? I guess I never noticed." Shade was shoving the biscuits around on his own plate, familiarizing himself with his breakfast before eating it. "I mean, those fuckin' plaids you're always wearing, How, they make bein' super-chunky seem sort of secondary."

"Uh-oh! You're on to *all* my secrets now."

Over the next few minutes Shade managed to eat a biscuit or two and Blanchette cleaned his own plate. They sipped coffee and Blanchette probed his teeth with a mint toothpick.

Rosten came down the counter and stood near them.

"What's new, How?"

"Well, actually," Blanchette said, "I'm glad you asked that. I want the two of you both to hear this at once. I don't play favorites." Blanchette rested the toothpick in the corner of his mouth, pulled his hat off and fanned his face with it. "Look, fellas, last night, it was a good night. The weather was decent, the Cardinals won, and I was hungry."

"Imagine that," Rosten said.

"Hush up," Blanchette said. "This is hard enough, man." He put his hat back on. "I was *hungry* so I went to Paquet's and had me some shrimp boiled in beer, and some of that yellow rice and a gallon or two of some kind of wine they had that I found out I could stand to drink, and right after stiffin' the waiter for bein' such a snot, I leaned over and asked Molly Paddock to marry me."

Rosten responded by shaking his head as if there were a terrible buzzing in his ears.

Shade said, "Man, what brought this on?"

"Well," Blanchette said, "I'll tell you what it was. What it was, is I been seein' Molly for three years and, let's face it, the young succulents were pretty good at brushin' me off and she doesn't. That attracts you to a person, when they don't brush you off and you're a guy like me. So, young succulents ain't gonna wet down my future, and I know it, and the other day I patted my middle. I patted my middle and my hand clinched around the fringe of a great gob of flab. It was then I said to myself—'How, you're so fat, you might as well go ahead and get married.'"

"That's a dandy reason to throw in the towel," Shade said. He thought of Molly Paddock, a decent, bland-faced shapeless cop-widow with a pleasant personality and no ambition at all. "I guess congrats are in order."

"Most people would think so," Blanchette said. "And what do you think about me gettin' married, Grif?"

Rosten put two long fingers to his chin and cocked his head sideways.

"I think it's a crime against women," he said.

"You shit head."

"I don't think you'll be indicted on it."

"You know-it-all shit head," Blanchette said as he stood. He tossed a bill onto the counter. He looked at Rosten. "You just couldn't say something nice, could you?"

"I want to," Rosten said, "but I'm cursed with honesty."

Shade tossed down a buck and a half and he and Blanchette shuffled out of The Grubbery and up the worn steps to the street. The whole workaday world was out and about, honking horns, grinding gears on produce trucks, walking along with eyes down.

When they reached the parking lot Shade said, "You got any ups, How?"

"I thought you didn't want any."

"I don't but I might need it. I'm pooped, man. I was drinkin' 'til four or five in the morning."

Blanchette pulled out his wallet and slid an Alka-Seltzer foil from a credit-card slot. He handed it to Shade.

"I only got this one," he said. "It'll put some zest in your fuckin' day, too."

As he walked to his own car Shade said, "I just want it in case I need it."

"Naturally, comrade," Blanchette said. "But I'll bet you do."

5

AFTER BREAKFAST Shade decided to cut the sensitive noses of the world some slack, and went home to take a shower. His apartment was a small historical curio, with furniture from the fifties, plumbing from the forties, on the second floor of a brick row house that had been built by French craftsmen who'd all been dead for a minimum of one hundred and twenty years.

Shade's mother lived downstairs and ran a poolroom from what had once been the dining and living rooms. Though still married to the ever-drifting John X. Shade, she had reverted to her maiden name for business, and called the modest establishment Ma Blanqui's Pool House.

When Shade stepped out of the shower feeling Irish Springy, he dried and dressed in light cotton. The heat would rise through the day so he selected white pants, loose and pleated, a yellow pullover that billowed out enough to hide the pistol clipped at his belt, and went sockless in his stinky white slip-ons that he felt he could run faster in.

Shade had lived in this same building for most of his life, here at the corner of Lafitte and Perry, and learned the hard lessons of the world on these hard bricked streets, within spitting distance of home. This was Frogtown, where the sideburns were longer, the fuses shorter, the skirts higher, and the expectations lower, and he loved it.

As he came down the back stairs he could see the river across the tracks, and a shimmery haze rose from it, making the farther shore a mere mirage. He slid into his car, fired the husky-sounding three twenty-seven, and headed toward the nearby abode of Willie Dastillon.

★ ★ ★

Willie Dastillon, like most good Americans, wanted to "have it all," and to him that meant having a door jimmy, a friendly fence, and a ten-minute headstart. He lived in a small frame house with green tar-paper siding on Voltaire Street.

When Shade came up the steps to the porch a small, bruised boy was wheeling a tricycle recklessly from rail to rail.

"Who you?" he asked as Shade approached.

"I'm looking for your dad. Is Willie home?"

"Mm-hmm." The boy jumped off the tricycle and reached above his head to the front doorknob. He opened the door with surprising ease. "Papa! Papa, a mister is here."

Shade stepped inside without being invited. Willie sat in the front room. His left leg was in a cast and propped up on a stool. He wore sunglasses and earphones, and held a long white back scratcher that he plucked at air-guitar style.

When he saw Shade he pulled the earphones down to his neck and Jason and the Scorchers rattled against his throat. He then shook his head and killed the music.

"Shut the door, Mick. Go back out and play."

"Okay, Papa."

Shade helped himself to a seat.

"Right, make yourself at home," Willie said. "Today must be the day of the party. I guess I forgot."

Willie Dastillon was rock-and-roll lean with a long shag of dark hair and from his left ear dangled a glittering shank of earring that might have pulled in a keeper bass if it were trolled near rocks. His nose was narrow with a sharp, balloon-busting tip, and his cheeks were blue with stubble. He wore a black .38 Special T-shirt and a pair of blue work pants with the left leg hacked off above the cast.

"Did you just drop by to watch me jam on my back scratcher, Shade?"

Shade leaned back in the soft chair and put his feet on the coffee table. His expression was flat and he stared unblinkingly at Willie.

"Is your whole band going to wear casts, Willie? I mean, I'm not up

to the minute on rock theatrics, but a whole band in casts, why, that'd
be a gimmick, but maybe not a good one."

"Hey," Willie said, "there's a thought. I'll bring it up with the guys.
I wouldn't mind puttin' the drummer in a full body cast, man. He
shows up on time but he just can't *keep* time."

Willie Dastillon was a thief and a gambler but he called himself a
musician. He'd had several local bands over the years but B&E busts
and the pursuit of bliss in powder form had kept any from lasting more
than a summer. The bruised child and wife who worked while he
didn't were both testaments to his callous vanity, for the man blew
enough on craps alone for them to live much better. He'd bet Betty's
next paycheck on a fighter he'd never seen before, or those splayfooted
ponies, or them rolling bones. He was a man with a tin-ear present
who dreamed of a rock-opera future.

"What happened to your leg?" Shade asked.

"The usual: I was backstage at a Stones concert out there in L.A. and,
you see, my buddy, ol' Jack Nicholson who is just a card and a half, says
to me, 'Willie, go on out there and turn your pipes loose on "Beast of
Burden," and shame Jagger off the fuckin' stage.' So, because me and Jack
are like this, I go out there and Keith Richards nods and smiles and Jagger bows at me and hands me the mike, and all these flowers are tossed
onstage and flashbulbs are poppin' and all I can see is a wave of young titties bouncin' in front of me, and I get confused and fall off the fuckin'
runway, break the leg. You can hear the pop on their live album, man."

"Yeah, right," Shade said. "I think I was there, too, singing harmony, wasn't I? Next time you tell it, could you mention I was there,
too, Willie?"

"Depends on who I'm tellin' it to, Shade. In some circles your name
ain't a charm."

Shade took note of the way the earring Willie wore flipped up and
down with his every head movement, and asked, "What is it with earrings, anyway?"

"Hunh?" Willie's fingers were touched to the shimmery ornament.
"It's fashion."

"That's all—just fashion?"

"Uh-huh. All my crowd has 'em."

"It doesn't mean anything? It doesn't mean, 'Hey, I'm for social justice,' or 'Party 'til you puke,' or 'Meet me in the men's room,' or nothing?"

"No, man. No. It's all about fashion." Willie turned his head to the side so Shade had a close-up view of the earring. "I just got this one, man, whatta you think?"

Shade pursed his lips and nodded slowly.

"It's very fashionable, Willie." Shade leaned over and tapped the cast on Willie's leg. "I got some questions for you."

"I knew you would." Willie pushed on the bridge of his sunglasses as if he were adding camouflage to a hiding spot. "I ain't the answer man, though."

"There is a rumor making the rounds that a cop did some leg bust- ing around here, either as a public service or a second job, I don't know which. But the rumor is he did some unlicensed chiropracty hereabouts with a fungo."

"Cops are here to protect us," Willie said, smirking beneath his Ray-Bans, "not to hurt us."

"Look, Willie," Shade said, "I want to know if a cop named Bell broke your fucking leg, so what I'm going to do is, I'm going to ask you, 'Did a cop named Bell break your fucking leg?' and that'll give you the opportunity to answer yes or no and if you do that and I believe you I won't have to go gorilla on you."

"I heard that's your specialty, Shade." Willie slid his hands up and down the back scratcher like he was strumming chords, and looked to the ceiling, lost in a silent solo.

"That's right," Shade said. He leaned over and shoved the cast off the stool. Then he stood and slapped the sunglasses from Willie's face. "I *have* been accused of being a brute before, son. Several times. I think you should know I lived with the shame of it all just fine."

Willie rubbed two fingers at the bridge of his nose, a gesture of impatience and disdain.

"You really think I'm goin' to do a bad-mouth testimony on one cop to another? Shit, man, you seem to have your mind made up anyhow. Here I am, crippled up 'til practically Halloween, and you're jerkin' me 'round 'cause I *might* be a victim." He retrieved his sunglasses from the floor beside him and slid back under them. "What gets you interested anyhow? He cut you out of your piece of the ice, man?"

Shade, who considered himself to be prey to many of the nasty passions, felt that while he could be brutish or dense, slow or too quick, he could not be bought by any valuable thing that had numbers on it. This quality seemed so mulish for a human to possess that he found perverse pride in the fact that his corruptibility took a form closer to the poetic than the crass.

So he slapped those cheesy shades from the man's face again.

Willie's face firmed into a somewhat impotent expression of anger.

"You fucker," he said and started to rise, crippled or not. "This is my house."

"Freeze on that," Shade said softly. "You ain't got the whiskers and we both know it." Shade shook his head and picked up the glasses and handed them back to Willie. "I'm tired, son, that's all. Forgive me." He sat on the arm of Willie's chair and patted him on the head. "Could you find it in your little nubbin of a heart to forgive me?" For the first time now the heavy-metal thief seemed scared. "See, Officer Bell was whacked last night, there, superstar, and under the first rock we turned over we found *your* name."

"Oh, shit, man, you can't think..."

"You see the spot you're in now, don't you?"

The sudden recognition of the spot he was in set Willie squirming, tapping the plastic fingered back scratcher against his cast.

"You know I couldn't do that," he said. "Let's face it, man, I know what I am. I'm a musician who never caught a break so I *find* tape decks in other people's cars and shit like that. I dig gamblin', too, and natch I love my tunes, but stealin's only just my way to platinum—you know I'd never shoot anybody, especially Gerry Bell."

"Gerry, huh?" Shade said. "So you know him?"

"Hey, lots of us small fry got to know Officer Bell, man." Willie put his hand over his mouth and squeezed his lips, then said, "Since he's dead I'll tell you, Shade. Yeah, fuckin' Bell broke my leg all right, right here in this room, in front of Betty, too. He come in here in his fuckin' *uniform* to collect from me and I was tapped for cash so he tosses a quarter at my face and says, 'That's for my ticket, punk, I always pay for a good time.' Then he did it, man. Hurt like a motherfucker."

"Did his partner, Mouton, come with him?"

"He sat out in the patrol car."

As Shade pondered the implications of Bell's brand of civic duty, the front door opened and in came little Mick.

"Can we eat?" he asked. There were scabs on his elbows, bruises on his legs and dirt in his ears. "Papa, I'm hungry."

"So eat," Willie said. "Get yourself a hot dog."

"Mom said I'm not s'posed to touch the stove."

"Then *don't* touch it, boy. Eat 'em cold. They're good that way. Wrap a piece of bread around one and eat it cold."

Mick padded off toward the kitchen, his head down, the slump of his shoulders giving an advance notice of his opinion on eating hot dogs cold.

"Willie," Shade said, "aren't you going to get up off your ass, stump in there and feed the kid?"

"This cast feels like a ball an' chain, man. Makes my hip hurt to walk on it."

Shade, who found that all bad fathers reminded him of his own, said, "Dastillon, shit floats and you're rising fast."

"He can fend for his ownself," Willie said defensively. "I always had to. Nobody fed me but my own sticky fingers."

"I'll go cook the kid a couple of dogs," Shade said and started toward the kitchen.

"You do that, Shade, but don't spoil him. The world ain't no day-care center and I'm teachin' him that now, while he's young, so he won't be all let down when he grows up."

There it was, Shade thought, the Frogtown ethic in one bumper-slogan line, The World Ain't No Day-care Center.

The kitchen was orderly and clean, a testimony to Betty's elbow exercise. Shade found a black skillet in the oven and set it on a burner. He opened the fridge and saw half a dozen short dogs of wine and back behind a container of yogurt he turned up a pack of red dogs of chicken.

"How many you want, tiger?" he asked Mick.

"This many," Mick said, holding up two fingers.

Shade turned on the gas beneath the skillet and dropped the dogs in. He found a fork in a drawer and used it to shove the links around.

"Hey!" Willie shouted from the front room. "Hey, put me on about three, too, uh? I'm laid up."

"I can't hear you," Shade barked back.

While the chill was grilled from the dogs Mick got out two slices of bread and squeezed mustard onto them. Shade had the heat on high and the dogs were soon sizzling. He turned the flame off and handed the fork to the boy.

"Bon appetit, tiger."

Shade went back to the living room and stood over Willie.

"Okay, Willie, the domestic shit ain't free. Who was Bell collecting for?"

"Come on, man, you're from around here—take a guess."

"Rudy Regot? Delbert McKechnie? Shuggie Zeck?"

"Yeah, Shuggie," Willie said. "Am I fuckin' up major tellin' you this? I mean, I heard you and him was runnin' mates back there in yesteryear."

"You heard that, huh?"

"Everybody has. I'll bet you were a troublesome pair of playmates."

"You're right, Willie, that's all back there in yesteryear." Shade once again sat beside Willie. "So what's his beef with you?"

"You know me, man. I thought I had me a new sevencard system, but, really, I guess what I got is a disease. That's what Betty says ten or fifty times a day. Nothin' out of the ordinary, I was tryin' to work the kinks out of the system and dropped a bunch of dinero I didn't actually have. Officer Bell encouraged me to come up with it."

"Did you?"

"You fuckin' A, I did. Sold the car, I only got two legs. Now Betty hoofs it to work. Lucky her, I'm crippled up 'til the wet season ends." He edged the scratcher under his cast and pulled it up and down. "The man took some pleasure in it, too. You'd've thought he was porkin' Tina Turner, 'stead of crushin' *my* bones, from the look on his face."

"You know for sure Shuggie sent him?"

"Well, it was Shuggie's game where I got the markers, but Shuggie is gettin' up there, Shade. He's like this with Mr. B. now I hear."

"Everybody's heard that."

"Gee, sorry to be a borin' snitch, man." Willie rocked back and plucked away at the back scratcher. "You find who killed this bad cop Bell tell 'em I'll play a benefit for their defense fund, huh?"

Mick had come to stand in the doorway of the kitchen, a hot dog in each hand.

"Did Bell work for Shuggie?"

"I don't fuckin' know, man. I don't really know the big answers but what I do know—duh-dun-duh-dun—is the blues. What else can I say?"

"Nothing good," Shade said. He walked to the door and opened it, and as he stepped out into the hot wet air of another tough day in river country, he heard Willie bark, "Come 'ere, give me one of those!"

6

THE POLICE station was on Second Street, a white-stone building erected along severely square lines, at hand-holding distance from city hall.

When Shade came up the stone steps, steps polished to a fine sheen by the somber gait of the guilty, the light dancing feet of the innocent, and the uncertain shuffle of the uncertain, he turned right toward the squad room just as How Blanchette came down the adjoining hallway from the Captain's office.

"What's up, How?" Shade asked. "Bell's partner here?"

"Yeah," Blanchette said, "he's downstairs." He held his hat in his hand and there was a pinkish flush to his face. "We been split up, Rene. Captain took me away from you and put me with Jesse Pickett."

"What?" Shade asked. "Am I in trouble?"

"I don't think so yet," Blanchette said as he shook his head and wiped sweat from his cheeks. "Officially, me and Pickett are supposed to say we're in charge of the investigation. Pickett's okay, I can live with Pickett, but I don't know why they broke us up."

"They?"

"Mayor Crawford's in there, too, baby. He's got a new look. When you go in there you'll notice it."

"I'm supposed to go in there, huh? When?"

"Now, comrade," Blanchette said. "And I think you better have an open mind."

★　　★　　★

The heavy wooden door to Captain Karl Bauer's office was open, so Shade looked in and said, "You wanted to see me?"

"That's right, Shade. Come in here and close that thing behind you." Bauer pointed at a chair directly in front of his desk. "Give your dogs a rest, Detective, we have a thing or two to discuss."

Shade sat in the chair, a bit tentatively since a vast range of unpleasant possible topics for discussion wisped through his mind like paranoid vapors.

"What's the deal, Captain? I already talked to Blanchette."

"Uh-huh. Good." Bauer was a large, flat-topped man, with pale skin that had been acned and pitted so that it resembled a cob cleaned of corn, eyes the color of snuff, and the general expression of a natural-born straw boss. "Officer Bell's murder is going to require a kind of unique approach, Shade, and you've been picked to make it."

From the far corner of his left eye Shade became aware of another presence in the room. He turned that way, and back there in a shadowy part of the office, seated on a straight-backed chair, he saw a gargoyle in silk watching him closely. Mayor Gene Crawford's silver hair was, as usual, combed just so, and his suit had that sheer and costly look, but his face was interestingly made over. His eyes were swollen nearly closed, with black half-moons below the slits, and a piece of aluminum had been taped over an obviously smashed nose.

"Look at me, Shade," Bauer said. "I'm the one talking to you."

Shade faced him across the polished mahogany.

"Yes, sir."

"Did you hear what I said? I said we're going to try a unique approach using you. How's that sound?"

"I'm listening, Captain."

"Fine. What do you know about Officer Bell?"

"I heard he moonlighted as a collector for a loan shark, and that he did the collecting in uniform with a nonregulation fungo bat."

"That's what you heard, huh?" Bauer leaned back in his chair, then rocked squeakingly back and forth. "Anything else?"

"Not yet."

"I see." Bauer leaned forward suddenly and put his elbows on his desk, making dramatic eye contact with Shade. "Here and now I'm going to tell you how Bell got his dumb-ass self greased, Shade. I'm telling you 'cause you'll need to know, and it's all true, what I'll tell you, but none of it's official."

This brought a nod from Shade, then he glanced back to where the Mayor sat, his legs sedately crossed, his hands clasped in his lap, and his face swollen and colored like a hoodoo mask that kept children in line.

"I'm your man, Captain," he said and looked back at his superior. "What went down?"

"What went down is this." Bauer began to do some vaguely threatening theatrical business involving his squeezing rubber balls in both hands, on the desk top, so that his forearms twisted with cords of muscle. "Some of the finest money in this region was on one of the finest tables in this region and several gentlemen of the first rank were seated around that table along with a couple of ramblin', gamblin' colorful types who were there to add to the adventure and..."

"No sarcasm," the Mayor said in an atonal basso wheeze.

Bauer nodded grimly and went on.

"...long about the witching hour three tough guys in ski masks come through the door. Can you fill in the rest yourself?"

Shade said, "The tough guys wanted that fine money and they had guns to take it with and Bell was the guard. Is that close?"

"Close enough. Bell was the guard, only he was also a bust-out gambler and pretty soon he was sittin' in on the game instead of watchin' the door for tough guys." Bauer really began to mash away at the rubber balls, his teeth grinding behind an open mouth. "See, Mr. B. has not been fucked with like this for a while, and everybody was gettin' lax. Now this has happened and everybody is pissed off and in kind of a spot."

"When Bell got shot," Shade said, "these pillar-of-the-community types who were there didn't want to be splattered by any shit, so they dumped the body at the hospital and called it a night, huh, Captain?"

"You got it," Bauer said.

"Who were they?" Shade asked. "I'd like to talk with them."

"I'm afraid that won't happen, Shade. I'm tellin' you all there is to tell, and it's all off the record." Bauer looked hard at Shade. "For the record Officer Bell died while off duty, probably in an attempt to halt a burglary."

"You think anybody'll buy that?"

From the shadowed corner came a flat, gasping answer. "It doesn't matter if it's believed or not," Mayor Crawford said. "It will wash."

"That's your opinion, Mayor."

"Yes, Detective Shade," the Mayor said, his voice thick with curdled civility. "It's only one man's opinion, but it's a man whose opinion means *just a little bit* in these parts."

Shade said, "You blew your nose, didn't you, Mayor?"

"Pardon?"

"One of these tough guys we been discussing belted you and your nose filled with blood and mucus, and your instinct was to blow it. So you did." Shade shook his head. "That's a case of an instinct misleading you, 'cause when you blow a busted beak it makes your eyes swell shut. Kind of like yours are."

"Why do you think I was there?"

"Because you're here."

Mayor Crawford was an almost unassailable political figure in St. Bruno. He had masterfully endeared himself to the rice-and-bean legions who all had one man, one vote, and he was personally liked for his roguish charm, laissez-faire approach to victimless crime, and his poon-hound exploits as a tea-dance heart warper.

The Mayor now swiveled his gaze from Shade to Bauer, and nodded curtly.

"Okay," Bauer said, "it's like this, Shade. Our little metropolis is run by a certain system and now some fuckin' cowboys are throwin' shit in the gears. That's not good for anybody. Several factions in this town could run amuck if we don't step in and settle this."

"Uh-huh," Shade said. "Like some of your gambler pals, huh, Mayor?"

"Detective," the Mayor said, "be an adult—you'll always have a lot of gambling wherever you have a lot of blacks."

Shade laughed.

"Come on, all your gaming pals are white."

The Mayor sucked wind through his mouth.

"Them, too," he said.

At this moment, Shade was sensing a request that would be officially above and beyond the call, but unofficially crucial, and sweat slid down his temples. He wiped the sweat away, and said, "Christ, this'd be good weather to make weight in. What is it you want me to do?"

"Get the bastards," the Mayor said.

"That," Captain Bauer said, "and if possible save the taxpayers the expense of a trial."

The Captain's comment caused Shade to suddenly believe a legend, for there had long been one told about Bauer during last call at FOP meetings, and around anyplace cop buddies saluted their secret heroes, for this bit of law-and-order mythology claimed that the good Captain had performed just such an assignment years ago, when the Carpenter brothers had risen up and challenged Mr. B. It came about that the then Detective Bauer and his partner, Ervin Delahoussaye, had found themselves in a remote grain bin that was empty except for four spreadeagled Carpenters, only to have the brothers get allegedly combative and thereby cause their own deaths. Each brother, the coroner said, was shot twice in the head, and the whole thing was ruled justifiable force. Bauer leapfrogged up to captain, and cops young and old praised his marksmanship. Delahoussaye, clearly not leadership material, snacked on his gat six weeks later.

It was all true, Shade now knew, and he'd best step carefully.

"Are you telling me to take them off the count, Captain?"

"Not by yourself. There are other people who want to find these motherfuckers, too. One of them will help you."

"There may be some money in this," Mayor Crawford said. "A covert reward."

"No," Shade said, "I don't want money. I'm independently wealthy, anyhow. I mean, I've been poor so long it doesn't bother me anymore, and that's as much peace of mind as a Rockefeller's got." The sweat on his face again required mopping, then he asked, "Does it have to be me?"

"It does now," Bauer said. "Plus, our outside friends specifically asked for you."

"I see."

"Detective," the Mayor said and strolled toward him, "you've been around. You're from Frogtown—does this all seem too far out of the ordinary?"

"I can't call ordinary, Mayor. I can tell weird, but ordinary is a tough call to make." Shade bowed his head, trying hard to foresee all the angles, then raised his face and met the Captain's eyes. "Who am I supposed to work with?"

"Shuggie Zeck," Bauer said. "You're doing the right thing, Shade, in the long run. Shuggie's waiting for you now, at your brother's dive by the river, there, The Catfish Bar."

7

OVER A bowl of guinea-hen gumbo, at a small white table in
Maggie's Keyhole, Wanda Bone Bouvier was pressed into service as a luncheon audience of one for Hedda Zeck's slightly slurred
tale of her past. As the ample Hedda, who disguised her ampleness
behind a billow of yellow summer dress, told it, her life up 'til she
hoisted this very bloody mary in her hand was a convoluted tale of
bubbly love gone flat, fine talents unnoticed and similarly woeful
bullshit.

"So," Hedda said, "Shuggie stands there, honey I mean he *stands*
there like somebody who's got the fuckin' *right* to look at me that way,
so evil, and he says, ' 'Til you sweat off some of that lard you're gonna
have to bend like cookie dough and lick it your own self. You're only
gonna get the ol' in-and-out until I see you in a dress that says size ten
on it.' " Hedda sucked on her smoke, ignoring her own bowl of gumbo,
shaking the ice cubes in her drink. "Would you take shit like that from
a man, Wanda?"

"You're not fat, Hedda," Wanda said. "Besides, Shuggie ain't exactly
a hunk hisself."

"He *is* chubby, isn't he?"

"He could sure enough stand to run some laps or something." Wanda
had heard such miseries from Hedda before, but up until Ronnie had
run afoul of Mr. B.'s organization it had mostly come out when the
men had gotten up from the table and swaggered into a dark corner to
talk business, as they put it. But now, with Ronnie an outcast from the

group because he had gotten just a little too indiscriminating about whose money he hustled, they met only here, on the sly, out of the way. "You want another bloody mary?"

"Oh," Hedda said, "I shouldn't but I will." Hedda Zeck had been born a Langlois, which was a good thing to be in Frogtown since everyone knew they were cousins to the Beaurains, and she was ten years or so further down the track than Wanda. Her lips were full and red, and her hair was dark and cut short. Her twin vices were hard liquor and baked sweets, vices that greatly contributed to her dimensions, which in turn led to her being less often laid, which could possibly force her to acquire another vice that consisted of motel rooms and trampy men. "Aw, Wanda, wouldn't it be a nicer world if God just grinned and everybody got what they wanted?"

Wanda sipped her beer, shrugged and said, "I think that could get sort of boring, really."

"Honey," Hedda said and laughed, "I declare you'd find fault with the land of milk and honey."

"That's right," Wanda said. "You can't dream up a world I won't criticize."

They signaled for more drinks and got them, allowing the gumbo to cool until a film developed on top.

Wanda actually did like Hedda, and in more flush days she'd found the older woman to be of some use in the selection of clothing, furniture, vacations and other matters that didn't mean squat since they got mad and fed Ronnie to the law. She'd had to sell off everything to pay lawyers and landlords. The high life had been snatched back away from her and here she was, in cutoff jeans, sandals, and a cheap cotton shirt with Technicolor vegetation on it, listening to a gal with a few wads in her wallet rambling on about the hardships in this torture called *her* life.

"Hedda," Wanda said, "I wish Auguste and Shuggie and them'd quit bad-mouthin' Ronnie all over town. These things get back to me sometimes and it don't make me feel too good." Wanda took a big gulp of her beer and gestured for another since she knew who'd pick up the tab. "I mean, they done run our name down to the goddam dogs. I'll admit Ronnie misbehaved. I admit that."

"Honey," Hedda said, squinting through a puff of smoke, "he cheated Auguste."

"Aw, Hedda, really now, that was just sort of an in-joke that got out. He was just seein' if he could do it, as, like, a security check."

"He took bets on races that were already run, honey. Auguste considers that cheating."

"Now, Hedda, come on," Wanda said. She stared sullenly into her mug of beer. "I bet there ain't a bookie south of Minneapolis who ain't took a post bet or some such shenanigans just to make ends meet once in a while."

Another beer arrived, along with an unrequested bloody mary that Hedda decided not to send back.

"Wanda," she said with a vodka stumble in her voice, "people get killed for what Ronnie done. I *love* you, honey. I *love* you like a little sister, and I screamed and screamed when that all came up, but if I wasn't kin of the Beaurains I think you'd've been wearin' *bl-ack* for a while."

"I know you went out on a limb," Wanda said.

"But I don't mind," Hedda said. "I *love* you."

Up at the bar a middle-aged woman with one leg, her crutches leaning against the rail beside her, did a merry-go-round number on her stool, spinning slowly enough that the I Can't Help It If I'm Lucky on her T-shirt could be read. Behind the bar a preened man in a brewery uniform was loading beer into the coolers, his gaze frequently circling around Wanda's way, as if he was hoping that regular blasts from his icy blues would prompt some spur-of-the-moment afternoon lushness to come into his arms.

The third time Wanda caught his Nordic Casanova act she flipped him the bird and he kept his eyes on business.

If this tête-à-tête had been strictly for friendship Wanda would've gladly gone awash on draft, but there were things that she needed to know and Hedda was her only source. The bloody marys were providing an assist, and Hedda seemed primed.

Wanda put some zippidy-doo-dah into her smile, and said, "But what else is new with you?"

"It's none of it new," Hedda answered, using both hands to tame the wobbling of her drink. "I hardly get to shop. Shuggie won't leave me the checkbook since, you know, since I like nice things and checks can be traced, right, traced and then added up by the tax man. The fuckin' tax man has ruined my life, 'cause now I gotta use cash and I gotta wait for fat-assed Shuggie to give it to me." She looked blearily at her audience. "Ain't I half of this marriage?"

"At least," Wanda said.

"He used to say for me to use good judgment, but now he just says forget it, no way."

"I'm sure he's busy nowadays," Wanda said amiably. "Tryin' to oversee all of Auguste's games and other interests. Crime is a job, when you get right up against it."

"Tell me about it. It's like a doctor, like Shuggie's an odd sort of doctor or something, the way they call any hour of the night. Like last night, it must've been, I don't know, late. Real late. I don't remember what time, but it was late, 'cause I was asleep and the TV was all static, and they called." Hedda fumbled for a cigarette, then lit it. "Some problem at the country club, they had some kind of uppity poker game or somethin'. Some problem, I don't know. They call anytime, day or night."

"Well, Shuggie can handle any problems," Wanda said. "He'll probably have it straightened out by now."

"Prob'ly. He ain't come home yet, when I left. He called. He's a good li'l boy that way, he calls home and tells me where he's at. It's in case he gets murdered, I think, so I'll know who to sick Auguste on." Hedda leaned toward Wanda, drunkenly sincere. "Do you think Ronnie fucked aroun' on you? Do you?"

"Not tremendously."

"But some?"

"I imagine. I mean, I'd eat a tame man up, and I couldn't eat him up."

"Does Shuggie fuck around?"

"I doubt it. He never came on to me, Hedda. I'd tell you if he did."

"You're a dear, you know it?" Hedda waved her cigarette around, and picked at some tomato juice that had slopped onto her summer dress and dried. "That makes me feel better about him and all them naked girls out there."

"Out where?"

"When he called he said to send messages out there to that place, you know, on River Road? Where them naked girls dance and bend over with their tushes in men's faces, trollin' for dollar bills to be stuffed in their garters."

"Huh," Wanda said.

"We went once, me and Shuggie, just for the hell of it. It didn't help." Hedda was swaying in her chair, becoming dangerous with the hot end of her smoke. "I imagine he's openin' a game there, or somethin', after that trouble last night."

"Is that The Rio, Rio Club?" Wanda asked.

"That's it. They wax their pussy hairs out there. I *saw*."

"Listen, Hedda, I got to get goin'," Wanda said. She stood, came around the table, and embraced her friend and unknowing informant. "I'll call you a cab, okay?"

"Ooh, I *love* you."

As Wanda pulled into her dirt-rut driveway she saw the men's car parked back behind the bougainvillea at the side of the house. When she came in the front door she heard a muffled pop and some hairy-chested guffaws.

She went into the sparsely furnished family room and immediately noticed a couple of dozen eraser-sized holes punched in the walls near the floor.

"What on earth?" she said, then looked closer and saw unshelled peanuts littered about. She heard the guffaws again and tracked the source to the side porch where she found Dean and Cecil in *her* underwear, waving Ronnie's pellet rifle around. "You fuckin' slobs," she said.

"Uh-oh," Dean said with a drunken smile, "the landlady's home."

Wanda extracted a recitation of the chain of events from Cecil and found that it all started when Emil went back to bed and Cecil decided to flaunt his worldliness by mixing up a batch of gimlets, four parts gin to a teaspoon of lime juice, the way muckety-mucks mix it in Clearwater, Florida, a place where he'd once had a bartender buddy. Anyhow, Wanda learned, you got to give the snooty sorts a tip of the cap on this, 'cause it's a flat-out monster drink and Dean, you know, Dean lets himself into your bedroom looking for a Band-Aid for the finger he cut after he'd dropped the first pitcher, that glass one with the fancy scenes painted on it, and down there in your closet where you keep a bunch of crotchless panties and negligees in that oatmeal box, you know, down there, he turns up this here pellet gun and says he can shoot better'n me. I told him I could hit an unshelled peanut from across the room, and, by golly, two or three times I did.

"Oh, man," Wanda said disgustedly when the whole thing had been run down to her. She looked at them as they hoisted their gimlets in green plastic cups, Dean in a pair of lavender French-cut panties, and Cecil in a pink pair with a red zipper down the middle she'd gotten mail-order. "You fellas go on and just *keep* them panties, hear? My treat."

Wanda's presence seemed to bring the fun buddies down, and pretty soon she got the gun away from them and they turned the TV on and cuddled up to get *au courant* with some soaps they'd missed since Braxton. Wanda went into the kitchen and Jadick came out of the bedroom in his pants, but shirtless.

She fixed him with a baleful gaze and said, "I hope to god the FBI ain't buggin' this house, Emil. They'll ridicule us in court."

"Bad day?" he asked.

He went to the kitchen sink and splashed water on his face.

"I found out what you wanted," she said. "Hedda was half lit when I got there."

"Oh, yeah?" Jadick said, suddenly intent. He held a dish towel at his face, poised to dry it. "Where?"

Wanda took a seat at the table and began to stack all of the empty beer cans.

"A tits and ass dance joint out on River Road."

"Is it Beaurain's?"

"I imagine, it's out this side of town."

"Hmm," Jadick went, and sat down across the table. "So there's liable to be a bunch of wise guys in there. That could be a problem if we come on too loose."

"I don't know about those things," Wanda said. Looking through the litter on her own kitchen table she turned up half a doobie and put fire to it. As she choked out a deep toke she asked, "You always been a stickup guy? Or have you did different things?"

Jadick smiled, and it was a shockingly pleasant, white-toothed smile. He held a finger to a flat part of his nose.

"I used to be a fighter," he said.

"Before you were a stickup guy?"

"Kind of in between," he said. "This was some years back, in Philadelphia. I had moved there to be a fighter, plus I was drawn' some heat in Cleveland. I knocked a grown man out with one punch when I was thirteen, so I always held it in the back of my mind that I could have a career down that line. So I went to Philly, and all these experts said a white dude couldn't stand up under all the shit they'd dish out in that bad town. But I didn't listen and became a sparring partner, which is to say a punching bag. They were all the time poundin' me 'cause I'd never had formal lessons or nothin', just instinct and a wallop." He shook his head wistfully. "Pun-kin, them niggers zapped my eyes shut, and never even sprang for a soda, just beat on me and said, 'Can't take it, can you, ofay?'"

"What'd you do?"

"I went back to the stickup dodge, gorilla work. I won't tolerate that shit from niggers. Fightin' niggers is like dancin' with a pig, anyhow, it ain't meant to be."

"That's a shame," she said. "You got a plan for The Rio, Rio Club? That's where the game'll be."

"I'll think about it."

"Well," Wanda said, "I was fixin' to intrude an idea of my own on you. See, the boy across the street works there. He's older'n me, really, so I shouldn't call him boy, but he gets a tent in his britches every time he sees me. I reckon he'd show me a good time out there if I acted interested."

"When could you do that?"

"Tomorrow. He's already there by now."

"No," Jadick said. "We'd have to cap him, then, or he'd snap to it after the rip. No." He leaned across the table and patted her hand. "I think you should go out there right away and apply for a job. I want to hit them tonight."

"Tonight? Tonight? Man, your gang is in the other room too drunk to wear men's clothes!"

"Nah, I can sober 'em up." Jadick stood and walked to the fridge. "If we hit 'em again tonight I think they'll be sort of freaked out, ready to fall."

"Emil, I'm no stripper."

"You got the raw talent," he said. "Just juggle it around."

The phone was on the wall by the fridge. When it rang Jadick answered it, listened for a moment, then said, "Yeah, we'll accept charges." He turned to Wanda. "It's Ronnie."

"You shouldn't be answering my phone," Wanda said. She took the phone from Emil and cradled it to her ear. "Hello, Ronnie. What? Yeah, that was him. He's here. Your relatives are here." She leaned against the fridge and watched Emil. "You heard that already? Up there? He was a what? What? Oh, man." She held the phone down and said, "That was a cop, Emil. You all killed a cop."

Emil shrugged and opened the refrigerator and took out a carton of milk. "Life goes on," he said.

"Yes, Ronnie. Of course, yeah. I'm a little worried now. Naturally I am. Uh-huh, I know I have to be strong. I understand."

Wanda hated the picture of her legal lover man she had in her mind, for she thought of him as jailhouse pale, chain-smoking Luckies, dressed in that bright white target uniform they wore at Braxton. She had this sad image of him at the same time Emil stood before her drinking milk straight from the carton, his stomach all muscled and firm, crying out for her fingertips to be stroked down it to the happy stick.

"You know I do, Ronnie. You know I love you. Uh-huh. I did what you told me." She began to twirl the phone cord around her fingers as Emil locked his eyes on hers. "Uh-huh, you told me I should. Well, that's why I did. Ronnie, I ain't going to lie to you: I dug it. He's younger'n you. You know he's real built, big arms and all."

Jadick, realizing that he was under discussion, fell back against the kitchen counter, his legs spread, his chest puffed.

Wanda could not take her eyes off him.

"Uh-huh, Ronnie, yes. I'll do what he wants because it's for you, really, it's for you. Everything I do is for you. Uh-huh. Okay, I do like him. Well, you know," she said, her eyes going to Emil's, "he's a little bit sentimental and a little bit mean: in other words, just right. Okay, Ronnie. You know I love you and that's no shit, neither, baby." She hung up the phone and sighed.

"He says to go on, keep doing what you need."

"I knew he would," Jadick said. "Ronnie knows what it takes, punkin. Not everybody does."

"Uh-huh." Wanda felt flushed by the conversation and the manly aroma of a sweaty Jadick. "Let's don't kid each other," she said, "the bedroom's thisaway."

Jadick laughed and took her by the arm in a nearly courtly manner.

"There you go," he said. "I'll get you good and limber for your audition, pun-kin."

8

THE CATFISH Bar was on Lafitte Street, the main artery of Frog-town, a short stroll from Shade's apartment. He left his car at home and took the railroad-track route, the back way to the bar. He passed two old men who were hauling a stringer of channel cat home from a slough, and a smattering of drunks dozing it off in the sun. Up the tracks at the bridge he saw a group of neighborhood lads, neophyte sadists in dirty Air Jordan sneakers and fresh scowls, prowling for ethnic winos or solvent strangers to ratpack. As he reached the dirt alley beside The Catfish he passed a young man and a mature woman sitting in a candy-colored four-barrel muscle car, friskily familiarizing themselves with each other's anatomy.

The Catfish was a place of raw wood and a colorful past, the chief neighborhood rendezvous for as long as Shade could remember. His grandfather Blanqui had hung out here when the floors were saw-dusted, free lunches did exist, and the Kingfish was everybody's hero. Little had changed over the years except ownership, and that had passed into the hands of Shade's older brother, Tip.

When Shade came into the bar Shuggie Zeck was sitting on a bar-stool talking to Tip. They both turned toward the sunlight that came in the open door.

"Well, well," Shade said, "I'll be dogged if it ain't Joe Shit, the ragman, live and in person." He sat on a stool twice removed from Shuggie. "How you hanging?"

"You talkin' to me?" Shuggie asked. "I don't believe you're talkin' to *me* like that."

"Believe," Shade said. He nodded then at his brother. Tip was an up-and-down sibling, into a lot of secret this-and-that, and the brothers were not close. "You're looking good, Tip."

"Hey, you, too, li'l blood."

Tip Shade was large and pock-faced with a heavy dose of the sullens and long brown hair.

"I'm the one you're here to see," Shuggie said. Shuggie was a hybrid of flab and flash, who, try as he would to upscale his image, could not groom himself past looking like six feet of Frogtown funneled into pinstripes. He had a Lafitte Street yen for gaudy rings and wore two to a hand. His hair was dark and curly and his face was like that of a bulldog who smiled easily. "We're goin' to be pals, right, Rene? Like the old days, huh? Remember the old days?"

"Yeah, I remember," Shade said. "Every time I look into the holding tank."

Shade and Shuggie had shared an inkish youth, an adolescence given over to the moiling passions of white-trash teens, and on nights fueled by fear and anger, pride and chance, they had done many things criminal and a few just plain mean. As serendipity would have it, Shade escaped charges on all counts, was only stomped by cops once, and outgrew his criminal aspects when he devoted himself to boxing. Over his sporting years Shade drifted apart from Shuggie and Tip and a street-corner choir of other accomplices. He had since endeavored to go down that endless crooked road that was somehow misnamed the straight and narrow.

"Want a beer?" Tip asked.

"Sure. Très bien, big bro." Shade reached into his pocket and pulled out the black beauty cached in the Alka-Seltzer foil, and popped it into his mouth. Tip handed him a draw in a mug and he took a swallow. "Merci."

"What was that you just ate?" Shuggie asked.

"Sinus tablet," Shade said. "This humidity. So, Shuggie, let's get it right straight from the giddyup—I'm going along with you as long as it seems to be going somewhere."

"I'll be going somewhere, all right." Shuggie smiled and beckoned to Tip. "Tell your hard-on brother what you seen over at Frechette Park, Tippy. Tell him where I'm takin' him."

"Well," Tip said, and leaned against the bar, his massive arms folded, "I was over there in the park, there, Rene, up above Bum's Hollow, there, and at a picnic table I seen Bobby Gillette and two other fellas. This was yesterday, and they were all huddled together, you know, fomentin' something for sure."

"Bobby Gillette, huh?" Shade said. "Who the fuck is Bobby Gillette?"

"He's a fella who never learns," Tip said. "That's what I'm tellin' you, I know the dude, and he never learns."

"There's a lot of that going around," Shade said.

"Hey look, don't you remember?" Shuggie asked. "A couple of years ago? You don't? Well, Bobby Gillette was the one who knocked over a game Delbert McKechnie had, then he did one on me. He's a tush hog, lives out in the country, on a spit of soggy dirt out there called Gumbo. Know the place?"

"I've been by there."

"Back then, Mr. B. was worried about Mayor Gene's election that was comin' up, so we had to play it smart. So Gerry Bell ended up nailin' Gillette in the act of a burglary he never heard of, but the beef stood up in court." Shuggie sipped from his own drink, his pinkie rings bright in the tavern gloom. "Tough guy did a bit on Trahan's Farm, got out a month ago."

"I never heard about those games being hit," Shade said. "I never heard a thing."

"That's the price you pay for bein' standoffish," Shuggie said. He spun on his stool to face Shade. "If you were still my friend you'd hear things like that."

"I'm sure I'd hear things all right."

"If we were friends you'd hear the *right* things, Rene."

"You don't know any right things, Shuggie."

"Jerk," Shuggie said. Shuggie Zeck, who considered himself to embody the Horatio Alger myth, if Horatio had been as wise to the angles and had his connections, but who did not feel that ambition necessarily required deceit, said, "Did I ever lie to you? *Ever?*"

Shade, whose sense of trust had been badly singed by experience, sucked down some suds, then said, "That time we stole four cases of Old Grandad from Langlois' Liquor and hid them under the bridge you did. You said somebody else ripped it from us, but I always have figured you beat me out of it."

"Jesus," Shuggie said with a wince, "that's really goin' back there, man. But I told you the real deal then, and I'd tell it to you now, once in a while, if we were friends."

"I'd come in handier than Officer Bell, huh, Shuggie?"

"I doubt that," Shuggie said. "Bell had motivation, and you don't seem to."

"I seen a good ball game up in St. Louie," Tip said out of the blue. "Jack Clark belted one I just missed by two rows."

"I'll never work for you, Shuggie."

"Ah, you don't want to 'cause you know me and familiarity breeds contempt."

"Familiarity with *you* certainly does."

"Clark is the best power hitter they've had since Stan the Man if you ask me."

"Fuck you, Shade."

"Fuck *with* me, Zeck."

"Give him a heater on the inside of the plate and somebody gets a free ball in the cheap seats." Tip suddenly slammed a palm on the bar, the boom startling even the drunks nodding in the far corners of the room. "Shuggie," big Tip said, "this is my li'l blood, Rene. Now, Rene, you li'l piglet, you, this is Shuggie. You two start over from scratch, huh? What's buried in the past is dead and already returned to nature, such as shit does. If I was you fellas I'd be friendly first; then, if and when that don't work no more, then go ahead, what the fuck, settle it at Knuckle Junction."

One of the drunks who'd been startled awake by Tip's conciliatory boom began to sing some crazed gimmick song from way back that claimed the singer was entangled by incest and was in fact his own grandpa. His drinking buddy shooshed him but made no effort to leave, and soon joined in on the sad family refrain.

"Come on," Shuggie said. "Tippy's right. Let's go, there's somebody who wants to meet you who I think you ought to meet."

"As long as it goes somewhere," Shade said. He then patted his brother's shoulder and asked him, "If I wasn't with Zeck would you've told me about Bobby Gillette?"

"You know I wouldn't, Rene," Tip said. "It wouldn't really be the right move for me if you think about it."

"I knew that," Shade said as he followed Shuggie to the door. "I just wanted to be reminded."

9

As the sliding doors to the pool area were opened and Shade and Shuggie entered, a loud voice was raised: "Solve the riddle! Solve the riddle! Don't spin the wheel, Miss Greedy, solve the riddle!"

Auguste Beaurain sat at poolside on a wicker chair that had Tahitian pretensions but had been made in Memphis, watching a game show. The swimming pool was enclosed by glass, roofed with same, and plants of several sizes were growing from pots on the parquet floor. Beaurain wore a white suit with a blue shirt and a jaunty yellow tie. The pool was calm and empty and the air conditioner was on.

"Afternoon, Mr. Beaurain," Shuggie said. "This is Rene Shade."

"I know," Beaurain said. He did not take his eyes from the TV until the contestant went bust, then he growled, "Greedy people get what they deserve *sometimes*." He then snapped the TV set off and said, "Detective Shade, do you understand the world you live in?"

"Which part of it?" Shade asked.

"The whole of it."

"No, I don't. And neither do you." Shade sat down on a nearby chair and set his feet on a small, glass-topped table, thereby establishing his insolence. "Mind if I sit?"

"Of course not." Beaurain lifted a bowl of nuts and held it toward Shade. "Help yourself. I particularly like the cashews, myself. I'd appreciate it if you left them for me."

"No thanks."

"Okay." Beaurain set the bowl down. "Shuggie, sit, be comfortable." Beaurain measured five foot seven standing on your neck. He had a lean but lined face, with a pleasant arrangement of features, and a nearly constant smile. His hair was gray, thin, and carefully combed. He had all the attributes of a "Disney Hour" grandpappy but his was in fact the whip hand held over the insolvent and indictable of St. Bruno. "We've met before," he said to Shade. "Twice. Once when you were a small boy. Your daddy is John X. Shade, isn't it? You were with him, years ago. There were three of you boys, one not so little. Your daddy used to book bets for me, Detective."

"He ever give you a short count and lam out on you?"

"No, he never did."

"Then it must've been a different John X. Shade, Mr. B."

"You really *don't* understand the world you live in, do you? Ah" — Beaurain shook his head like a displeased schoolteacher — "that will make this harder."

"He's a knucklehead," Shuggie said. "I've known him since we had to stand on a bicycle seat to sneak through a window."

"You told me that," Beaurain said.

"You said twice," Shade drawled. "When was the other time we met? I don't remember it. I've seen you around, but I don't remember meeting you."

"Well, you were sort of distracted the second time. The first time you were a child and the second time you'd just encountered Foster Broome in your one chance at the title. I'm not certain you could even see, your eyes looked like tomatoes squashed on cement." Beaurain laughed. "That nigger whupped you like he'd caught you stealing chickens, didn't he?"

"He was a great fighter," Shade said. "I was offered a shot at him so I took it and he kicked my ass. Big deal."

"I knew you'd take the fight," Beaurain said. He extracted a cashew from the bowl and ate it. "And I knew you'd lose."

"What do you mean, you knew?"

Beaurain laughed and said to Shuggie, "He really is a knucklehead, ain't he?" He then turned to Shade, looking disgusted. "How do you think you got that fight, asshole? Your record was what—eighteen and seven?"

"Eighteen and six at the time," Shade said. "I ended up twenty-four and nine."

"Whatever. I put up the guarantee for that fight, Detective. I wanted to see a local boy get a chance at the big brass ring. I guaranteed Broome's purse so you could get it."

"Why?" Shade pulled his feet off of the table and sat up straight. There was nothing insolent about him now, and he needed to know more. "Why would you do that?"

"Like I said, I knew you'd lose. But I remembered your daddy, and I always liked him, and I knew every redneck, half a wise guy, and straight citizen from this town would bet on you. It got even better when the niggers went for you, too. That surprised me, but they bet you probably, oh, sixty percent. Go figure, you see. That's why it's called gambling."

"Well, I came through for you," Shade said. "I lost."

"Yes, but you were given a chance. I want you to note this, too. It wasn't the nuns at St. Peter's who got it for you. It wasn't a group of lawyers, judges, doctors and poets who got it for you. No, Shade, there was not a consortium of moneyed saints and sporting bankers from Hawthorne Hills interested in seeing a Frogtown boy like you get a chance to punch out a place in history. No," Beaurain said with a slow head shake, "the good people of St. Bruno stood apart from you, but I didn't."

This was all news to Shade, and it went back to a not so distant phase of his life when he'd been on the cusp of both worlds, straddling the street and the straight and narrow, and it was the fact that he'd actually, miraculously, been given a title shot that had convinced him that the world was benign more often than he'd given it credit for. He was not old now by any calculations other than the athletic, but he suddenly felt like an ancient dupe, a moron, a man who couldn't tell fresh creamy butter from pig fat.

"I hear you," he said, "but I don't think I owe you shit."

"Oh, no, you don't owe me anything. I'm just helping you toward understanding the world you live in." Beaurain clapped his hands and said, "Norman, bring us some drinks!"

A pale, round-faced man came out from behind a green curtain of plants. He was bald and wore a shoulder holster.

"Who's that?" Shade asked.

"That's my son-in-law, Norman the Jew. He watches over me here, him and my daughter. This is a bad neighborhood, you know."

All of the men chuckled, for none of them had ever willingly lived anywhere else. Beaurain's house was very modest when viewed from the street, but the interior was richly furnished, and he'd added on the pool room in back. He had the down payment for a palace anywhere but he stayed here, in Frogtown, not two full blocks from the house he'd been born in.

Presently, Norman came back carrying a tray of drinks. He set the tray on the table and went silently back to his sniper blind behind the plants.

"I only drink tonic water in summer," Beaurain said. "The quinine, you know."

Shade was feeling the first tingling waves of illegal alertness. He lifted a glass and gulped from it.

"You ever been arrested?" he asked. "I heard we've never popped you for anything."

"That's right," Beaurain said. "I'll go to heaven. My record is free of criminal charges."

"That's amazing."

"Well, I'm a likable person, Shade. People seem to want to be nice to me. Plus, I'm not greedy, so I don't make enemies the way you'd expect."

Mr. B.'s rep, though clangorous and fearful, was, Shade knew, that he was a fair-minded breed of gangster. Street slime and sly businessmen considered him to be more decisive than the legal system, a good deal more fair, but when he convicted someone his sentences tended to be forty-five caliber.

"Maybe I'll nail you," Shade said. His teeth were grinding and he had a black-beauty sense of optimism.

"Jerk," Shuggie said.

"What would be the point?" Beaurain asked. "I'm a good governor. Let me tell you, Detective. Let me tell you about greed, which I don't have. Down on the south side here, there's Del McKechnie and Benny Kreuger and Georgie Sedillo, and, oh, one or two others. Do I fuck with them? Do I make life a heartache for them? No. No, maybe I accept a tithe, presents really, when they offer them to me, which is, frankly, always. Do I want more? Do I want it all? No, that'd be greedy. Greed makes trouble. So I accept a tithe and things go smooth. And over in Pan Fry Mr. Sundown Phillips has things pretty much under control but, still, I know people he doesn't and maybe he gives me a piece, a small percentage, out of respect. I accept graciously. I don't send Shuggie over there to make trouble, and I don't let Rudy Regot or Steve Roque or any of the Frogtown cliques go into the south side and come on rugged with the fellas down there."

"Yeah," Shade said, "and does everybody live happily ever after?"

"Jerk."

"Shade," Beaurain said, "if you weren't a cop, what would you be?"

"I might be you."

"Never, never, you don't even understand the world you live in, how could you be me?"

"I could dress spiffy and talk like a duke, too, if it wasn't that I'd rather wear rags and feel free to spit on dukes."

"I'm sorry, Mr. Beaurain," Shuggie said. "This is how he always is."

"Oh, don't be sorry," Beaurain said. He ferreted out another cashew and put it in his mouth, then sucked on it behind a smile. "He's what you said he'd be. Shade, I wonder, are you a good Christian?"

"My case is under review."

"Ah, but I think you want to be. I admire that. The higher-calling angle, you see, can inspire men toward greatness. It can also delude them. Ponder it." Beaurain hunched forward, his hands on his knees. "I'm glad to have met you. But now is business. As you know there are some ruffians going around, hurting people, fucking things up. They're greedy, they're stupid, they're going to pay. Your team feels the same as my team, Detective, and it's all of us against the umpires."

"So I was told," Shade said. "I'm not a fuckin' hit man, though."

"Jerk."

"Shuggie, you call me a jerk again and I'm gonna kick your fat ass in front of your boss."

"Come on *with it*, Rene."

"Shut up," Beaurain said with a wince of offended elegance. "Both of you. I feel like I'm a kid again, with all this fistfighting shit, and, believe me, my kid years are *not* my favorite memory." Beaurain looked over his shoulder toward the gun position behind the petunias. "Norman, show these gents the door." He then quickly spun back to Shade. "I don't want to see you get hurt, Detective Shade, but you don't know enough about the world you live in. I could tell you, but I don't have time."

Shade stood and shook his legs loose and felt the pleasant amphetamine back beat of his heart.

"They whacked one of ours, Mr. B., and I'm in it because of that. But later, I might get on you just to see your moves." Shade extended his hand to the overlord of his town.

"Very well. Bonne chance. I look forward to it." Beaurain stood and shook Shade's hand. "Just remember the birds-and-bees of business—I fuck you or you fuck me. And there aren't many birthday parties for fellas who've fucked me."

Shade smiled widely and stared hard into Beaurain's face.

"You talk a lot of shit about knowing the world we live in, Mr. B., but you're dangerously fuckin' confused about me. I want you to know that up-front."

10

As it had been on so many key days in Wanda Bone Bouvier's life, the sky above her head was murky, backed up by soiled wads of cloud. She drove west from home looking for a through street to the north. A smoking stick of boo was in her left hand, clasped to the steering wheel. Her right hand held a bottle of Pepsi that she'd clogged with salted peanuts and called a late lunch.

She hit River Road and jumped on the gas, prompting gut checks in oncoming motorists when she passed the old pokies in her path. She sucked on the doobie, chomped and swished her southland snack, speeding on by a seedy stretch of small businesses and stores where the cashiers tended to keep their hands beneath the counter when strangers came in.

It was a gray, hot, horsefly afternoon, and her skin felt slick with sweat when she pulled into the parking lot of The Rio, Rio Club. The joint was a large prefab aluminum concoction, guaranteed to go south in a heavy wind, with a sign above the door that said, BUSCH ON TAP, ROOMS TO LET.

Wanda had pondered several themes she might embody and had opted to attempt the fresh-out-of-high-school-but-willing approach. She wore a pale green and yellow summer dress, with fifty cents' worth of pearls around her neck, red lipstick and yellow spike heels. When she came in the club she saw a round stage with a light above it, and a woman lying on a blanket doing splits. Jerry Lee Lewis, a regional hero, was booming from the speakers, "The Killer" singing a vigorously sad song about bad love gone worse, and beating his piano like he was married to it.

Wanda took a seat up against the stage and studied the bare gal's performance. The audience was a steamy-eyed group therapy conglomeration of night-shift factory drones, expense account raconteurs and countrified shy guys. The dancer did her limber thing lying on a pink blanket, seemingly unaware that others were in the room, doing her gynecologically revealing calisthenics as if she were at home with the curtains drawn.

Wanda looked into the supine dancer's eyes and decided that the woman seemed so aloof because she *was* aloof, likely hiding behind a reds and daiquiri veil.

"What'll you have, sister?" the bartender asked.

"A glass of whatever's on tap."

The bartender was a husky old hustler, in a nice white shirt with a red bow tie. When he set the beer in front of Wanda he said, "Pardon me for askin', ma'am, but are you a dyke?"

"Does it matter?"

"It'd break my heart."

"I'm just watchin' her out of boredom—my TV's on the fritz." Wanda tasted the beer. "Mmm, good'n cold. Leon around?"

"Leon? Leon?" The bartender did a mock stagger, his hand over his heart. "You ain't gonna stop 'til you do break it are you?"

Wanda dealt the old boy a smile as a reward for still having the pluck to try.

"He's just a friend," Wanda said, coyly smiling, her eyes angled down demurely. "I only fuck elderly bartenders. Is he here?"

"Elderly? Girl, you are flat-out cruel." The bartender pointed to a loft ten feet above the front door where audio equipment was set up. "He's somewhere in there, honey. He spins the records. He'll be done after this tune for the girl's break."

As she waited for the music to end Wanda scanned The Rio, Rio Club, furtively memorizing the layout. Basically, it was a barn, with only one interesting door, back in the left rear. She thought she heard a hammer over the blues, then the music was gone and she knew she did. There was some hammering being done, back behind the interesting door.

"Hey, Wanda, I saw you come in," Leon Roe said. He sat on the stool next to her. "Want a beer? I can get you a free one."

"I got one."

"I'll make it free for you."

"Thanks, Leon."

Leon had a narrow face, with a shiny forehead perfectly halved by a well-trained spit curl. He had a hesitant way about him but he dressed like a cowpoke star who wanted to pull in a more fashion-conscious crowd. There was black piping on his lavender western-cut coat, and his eggshell shirt was capped off by a blue string tie held up by a turquoise clasp that resembled an extra-large spider. At some recent time he'd spent too much on a pair of rattlesnake boots, and he wore one of those silver belt buckles that made a statement about his favorite brand of beer.

"Well," he said, his cheeks flushing, "what you been doing?"

"Anything, and a lot of it," Wanda said.

"Oh," Leon said, smiling. He found her to have a rare, exciting psychology, and he watched her now, as always, with an expression of nose-to-the-glass fascination. "Ever been here before?"

"No. It looks sort of cheap."

"Uh-huh," Leon said, "I agree, see, but, you know, I'm only here for the experience. To learn the entertainment business."

"You call this the entertainment business?"

"I call it a start, the first step. Elvis once drove a truck."

Wanda noticed a few workmen coming out of the door that concerned her. She turned to Leon and put her hand on his thigh.

"I need a job," she said, staring him into a puddle. "Could you help?"

"Here? You mean, here, Wanda? I'll loan you some money," he said. "We *are* neighbors. That means something to me."

"I'd rather earn it."

Leon studied the toes of his snakeskins.

"This place is total nudity," he said. "Some of the stuff gets pretty tasteless."

"I noticed," Wanda said. "I'd bring up the level, I reckon. Don't you think I'd look pretty classy in the buff, Leon?"

"Oh, God," he said, "I think you probably look too classy, too fine, for a place like this."

She patted his thigh, her hand lightly, nearly accidentally brushing his crotch. He was so easy to play, she thought, sadly out of place in the nighthawk realm. The kind of guy who walked down Seventh Street in broad daylight and prompted muggers to look up and say "Bingo!"

"Leon, why don't you find your boss and let *him* decide if he can use a fresh face? Won't you do that for me, sweetheart?"

Leon ushered Wanda into the room behind the interesting door, and introduced her to Fat Frank Pischelle. He sat at a small table, hunkered over a plate of chili dogs. His black hair was swept straight back and he sported a long goatee with dangling streaks of gray.

"You ever done this before?" he asked.

"Sort of. At a party or two," Wanda said. Fat Frank's fatness was vaguely nauseating at this distance. "But never what you'd call professional."

"We strip to the crack here," Fat Frank said. "Are you sure you're up for something that new and different?"

Wanda jutted her hips and smirked.

"Mister," she said, "I bust a cherry every day gettin' some new kind of kick."

"I'll bet that's true," he said. He used a fork to chop off a mouthful of chili dog, then sat back and stared at her while he chewed.

Wanda spun on her spikes, slowly spinning so that her selling points were highlighted, and as she did this modeling turn her eyes took in the two poker tables and the craps box, the exit door in the southwest corner, and the shotgun perch that had been built up on the wall. She put her hands on her hips and went into that salesmanship spin again.

"I'm an interesting thing if you look at me," she said. "My figure's nice. I play basketball like a man so you won't find no cottage cheese on my butt. No sir," she said and patted her haunches, "this little fanny is harder'n married life."

Fat Frank's attention was split between the chili dogs and Wanda. His expression was dispassionate, cool and almost bored. He took in another bite of his meal that would've put two jockeys out of work.

"You gotta audition," he said. "Leon, put a quarter in the juke over there."

Leon was sweaty-faced and pale, silently pledging allegiance to Cupid, for his dreams were being answered. He gave Wanda a thumbs up and walked to the jukebox.

"What should I play?"

"A-seven," Fat Frank said from behind a mouthful. He pointed at Wanda, wagging his finger until he'd swallowed. "That's 'Love Potion Number Nine,' honey. I use the same song on everybody 'cause everybody knows it." He picked up a napkin and daintily dabbed at his mouth, then clasped his hands on the tabletop. "Let's see your version."

In the brief moment before the song began Wanda decided she'd improvise a narrative strip, an impromptu skin story with plenty of tits and ass to hold her audience. As the tune boomed she went with the lyrics, holding her nose between two fingers, closing her eyes dramatically, then mimed taking a drink. She hopped about on her high heels a little awkwardly through the part where she wasn't supposed to know if it was day or night, doing a wicked imitation of stunned innocence as she kissed everything in sight, and she loosened her dress and let it slide, slide, slide when she acted out kissing the wrong cop on Thirty-fourth and Vine, and her breasts were bared, revealing pink nipples the size of peach halves, then she kicked free of the folds, baring herself down to spikes, pearls, and red G-string panties, and bent over with her ass aimed at Fat Frank, her eyes on Leon, and she shook, shook, shook from side to side, then front to back in a crowd-pleasing mimicry of the thrusting arts, until the cop broke that little bottle of Love Potion Number Nine. She ended her recital standing straight, a hand on either side of her open mouth, in a wide-eyed gesture of surprise.

The song ended and she dropped her hands to her hips.

"Well?" she asked.

Fat Frank nodded slowly and said, "Corny interpretation, but lots of verve. I can use you starting a week from Friday. What's your name?"

"How about Sinful Cindy?"

"Naw. We already got a Sinful Suzie." Fat Frank raised his fork. "How about Moaning Lisa?"

Wanda shrugged.

"Kind of artsy, ain't it?"

Fat Frank nodded, then drove the fork deeper into the chili.

"That's the secret me," he said. "My face fools people. Leon, explain things to her, somewhere else. This is my mealtime."

Wanda picked up the wadded dress, then followed Leon back to the front room, her heels clicking on the cement. She went to the bar, naked still, and lifted her beer for a drink. The bartender stared at her, smiling, and all eyes in the place focused on her. She gave the bartender a direct deadpan gaze, snorted, then raised her arms and shimmied into her dress.

"Uh, Wanda," Leon said, "the pay here is good. Two bills a week plus twenty-five percent of your tips." He ran his tongue over his lips. "You, you'll be rich by Christmas. You got something special. I'm glad you did this, coming here today. I hope it wasn't an accident that you came to where *I* worked."

"Sweetheart," Wanda said and pinched his nose, "I never try *nothin'* unintentional."

On the back porch at home Wanda settled down with a can of Jax and said to Jadick, "It was easy. They pay better'n I thought they would, too."

Jadick stood in the doorway looking down on Wanda, who was stretched out with her feet in their regular resting spot on the window-sill. She'd shed the spike heels and the summery dress draped down between her spread legs.

"You get any cookies out of it?" he asked. "You get any kind of kick stripping off in front of them guys?"

"Oh, man," Wanda said, "lemonade has got more kick to it than bare-assin' it in front of men like them. I mean, if they knew what to do with a naked gal they wouldn't be out there studyin' up on it, would they?"

"You wouldn't think so," Jadick said. "The layout sounds a little hairy but I think we can handle it."

"We've got to sober up your desperadoes," Wanda said. "They been in the cold shower for ten minutes but that ain't going to get them sober." She stood up and started wearily toward the kitchen. "I'll have to heat up the fryer and feed them something."

"That's awful sweet and wifey of you," Jadick said.

Wanda laid one of her flattest looks on him, then ducked under his arm across the doorway.

"I'm in this thing way too deep not to want it to work," she said.

Thirty minutes later the deep-fat fryer was sizzling and Wanda was turning out a giant platter of golden brown home fries.

"There ain't no meat in the house," she said as she watched the fryer steam, and heard the grease pop and hiss. "Which is a pity 'cause I fry chicken so all-around special even you boys might take up with women."

Dean and Cecil sat at the table, having already shoveled away the first small portion of fries. Their plates were streaked with fat and ketchup, and Cecil used his finger to etch a heart in the congealing grease.

"I *been* married," Dean said, still shaky on his chair. "To a woman, I mean."

"What was she like?" Wanda asked.

"Pretty tight for a gal with three kids. What kind of question is that, though?"

"A dumb one," Wanda said, and meant it.

There was a pot of coffee on the table and Jadick made his cohorts partake heavily of it. He sat like an overseer, directing the fellas to eat more of them taters, drink more java, think more clearly and listen up.

"I wonder if you guys have been hearing me," he said.

"We heard," Cecil said. Even his voice was puny and pale as his skin and hair. "We done rougher things."

"The timing has to be just right," Jadick said forcefully. "A stickup man has got to have timing—like a comedian. Robbery and comedy have a lot in common, 'cause if the punch line is slow, then the joke is really on the teller. Rob someplace with your timing off a heartbeat this way or that and it ain't gonna be too damn much fun. You guys hear me?"

"We ain't in this for the fun," Dean said. His lips pulled back and his greenish teeth went on display. He laughed and Cecil matched his giddy wheeze with his own high-pitched screech. "We're in it for the glory, ain't we Cecil?"

The fun buddies went AWOL, lost to some secret mirth, and Jadick stood up and went onto the porch.

Wanda poured the last basket of fries onto the platter, then set the platter on the table in front of the still cackling men.

She went to the porch herself, then, and found Jadick sitting on the chair arm, bent forward in the thinker's pose, with his chin resting on his fist.

"What you thinkin'?" she asked.

"A deep thought, pun-kin."

"Oh, yeah? Which one?"

"The one where I like to imagine the sun rising tomorrow and me still bein' alive to see it."

"Oh," Wanda said, and waved her hand at him with disappointment, "*that* one."

11

In the year of 1753, way downriver in the Crescent City, the Marquis de Vaudreuil was the appointed governor, and under the stewardship of this grand and elegant European one of the first truly successful ongoing criminal enterprises in North America flourished. The marquis's soldiers shook down the *cantine* owners along the docks, taking wine and rum as payment, and they patronized the bordellos where "correction girls," who'd been imported by the romantic governor, charmed these law-and-order types gratis, and with enthusiasm. There was tremendous eighteenth-century skim from all the city's affairs. The soldiers arrested or murdered any of the citizenry who defied them or insisted upon their right to two-step to the screech of a different fiddler, and soon this noble corruption spread and several of the soldiers turned sullen with success and began to hold out on the Grand Mamou himself.

Marcel Frechette, a Gallic entrepreneurial sort from near Calais, had enlisted under de Vaudreuil partly because his sales techniques had become too celebrated in the old hometown, but mainly because he liked the soldiers' hats. In the New World he very quickly found that being the law bore fruit that no mere gimmick could ever bear, and he shook down the pimps and the prostitutes, grogshop owners, and aristocrats with secret pastimes they preferred to keep that way. Frechette's zeal in his pursuit of other people's do-re-mi soon led him to decide that the governor's piece of the ice was too large, for wasn't he the one who parried the blades and bludgeons of those who were slow to pay?

The Marquis de Vaudreuil, famed for the haute couture he and his wife flaunted on all the gay occasions, had standards to uphold, so he sent a squad of good, loyal policemen to bring him this insolent Frechette, an alligator, and a bamboo cage.

In an upstairs rumpus room on Rampart Street, Frechette learned of the shift in the marquis's sentiments from a love-struck fourteen-year-old whore, and set off quickly toward the river where a demonstration of fine Spanish cutlery was required to secure a canoe for himself and the girl, who went by the name of Nathalie. They scurried upriver from the Gulf, paddling close to the bank day after day after day, until he saw a few modest mounds rising from the general soak. He called the hills Les Petites Côtes and appointed himself seigneur of the mounds, the marsh, and that stretch of the river. With the aid of the robust and uncomplaining Nathalie, Frechette hacked out space for a house and built a home overlooking the swamp.

He entered the fur trade and fucked the Indians via pelt prices that fluctuated downwardly from drink to drink, and soon he prospered. Alas, he did so well that other rugged entrepreneurial types paddled north and muscled in on the fur biz, and Frechette's aromatic past caught up to him in the person of one Pierre Blaise whose downriver brother had been slashed to death over a canoe. Blaise's harsh comments forced a duel on the mound that was to become known as Frechette Park, in commemoration of the better shot.

Marcel and Nathalie spawned a slew of children who would make river travel dangerous for another generation, and the old man lived on and on, and a town named St. Bruno wobbled up around him, and in the last summer of his four-score-and-two life, he saw the old French-town streets paved with the red cobblestones that still stood up to modern traffic.

Detective Rene Shade now buzzed over those thumpety-thumpety brick streets, riding on the passenger side of Shuggie Zeck's showboat El Dorado. Shade slumped in the seat and lay back, his eyes steady, staring out the window. The car sped past the cracked sidewalk, loitering corners of Frogtown, where the anarcho-capitalism of the street daffies was theorized, praised, and practiced. Misery was the lectern, and a gin rage the motivation, for meandering, harshly phrased harangues, and Shade and Shuggie had come up that way, hearing them all, believing most. In the thick summer offensive of heat and humidity, the cop and the hood rode in air-conditioned plushery through the worn, slick streets where the T-shirted sweaty backbones of democracy staggered about, drunk with despair or loaded on imported hope, game for any free enterprise that resulted in cash.

"How far to Gumbo?" Shade asked.

"Twenty minutes," Shuggie answered. "Unless the water's up."

They rode the blacktop north, parallel to the river. The land was flat and sogged with swamp and overgrown with indistinct greenery. The road slithered through the backwater country in a series of curves and loops necessitated by the need for solid ground. On either side of the paved surface the sloughs were coated completely by lily pads that gently heaved on the water like breathing ribs.

"Shuggie, you figure we'll have to butch down on this tush hog Gillette?"

"If we find him." Shuggie pointed to the glove box. "There's a pint of cherry vodka in there—hand it to me, uh?"

Shade opened the glove box.

"Cherry vodka? You still drink cherry vodka?"

"What's wrong with that?"

"I haven't had any for a long time, that's all." Shade handed the bottle to Shuggie. "I think it was when the Twist was new, the last time I drank cherry vodka."

"I'm proud of how you've grown all up, Rene," Shuggie said as he unscrewed the top. He took a gentlemanly swallow. "I happen to have a sweet tooth, and I *ain't* apologizin' for it."

As the car whipped down the back road Shade thought of his brother, Francois, who was an assistant D.A., and wondered if li'l bro Frankie could bail his ass out if this thing went Byzantine on him. And somehow the thought of Francois rewound the years and Shade was remembering a time when he, Francois, and this very same Shuggie had set off on an adventure together. It had been the fourteenth birthday of big brother Tip, and Shade, nine years old and earnest, wanted to find a present suitable for presentation to an idol. For this was in the time when Tip, with his already deep chest and huge arms, his street-stompin' rep that was even then spreading beyond Frogtown, was his hero. He sort of worshiped his own brother because didn't grown men, hardasses themselves in some cases, nod to Tip and give him wide berth? And Tip, with his variety of sucker punches and his horseshoe-tapped army boots, had the back-alley swagger that inspired young Rene and Francois and Rene's good pal Shuggie.

They would watch Tip as he stood on the roof of the row house putting pigeons, his odd choice of a hobby, through tumbles and tumults and a whole vaudeville of tricks. And on this birthdate it had been Shuggie who'd solved the gift mystery for Rene by saying, "He loves them birds on the roof—I know where we can get some more."

Young Isaac "Shuggie" Zeck led the expedition to Second Street and St. Peter's Cathedral, where he leaned against the bricks that had been faded by several generations of weather, and said, "Let's climb." He latched onto a drainpipe, then with blubbery bravado mountaineered up the cathedral wall until he came to a section where brick ornamentations jutted out, making for excellent handholds.

Once the trio was on the roof, in between the steep peaks, they began walking in the rain gutters looking for nests and trying not to stare down to the sidewalks where they would certainly splatter if they fell. Flocks of pigeons winged about overhead, scudding like cannon-shot clouds, while the boys kicked through nests, coming up with only two possibly rotten eggs. They put the eggs in a brown lunch sack, then sat at an angle on the steep peak, below the huge cross, their sneakered feet braced in the gutter. They were forlorn, for two paltry eggs were clearly insufficient gift for an idol.

Soon Shuggie began to swivel his head, staring here and there, down, and then up, where he spied a veritable thatch of nests on the flat space beneath the cross. He brought this to everyone's attention. "I don't think so," Rene said. He held the sack with its miserable offering, then studied the path to the cross, the climb up the steeply angled slippery roof, and said, "No way." Li'l brother Francois concurred mutely, merely running his bug eyes to the nests and shaking his head.

"Aw, give me the sack," Shuggie said, snatching it from Rene. Then he set off. He went up fast and low, his fat heinie bouncing with each step of his short legs, the laces of his high-tops flopping loose to the sides of his feet. Rene watched open-mouthed, his mind envisioning the one misstep on the steep incline and Shuggie sliding down, beyond control, whooshing off the roof in a deadly plummet, wafting to the sidewalk like something spit from the steeple. But, no, young Shuggie humped up the daunting path with a positively inspiring disdain for consequences. He breathed hard and his cheeks flushed, but he reached the nests and pillaged the eggs. For his descent he sat on the tiles with the sack at his side, inching down, but then, his feet raised, he flopped onto his back, and accelerated. There was hardly time to react. Rene and Francois stood motionless, shocked, expecting to be clipped by the tumbling Shuggie and dashed below.

Shuggie put his feet down like brakes and stopped on a dime. "I wish you could see the looks on your faces," he said, laughing. He opened the sack and checked on the looted eggs. "I didn't break a one. Let's go."

Big Tip, the birthday boy, was run down on Voltaire Street, outside The Chalk and Stroke, where he occupied an exalted spot against the wall, surrounded by lesser badasses. Rene approached him with the sack and held it to him. "Happy birthday from us guys," he said, gesturing at Francois and Shuggie. Tip stayed against the wall but held out his hand and accepted the gift. When he opened the sack, Rudy Regot and Harky Gifford and Lou Pelitier rubbernecked over his shoulder. Tip spit, then closed the sack and twisted the top. "Them's mongrel eggs," he said, then whipped his arm like he was snapping locker-room butt with a towel and smashed the sack against the bricks. He then lifted the sack by the bottom, turned it over, and drained the mongrel muck to the hot sidewalk, where it made a stain that lasted for months.

When Shuggie wheeled the El Dorado off of the hard road and onto the dirt, the jolt pulled Shade out of the past.

He looked at Shuggie and asked, "Do we have a plan, Shug?"

Shuggie wagged his head but kept his eyes on the narrow dirt road.

"We'll try the classic approach, man," he said. "Hustle in through the door with our guns out and see what runs."

"That's asking for disaster," Shade said.

Shuggie groaned. He raised the cherry vodka and treated himself to a nice long drink.

"Man, send out for some balls," he said harshly. "If these are the tush hogs we're lookin' for you're goin' to be *glad* you got that gun out."

"And if it's *not* them?"

"Uh, well, we'll make a strong first impression on 'em." Shuggie grinned. "That's one of the keys to a new relationship, you know—the first impression."

A few minutes later they began to pass houses built on stilts, raised aloft in recognition of the region's regular floods. Shuggie slowed before a yellow house made of thin, warping wood planks. There was a dirt yard worn down smooth as a defendant's bench. The windows were *sans* screens, allowing open-range rights to an occasional bat and all manner of smaller, winging specks of misery.

"His truck ain't here," Shuggie said. He leaned on the gas. "We'll go on down the road to The Boylin' Kettle. That's the local watering hole."

The bar looked just like any other house except for the gravel parking lot and a handpainted sign nailed to a lob-lolly pine that read THE BOYLIN' KETTLE. Shuggie parked behind a pea-green truck, raised high on swamp tires. There was a sticker on the truck's rear bumper that said Coonasses Do It in the Dark.

"That's his pickup," Shuggie said. "We got him."

Shade checked his pistol, knowing that there were no dull followers of the law out here, and that the local populace was mightily leavened by 'backy-chawin' muskrat bashers, whose business lives were attuned to the illegal games markets, St. Brunians' vacation schedules, and the low-flying international aviators who patronized their modest backwoods landing strips.

"If there's more than six coonasses in there," Shade said, "we should give it a skip and catch him alone. I don't have any jurisdiction out here."

"For Christ sake," Shuggie said disgustedly, "did somebody buy you a subscription to *Redbook* since the old days, or what? Geez!" He reached under the front seat and brought out a well-cared-for sawed-off shotgun. As he slipped shells into the chambers he said, "Man, I bet you can do seventy-seven clever things with tuna now, too, can't you?"

It was at this moment, chided by his old and present rival, that Shade decided it was time to revert to the shitkicker verities. Brazen dash, rough talk, and an ounce or two of mean were clearly required.

"I should be on vacation," he said, "and maybe I am. Trade with me." Shade held his pistol toward Shuggie. "Let me swing that cannon."

Shuggie asked, "Why?"

"Hey, look," Shade said, "you know Gillette when you see him and I don't. That means I've got to take your back, man, and cover your fat ass. There might be a passel of tush hogs in that dive, and I want something *seriously bulldog* in my hands when I come through that door. Now give me that double-barrel."

A slow, tense smile moved onto Shuggie's face.

"I hear you, man," he said, and they made the trade.

By the time they'd stepped out of the car, Shade had adopted a shrewd personification of those ancient shitkicker verities, and went toward the door with his shoulders back, chin up, eyes straight, in the long striding saunter of the rough n' ready.

"Now I recognize you," Shuggie said, walking beside Shade with the same stride and posture. "Now you look like the Rene Shade I used to know. Man, it's good to see you again."

The sun was behind the high branches of the tall timeless trees, giving a nice shadowiness to their movements as they went up the three slabwood steps to The Boylin' Kettle.

"Come on," Shade said. "We'll cut through these tush hogs like a rake through shit."

★   ★   ★

Bobby Gillette looked like a boy soprano who'd fallen in with the wrong crowd for twenty years or so and liked it. He had a frothy wave of sandy hair breaking down his forehead, and big soulful brown eyes and thin lips. When lying down he would've been perfect for measuring off two yards of cotton muslin, but when the bad-news duo came in the door he was sitting at a round table in the center of the room, nursing a Michelob, reading a copy of *Outdoor Life*.

"P'pere," he said to the old man behind the bar. Then he recognized Shuggie and added, "Oh, pas de merde."

Shuggie cocked the police .38 in his hand and held it barrel-up, palm toward Gillette.

"Bonjer, Bobby," he said, and stood over his target. "Some fool bizness went down in town, there, Bobby. Are you the guy who done it?"

Gillette turned a page of the magazine, aping nonchalance, and said, "I don't know, I might be. I'm a nasty motherfucker on a regular basis."

Shade stood just inside the door, his hand on the shotgun, the shotgun resting on the plywood surface of the bar. He looked at the old man behind the rail and the trio of drinking men in sweat-soaked shirts at the other end of the bar.

"Keep your hands where I can see them, Jethro," he said to the bartender. "That goes for you fellas, too. I filed the trigger on this sucker, so it'll spring off if I breathe too deep. I thought y'all should know that."

In the center of the room Shuggie was gently tracing a part in Gillette's hair with the pistol barrel, gentling the blue steel along the top of his skull.

"Whoever done it killed a man," he said sweetly.

"C'est triste," Gillette responded.

"Speak English, coonass," Shade barked. Shade was half-and-half, Franco-Irish American, but at the moment it was the Irish side he identified with. He spoke no more French than "bonjour," "merci," and a few other phrases, and thought the whole business of bilingualism was a trendy gimmick. "Or I'll give you something to 'c'est triste' about."

"Better listen to him," Shuggie said. "My man over there'll chew your face off and shit it in your mommy's roux, you mess with him."

Gillette sat up, stiffly erect, his hands on the table. He said, "I feel another phony burglary beef comin' on, Zeck."

"Worse," Shuggie said. "You know what worse adds up to, don'tcha, Bob? Huh? Worse means you could be chunked out and baitin' a meaty trotline by dawn."

Still stiff, as the police .38 rested on his head, Gillette said, "Man, I didn't do it, whatever it was. That other thing, back you know when, I did do. I did that. But I ain't done nothin' in St. Bruno since."

The Boylin' Kettle was basically the living room of a three-room house, with two refrigerators for coolers and a flat piece of plywood laid over three flour hogsheads to make a bar. The walls were the same color of green that would have set in on yesterday's fatally wounded, and there were half a dozen mounted fish on them gathering dust. A large upright radio quietly played some Belton Richard chanky-chank.

"Come on this side of the rail, Jethro," Shade said to the bartender, who was an impressively moustached man, pushing seventy and slowly wasting. When he had joined the three patrons, Shade said, "Get on the floor, hands behind your heads." The quartet of bossed boozers acted as if they might raise an objection to these proceedings, but this notion was promptly overruled when Shade bandied the shotgun about. "Facedown," he said, and they silently obeyed.

Now in control of things, Shade scanned the room and the bar and noted that every one of these swamp rats had been drinking bottles of Michelob and that there were cases of the same stacked between the refrigerators. Instantly curious about this astonishing market penetration by such a Yupscale brew, Shade asked, "Y'all hijack a beer truck lately, or what?"

The answer came from Gillette, who said, "If we did it wasn't in St. Bruno, man."

This brought Shade to Shuggie's side, and he nodded at his partner. "Ask him some pointed questions, Shug."

"Were you in town yesterday, man-sewer?" Shuggie asked.

Gillette was doing a fair imitation of stone, and only his lips moved when he answered, "No, man. I been here, swillin' the Michelob, all this time."

Shuggie grabbed Gillette by the collar, then booted the chair from beneath him and pulled on the collar simultaneously, toppling him to the floor, jamming his face to the wood.

"Lie!" Shuggie said loudly, then fired a shot next to Gillette's head, raising an energetic billow of dust. "A little birdie seen you, Bob. Little birdies don't lie. They ain't got it in 'em. You do."

Gillette's lips had split when his face met the floor and an elastic blood drool stretched down his chin and back to the ground. He shook his head groggily, whipping the bloodstrand like a lariat, and flinched when Shuggie blasted another round.

Shade turned to the cowering quartet and said, "I could grind all of y'all with one twitch, so stay down." Then he leaned to Gillette. "See here, sport," he said, "I don't want to have to watch you stain this nice wood floor from wall to wall. Y'all got yourselves a sweet drinkin' spot here and it'd be a shame if in years to come ol' P'pere over there had to bore himself and every new patron with a long sad explanation for your stains, man. So answer up and I'll hold Shuggie off you."

With bright, glassy eyes Gillette turned and faced Shade, one hand on the floor, the other swatting at the elastic bloodstrand, strumming it like the E-string on an upright bass.

"You changed parts," he said. "First he was Jeff and you was Mutt. Now he's comin' on Mutt and you get to be Jeff." He laughed. "I seen this good man-bad man thing before."

Shade stood tall and straight and kicked Gillette in the stomach. He then lifted his leg with his knee held out before him and jabbed his toes into Gillette's chest.

"It's Mutt and Mutt time, coonass!" he said.

Shuggie put some Italian shoe leather to work on Gillette's back, and Shade flicked his toes into his belly, keeping up the thumping reel until the tush hog tuckered out and collapsed on his side, moaning bluesily and sucking for sweet air.

Shade took a glance at the four prone bystanders and said, "Y'all be still and mind your own business." He then bent forward and leaned over Gillette. "We ain't near tired yet, so you best tell us something secret that we really, *really* want to know."

"Aw, man, I heard, I heard about it," Gillette said. He held his hands to his belly and curled his legs up to block any further dance steps to his guts. His head was sideways to the floor and crimson slobber was smeared on his cheeks. "There ain't no problem with my left tit," he said and tapped some fingers to his heart. "My left tit ain't got no dog in it, but I ain't doin' no more time for another crime I never even got the fun of pullin'."

The radio crackled with D. L. Menard droning "The Back Door," and a long beam of light from the sliding sun came through the southwest window and glinted off the cases of beer stacked between the refrigerators. The four men who stood a good chance of becoming possibly innocent victims, kept their hands on their heads and their noses to the wood and their opinions to themselves.

"I heard today what happen last night," Gillette said, "but day last I seen a man I know who whisper to me that a man he knows is in town who shouldn't be." Accompanied by a couple of convincing grimaces, Gillette sat up. "Oh, you town dudes—I don't fuck with you. Believe you that. This man who is in the town was not so long ago in the federal place, eh? Braxton. What I am told is that he run with a prison clique calls itself The Wing."

"Where'd your friend see this fella?" Shuggie asked.

"Buyin' gin and lime juice at Langlois' Liquor, there. In town." Gillette spit a heavy globule of blood and saliva that spun through the air and hit the wall a good ten feet away. "He had a partner, and this clique is s'posed to be dangerous more than a little."

"Are they the fellas we're lookin' for?" Shade asked.

"That I don't know for positive," Gillette said. "But they was in town, here, and they don't belong here."

Shade and Shuggie exchanged glances and with barely perceptible nods they agreed to several things: that Gillette's info was interesting;

that he was probably not involved; and that they wouldn't be capping anyone in The Boylin' Kettle.

"You hear a name on the out-of-town dude?" Shuggie asked.

"Well," Gillette said, "it was Cecil something." Gillette kept his face down and used his fingers to swab at the blood drools on his face. "Don't hit me no more, eh? Could be I don't know nothin' else."

"Okay," Shade said and walked over to the prone men. He stood near their feet with the shotgun loosely aimed at their backs. "Cough up all y'all's car keys, hear me? One at a time you're going to reach into your pockets and fish out your keys and toss 'em on the floor." He nudged the man on the left with a foot to the ankle. "Startin' with you, sport."

While Shade did his forcible valet thing, Shuggie lifted the chair from the floor and said, "Have a seat, Bobby. You got lucky last time and I don't believe you'd be stretchin' your good gris-gris this tight again." Gillette sat in the chair and slumped forward onto the table, a small afterflow of the crimson juice flecking the magazine he'd been reading peaceably when the day had so suddenly gone awful on him. Shuggie said, "But as you see we *can* find you, and if you bullshitted us we'll be back, *Rowbear*. And prob'ly we'll be all bummed out and hurt, too, hurt that a *confrère* like you would mislead us."

"I didn't, Zeck."

Shade had scooped up all the keys except Gillette's but the stomped man put his on the table without being asked. Shade stuffed all the keys into his pants pockets.

"I'll drop 'em in the middle of the road just before the blacktop starts," he said. He then rapped the sawed-off barrel on the tabletop, drawing Gillette's eyes up to his. "Now don't even think about loadin' up and comin' into Frogtown lookin' for us, man, 'cause your luck might run out and you'd *find* us."

With that the inquiring duo backed to the door where Shuggie paused and said, "This was only bizness, guys—no hard feelings, all right?"

From The Boylin' Kettle to the paved road Shuggie's El Dorado whipped up a dust trail and slalomed through the curves. He hit the brakes when he sighted blacktop and Shade rolled his window down and tossed a jangling variety of car keys into the dust. Then Shuggie tromped on the gas and swung off the soft dirt and onto the hard road, and roared toward town, displaying a road-hog outlook by taking the middle of the blacktop for his lane.

"We done good," he said to Shade. "You ever heard of this thing, this gang—The Wing?"

"No," Shade said. The shotgun rested on the floorboard between his feet just in case the coonasses knew some secret shortcut and lay in wait, fomenting an unpleasant reunion. "There's dozens of those prison cliques, Shuggie. The Wing I don't know."

"We'll ask around," Shuggie said. The pint of cherry vodka was on the front seat and he lifted it. "I gotta say, that was purty damn slick," he said, laughing. When he saw that Shade was unsmiling, he added, "Cut the long-face phony thing, Rene—I know you. You were wired and primed back there, man. You had your rumble hat on and don't bother tellin' me I'm wrong."

Shade did laugh and stretched his legs and leaned back in the soft plush seat.

"That business points up a po-lease man's constant dilemma," he said, laughing with a combination of relief and exhilaration. "Anybody who's ever done any crime knows that it *can be* a fuckin' hoot."

"We both been knowin' *that* for a while," Shuggie said. "Sometimes I recall things we done years ago, Rene, when we was a team and hungry." He slowly shook his curlyhaired head. "I never feel ashamed *at all*."

"I believe you," Shade said, mirthlessly, staring out the window. "But sometimes *I* do."

The day had zipped by Shade, lulled as he was by fatigue, propelled as he was by speed, and as the sun dove behind the tall marsh trees and the shadows loomed long and deep across the road he traveled down, he retreated once again into memory. It was the day of Shuggie's wedding to his astutely chosen bride, and St. Peter's was SRO, for the Langlois clan was large and widespread with kin in every quarter of the city, and the Zecks had a few friends, too. Shade had been put into a tux as a groomsman, along with Rudy Regot and Kenny Poncelet, while Shuggie's older brother Bill had been best man. That had been the last time Shade and Shuggie had been close, and after Father Marty Perroni had legally linked Zeck to Langlois, they'd all gone to a reception in The Huey Long Room of The St. Bruno Hotel and everyone was there: Auguste Beaurain sipped a glass of Champale while his then chief lieutenant, Denis Figg, who was soon to disappear during the unpleasantness with the upriver dagos, hovered nearby; and old Mayor Atlee Yarborough had acted real "just folks" and goosed a teenaged bridesmaid, repeatedly, to her consternation and the voters' joy; and Shade and Shuggie and Kenny Poncelet who died at Quong Tri and Tip and How Blanchette and the whole cast from the melodrama of childhood, had put Cold Duck away until the cows came home and the groom had required pouring into a rented black sedan, and Hedda had driven off toward a supposed honeymoon at Panama Beach.

Now, straddling that little white line toward Frogtown, Shade said, "You ever tell your father-in-law about all the times we ripped him off?"

"No, I never did."

"You don't think he'd find it enlightening? Or funny?"

Shuggie grunted, smiling.

"Actually, Daddy Langlois has bitched about the neighborhood thieves plenty, but I never say anything, although Hedda knows. I thought it might seem endearing, you know, like an old movie, so I told her one time." Shuggie took a sip of cherry vodka. "She's been holdin' it over my head ever since."

"I haven't seen Hedda to talk to in years," Shade said. "She always says, 'Hi, Rene,' and keeps going when I run into her."

"What'd you expect? You're a cop. Nobody likes cops. Cops cause nothin' but trouble."

"Yeah, yeah, I know," Shade said lightly, "but how *is* Hedda?"

"Fine, fine. She still likes to grease up and sit on the hog of an evenin', but we been married forever it seems like, man."

"Since what? Nineteen?"

"Yeah. Since the fun old days."

Soon they were within the city limits, back in Frogtown, rumbling over those thumpety-thumpety bricks that had been laid down so long ago, and Shuggie said, "Someday you're goin' to explain to me why you're a cop. Why that is, is because I can still remember when you and me plotted and plotted in our kid way, you know, dreamin' of growin' up and shovin' Mr. B. and Steve Roque and all those bossmen out of the boat and into the river."

"And we'd be top dogs," Shade said. "I remember when we dreamed that trash."

There were a couple of inches of sweetish booze left in the bottle and Shuggie held it in his hand.

"We figured we could outsmart 'em and take 'em off once we got seasoned."

Shade nodded and said, "I know we did."

After a swallow Shuggie held the bottle toward Shade.

"We still could," he said.

Smiling tightly, Shade looked out the window, then turned to Shuggie, who watched him intently. Then both men laughed and Shade wordlessly took the bottle, raised it and drained it, dropping the dead soldier to the floorboard where it slid with a ding into the sawed-off shotgun, and laid there.

12

MOTHER NATURE was laying down some Law out there in the bayou night, and as befits the order of things, large feathered creatures dove off high branches, swooped low and stuck talons in smaller furry meals, and bandit-eyed coons came stealthily out of hollow logs and glommed finned, scaly chow from the still, brackish shallows, while all those things that slither waited, coiled, for the passing appearance of any prey absentminded, and where the bayou waters butted against land and a screened porch overlooked the boggy stage for these food-chain theatricals, Emil Jadick sat on the arm of the couch and wrapped up a lecture that had been real Type A in tone and content.

He said, "And if either of you fucks up because you ain't been listenin' to me, I'll take you off the calendar myself, understood?"

Dean Pugh and Cecil Byrne sat on the couch, forearms on knees, heads down, sullenly nodding.

"We listened, Jadick," Dean said, raising his head. "And we been here before, Mr. Boss Hoss."

"You got caught before," Jadick said. "I'd like to avoid that—so don't fuck up."

Pugh and Byrne were both essentially state-raised social problems, government-parented misfits. They'd lived the institutional life in different places, Dean from age eight in Maryland, and Cecil from age four in Florida, and met at what somehow seemed to them to be the bosom of their family—the federal pen. Both men moved with that odd, fearful underdog gait, jerking around like disoriented lizards, gawkily uncoordinated, stoically confused.

"We're gonna back you up all the way," Dean said. "'Cause what is it that *always* flies above the shit?"

"The Wing," Jadick said in unison with Cecil. "The Wing soars above it."

"There it is, brother."

Wanda was in the kitchen where she'd listened to Jadick's pep talk while doing the dishes. She began to dry the plates and silverware with a towel, and Jadick walked up behind her and cupped her breasts.

"Do all men do that?" she asked, not missing a stroke.

"Do what?"

"Get the hots for women in the kitchen." She shook her head quizzically. "Every man I ever been around gets all touchy-feely when I do dishes or cook."

Jadick backed away and sat at the table.

"I'd have to think about that," he said.

Wanda put the dried dishes in the cupboard, then got herself a cup of coffee. She leaned against the counter, holding the cup.

"Is your gang up to it?" she asked in a low voice.

Jadick shrugged.

"They're givin' the right answers," he said.

"Oh, man," Wanda said, "I've heard beer farts that made more sense than them two."

"Shut the fuck up," Jadick said. He studied her closely, eyes narrowed. "Don't plant bad seeds, pun-kin. Don't plant no bad seeds in me when you *know* we got a job tonight."

She blew on her coffee and looked at him over the rim of the cup.

"I'm just concerned," she said. "That's all."

"Now, look," Jadick said, "the upshot is..."

"...Oh, I dread that," Wanda said, turning away.

"Dread what?"

"The upshot. Man, I dread that motherfucker."

At this moment Dean and Cecil came in from the porch, grinning and bouncing with criminal vim. Dean put an arm around Cecil's shoulders, face beaming, and said, "You know, I *like* my life. Really, I do. Lots of people would say it's a shitty kind of life, but I don't. I like my life, you know. Things happen in it. I don't see how as that should be considered shitty. Everybody has things that happen in their life, but I *like* the things that happen in mine."

Jadick slowly swiveled his gaze from Dean to Wanda, then he pointed an admonishing finger at her.

"You got anything to say to that, pun-kin?"

Wanda leaned back on the counter and raised her eyes to the naked bulb on the ceiling, shuddering though smiling, and said, "Well, now, ain't *everything* just *beauti*ful, in its own way."

When Shade came trudging up the dark sidewalk and in through Nicole Webb's front door, Sleepy LaBeef was cranked up on the speakers, singing a wry and lively country boogie about the path he'd taken to The Wayside Lounge. Nicole was in the kitchen leaning over a pan of boiling water, turning crawdads into food. She wore a long cotton country dress that was festooned with flowery things that had been paled by repeated washings. Her feet were bare, her long hair was a dark unbrushed bramble, and she wore her black-framed reading glasses. Her back was turned to Shade, her eyes were focused on the reddening mud lobsters. She said, "I heard you come in, Rene, so don't bother sneakin' up behind me and grabbin' my butt."

"I don't like sneaks either," he said. He walked over and reached below the hem of her dress and raised his hand to the split where it lingered. "Sorry about today," he said into her ear. "A cop was shot."

"I heard," she said. She put stove gloves on her hands and raised the bucket of crawdads. "Now watch out," she said, "they're done."

Shade opened the refrigerator and saw a stock of longnecked Texas beer, and selected one, then sat at the kitchen table. As was the case with most flat spaces in Nic's house, the tabletop had several books laid open to the spine on it. *The Women at Point Sur, A Moveable Feast*, something about Vermeer and two novels by Shirley Ann Grau were spread out for handy reading while cooking.

"What're you making?"

"Crawdads, yellow rice and sliced tomatoes—any complaints?"

"No."

"That's damned good news if you feel like eatin'. 'Cause this is it."

From birth to the age of eighteen, Nicole had called Port Lavaca, Texas, home. She'd been raised up smelling the salt air of the Gulf and it seemed even now that her gaze was naturally trained on the distant horizon. During her final year in high school, she'd busted her hump both before and after class peeling shrimp at the dock, saving every penny for postgraduation flight. It was Italy that she fled to, along with Sandy Colter, her lifelong best friend. But after eight weeks Sandy said she had some problems with the water, the men, the women, the dogs, the motor scooters, and "all the fucking garlic," and went home. Nicole stayed on alone and tried to go native in Trieste. Months later on a rambling excursion to Greece, she took the ferry from Brindisi to Patras and overheard two longhairs speaking with Texas accents and suddenly the sky opened and she was hunkered down with them beneath a rainslicker, sucking on a bottle of ouzo while puddles developed around their feet.

The more charming Texan was named Keith Goodis and he claimed he was a stock-car driver in his mind, and would soon be so in fact. Two weeks later she was back in Trieste by herself, and behind a sense of heightened loneliness she began to find the Old World to be crotchety rather than charming, and flew home.

In Port Lavaca she stuffed the necessities of her life into an army surplus duffel bag and thumbed to Austin, where she presented herself on Keith Goodis's doorstep, and was welcomed. For the next three years, while Keith tried to prove himself on the oval dirt tracks of the South, she went to the university with the vague notion of turning herself into something decent, like an English teacher. But as time went by a certain sour melody sound-tracked her days, for good ol' Keith had fallen into the trap of loving a life he had small talent for, and after seventeen straight Sunday finishes out of the money he blamed her and domesticity for leeching from his soul the wildness required by his career, and she responded with an unkind comment or two concerning hand-eye coordination and pudding for brains.

The next day she deep-sixed education and called her old friend Sandy, who told her she'd finally found her true self in St. Bruno, where she lived with her friend Kathleen and had a neat little business renovating and refurbishing old houses. Come on over, she said, and Nicole did. Nic worked with Sandy and Kathleen until Kathleen began to resent her for having known Sandy since infancy, and she went hungry for a while, then took a job at Maggie's Keyhole. She was now twenty-eight and at home in Frogtown and at ease with Shade, but there was still something quietly unsettled about her that made it seem she was only marking time.

As Nicole set the bowl of crawdads along with rice and tomatoes on the table, Shade said, "What's with the fridge full of Texas longnecks?"

"Oh, now and then I can't help gettin' sentimental for some Lone Star."

"Uh-huh," Shade said. He filled his plate with a glob of everything, then belted back some brew. He was pulling the tail off a crawdad when he said, "I'll bet Lone Star was ol' *Keith's* favorite pabulum, *wudn't* it?"

"Don't do that," she said. "Please—it knocks you down in my eyes."

"All right," he said. "I hear you." Ever since she'd made the mistake of telling him the details of her previous major fling he'd needled her about it, usually by implying that she'd been love-suckered by a crybaby. "The mud lobster is done *just right*," he said.

"Thank you."

While dinner was eaten Nicole told Shade that How Blanchette was looking for him and would be at Ma Blanqui's early, early in the morning. She then segued into a pretty passionate explanation of Robinson Jeffers's "inhumanism" and he nodded cunningly as her whole theory whooshed right past him. During a lull in her explication he explained to her that he was flattened out from postspeed-sag and fatigue and that he might have to get back on the street in a few hours. What he needed was to relax.

After the meal Nicole put a stack of Nanci Griffith albums on the stereo, filled a yellow salad bowl with ice, then stuck in bottles of beer. She went into the bedroom and came back with two joints and a lighter and said, "Come on into the backyard, Rene, and smooth your ragged self out."

Shade followed her outside and they sat on the concrete blocks that served as back steps. The yard was not much larger than a regulation billiard table, squared off by the neighbors' fences, screened in somewhat by the honeysuckle that grew on those chicken wires. Several cottonwood trees rose up and spread out, partially blocking the light cast by a half-moon on a clear, delta summer night. The previous tenants of this cozy but ramshackle house had had their union blessed by a set of quickly spoiled twins, and a few obsolete toys were trashed along the fencerows, and a pink wading pool with penguins painted on the side sat in the center of the yard.

Shade drank while Nicole smoked, joining her for only two or three tokes out of a sense of etiquette that was a holdover from his teens. In less time than it takes to drink one cold longneck on a hot night, while Nanci Griffith sang "Spin on a Red Brick Floor," Nicole began to go gypsy beneath the moonglow, dancing exuberantly in a tight circle, spreading her skirt, her rhythmic jostles causing foam to rise from the lips of her bottle and spray about. Soon she came back to the steps and picked up the yellow salad bowl of iced brew, and said, "I feel like a dip in the pool."

The honeysuckle scent flavored the night breeze, and voices laughing at "The Late Movie" carried from nearby houses. Distant hounds howled from pen to pen, relaying the nocturnal edition of the dog news.

Nicole shimmied out of her dress and plopped into the shallow pool.

"Aw, I filled it fresh at dark," she said. "It's cool—come on in. Surf's up."

Shade stood up from the steps and walked over to the pool. He looked around and saw a few upstairs lights on in rooms that had a view of the pool. He drank from his bottle, then looked down to where Nicole reclined, using her hands to cup cool water and splash it onto her chest.

"Rene, don't be bashful," she said, "there's no X-ray eyes around here."

"I'm kinda tired," he said.

"I wanna have fun, Rene."

"Okay," Shade said, and kicked out of his slip-on shoes, then pulled his shirt off and unbuckled his britches, letting them fall, then stepping free. He stood there in his birth suit, drained the beer and tossed the empty into the undergrowth by the fence. "Darlin'," he said as he crouched into the water, "you're fixin' to have yourself *multiple* funs, hear?"

Nicole chuckled and said, "I believe in the deed, honey, not the threat."

A shared beer later, there in the children's wader, beneath the sweet night sky, Shade admitted to feeling chemically limp, and turned to the tongue for amusement. "It must be the French in me," he said, then slithered across the slick pool bottom. He put his hands beneath her hips and raised her pubis to the waterline. He crouched forward, knowing that there were certainly nights, and he'd experienced many of them, when he'd rather be right where he was now, buried in muff, exercising a learned tongue, licking her breathless, his own rocks on hold.

The Wingmen rolled to a stop in the white rock-dust of The Rio, Rio Club parking lot. They'd appropriated a black Trans-Am from the employees' parking lot of an open all-night Kroger's. Cecil sat behind the wheel, the engine running, the headlights doused. The low rumble of the engine heightened the sense of coiled readiness that filled the car. Jadick said, "Masks," and the three of them pulled ski masks on, adjusting the eye slots into satisfactory position. The car rocked while idling and Jadick, from the backseat, said, "Who is it?" and the proper response, "The Wing," came from the front. Jadick then leaned over Dean and opened the door.

"Let's fuck 'em up," he said, and The Wing climbed out, and swooped.

13

"THIS IS the part I like," Shuggie Zeck said with a wide smile. He patted Hedda's knee and leaned close to her on the couch, pointing at the TV screen. "Watch this—Red Skelton just has always cracked me up. See?"

Shuggie was in a blue robe, freshly showered and shaved, smelling of Old Spice. He watched the screen with lips parted in a small, constant smile. "I should get back to the club," he said, "but I love this guy."

On the coffee table in front of the couch there were two snifters containing Frangelico over ice. Beside the snifters sat two empty bowls that had a thin coating of ice cream and a few crumbs of peach cobbler growing sticky on the sides.

In the movie Red found himself in Cuba where he was helping a New York society dame get settled into the vinecovered, shutter-slapping spooky mansion that was her haunted inheritance. Skelton's spaz reactions to the living dead who abounded on the estate caused Shuggie to roar and Hedda to smile serenely. In between guffaws Shuggie pulled his socks on, then stood and stepped into a pair of white slacks.

"The hell with it," he said and sat back down. "So I get back to the club a little late—I gotta see the end of this one again." He wiped laughter-tears from the corners of his eyes. "Christ, I loved Red Skelton movies since I don't know when."

"I know since when," Hedda said. She was also in a robe, a red one, and a pink bandeau covered her hair. "Since childhood."

"Yeah," Shuggie said. "I s'pose that's so."

The movie plot had dragged the ever jittery Red Skelton to the house of an old crone who wore silver-dollar earrings and a secretive mien, and Shuggie was watching contentedly, when the phone rang.

On the third ring Shuggie reached to the end table and lifted the receiver. "Yeah," he said. "What? When?" He listened for a few seconds, then said, "Keep the lid on and line up the employees. I'm not happy." He hung up. He turned back to the TV and took a lingering look at the supernatural antics going on, then turned away and stood. He untied the robe and dropped it. He went into the bedroom to finish dressing. As he buttoned his shirt he shouted to his wife, "Hedda, get me that gun that's downstairs behind the furnace!"

"Which gun?"

"The one I filed the serial numbers off!"

Fat Frank Pischelle sat on a barstool in The Rio, Rio holding a bloody towel to a long, vertical gash in his forehead. There were bloodstains on his shirt and on the floor near his feet. Above and behind him there was a huge, splintered hole in the lookout perch on the wall, and smeared, modernist trails of blood streaked down abstractly.

"For the tenth time, Shuggie," Fat Frank said, "they was in the door and pullin' triggers before we even seen 'em. The man with the shotgun, the son of a bitch who bashed my forehead, cut loose on Eddie Barnhill, up there on the wall, *immediately*. He seemed to know right where to shoot." Fat Frank looked up shaking his head. "They wore masks, and like, you know, duck-hunting shirts or whatever. It made them look like they might be efficient or something. They were in charge from the get-go."

Leon Roe came over with a handful of ice and handed it to Fat Frank. Fat Frank said "Thanks" and wrapped the ice in the towel. He leaned forward, gash on the ice, and said, "And like I said, Shug, there ain't been nothin' unusual today. The workmen is all."

"Christ," Shuggie said, slapping a palm against his forehead. "Who is it? Who the fuck are these guys? Hey, they *were* definitely white, right?"

"Yeah," Fat Frank said. "They were white. Man," he said and glanced up at the shotgun perch, "poor Eddie. Poor Eddie."

Shuggie had already spoken to everyone who'd been there who hadn't split, except for Leon Roe. Leon had been making himself useful, getting ice for Frank, a sloe gin fizz for Shuggie, and he'd helped a gambler named Ralph carry Eddie Barnhill's body outside to a pickup truck.

When Shuggie approached, Leon was sitting by the jukebox, his eyes still expanded by the new sights he'd seen, his hands absently rubbing a wet rag on his red-spotted clothes.

Shuggie stood over him. He said, "I talked to Luscious Loni and Panting Patti, kid. They said Sinful Suzie told 'em you'd brought in a new girl today—I guess you forgot that."

"New girl?" Leon said.

Crouching down so that he was eye to eye with Leon, Shuggie said, "So, kid, you ever seen a flick called *Rolling Thunder?*"

"No. No, sir."

"That's too bad. There's some good torture scenes in it. So, kid, tell me about the gal who came in today. You bought her a beer. She's a bricktop gal."

"Bricktop?"

"A redhead."

"Oh."

From his barstool beneath the wall tapestried by gore, Fat Frank said, "Hey, that's right. I forgot about that, Shuggie."

"What's her name, kid," Shuggie said. "This is probably a coincidence, but tell me her name."

"Her name? I think it was, I don't know, Moaning Lisa."

"That's it," Fat Frank said.

"No, no, no," Shuggie said angrily. "Not her fuckin' striptease name—her real name."

"Her real name?" Leon looked down at the tips of his snakeskin boots. "She said it was Wanda."

"Wanda? A bricktop named Wanda?" Shuggie sprang to his feet. "What's the rest of her name?"

"I never knew," Leon said. "I just seen her, you know, at the Kroger's store in Frogtown, there, a few times. She was buying chickens and me, too. I tried to chat her up."

"You know where she lives?"

"No. I guess over by Kroger's."

Shuggie paced up and down the room for a minute or two. He had his hands in his pockets and his head down. Finally he paused.

"This redhead—she about this tall? Big jugs? A few freckles buckshot across her face? She always have this sort of expression on her that says 'Fuck me if you dare'? You know what I mean by that? Is that her?"

Fat Frank lowered the bloody towel from the split in his head, his fingers thoughtfully stretching his salt-and-pepper goatee.

"Oh," he said, "you must know her."

The living room was illuminated by the imageless screen of the television when Shuggie stomped in. The Frangelico bottle was nearly empty and Hedda was stretched out on the couch, facedown, snoring. Shuggie grasped the back of her robe and spun her onto the floor.

As she came awake he stuck two fingers in her mouth, causing her to choke, and said, "Spit it out! Spit it out!"

She slapped at his hands until he removed his fingers from her mouth. Her eyes were bleary but wide and her chins shook.

"What? Shuggie! What?"

"Spit out that bridge I paid eighteen hundred dollars on. I don't want to break it, but I *am* goin' to slap your face, Hedda."

Liquored up and confused as she was, Hedda instinctively began to slide away across the carpet.

"Honey—what?"

"Put your bridge on the table!"

Hedda was trying to do a crab-slide around the coffee table. The TV glow seemed to throw a spotlight on her.

"What'd I do? Huh? What'd I do, honey?"

"Take your bridge out," Shuggie said, then began to slap the back of her head. "Take"—slap—"your bridge"—slap—"out."

"Okay, okay okay okay." Hedda hunched forward and slid the bridge out. The bridge included her two front teeth and she set it in one of the empty dessert bowls. "Now what'd I do?"

He leaned over her, hands clasped behind his back, then his left palm came out of the darkness and slapped her across the mouth, and when she pulled away his right hand followed up and bloodied her nose.

"You got a man killed!" he yelled.

"What?" Her face reflected her terror. In fifteen years together Shuggie had never struck her and very rarely raised his voice to her. "I didn't," she said, baffled. "I didn't—what? Kill? Me? No, no, no."

"You been seein' Wanda Bouvier, haven't you? I told you never to talk to her or see her again, but you did, didn't you? I sort of knew you were. I figured you were. I figured you were *despite* what I told you."

Her head was shaking in the negative, blood drizzling down across her lips.

"Who said that? Honey, they're lyin'. Who told you that? I mean…"

He backhanded her high on the cheek, and her left eye instantly began ballooning closed.

"It had to be her," Shuggie said. "And that means it had to be *you*. You and your big, floppy-lipped mouth." He collapsed onto the couch, sitting up. "The country club game, that was goin' on for years, so everybody knew about it. Ronnie, too. But this game at Rio, Rio, why, only a few, only just a few knew about *it*." He pointed at his wife's head, his index finger and thumb making a pistol. "You saw her today, didn't you baby? Huh, sugar plum? What was it, lunch, or just a beer? Tell me, sweet lambikins, you meet to eat or just to hoist a couple?"

"Both," Hedda said, dully. The hot urges her husband felt had led to an ominous melt of his facial features, they sagged flat and mad. She was a bloodied heap on the floor. With one eye swollen shut she had to swing her head around to keep him in sight. "You knew all along how I feel about her. She's a good kid, like the li'l sister I never did have. I love her."

"Uh-huh," Shuggie said. "I guess I should keep that in mind. Say, do you remember one time when you and me went to Miami with Eddie Barnhill and his wife—what was her name?"

"It's Emily."

"Yeah," Shuggie said, nodding. "That's it. Emily. Emily's a widow now. As of a couple of hours ago. Eddie's a fuckin' design on the wall at The Rio, Rio and your *li'l* sister who you *love* did it!"

Hedda seemed dumbstruck, mouth open, eyes squinched. Her head shook and she had the look of a woman who had sunk chin-deep in the mire of unsuspected spousal dementia.

"What on earth are you talkin' about? Wanda? Killing people?"

"Yeah," Shuggie said. "She cased the place for a few tush hogs to knock over. My guess is that Ronnie made hisself some new friends in Braxton. Ol' *Ronnie's* song is sung. Know what I mean? He's a dead man but it might be awhile before his heart gets the news."

Shuggie got up from the couch.

"Now, honey-bunchkins," he said, "I want to know where she lives these days. I'm gonna *suggest* that you tell me, too, *right now.*"

"Oh, Shuggie, she never told me. Don't hit me! She never told me, you see, 'cause she thinks maybe you'd, you know, make trouble for her. 'Cause of what Ronnie done."

Shuggie stood between his wife and the illuminating TV, casting a huge shadow over her, his hands clasped behind his back.

"You seem like you expect me to believe that."

"Oh, I wish you would!"

"Well, you know the truth about wishes, don't you, sweet pea?" he said, and his hands flew.

Later he sat down and stared at his wife. She was curled in the fetal position. A few of her hairs had been pulled out and stuck to his hands. She whimpered and sobbed, her face to the carpet.

"All right," he said, "maybe you *don't* know where she's stayin' anymore. That might make sense. To her it might make sense. But you do have a phone number—right?"

Though this comment was a relief, Hedda suddenly shrieked louder, and slapped her fists against the floor.

"Hush up, honey. I got to think. I got to make a phone call. I got to figure things out." He reached over to the end table and lifted the phone. He dialed a number. "Hello," he said, "Karl? Shuggie. I know, I know, I'm sorry to wake you. Are you awake enough now for me to tell you something? Uh-huh, we did. Yeah. No, we ain't got them yet but I got a lead. Look, Karl, that's what I'm callin' about. I don't think Shade is the man we want on this. Just a sense I have. It's goin' to get nasty. Hear what I'm sayin'? Yeah. Shade might get in the way. You better get me Tommy Mouton. He'll do whatever it takes. Okay. Yeah. And Karl, have him come in a squad car, all right?"

Shuggie hung up the phone. Hedda was still sobbing into the deep shag carpet. There was an inch or two of liqueur left in the Frangelico bottle that they'd shared earlier while watching Red Skelton and the Cubano zombies. He raised the bottle and had a sip.

"Hedda, honey," he said softly. "I'm goin' to tell you what to say, then you're goin' to give Wanda a call. When you give her this call you know what it is you're goin' to do?"

Hedda raised her upper body from the carpet and quickly turned toward her husband, her expression fearful, her face colorized by red smears, lumpy white swells, and blue bruises. She said, "Whatever you tell me, Shug."

14

WANDA BONE Bouvier was being caressed and cuddled on the mottled pink mattress in her bedroom. She was having to endure Emil Jadick's oversqueezing of her ribs and the quick darts of his tongue into her ear. He was talkin' all kinds of trash to her. He was trying to insinuate himself into her future via an interesting cross of sweet syntax and menacing pillow talk. He was giving her the old "I been there and I been here and I been here and there and nowhere did I meet a gal who loves me like you do, so strong and tasty and smart, and if you don't be my lovin' woman from now on out I'll *hurt* somebody *bad.*"

The candle was lit and flickering in front of the mirror. Wanda wore a red wraparound skirt and one of Ronnie's black T-shirts that stretched down to her knees and said Jack Daniel's Field Tester on it. Emil was curled next to her, still in camouflage. The St. Bruno High Pirates gym bag was at the foot of the bed, open, drooling dollar bills.

"I don't know about hearin' that kind of talk," she said. "I love Ronnie true, Emil. That's a big deal to me."

"You can still love him," Jadick said, his lips skimming along her neck. "You can still love him but second instead of first."

"Uh-huh. You'd be first?"

"Sounds good don't it."

When it came to men Wanda felt like she was basically a highly prized household convenience. Oh, they birddogged her sweet and breathy with promises and presents, but only Ronnie stayed sweet after he'd had her awhile.

"I think Ronnie might object to that," she said.

"Not if he was gone."

"What do you mean by that?"

"Well, pun-kin, when Ronnie gets home he could be out here on this river, breathin' free air again, and have himself a fishing accident— couldn't he?"

"I don't think so." Wanda squirmed out of Emil's arms and got off the bed. "I don't believe he could have a fishin' accident—he's strictly a meat-eatin' man."

Wanda started toward the kitchen and Jadick rolled off the bed and followed her.

"You ever seen that much money?" he asked her. "You ever seen the kind of dough The Wing brings in?"

"No, Emil," she said. In the kitchen she opened the cupboards and shoved the yellow-labeled cans of generic soups around, rooting for a snack. "I'm nervous but I'm hungry."

Emil corralled her from behind and bumped his groin to her ass.

"Hungry, huh?" he said. "What are you hungry for?"

She shook free of his arms, went to the fridge. When she opened the door the light flashed in her eyes. She said, "Would a tiny taste of *everything good* be out of the question?"

Though she had her head in the brightly lit fridge he smiled at her. He bobbed his chin. He said, "You weren't actually talkin' to *me* there, were you, pun-kin?"

She closed the fridge door.

"You're right," she said.

"You were talkin' to whatever it is I talk to whenever I say, '*Why me?*' Weren't you?"

"I suppose so," she said.

"And you never get no answers do you, Wanda?"

"No," she said. She sat at the table and braced her chin in her hands. "But I think that might be just as well."

When the phone rang Wanda jumped up, startled, and looked at Jadick. After another few rings she shook her head in bafflement, and lifted the receiver.

"Oh, hello," she said.

Jadick went onto the porch. It was beginning to be his favorite spot. He gazed out onto the black bayou and imagined that all the shadows were silhouettes of living things and that all the chirping, buzzing, whirring, splashing sounds were coded human communications used by those silhouettes as they studied him from the bog.

For ten minutes he sat there, hearing Wanda's side of a crazed conversation, imagining himself to be encircled by a band of enemies who mimicked the natural world precisely.

After she hung up she joined him on the couch.

"Who the hell was that callin' you at two forty-five A.M.?"

"Oh, man," Wanda said with a long sigh, "it was my friend Hedda. The one I had lunch with. She's drunk as a lord, man."

"What'd she call you for?"

"I'm her friend. Her husband's Shuggie Zeck, you know? She heard about the Rio, Rio deal and she can't get ahold of him."

"Uh-huh," Jadick said. "She thought he'd be here?"

"No, man, no. Christ, I wouldn't fuck her husband. He's at a big poker game up the road a ways. At the bathhouse at Holiday Beach. There ain't a phone out there and she says he's playin' for the long green, big money." Wanda wagged her head thoughtfully. "She's afraid you all will hit that game, too, and he'll get hurt."

"This place is up the road a ways?"

"A mile. Maybe two."

They sat there silently. The toilet flushed. Bare feet padded in the kitchen. A loud bark wafted over the water. Something splashed. The refrigerator door opened and Cecil said, "Shit, there ain't nothin' to eat."

Jadick said, "Long green, huh?"

"Oh, man, this is too much."

"Big money, huh?"

"Emil? Oh, man, I feel hinky about this. Really I do."

"Put on some coffee," he said. "Quick."

"Coffee?" she said. "Oh, man, you're gonna go for it. Man, you're pushin' it too hard."

"Darlin' girl," Jadick said harshly, "do you know what the Fates are? Huh? Do you?" Jadick squeezed her knee until she writhed. "Well, I'm out to test 'em."

There was one light on when Shade walked into his mother's pool-room. Monique sat on a tall stool near a large red Dr Pepper cooler, vigorously brushing her ankle-length gray hair. In daytime she wore braids circled and pinned up like a crown, but at night it all came down and gave her the appearance of a witch.

"Hey, Ma," Shade said. How Blanchette and Francois Shade stood leaning against a pool table, rolling the balls against the rails. Shade said, "This better be important, guys. I was *finally* asleep."

"Son," Monique said as she continued to brush the yard and a half of her hair, "they didn't drag you out just to mess with you."

"Uh-huh," Shade said. "So, let's hear it—how is it I'm jammed up?"

"No one said you *are* jammed up," Francois said. He looked none too thrilled to be out at this hour himself. He was taller than Shade by a few inches and when tired, as now, he slouched. His hair was dark and razor-cut and within a flippant curl or two of being too hip for the D.A.'s office. There was blue stubble on his lean, sanguine face and he wore a plum-colored jogging suit that was unstained by sweat. "We got you out at this hour to tell you that you better watch your step." Francois shoved the eight ball against the far rail and it banked around the table in an ever widening pattern of caroms. "Rene—I heard something today. Then How called a little while ago and we put it together."

Shade stood next to the pool table and caught the eight ball as it died against the rail. He hefted the ball, shifting his head from side to side.

"How much do you know?"

"Rene," How said, "how much do *you* know? Huh? That's the question that's got us out of bed."

With his mother's brushstrokes rhythmically sounding behind him, the green-shaded light above the table shining on his hand, his hand holding the black ball, his face in shadows, he said, "Enough to take care of my ass. It's touching that you guys are concerned, but..."

"You ever heard about Captain Bauer and the Carpenter brothers?" Francois asked. "You must've eh?"

"Sure. I heard it. I think it's true, too."

"Good," Francois said. "You know who his partner was on that?"

"A cop named Delahoussaye, wasn't it?"

"That's what I always heard," How said.

Francois leaned back on the rail, then rubbed his eyes wearily.

"That's right," he said. "Plus Larry Carpenter."

"Larry Carpenter?" Shade said. "Whatta you talkin' about? Larry was one of the dead ones."

"He was the oldest brother. Rene, Larry Carpenter had a bourbon-whipped liver and two daughters and a wife who'd flipped and he'd started a war with Mr. B. that he'd come to realize he just couldn't win. He set his brothers up for Bauer and Delahoussaye to *arrest* them, but, as you know, funny things happen when you're in the dark with Karl Bauer."

Still on her stool, Monique said, "Karl was scary since as long as I recall." She looked like a veteran necromancer, wreathed by smoke from a long brown cigarette. "He's been mean ever since pantyhose ruined finger fuckin'."

"When would that be, Ma?" Shade asked.

"Oh," she said, "a good while." Monique wore a white smock and pink fuzzies on her feet. "That was about when I had Tip."

How Blanchette's pale face flushed, as it did when people he still thought of as "parents" talked bluntly. Monique Blanqui Shade had caused more blushes than Revlon.

"Frankie," How said, "is that why Delahoussaye committed suicide?"

"I'm going to answer that for your benefit, Rene. There was some teamwork involved in Delahoussaye's suicide. Paul Lowell was D.A. way back then, and he told me this: Delahoussaye was talking to somebody in the state attorney's office." Francois then leaned over and punched his index finger at Shade's chest. "You look like the Delahoussaye in this deal, Rene. If it blows up, man, they're going to send your ass down for it."

"Or worse," Shade said.

"That's right."

"And comrade," How said, "there's more news. You know Ralph Duroux from Tecumseh Street? Well, he's got some problems he wants help on. He called me out of bed and tells me Shuggie Zeck had a game knocked over tonight. At a strip joint out there, The Rio, Rio. A man was killed."

Shade groaned and said, "Oh, that sly shitass."

"You been with Shuggie all day, ain't you? It's you and him on this, right?"

"Yeah, it's me and him."

"Watch your ass with him," Francois said.

"I am."

"Did he call you?" Blanchette asked. "I mean, this killing was around eleven or so. He call you?"

"No."

"You're partners and he didn't call you? What's that make you think?"

What it made Shade think was hot things, then cold things, then calm things. He squeezed between his mother and the Dr Pepper cooler and went to the phone. He dialed a number and waited. And waited. After twenty-seven rings he hung up.

He rejoined How and Francois.

"Well, it stinks," he said. "Shuggie's snowin' me, ain't he? It stinks. He's not home, either."

How Blanchette was spread out against the pool table, chewing his lips, using his choppers to delicately skin himself.

"Rene," he said, "you want I should come with on this? Huh? Don't trust Shuggie, man. I know him, too, and that's my advice."

"No, man, no," Shade said. "Stay out of it and clean."

Francois said, "Keep me up to date in case I need to do what I can. Rene, tell How what's what and I'll get it from him."

"Sure, counselor," Shade said. "You don't want any calls from me in your phone log."

Francois smiled.

"Damage control," he said.

Shade nodded, then walked over to his mother and pecked her on the cheek.

"Time to be hard-nosed," he said. "Like you raised us."

"Try not to get caught out in the shit trap," Francois said. "It's liable to get deep fast."

"I hear you. I hear you. I'll try to keep the Shade name clean so you can run for mayor someday, *Frankie*."

"Someday might come sooner than you think," Francois said sharply. "If this thing goes awry but awry *correctly*, it could be pretty *damn* soon. Hear me? And if I was ever to be elected, well, it wouldn't be the worst thing that ever happened to you two."

Monique hopped off the stool, her hair hanging down and around her like a witch's cloak, and rapped her hairbrush on Shade's back, and when he turned she pointed the ebony-handled boar bristles at him.

"Listen to your brother," she said. Her arm was fully extended and the brush was aimed between Shade's eyes. "I wouldn't tell you to squat when you pee or curtsy to hoodlums or kiss any man's ass—but son, I'm askin' you to listen to your brother. It's not too much to ask of you, is it?"

St. Bruno, being north of the French Triangle but south of the Mason-Dixon, below the deep-freeze belt but above the land of tropical ease, was not naturally endowed with beaches. Therefore, north out of town, past two miles of slushy terrain, cinder-block roadhouses, and white-washed shacks, one had been made. Golden Rule Creek, a sluggish stream, had been diverted into a long shallow trough, surrounded by trucked-in white sand. The place was called Holiday Beach and, for ten bits a head, the citizenry could recline on sand as alluring as any in the Caribbean, there to sip various fruit-based elixirs, eat grilled prawns, and take bold dives into the unfortunately brown lagoon.

Only one road connected Holiday Beach to the highway, and Officer Tommy Mouton used the spotlight on his squad car to find a place where he could safely back off of it and hide.

"That looks okay," he said, spotlighting a fairly flat area between two gullies.

"Sure," Shuggie Zeck said, without bothering to look. "Whatever."

Mouton backed into the spot, then doused the lights. He was hooked on menthol and lit one of a constant chain of Kools.

"After this I'm the iceman, eh?" he asked. "For sure?"

"I said you would be." Shuggie had the sawed-off shotgun resting on his lap. His left hand was swollen from contact with his wife's hard head. His tone of voice was somber. "Quit actin' like you don't believe me. When I say it I mean for you to believe it."

The bright glow of the cigarette lit Mouton's features expressionistically, like a jack-o'-lantern.

"I can use the money," he said. "I really can. My old lady's pregnant again." Mouton considered himself to be a sharply packaged brand of manhood: slim, square-chinned and dusky, with a go-to-hell moustache and razorblade eyes. "So's my girl friend. I can *definitely* use the money." He tossed the butt out the window and immediately lit another. "They cost me, but they're both fun, you know what I mean?"

"No," Shuggie said crisply, "I don't."

"That's too bad," Mouton said. "It's the one thing I agree with the professors and radicals on, you know. Smash monogamy. It's more natural to the human animal to smash monogamy. Smash it into pieces— get it? That's what *they* say. I'm willin' to go that far with the hippies and the eggheads, but no further. Past that point they're full of shit."

Shuggie sat calmly, staring out the window toward the highway, waiting for oncoming headlights. He'd taken a pint of peppermint schnapps from the trunk of his El Dorado, but had yet to break the seal.

"When they come, swing up beside them—fast," Shuggie said. "No cherrytop, no nothin'."

"Gotcha," Mouton responded. "So, Rene Shade ain't got it in him,

huh? I always heard he was a tough guy. Like Tip. I know Tip from
around The Chalk and Stroke years ago. He's a brute. I always heard
Rene was, too, only smaller, weight-wise."

"He's not the right man for this," Shuggie said. "He might go soft
when you least expect it. He ain't got your stones, Tommy."

"Who does?" Mouton smiled. "Some of those hunchbacks maybe
do. Hah, hah. It takes a strong spine to lug around a set of..."

"Shut up, Tommy. I don't like men who talk about their privates all
the time. It's better if it's girls talkin' about a man's rigging, Tommy.
When a man does it it's like—'I hear the sizzle, and if you show me the
steak I'll belt you.'"

"Wow," Mouton said. "That's pretty harsh." He inhaled some more
Kool smoke. "I guess the sixties musta just passed you right by."

For the next several minutes the men sat quietly, watching lightning
bugs and listening to tree frogs. The moon was dropping away and
stars paling. A pleasant breeze shook the trees and across the beach a
cock mistimed sunrise and began crowing prematurely.

"So," Mouton said, "the bottom line is, all these punks have got
to go."

Shuggie exhaled wearily. "Tommy, what did I tell you?"

15

THERE WAS a mailbox at the curb atop an ornate piece of black, pseudo-French grillwork, and on the side, in fancy script, it said, The Zecks. Up the short driveway from the street was a refurbished house that had once been a duplex of shotgun apartments. Now the place was nicely painted a shiny yellow, and a broad, rounded, black and white awning spread over the two original doors.

Shade parked a ways down the block, then walked along the drive to the house. Despite the unanswered phone call he thought Shuggie might be at home. He didn't see the El Dorado on the street but went on up to the house anyway. On the porch, under the awning, he saw that the inside door was open, so he pulled on the screen, and it was unlatched. He let himself in and found himself to be in a wide parlor that had been made by busting down some walls. All walking in here was done on carpet, and he went quietly into the other rooms.

At the kitchen he smelled alcohol and pie. For some reason he wanted his pistol out, and quickly it was. There was a short counter between the kitchen and dining room and he paused at it.

That's when he heard ice cubes clicking and water dripping. All of the house was in darkness and he was tired enough to suspect himself of hallucinatory vision, but he thought there was someone sitting at the table. The whatever it was he saw seemed to bend forward and make sputtering noises.

Shade crept forward, hand on the wall. Halfway there he happened across the light switch, and flipped it up.

Hedda Zeck sat at the dining table, her face submerged in a clear glass mixing bowl full of ice and water. There were wisps of blood sloshed among the ice cubes. She raised her head, looked blankly at Shade, then said, "I didn't holler cop."

"Jesus," Shade said.

She had Killer Bee—stung lips and her visage had been brutalized into asymmetry. The left side was puffed out to here and the eye on that side would be winking purplish at the world for a while. Finger-sized bruises were imprinted on both cheeks and high on the throat.

"Did you hear me?" she asked.

"God damn, Hedda," Shade said. He holstered his pistol and stepped toward her. "Shuggie whipped you like that?"

She gave no answer but the dropping of her face into the ice bowl. When she pulled up out of the bowl Shade repeated his question. She answered, "Of course not. I bought a case of bad makeup, you dumb fuck." Then she resubmerged, trying to hold down the swelling.

Shade went to the phone and found that the cord had been yanked from the wall. He went back to Hedda, pulled out a chair and sat next to her. When she paused to breathe again, he said, "Want me to run you to St. Joe's?"

"Oh, Rene," she answered and started to weep. She turned to him and he held her. "He was mean, *so* mean. I did something wrong, but he was *so, so* mean."

During the long, slow courtship of Shuggie and Hedda, Shade had been a fairly constant witness to the proceedings. He'd sat one seat removed in the balcony of The Strand Theater while the lovebirds had experimented with tongues and touches and fingerbanging, and he'd been the fella with the bottle and the weed on the night Shuggie popped her cherry on a picnic table in Frechette Park while he sat at the other end, drinking peach brandy, too close to ignore their sounds, too stoned to want to.

"I didn't think he could do this," Shade said. She held him tightly, water dripping onto his shoulder. "I never would've believed it." He stood and raised her alongside. "Come on, I'm going to run over to St. Joe's. You ought to be checked out."

She pulled loose of him, her head shaking wildly.

"No. No. Huh-uh. He'll kill me. No. Or my dad'll find out and shoot Shuggie." She backed away, hands up. "I did wrong."

"Maybe so," Shade said, "but now you're a victim."

"Well," she said, as if pondering a multiple-choice question, "well, you know, the weak, the *weak* are notorious for bein' victims. There's a chain of events involved."

"Where is that motherfucker now?"

"Uh, well. Well, Rene, I got a friend, a good friend, I *love* her, really. Her name is Wanda. Shuggie's gone to kill her."

"Why?"

"Oh, he thinks she's in with a gang, or whatnot. He thinks they robbed his games, you know?"

"Who is she?"

"Wanda Bouvier, Rene. That's her name."

Hedda began walking toward the couch, walking with the abysmal choreography of a woman who was out on her feet. "She's married to Ronnie Bouvier."

"I get it," Shade said. "I get it now. How do I find her?"

Hedda stumbled over the coffee table, dumping the Frangelico bottle, dessert bowls, and her bridge to the carpet. She sort of drooled down to the couch, a slow caving in.

"I wouldn't tell him," she said with a faint tone of pride. "But I'll tell you, I'll tell you."

16

ALL KINDS of bad feelings had huddled around Leon Roe in the lonely darkness of his house and tormented him. He sat on a metal folding chair near the window that faced Wanda's place, peeking out through the curtains. His hair was disheveled from the several times he had grabbed it and jerked his head around, punishing himself. On his lap sat an open bottle of Fighting Cock bourbon, which he usually kept under the kitchen sink and only dusted off when his mother visited. But tonight, feeling sneak-punched by love and hope, he had suckled down a few inches of hundred proof.

A couple of swigs ago he had seen a car leave Wanda's drive with three people in it, and now he tapped the toes of his boots to the floor in a fast upbeat tempo, impatiently waiting to see if anyone else came out. He didn't know if Wanda had been in the car or not, but he didn't think so. As he put the bottle to his lips there were tears in his eyes, for the prettiest girl in Frogtown clearly didn't know or care how much he dug her, *no, more* than dug her, *grooved* on her. All he wanted was to win her heart and take her away from all this and give her nice, soft, silky things to wear and write songs based on her bein' a spike of honeyed sunshine in a lonesome rockabilly boy's life and play with her tits whenever he wanted. But she refused to see this. She didn't see it at all. She was with *them*.

Swig, sniffle, and sigh.

And they were bad.

Leon rose up from his chair and, bottle in hand, went outside. Between the swaying limbs of trees he could see a light on across the street. He went toward it, sidling a bit to the left of straight, unaccustomed as he was to heavy drink. But he felt like a new man, or at least a man, and staggered right up the steps and in the front door.

He knew the layout of the house from visits he'd paid to previous tenants. The rooms had hardwood floors and were sparsely furnished and his footsteps seemed to drum out. He swilled more liquor and dribbled some down his chin and onto the nice shirt that was already stained by blood, so what the hell.

A narrow hallway led past the john and that's where he heard her. She was in there tootin' and turnin' pages.

The door was open a crack and there she sat on the commode looking at the fashion pictures in an old waterstained *Cosmo.*

He shoved the door open and her eyes turned to him, and with the Fighting Cock in his hand he pointed at her. He said, "Wanda, you put me face-to-face with death tonight. You put me in a horrible place." He burped and wobbled. "My quick thinkin' saved *you*. For the moment."

"Is that so?" Wanda said. "By the time I wipe my ass you better have done some more quick thinkin', Leon. *Boy.*"

Instinctively courteous, Leon turned his back and listened to the toilet paper roll on the spindle. Then, after the flush, he said, "Shuggie Zeck is gonna kill you deader'n Elvis."

"What?" she said. She squeezed past him and walked toward the kitchen, her face hot and her step panicky. "Leon, why would he..."

"Because you're guilty." She stood by the wall and he sat at the table. He shoved empty cans off the tabletop, pinging them to the floor, and set the bottle down. "That's a plain, plain fact, Wanda. You're guilty as hell." He stared at her feet, chin on his chest. "But I ain't givin' up on you yet. Not just yet."

Wanda went to the sink and turned on the cold water. She held her head under the tap trying to cool her brain, for cool thinking was called for here. When her head was thoroughly soaked she stood erect and swept her red hair straight up and back, using her fingers as a comb, and fashioned a dripping, jumbo pompadour.

Then she sat at the table, and said, "You better tell me all about it."

The Wing was driving slowly and hee-hawing in the car toward Holiday Beach. Though the turnoff was clearly marked they'd missed it twice. Dean Pugh drove, Cecil Byrne rode shotgun and Emil Jadick sat in the back. They were riding high, feeling strong, frequently comparing themselves to fantastic miscreants of the past. Several tortured parallels had been drawn between themselves and The James Gang, Dillinger, Lieutenant Calley, E. F. Hutton and Al Capone.

When Pugh turned down the road to the beach he punched the lights off. He hunched toward the windshield, following the road as nearly as he could.

"You know," he said, "I'm glad we're flippin' off the mob here. In a special sort of way it makes me feel good, flippin' off the mob."

"This is a mob," Jadick said, "but not the dago mob."

"This is a peckerwood mob," Dean said, "but it *is* a mob."

"Sure it's a mob," Jadick said. "But flippin' off the dago mob is where we'll come into the real, *real* money."

"I always stood aside from them," Cecil offered. "The Mafia, I mean."

Jadick made a sarcastic bodily sound.

"Fuck the Mafia," he said. "The Mafia is just all these short tubby greasers who wouldn't last a week on The Yard if you didn't know their friends on the outside would kill your whole family."

"I was in Marion when Roy-Roy Drucci was," Dean said. "He was only about yea tall and plump, and one time this big nigger named Blue went after him." Dean shook his head. "Roy-Roy chopped big bad Blue down like he was a weed, man. Took a wood chisel to his head, skinned him like a turnip. Sort of awesome, really."

"All right, all right," Jadick said tartly. "I didn't mean none of them was rough, just in general."

Pugh put on the brakes. He pointed down the road a ways, and said, "Is that the lights? Is that it?"

And they all leaned forward and peered out the windshield and something came roaring up beside them.

The squad car was all smoked up when Officer Tommy Mouton said, "Hey, look."

"See lights?" Shuggie asked.

"No, but there's a dark shape on the road, movin' slow this way."

"Lock and load," Shuggie said. "We own 'em."

The slow-moving shape was opaque and humped, grumbling on the gravel. Despite the snitching glow of moonlight, the dark car felt its way down the road, right past the black and white. When it was but a few lengths beyond the ambush, Shuggie said, "Let's straighten 'em out," and Mouton fired the engine and whipped up alongside The Wingmen. When Shuggie was abreast of Pugh and Byrne, Mouton flashed the spotlight in their faces, and their expressions of surprise were superb, authentically loose-jawed with eyes stunned wide, and fatal, for that long elastic second of shock allowed Shuggie to aim.

By no design other than sheer opportunity, Shuggie saved both Pugh and Byrne from a period of bereavement, for he saw to it that they died together. With just one pull on the twin-triggered blaster he shredded them in tandem, the spotlight illuming their corporeal dispersal against the dash and windshield. And now, rudderless, The Wing mobile oozed off the graveled road and went nose-down in a shallow gully, slamming the grill against a ripple of earth.

The jolt hurled Jadick against the front seat, pounding the air from his lungs. Without time for a good breath, he acted. He climbed wheezing over the seat, sliding down on the fabric chummed with his gang. There was stench from sphincter release and blood and it was on his arms and he opened the door on the driver's side and shoved Dean Pugh from the car and the body flopped under the wheel, but Jadick slammed the shifter to R and backed over it and up the gully.

The spotlight was swinging around as the squad car pulled a U-turn and this soured any chance for secrecy as it beamed on Jadick. He flipped on his own headlights but couldn't see through the crimson muck on the windshield so he wiped a peephole clear and tromped the gas. The shotgun sounded again and metal tore, but the only hope was flight.

The road was fairly straight and Jadick took it fast, grinding the gravel beneath his wheels, billowing a dust trail. Where the road met the highway there was an antique store with a streetlight near it and Jadick swung wide through the parking lot, beneath the light, and he saw Cecil Byrne in a wad on the floorboard, his head a frayed mop, and a glance in the rearview told him that his current problems drove a St. Bruno police car. And he slid back onto the two-way blacktop and screamed a great, thick-necked, tendon-stretching cry, for he instantly understood just how potent Mr. Beaurain's "protection" was in this chitlin' city.

He picked up Pugh's pistol from the seat beside him and sent a forlorn shot in the other direction.

Foot to floorboard he raced toward town, recognizing all too clearly, but not at all sadly, that he was in yet another of those life crises where the odds for success were the ubiquitous slim and none.

When he was a few hundred yards from the turnoff to Wanda's the rear window shattered. Much to his own surprise he freaked at this, and warm piss ran down his leg.

They were on him. Aiming, he could see. Ready to shred the final Wingman, and he leaned hard on the steering wheel and flew the car off the low bank of the road, and into the bayou.

He bailed out as the car sank to its wheels, for the water here was not deep, and the squad car squealed to a stop. As the spotlight spun on its swivel and beamed on the wet surface, he submerged.

And with each underwater stroke there was a chant in his brain. It went—Set up. Set up. Set up.

17

SHADE WAS rediscovering all sorts of old skills this night, and as he crept along the narrow walk that ran behind Wanda's house to the back porch he utilized the style of stealth that he'd learned at age twelve when it came to his attention that Connie Pelligrini's knockout momma liked to take her evening bath with the curtains parted in hopes of a breeze. He edged along the brick walkway, inches from the bayou, then quietly went up the steps to the porch. At window height he paused and looked into the kitchen. There was a man in rustic finery and snakeskin boots bent over the sink, retching. An open suitcase sat on the table and every few seconds the bricktop beauty came whirling over to it and stuffed something in.

Despite the myriad night sounds Shade could hear Wanda saying "Oh, no," with every trip to the suitcase, and the retching man came across loud and clear. Shade was waiting to check for more people in the house before making an entry, and he had leaned against the porch door, settling in, when a splash sounded behind him. Then dripping sounds. He heard a breath, and when he turned toward it he looked down a pistol barrel that was backed up by a stocky, swamp-scented creature who said, "One of Mr. B.'s boys, I presume."

"Me? No, no."

"No, no?" Jadick patted Shade down and removed the pistol from his belt holster. "These things are dangerous. You a hitter for Mr. B., huh?"

"No," Shade said. "Ronnie, man. Don't bust that cap on me, man. Come on, I'm a friend of Ronnie's."

Jadick pushed the barrel against Shade's nose.

"A friend, huh? That's interesting."

Mud and leaves and mossy hairs were stuck on Jadick. His eyes seemed to be glowing spots in a bucket of primordial ooze.

"Up the stairs," he said. "In we go."

Shade opened the screen door and stepped onto the porch. A pistol bumped against the back of his head. At the kitchen door he was belted on the neck, then shoved to the floor. As he skidded across the linoleum, Jadick said, "Set another plate, pun-kin. We got company."

Wanda was frozen, bent over the suitcase, her lower lip covering the upper, a long black dress dangling from her hand.

"What's that?" Jadick asked, waving pistols in both hands.

"Oh, man, it's my good dress."

"Not that. The suitcase. What's with the suitcase?"

"I'm packin', Emil."

"So I see." He gestured at Shade. "I don't know who this guy is, but he was scopin' you through the window. I don't know who the other guy is, either, but I'm pretty sure you'll have an explanation."

Wanda turned and dropped the dress into the suitcase. She swept her hands back and across her jumbo pompadour, looking like a very showy juvenile delinquent from a gone era.

"Oh, Emil. Emil. I got scared. Man, I just started to shake, I didn't know what to think."

Jadick walked past Shade and over to the counter. He plugged the deep-fat fryer into the wall socket. "I'm hungry," he said. "I can't wait. You southern coozes, you don't think it's food if it ain't fried, do you? Huh? Travel has broadened me." As he walked past Shade again he bashed him above the eye.

Shade felt the skin part, as the barrel broke open an old boxing scar. Instinctively he reached out, only to be hit on the ear. He fell dizzily back against the wall. Shade tried to focus his eyes, but the right orb was awash in his own blood. The eyeball seemed to slide. This was an old ring sensation, partial blindness was, and the haunted rules of the past came pointlessly to mind: get on one knee; take an eight count; cover up. Shade slumped sideways.

"Something about him unsettles me," Jadick said. He then gestured at Leon who was curled over the sink. "Hey, you. Yeah, you. Get on the floor with Droopy, here." When Leon had obeyed and sat beside Shade, Jadick said, "So, pun-kin, what *was* it that got you so scared?"

"I realized it was true," she said. She shrugged her shoulders slowly and looked down. "I loved *you*, man. I loved you more than Ronnie, and like the thought scared me."

"Aw, Wanda," Jadick said wistfully, "I know some things about *love*, and what you did to me ain't it." He shook his head, mud clumps and twigs falling from his hair. "It ain't even close. You set me up."

"What? No, man!"

"Sure you did. Dean and Cecil are dead now." He nodded at her several times. "That part of your plan worked fine."

"I can't believe this," Wanda said.

"You can't believe I ain't dead is what you mean." He swiveled and aimed pistols at both of the men on the floor. "So, which one of these guys is your boyfriend?"

"You're my boyfriend."

"No. You're a tramp. You set me up."

Wanda's fingers pulled her T-shirt taut, and she turned partly sideways, and breathed very deeply.

"You got a stigma in your mind on me, Emil. I never set you up."

The fryer began to give off faint simmering sounds in the background.

"I was open with you, Wanda. I was revealing of myself. You've come to sort of know me, ain't you? That's what you used to set me up."

Dizzy on the floor, Shade put his palms to the linoleum to steady himself. Jadick's blows reverberated through his head, causing his thoughts to meander. He closed his right eye and focused with the left, gaining a lopsided view of things. The man next to him stank of bourbon-based vomit, and on the counter grease sizzled, and standing in a shadow the bricktop beauty was engaged in a menacing minuet with what appeared to be the Missing Link.

Jadick said, "Get out some eggs and cornmeal, Miz Bouvier."

"Huh?"

"Eggs and cornmeal, pun-kin. I want that golden batter. It's the truth I'm after, and I'm gonna fry your fingers to get it out of you."

The kitchen was lit by a single bare light bulb. Shade felt suddenly alert as he watched what was happening in the shadows around the edges of the room. Thus lit, the whole room, and every gesture made in it, had a quality of the surreal.

Wanda stepped backward into the light. The pink drained from her face. Her hands came up to her chest, palms out.

"Man, you're serious." She breathed hard and fast. "You'll kill me, won't you?"

"You know I would," Jadick said. "That's why you were packin'."

"Oh, man. I didn't cross you."

Leon Roe had puked himself nearly sober. He squatted on the floor, his legs crossed beneath him, his shirtfront soiled a couple of different ways. In his head one of his dreams was being run. Leon's secret dream was the lurid, darkly lit one, wherein a decent but necessarily dangerous lad had lived the sordid, stray tom life, being no better than he oughta be and often worse, especially where heartbreaking was concerned, until his prowling led him to the back door of an ivory-skinned, clear-eyed earth angel and he unexpectedly succumbed to love and reformation. In the third reel of this tear-drizzler the ex-scoundrel was ratpacked by circumstances and forced to employ various skills from his unsavory past to safeguard the fair lady, her crippled brother, and, in some versions, The American Way itself.

With this dream playing continuously in his mind, Leon began to conjure solutions to the problems of the prettiest girl in Frogtown.

Across the room, Jadick stood before the open doorway of the refrigerator. He turned and shoved a carton of eggs down the counter. He reached to the telephone that hung nearby, and tore it from the wall.

"No help from that quarter," he said, as the phone slammed to the floor. "Get an egg in your hand."

Tears were thinly pouring from Wanda's eyes, and tears were strange to her, but she opened the carton and extracted an egg. It was a brown-shelled egg and she held it in her fist, her face down.

"Squeeze," Jadick said.

As she squeezed the egg and the yolk gooed between her clenched fingers, Wanda reached the last ditch and said, "Emil, don't hurt me—I'm with child."

"You're what?"

"I'm carryin' your baby, man. I'm pregnant by you."

"How could you know that?" Jadick's head shook sternly. "I only been humpin' you a week, how would you know you're knocked up?"

Wanda brought both hands to her lower stomach and clasped them, yolk and shells falling to the floor.

"A woman can tell these things. Emil, a woman just *knows* sometimes. I felt it when you fucked me."

"Let me feel of it," Jadick said. He advanced on her and touched the barrels of both pistols to her tummy. "That's where the little critter is?" he asked.

"I know it is," she said. "I know it is."

"Huh," he said, then slammed a pistol butt to her belly. As she slumped to her knees, he said, "Welcome to Daddy's world."

Reviving from his tearjerker dream, Leon embarked on an act of solo bravado, and sprang forward and grabbed Jadick at the knees and pulled him to the floor. Jadick banged him on the head with the pistol then rolled away from him.

Then he shot the rockabilly boy in the stomach.

And Wanda reacted despite the pain in her gut, and raised up and swept the hissing fat fryer off of the counter and onto Emil's mid-section.

The pain caused The Wingman to drop both pistols and scream, his eyes rolling back in his head.

Wanda stood, transfixed by the steaming man below her, and the gut-shot man across the floor.

Shade knew good fortune when he saw it and rose to his feet, then retrieved his pistol. Jadick was going into shock, his voice locked in a steady, monotonous, "Uhhhh..." A pool of grease smoldered on and around Jadick's legs and hands. Burning flesh scented the room.

Shade straddled Jadick's shoulders, wiping the blood back from his own eyes. He leaned over the prone man, the man he'd been told to hit, cocked his pistol, put the muzzle near the forehead, then, for reasons he would long wonder about, he did not shoot. He eased the hammer down, and stepped back.

"Oh, man," Wanda shrieked. "Who are *you?* Do I know you, man? Oh, man, tell me, who the fuck are *you?*"

His thoughts were still fuzzy around the edges, but Shade said, "As much good luck as you could ask for." He gestured at the two men on the floor.

"They might make it. Help me get them to the car."

But Wanda Bone Bouvier just stood there, stalled by the crimson events, until Shade spun her about and kicked her hard on the ass, the jolt bouncing her against the kitchen sink.

"Help me get them to the car!"

18

I THINK Leon's dead," Wanda Bone Bouvier said from the backseat. She sat between the two wounded men, smeared with gore from fingertips to forehead. "Oh, man, he's dead."

Shade was driving, trying to see through the film of his own blood running into his right eye, his right hand held to the rip in his brow, attempting to divert the flow.

"Which one's Leon?"

"The boy. Man," she said, her voice hitting awkward, brittle notes, "Leon is the boy."

Jadick was in shock, his hands blistered rare, eyes rolling in his head.

"We'll be at St. Joe's in a minute," Shade said. Pain and blood and punishment; he knew these things, he had no confusion when confronted with them. "I'm a cop," he said, "in case you're too fuckin' stupid to know that."

"Oh, man, my life has turned out just like Momma said it would—a screamin' mess of shit. She said that to me, way back in time."

That's when the cherrytop appeared in the rearview mirror, the light revolving, stabbing beams of red into the car. He watched the redness infuse Wanda's face, which had suddenly become still.

"Zeck," he said under his breath, certain somehow that Shuggie was behind him now. "Mouton."

Leon the dead boy lay with his head on Wanda's shoulder. She moved him away and turned to look out the rear window.

"Oh, man, it's him—it's Shuggie Zeck!" Her voice came out in a flat whine. "Oh, man, oh, man, oh, man."

Shade punched the gas pedal and the blue Nova shot forward. The wheels skimmed over the hard cobblestone street, sounding like a jet distant in the clouds. He turned hard left up Voltaire Street.

Wanda lurched forward and clutched at his shoulder blades, her fingernails biting in. "You can't give me up to Shuggie, man. You can't do that! He'll turn me inside out!" That close she had a strong metallic odor of blood and fear-laced sweat and some lingering jasminy perfume. "You gotta promise! You gotta—"

"Shut up!" He stole a look into the rearview mirror. "Sit back and keep your fucking head down."

His mind shifted into another gear where action came independent of precise thought. He floated the car over a blacktopped rise in the road, then turned into a used-car lot, cutting toward the alley. It was Laughlin's Car Lot. A part of the neighborhood. He and Shuggie, here at night after seeing *Love Me Tender* at The Strand, hair slicked into a duckass, and they'd been jamming an unwound wire hanger through the window seal of a highly coveted '57 Chevy, yearning to cruise the backroads with the wind in their hair, when Laughlin himself had fired a shot over their heads, and strong young legs had carried them to safety. And Shade's thoughts that night and this had centered on the issue of bad companions, bad choices, and questionable self. To be alive, alive to the bone, is to make mistakes, but to stay alive you must learn from them. Then and now.

Shade's Nova was small and light and overhorsed and it maneuvered easily through the maze of parked cars. Wanda's sobs and invitations to the deity to save her were constant background noise. He pulled onto Second Street, going the opposite way, and her voice pitched higher as they jolted over the curb. The patrol car was still on him, right there, behind by a few lengths. St. Joe's Hospital was in sight, a tall pale stone building that rose into view just beyond the dark brick of St. Peter's.

Would they dare make a hit in front of the hospital?

From the backseat Wanda wailed, "Those cops will blow me away! Look, look, you can't—"

"Shut up!"

Shade shook the steering wheel, surprised by the frantic heat of his own voice.

The tires squealed musically as he swerved around a corner on Second Street. The sky was lightening and there was some traffic farther up the street. The street itself, with its bumps and holes, formed a useless kind of jolting litany. Memory has a rhythm all its own, and Shade's lips moved soundlessly as his mind flashed back on the mournful quality of a certain rainy afternoon when they'd fought on a sandbar below the highway bridge, but he couldn't remember why . . . and the warm expansiveness of a spring evening when their feet clapped down this street, this very street, outrunning Father Geoghegan who'd made an irresistible target for their peashooters. Memories came one after another, like the ruby beads on his rosary which he'd once known how to use. And all the time Shade could hear a bubbling, gurgling sound from the wounded man, Jadick, in the backseat, like a fish drowning in air.

There was a shortcut through the church parking lot that he'd used all his life, especially after having learned to drive. By following it youths could fashion a circular racing track without resorting to an actual road. Many scores had been settled here and many grudges born.

Shade wheeled into the church parking lot, instinctively taking the path he'd used so many times before. He swung past the jungle gyms and the swings with crooked seats. He raced toward the alley behind the dumpster, between the church and rectory, hoping to put distance between himself and the pursuing red light. He was well into the alley when he saw that a line of cement posts now barricaded the passageway. For a brief moment the posts seemed unreal to Shade, they didn't belong to the landscape that he knew and his mind rebelled. The loud scream of his brakes brought him to. The Nova fishtailed as it came to a halt.

Then he remembered having heard that Monsignor Escalera had erected the barrier a year ago to stop the traditional youth races.

The patrol car was squeezing down the alleyway behind them. Shade opened the door and got out. He shoved the seat forward. "Beat it!" He pulled Wanda over Jadick, and out of the car. "Find a place to hide," he said, but Wanda froze at his side, staring dumbly at the dark windshield of the St. Bruno patrol car. "Hide yourself in the goddamned church," he said harshly, and her legs began moving away from the red light.

When the patrol car came to a halt Shuggie Zeck came springing out from the passenger side. Shade watched Zeck lumber up the church steps. Shade pulled his pistol and held it down near his thigh. He glanced into his car at Jadick, who still breathed though he might have preferred to be dead. The patrol car moved cautiously up to the rear bumper of the Nova. Shade approached the driver. A strange veil of calm had descended over him.

"You're Mouton, right?" he said loudly. "I been lookin' for you."

Officer Tommy Mouton stepped out of the dark cab of the patrol car. He did not wear a hat and his hand rested on the butt of his pistol.

He said, "You been lookin' for *me?*"

"Yeah," Shade said. "I was hopin' to find you before it was too late." Shade planted his pistol inside of his waistband, then swept one hand over his bloody brow. "I got the son of a bitch. Come on, he's in the car."

There were a few cars pulling into the parking lot slightly in advance of the early mass, and Shade was gambling that Tommy Mouton wouldn't back-shoot him when visible to them. At the Nova, Shade placed both hands on the window and looked into the backseat.

"I'd like to bust about three caps in his head right now, but Mr. B. doesn't want it that way."

Mouton looked in on the backseat, took in Leon's body and Jadick. He said, "Who's the other guy? There's only supposed to be one more."

"He was with them and he got in the way."

Mouton stepped back and nodded slowly. "You *are* a brute."

Shade kept his head down and said, "Mr. B. wants him alive. There was an inside man on this, and he wants to find out for sure who put the finger on the games."

"The *girl* did that," Mouton said, "and that's why the girl and this cat have to go."

"Shuggie tell you that?" Shade said swiftly. "I bet he did. Sure he did. *Shuggie* set the games up, sport. That's why he don't want nobody livin' through this but *him*. He knows Mr. B.'s smart."

Mouton said, "Are you shittin' me? I think you're shittin' me."

"Christ, why do you think he cut me out of this?" Shade said.

Mouton eyed him nervously. "I don't know," he said. "I don't know about this."

"Shit you don't know fills libraries, Mouton," Shade said. "I just came from Beaurain's this morning. You wanta be on the right side of the man, you listen to me. You wanta be on the wrong side of the man, you just keep thinkin' you're smart."

"You don't sound like you're shittin' me."

"I'm not," Shade said, taking a step back from the car. "Get the burned guy here over to the hospital quick. I'm gonna get in there after Shuggie before he has time to cap his secret squeeze."

"This ain't what Shuggie said."

"I'm sure it ain't," Shade said. "Who do you think woulda been the last guy he had to waste, ya dumb fuck? He's got you in way deep now."

Mouton's sharp presence seemed to dull upon hearing this, his feet shifted uncertainly.

"I wanna be on Mr. B.'s good side," he said.

"Smart," Shade answered, then turned his back on Mouton, walked up the alley and into the church.

A weak broth of light fell through the vaulted windows of St. Peter's and spilled across the dark tiled floor. Shade edged along the near wall, then stood quietly. He took a step and his shoe squeaked, the sound echoing up to the Gothic ceiling. A permanent smell of incense wafted from the walls and pews, a sensual link to an older sensibility. A couple of tapers burned in front of an icon of the Virgin, the flames flickering with the currents of air. Perhaps some old woman had been here before dawn, or maybe even Wanda Bouvier had paused in her haste to light a candle before she hid.

Suddenly Shuggie was right beside him, loosely holding the sawed-off. He'd been standing in the shadow. Shuggie nodded at him knowingly.

"She's a bad cookie, Rene, we both know that." Car doors slammed outside the building, the sound muffled through the brick walls. "She's *very* bad cookies now. She's gotta go. Understand? I don't want to have to kill you, but I will if you push it. This comes from high up."

Shade smiled at him then.

"Don't count on it," he said.

"Rene, you're buckin' the big boys on this. You ain't slappin' the shit outta some coonass like Gillette. This is Mr. B. You're gonna get hurt bad."

Shade held his hands spread wide, laid his head onto one shoulder, smiling, and said, "Ain't that the point?"

"Jerk."

"Where is she?"

Shuggie shrugged. "Somewhere in here. I laid on the floor and looked under the pews. I can't see her."

Shade said, "You don't want to kill a cop, Shuggie. I'll find her."

Shuggie snorted at him and the sound expanded with resonance.

"Be smart," he said.

"Be smart? Smart like you?" Shade punched a forefinger at Shuggie's chest. "I saw what you did to Hedda. I was over there. Yeah. You fuckin' punk. *I ain't Hedda.*" Shade grasped but did not pull the pistol in his waistband. Shuggie blanched. He looked away. His mouth opened wide and he rocked his head back on his neck.

"I didn't want to do that. I wish I didn't, but I had to. Her talkin' was out of control."

Shade spit onto Shuggie's pant leg. "Take off, sport. Just go. I wanta see that fat ass of yours framed in that doorway, going out."

Shuggie took a few paces backward. The shotgun was aimed down and it wavered in his hand.

"I don't know if you can back that shit up, Rene. I could kill you."

"You reckon?" Shade answered.

"Well," Shuggie said, smiling almost wistfully. "We always wondered about this, ain't we?"

Shade nodded and turned sideways to Shuggie.

"I guess so."

They stared from shadow to shadow, then Shuggie turned away.

"Fuck this. I'm goin'. We can take care of her anytime."

As Shuggie walked away, Shade sat on the last pew and used the polished wood seatback for a gun rest. He cocked his pistol and took aim at the center of Shuggie's back.

"I know you're going to go for it, Shuggie."

"You think I'm a fool? I heard that pistol cock."

"I think you're gonna go for it, Shug," Shade said and put both hands onto his pistol. "Whatever that means."

Shuggie's laughter resounded throughout the cavernous room and Shade watched with a sense of incredulity as Shuggie walked to the door and out.

For a moment Shade just sat there breathing deeply, his hands clenching.

From beneath the altar came a low, scuffling noise. Then he heard Wanda's voice as she said, "Oh, man—what now?"

He heard the explosion then, a single shot fired in the alley. He went quickly to the door and cracked it open, pistol at the ready, then he swung the door wide and stepped out, looking down on Shuggie. There below him, belly to the asphalt, Zeck lay already dead, a fist-sized piece of his skull swinging open as if hinged, a rush of blood and brains running down his back.

Officer Tommy Mouton stood a few feet away. He jerked his thumb to his chest, his face clutched in a terrible sneer.

"*I'm* the iceman, now," he said. "Put me right with Mr. B., Shade, don't you take credit for it. Don't try that. *I'm* the iceman now."

Shade was choking on his own breath. He raised his face straight up, and there, at a dominating height above them all, he saw the first light of the new day glinting from the cross atop the steeple. And as he followed the trajectory from that shimmering point to the bloody asphalt below, it seemed that Shuggie had been spit from precisely there, to come to rest, inevitably, just like this.

And in the next instant Wanda Bone Bouvier, bloodstained and otherwise soiled, pulled at his shoulders, gasped at the body, and said, "Oh, thank you, Jesus, just this once."

THE ONES
YOU DO

For Katie and Leigh

"If it weren't for the rocks in its bed, the stream would have no song."

—CARL PERKINS

Part I

Criminentlies

(cry-men-ent-lees)

1

AFTER HIS wife stole the gangster's money and split on him, she wanted to rub his nose in her deed, so she sent him a note. John X. Shade was sitting on a stool behind the bar in the main room of Enoch's Ribs and Lounge, his gray head bowed, his lean shaky fingers massaging his temples. The safe gaped open and empty behind him, and a bottle of Maker's Mark, sour mash salvation, sat sealed and full on the bar top before him.

The note that was meant to make him feel pitiful as well as endangered was delivered by his ten-year-old daughter, Etta. She came in the side door and through the sea shell and driftwood decor of the lounge where her mother had been the musical entertainment before taking up thievery, carrying a small pink vinyl suitcase that had a picture of Joan Jett embossed on the lid. The girl had thick black hair cut in a fashion her mother, Randi Tripp, considered hip, this being a feminine sort of flattop with long rat-tail tresses dangling down the back of her neck. She wore a green T-shirt that was pro-manatee and raggedy jeans that were hacked off just below the knees. A black plastic crucifix hung lightly from her right ear. Her actual name was Rosetta Tripp Shade, but she preferred to be called Etta.

"Mail call," she said and tossed the envelope onto the bar beneath John X.'s chin. She climbed up onto a stool across the rail. "She said you should read it pronto."

Enoch's wasn't a popular spot until late at night when last-call

Lotharios from along the Redneck Riviera would fill it up, rooting around after pert and democratic Yankee tourists whose off-season dream vacations had yet to be consummated. It was not open at all this early in the day, so the two were alone. Hot Gulf Coast sun beat in through the smoked windows, warming the joint. On the walls there were community bulletins announcing upcoming fish frys, Gospel shows, ten-K runs for various Mobile charities, and several large, glamorous glossies of Randi Tripp, the 'Bama Butterfly.

John X. started to rip the envelope, then saw the sweat on his daughter's face and felt a trickle stream down his own temples. He shoved the shiny beverage cooler open and said, "I ain't King Farouk, kid, but I'll spot you a bottle of RC."

Etta grinned and grabbed the cold bottle of Royal Crown Cola that he slid to her.

"Well, I ain't Madonna, neither," she said, "but I could drink one."

He opened the envelope and unfolded the letter. It was on yellow paper scented with lilac, and he spread it flat on the bar to read.

John X. (no dear for you),

  You are not a clean fit with my future. I have made a choice and it was in favor of following my dream as you by now know. I leave special Etta with you on account of my dreams, for it is a lonely road I must travel to the top. Here I am always Enoch Tripp's daughter and many say that's why I am always featured singer here. I have talent! My voice fills a room to capacity with any advertizing at all. Motherhood is one thing but what is that compared to the many gifts of song! You know this too. The money I have borrowed for good to invest in my dreams was only a killer's loot. What good fine thing would he ever do with it? Europe loves ballads of amore and shitty luck and am I ever the thrush for them! I realize Lunch will think the money is still his but having it is nine-tenths of the law and all of spending it. You have a silver tongue, shine it up and maybe Lunch will believe your tale of innocence. Many is the time I have. Enoch is on those sad last legs and I have told him ciao.

                                                              Randi

P.S. I have a sense of my own destiny now. My sense of my own destiny is that you're not anywhere in it. I was young and married old, a classic story. But Etta will fit in with me down the road — I'll have my Lear jet fetch her to me where the nights are sweeter than sweet and full of music and could be she'll like it like me someday.

John X. wadded the letter into a ball and pitched it at a photo of the 'Bama Butterfly. Great lakes were being formed on his white shirt by flop sweat.

"Did I have this comin'?" he asked.

Etta retrieved the letter, then lit a match and set it afire. She dropped the flaming ball into an ashtray, and watched the flame rise before returning to her stool.

John X. looked at her sadly, then raised the bottle, cracked the red wax seal, and filled a juice glass with whisky.

"Criminentlies," he said, "but your ma is some gal, kid."

"I reckon," Etta said. "She put me off at Shivers Street and told me to walk here. That gives her time to get gone, huh, Dad?" She held the soda bottle with both hands, her body hunched over the bar, eyes down, like a precociously forlorn honky-tonker. Cosmetics were not foreign to her young face, and turquoise was the lip color of the day. "Mom let me pack first, at the trailer."

"What a gal," John X. said.

He pulled the tumbler of whisky close and Etta watched the glass, then said, "She predicted you'd do that."

"Do what?"

"Pour a giant whisky and have at it."

"Oh," he said. "That didn't call for no crystal ball." He raised the glass and put the bourbon down in one constant swallow. "And after a drink what'm I goin' to do?"

"She figured we'd go runnin' to the hospital'n see Grampa Enoch."

As he poured himself another dollop John X. nodded and said, "Then what?"

"Well, she wasn't sure for sure, but her best guess was, flee. She figured we'd flee."

Lunch Pumphrey was called Lunch because if he had a chance to he'd eat yours for you. The stolen money had originally been won down at Hialeah on a horse named Smile Please by two hunch-playing dentists from Baltimore and then tushhogged from them in The Flamingo Motel by Lunch, the thirtyish badass who was a silent partner in Enoch's Ribs and Lounge. Lunch was a loud partner in a bunch of nasty this-and-that along the Gulf Coast between Biloxi and Tampa, but his home port was here in Mobile. It was said of him that he hurt people over business, or pleasure, depending on opportunity, and that his services as a pistolero were in some demand in distant parts of the nation where his face rang no bells. The loot Lunch had taken from the two hunch-playing dentists who'd briefly considered themselves lucky had been invested in the national pastime and doubled when the Cubs eked one out over Doc and the Mets, then doubled again when the Cubbies beat the Cards two straight. The money had spawned to the amount of forty-seven thousand dollars and was stored in the safe. Yesterday the word got around the lounge that as the season wound down all forty-seven K had been put behind the Cubs, the cable team of Lunch's heart, and lost when the Atlanta Braves found some miracle broom and swept them three straight at Wrigley. Lunch had gotten this stunning series of losing bets down with Short Paul of Tampa, who was allegedly wired up asshole to belly button with Angelo Travelina, kingpin of the dangerous dudes in sunkissed country and an aggressive debt collector. When Lunch came in today for the cash to pay off Short Paul and found an empty safe, he could well decide that both business *and* pleasure dictated that he hurt a few folks in some marvelously painful manner.

"Criminentlies," John X. said with a groan. He pulled a cigarette pack from the heart pocket of his shirt and lit one of the fifty or sixty Chesterfield Kings he inhaled daily. He lit the smoke with a gray flip-top Zippo lighter that had the outline of an eight ball etched into it. After exhaling, he said, "I'm not *whelmed* by this, kid. Don't think I am."

"Dad, I don't think you're whelmed."

"Kid, I refuse to be *whelmed* by this." John X. Shade had long believed that the key to life was cue ball control, but lately his stroke was so imperfect on cue balls and life alike that his existence had come to seem far too much like the stark moral to a cautionary homily he'd chosen to ignore. He was in his sixties, a decade of his life that suddenly had more miscues and comeuppances in it than he could construe as merely accidental. His hair was wavy and thick and partly gray but leaning more and more to pure white. The physical aspects of his life had taken wicked turns over the last few years, and now his blue eyes had weakened to the point where they watered over if he stared at an object ball for more than five seconds, a pitiful development for a career billiardist. He also had complaints from his liver, a creaky left knee, fallen arches, gummy sinuses, and, to finish off the organic revolt, his hands trembled almost constantly. The trembling hands meant he had to shakily swat at the cue ball in less than the five seconds it took his eyes to water over. This series of afflictions had led to his being victimized by other career billiardists down to the last copper cent, and thus to his becoming a bartender slash son-in-law mooch six nights a week in Enoch's Ribs and Lounge.

"Oh, kid," he said, "it's bum luck you're stuck in this mess with me."

With her thonged feet on the rung of her barstool, Etta leaned out across the bar and patted the old sport who was her father on the head.

"You're not totally responsible, Dad."

John X. sat up straight and lifted his chin and stared into Etta's big 'Bama browns.

"Hell, I know that," he said. He scooted away and shook open a Winn-Dixie grocery sack. He bent below the bar to the reserve stock and began to set bottles of booze into the sack. He showed his loyalty to the Maker's Mark brand up to four bottles, then impetuously included one bottle each of gin and rum so that in the weird event he should want a change from bourbon, he'd have it right there with him. "People fall out," he said as he lifted the sack to the counter, "and life rolls on down the road even after the tread is gone."

Etta jumped from the barstool and went to the wall by the side door, and there she carefully took down a photo of her mother. In the photo Randi Tripp was darkly lit and wreathed in artsy webs of smoke, her eyes cocked in the manner of a self-aware cutie who had just thrown out an especially provocative gambit, and her magnificent cleavage and full lips seemed to promise a bounty of luscious succor for the man with the winning response. Her hair was black as a crow wing and aloft in a timeless bouffant.

Back at the bar Etta opened her Joan Jett suitcase and put the photo on top of her clean underthings and the precious trove of bass lures Grampa Enoch had given her over the course of several holidays.

John X. reached deep into the floor cabinet for the stiff leather case that held his Balabushka cue, a cue he'd lived with for thirty years, and pulled it out. Dust coated the case, and old pawnshop tags were still stuck to the leather. John X. was studying the tags and the dust when he heard a key going into the front door lock.

"Uh-oh," he said, then spun around and shoved the safe door closed. There was a Budweiser mirror that concealed the safe, but it was on the floor and the front door was opening. John X. looked that way and said, "Hey, Lunch, how're you hangin'?"

"'Bout a quart too full," Lunch Pumphrey said. His speech was hardy and roughly stylized, with a tangle of Appalachian underbrush in it. He was about five and a half feet of condensed malevolence, wearing a snap-brim hat of black straw, black half-boots, black pants, and one of the long-sleeved black shirts he favored in any weather because they covered the mess of ridiculous tattoos he doodled on his arms when drunk. "Why for's the safe uncovered, Paw-Paw?"

As Lunch came around the bar John X. said, "Flyshit, Lunch. Christ, there was flyshit all over the mirror and gals kept lookin' in it and runnin' out of here thinkin' their lips had sprouted chancre sores. Bad for business. I had to wash it."

Lunch paused with one hand on the bar. His skin was pale and clear of worry lines, his face angular and bony, with dark, sepulchral eyes.

"Still hot," he said, then looked at Etta. "Whew! I bet that there dog won't hunt."

"She don't want to hunt, Lunch," John X. said.

"Just teasin' the child," Lunch said. "My sis used to always pick on me by callin' me bad things, up 'til one day when she stopped callin' me anything at all. What she done was good for me, really, over the long haul." Lunch fanned his face with his hat, then set the hat on the bar. "I got to get somethin' from the safe, Paw-Paw, so back away from there."

John X. looked at Etta, then looked at the whisky bottle on the bar, then looked at the tiny bald spot amid Lunch's burr-cut red hair as Lunch bent to the safe.

"Tonight ought to be quiet here," John X. said as Lunch twirled the combination. Then he grabbed the Maker's Mark bottle with his right hand and smacked it briskly against Lunch's jaw from behind, just below the ear.

Etta screamed as Lunch sagged sideways, his hands clutching at the bottles behind the bar, sending them tumbling to the floor.

The air was soaked with scent from the shattered liquor bottles and Lunch was on all fours, grunting in the eighty-six-proof mire.

"Be human, for cryin' out loud," John X. said, then stepped up and smacked Lunch again. Lunch went out this time, and landed on his chin. John X. spun to face Etta.

Etta's hands squeezed the RC bottle, her eyes shocked circles.

"Get your stuff," John X. said, and she nodded slowly. "We gotta go to the hospital and see if Grampa Enoch knows a way out of this."

He tapped the cash register for the seventy dollars that were in it and added them to the nine bucks in his wallet. Beneath the cash register, on a handy hook, there was a Bulldog .38, and he slipped it off the hook and into a pocket of his light blue shorts. He found a box of shells and took them too. He stuck his pool cue into the sack of liquor and hoisted the load. He came around the bar, opened the front door, and checked the parking lot.

"I hope to God Enoch has some magic in his pocket. Let's get our heinies hoofin' over there and see, huh?"

"I don't have any idea where she run to," Enoch Tripp said. Enoch was a widower, father, father-in-law, grampa, and scoundrel, but he'd been whittled down to a moot point by cancer. His face was bearded, his white hair was matted, and, low in weight as he was, his eyes seemed huge in his thin face. A Bible was clutched in his hands for the first time since Iwo Jima. "Far away I hope."

John X. stood by the window looking out over other wings of the hospital to Mobile Bay. He had a cigarette going.

"We can rule out Europe, I'm pretty damned sure of that," he said.

"She ain't but twenty-eight," Enoch said in a weak voice. "It's good she caught a break."

Etta sat on a chair, pink suitcase on her lap. She had a problem looking straight at Grampa Enoch, who'd taught her many things about the largemouth, the spotted, the redeye, and even the Suwannee basses, back when he'd been seventy or eighty pounds more alive.

"This is a hell of a note at my age," John X. said. He was rubbing his chin, gazing out at the Bay, watching the regular afternoon rains blow in from the Gulf. Clouds were dark and bunched together, rolling toward land. "Criminentlies, Enoch, I'm two years older'n *you*. Let *that* sink in."

"It is," Enoch said. "It's *all* sinkin' in, Johnny. Every goddamn thing is sinkin' in." He paused to take two deep snuffling breaths. "But Randi could go off and make the Tripp name mean somethin' to the world. Think on that like a dyin' man, would you?" Enoch raised his head from the bed, the weight wobbling atop his weak neck. "Save Etta, Johnny. She's the good thing I've known lately. She's got to where she can cast 'tween twin lily pads, perfect." His head flopped back on the white pillow like a carp tossed on the bank to die. "You got a lot of moves, John X., dust 'em off'n save her."

"Now how can I save us?" John X. asked in a tone of lilting frenzy. He gestured at his feet where there were black low-top sneakers, then his knobby knees and no longer athletic thighs that were visible beneath blue golfer shorts. He plucked a smoke from his heart pocket and lit it with the butt he still had burning. "This's all the clothes I've got. Randi took the car and I've got under a hundred bucks, *E-noch. Buddy.*"

Enoch propped his left elbow on the bed and levered his hand upright. He aimed a finger bone at the closet.

"Take my suitcase. It's got clothes. The truck keys are in this drawer here." His hand fell. "My gift, and welcome to it."

John X. retrieved the suitcase and the truck keys. He could feel the pistol sagging his shorts, and cigarette smoke rose from between his fingers.

"Later on, Enoch."

"Uh," Enoch grunted. "You were my best pal, Johnny, and I couldn't make her *not* do it, so that's that. Randi's blood, and I can't rat out blood."

John X. shrugged and, with down-home grace, waved his cigarette in a gesture of dismissal.

"Aw, forget about it," he said. "Que sera and so on, you know."

Enoch's eyes closed and he said, "See you at the back table on Cloud Nine, Johnny."

"Sure 'nough," John X. said. "I'll stick the balls right up your ass there, too."

"That's good. You always did do that."

John X. gestured at Etta to kiss Enoch good-bye.

"On the cheek?" she whispered.

John X. nodded, then watched her plant one on Enoch's beard. Then she hugged his sick, weary head, but it seemed he didn't care to notice.

As they went down the brightly polished floor of the hallway they did not speak. On the elevator Etta asked, "Why'd she leave, Dad?"

"Well, kid, I always was more Spanky, you see," he said philosophically, "and she was more Alfalfa in type, and that mix ain't good forever."

"Huh," Etta grunted. "She said she outgrew you."

"That's incomplete."

They walked through the lobby and stepped out to the street just as the first fat drops of rain began to fall. Trees shimmied in the Gulf breeze. The streets gave off that nice hopeful smell of fresh rain on hot pavement.

"What's our stragedy, Dad?" Etta asked, using a coined word that was a favorite of his.

He shrugged, then smiled, and his face was briefly as handsome as it had ever been: blue fuck-me eyes, strong chin, proud nose, terrific come hither grin.

"First, find the truck," he said. "Second, flee."

The truck was orange and in sorry condition. The color was owed to a half-price paint sale and the condition to simple neglect. The pistons sounded like a family squabble. A fist-sized gap had developed in the rusted muffler so that exhaust rose into the cab at stoplights. The windshield on the passenger side was webbed with cracks surrounding a .22-caliber hole that resulted from a night when Enoch had taken his coonhounds on a moonlit run across property he'd been warned to stay clear of. The tires were iffy, but the radio worked and all the buttons moved the dial to different country stations. On the tailgate there was a big bumper sticker that read, I Don't Give A Damn *HOW* You Did It Up North.

The liquor was in a plastic ice chest that Enoch had left in the truck bed, minus one bottle that rode in the cab. The two suitcases were on the floorboards under Etta's feet.

The truck was now pulled over on the shoulder of a blacktop road that had a view of The Breeze-In Trailer Park. There was a drizzle of rain and sirens filling the air. John X. reached blindly for the bottle, his eyes steady on the twenty-foot flames rising from his trailer.

"I didn't kill him," he said as his hand found the bottle. "Or hurt him much, either, I don't guess. That there's the sort of thing Lunch does whenever there's a chance of it."

Etta's face was pale, her mouth open. She hadn't looked away from the flames since she first saw them. Her arms were wrapped around her shoulders, hugging herself.

John X. poured two fingers of whisky into a bar glass with pink elephants on it that he'd always kept in Enoch's glove box. He swished the whisky around his mouth, then swallowed. The trailer walls had collapsed inward, and as flames destroyed his most recent home John X. closed his eyes to the awful fact and symbolism of the sight.

"Well, kid," he said sadly. "I'm feelin' the call of the open road. Whatta you think?"

Her eyes stayed bugged on the fire, and her tongue flickered over her young painted lips.

"You're drivin'," she said.

Three hours later the afternoon rains petered out and the sunset was pink and promising. After Pascagoula they'd left the big Gulf Highway for a smaller one that cut away from the coast and was flanked by loblolly pines, barbed wire fences, and chicken shacks.

"Fix me up with a tiny angel, angel," John X. said.

"Just a sec," Etta said. She'd been painting her fingernails out of boredom, and at present her hands hung from the window to dry the purple polish. The wind blew the black crucifix straight back from her ear. In a few seconds her nails were dry enough, and she pulled her hands in and poured him a tiny angel of Maker's Mark in the pink elephant glass. When she held the glass toward him she said, "What'll he do if Lunch should find us?"

"Now don't you worry about that," he said as he took the glass from her hand. "That's my department." He drank the whisky and set the glass on the seat. "I don't want you worrying about that." He kept his eyes on the road and straightened up like he meant business. "I realize I'm a little bit askew as a daddy, but, girl, I want you to know, if anyone messes with you or me, why, I'll get P.O.ed pretty good, and, darlin', when I get mad I'm just like *Popeye*."

2

Over in the delta where the Big River flows brown and strong and sluggish sloughs lurk outside its channels, Rene Shade reclined on a blanket in the small backyard of Nicole Webb's place in Frogtown and watched the sky. He was watching the autumnal parade of millions of birds wending south along the Big River flyway. They followed the river from the near and far north, and now they dominated the sky, coming on in lively legions, in wide variety, honking, tweeting, migrating to wherever. The yearly panorama above was wistful but reassuring to Shade, whose own world had flip-flopped when he'd been suspended from the St. Bruno detective squad for ninety days. The charge was insubordination, but the fact was that he'd failed to cap a disarmed suspect who'd killed a cop.

They'd confiscated his gun and badge and something else he couldn't quite name.

This was his eighteenth day on suspension and there was a jelly jar of tequila sour nestled between his legs. Next to him lay a pile of newspapers and on it there rested a freshly cleaned, unregistered, and thoroughly illegal Taurus .38. His blue eyes had been brushed with redness, and a fresh pink scar had been added to the old familiar ones over his brow. He stared up at the avian parade across an afternoon sky colored heartbroken blue, lifted the pistol in one hand, the jelly jar in the other, and said, "You know, I'm very near to bein' normal, but I just can't get over the hump."

"Well, I like you," Nicole said. She was sitting in a chair against the chicken-wire fence that surrounded the yard, reading a book. The scent from honeysuckle withering on the fence wafted about her. Nicole, out of Texas by way of romance and wanderlust, had been going through a psychedelic cowgirl phase, and she was wearing a sleeveless electric blue shirt with a pearl yoke, red boots with black eagles on them, and faded jeans that were worn to a wispy whiteness and fit her rump as aptly as the word nasty. She was tall and lean and olive skinned with long dark hair pulled back into a great, puffy ponytail. Black-framed reading glasses perched on her nose, but otherwise she came across pretty much like a cowgirl who might've ridden the purple range in some pre-Raphaelite's fever dream. "I like you fine, Rene, but then, I'm partial to sociopaths."

"That's a piece of luck," he said. Shade wore only gray track shorts and a demeanor that was both sullen and mystical. On tiptoes he was a six-footer, thick in the shoulders and arms, bodyshot firm at the waist. The archaic angle of his sideburns and the dead-end-kid swoop of his long brown hair raised some upfront doubts about his good citizenship that his face did nothing to allay. His eyes were blue and challenging, and his nose had been dented artlessly meeting those challenges. Mementos of his free-swinging past had been stitched around his face, the most recent scar still pink above his right eye. Despite his scuffed look there was a ragged allure to his features, and a democratically dispensed "up yours, *too*" aspect to his person that certain neighborhoods took a shine to.

"Maybe I'm where I ought to be — off the cops and back home in Frogtown."

Without looking away from her book Nicole said, "Give it a rest, Rene. You're bad mouthin' yourself into something you'll regret."

It was still warm by day this far downriver but leaves were beginning to fall. The weaker leaves quietly retired from limbs, giving up the struggle in ones and twos, coming down in sad wafting swirls. There was an old children's wading pool in the yard and dead leaves floated on top of the rank water. From a nearby neighbor's porch a radio droned with a college football game, and somewhere down the block a nascent biker gunned his engine like the roar was a symphony to all ears. Shade listened to the symphony and thought that maybe he *was* giving in to fruitless introspection. He set his pistol down, had a swallow of his drink, and asked, "What're you readin', anyhow?"

Her eyes stayed intently on the page.

"It's a collection of short stories about what shithills men are," she said. "It's been gettin' *great* reviews."

"I don't doubt it," he said. He dropped a hand to his crotch and hoisted his rigging. "But that won't change certain facts."

Nicole looked at him and smirked, then raised a hand from the book and pulled the buttons on her shirt open, flashing a pert bare breast at him.

"No," she said, "I reckon it won't." She broke off a blade of grass from the ground beside her and used it as a bookmark. With her arms overhead and her legs stuck out, she stretched and sighed. Then she looked at the pistol and said, "Rene, that pistol is gonna be trouble. You're liable to get caught with it somehow."

Shade shrugged.

"I'd a lot rather get caught *with* it than get caught *without* it."

"Alright. I heard you. I'm not goin' to rag on your ass about it."

The traffic on the flyover once again compelled Shade's interest. He'd loved this sight all of his life and certainly he'd seen many of these exact same birds before. They always returned until death, taking the same path toward the same winter place.

Oh, yeah, they came back and back and back.

"Rene," Nicole said, "you're gettin' that strange moody look again."

"Well, color me weird," he said.

"I don't want to color you weird, I want you to pep yourself up." She put the book down. "I know you've got things on your mind this evening, but I want some fun time, and you ain't fun when you've got that strange moody look on you."

On the bed, in twilight, Shade lay on his back and stared out the window, watching birds float down to roost in nearby trees. "In Memory of Elizabeth Reed" was playing on the stereo and Nicole was playing with his body, using tongue and touch to bring his passion up to scratch. She'd coated him with oil, rubbed his back, fetched him a fresh drink, told him his pecker was pretty, and put in many kind words trying to raise his spirits. Now, her dark hair blooming out wild around her like a swamp shrub that might have stickers on its stems, she straddled him, nuzzling her bush to his nominally stiff dick.

She said, "Oh, sweet," and slid down on him.

His thoughts were out the window, roosting in nearby trees. He said, "Only Redwing blackbirds are in the one tree, and only grackles are in the other."

From her position astride him Nicole shoved a palm firmly against his cheek, pushing his head to the side, then pulled loose and rolled quickly off the bed. She grabbed a T-shirt from the dresser and held it in the hand she shook at him when she said, "Look, you son-of-a-bitch, we ain't been together long enough for you to start passin' out *courtesy* fucks! You hear me?"

"What're you yellin' about?"

"Hey," she said, standing there naked with her hair all akimbo and her hands on her hips. "When we fuck I want your mind on *me*, not on some other fuckin' *species*, Rene. For pity's sake, man, I ain't desperate enough to take charity pokes from the likes of you, or anybody else."

"I'm tired," he said. He sat up on the edge of the bed and again his eyes strayed to the window. "I guess that's what it is."

"You've been this way ever since you got suspended."

"What're you sayin'? You sayin' that I'm a lousy lay now, or what?"

"Oh, geez," she said, and the steam went out of her. She sagged against the dresser. "I don't believe we want to start tossin' those sorts of bombs around, Rene. Or do you?"

He looked down to his feet on the hardwood floor.

"No, I don't suppose," he said. He conjured up a smile. He patted the bed beside himself. "Come on over here and we'll make love nice, Nic. Set yourself down right here."

Nicole picked her jeans up off a chair and said, "So, you want to make love now, huh? Why don't you get on your knees'n crawl over here and *kiss my ass* and we'll *call it* making love."

Then she went into the bathroom.

Undisturbed now, Shade crouched to the window and stared at the trees where every limb and branch held birds that had come to rest for a night during their long instinctive flight to some destination that was mapped in their bones. The trees and birds were in stark silhouette against the fading light of the sky, and the vision was elemental and exhilarating and comforting.

When Nicole came out of the bathroom in her cowgirl garb and a scowl, Shade went in and took a shower. Then, while some blue grievances were stroked from a fiddle and blasted by the stereo, he shaved and dressed in white pants, white shoes, and a short-sleeved black shirt. He combed his wet brown hair straight back to dry.

He went to the bedside table and lifted his jelly jar for a slosh of tequila but found it to be empty except for ice cubes. He then crossed the flood-warped wooden floor to the kitchen, jar in hand, looking for a refill.

The kitchen was small, as befits a shotgun house, with the stove, sink, and fridge on one side of a narrow aisle, and a high cupboard, shelves, and a small table on the other. The floor was aged linoleum and creaked when Shade walked across it to the freezer.

As Shade dropped ice cubes into the glass and reached for the tequila, Nicole sat at the table facing away from him and said, "You know, from teenaged pink on I always did have the desire in me to be a wanton woman, but I needed to go off and find the right lover to show me how."

"Oh, yeah?" he said, pouring tequila over ice.

"Yeah," she said. "But I ended up meeting you, instead."

"Uh-oh," Shade said. He sensed another one of those a-gal's-gotta-do-what-a-gal's-gotta-do fusses coming on, and he chugged at his drink. But he said, "Your feet ain't nailed to the floor, sister."

She said, "Thinks you."

"Thinks me?" He stared at the back of her head and the olive skin of her slender neck. "Come on, Nic, why don't you roll a couple of joints and listen to the headphones or something?"

"I can't," she said.

"You can't?"

"Not in my condition."

Slouched against the wall, Shade held the jelly jar with both hands in front of his chest and said, "What condition is that?"

Nicole turned, then stood and faced him. She had a lean, muscular, girl-hoopster body, and eyes of a sea green hue that gave an impression of vastness.

"Well, now," she said, "my condition is I'm pregnant."

The jelly jar shook in Shade's hands. He looked down into it, face lowered, blankly studying the swirling cubes of ice until, finally, he said, "So, what do you want to do about it?"

"Aw, man," she said, then, lowering her head, she used both hands to shove him aside, the contents of his drink splashing onto his shirt as she scooted past him.

He stood there for a moment, alone, absently patting his wet shirt. Then he spoke toward the front room where she had gone, saying, "Good thing I'm wearin' black tonight, or I'd have to go change."

3

WHEN JOHN X. Shade was twenty-three he knocked up two girls in the same summer, so he married the fourteen-year-old. Almost everyone said he'd done the right thing. They were hitched quietly before Labor Day, and the nineteen-year-old left St. Bruno, headed west, and he never had heard if she'd been carrying a son or a daughter. His bobbysoxer wife was named Monique Blanqui and soon gave birth to a son, the first of three. The boy was christened Thomas Patrick but called Tip from the start, and he'd be about forty now. After five years of staid rhythm, the next two sons were born in jump time. John X. had by then ducked out on all but the most salacious domestic responsibilities, leaving Monique to tag names on the new kids, and her tastes ran more to the Gallic than Gaelic so she'd come up with Rene, then Francois.

As John X. came rolling toward St. Bruno on the blacktop from the east, he was thinking that, so far as he knew, Monique and all the boys had stayed put here, on the west bank of the big river, leading different sorts of lives on these narrow, bumpy streets. The old bridge fed his sputtering but still moving pickup truck across the broad murky expanse of water and into town.

Etta was worn out from the five days they'd been sleeping in state parks, eating Spaghetti O's straight out of cans, trying to figure where to go. She lay against the passenger door, dirty and asleep, snoring in a sweet childish tone.

For the last hour John X. had been able to tune in the All Big Band radio station from upriver, and somehow it seemed exactly right that he was slipping back into town while Helen Forrest sang "Skylark." He'd always had a hot, hot attitude toward Helen Forrest, and listening to her now he realized that he pretty much still did.

The music of yesteryear kept playing while John X. scanned the streets, and it seemed that they were the same as in yesteryear, too. He'd lived here 'til he was fortyish, and it was on these combustible streets that he'd been a rascally kid, a nasty teen, a thief, and eventually a damned fine pool player with a major in one-pocket and a minor in nine-ball. Behind one of these storefronts he'd booked bets for Auguste Beaurain, and in a dirt alley off Lafitte Street he'd taken a straight-razor to the chest and tummy of a burly Frogtown gangster who he was forever thankful he hadn't killed. Almost every rowhouse or clump of bushes put John X. in mind of past sexual encounters. He'd rutted around this neighborhood nearly nonstop from the age of twelve and a half on up, and after Monique had put the seal of approval on him by marrying him, the opportunities came even more brazenly, mainly from her friends, in irresistible variety.

John X. drove slowly on these streets, for they were as familiar and warm to him as a mother hug. As he rolled along he spotted the vacant brick hulk that had once been The Sulthaus Brewery, a hulk his own father had trudged to and from for thirty years, six days a week, even during Prohibition, but he'd never been promoted from the loading dock. John X. slowed to look at the boarded-over entryway. Sulthaus Beer had come in black bottles with green labels, and was known for having a smoky taste. Old Thomas Parnell Shade had once saluted his only child by hoisting a black bottle and saying, "Johnny Xavier, all a man can hope for is an occasional cool drink, which I have, a clean life, which I strive for, all capped off by a Catholic burial, which I await."

John X. drove on, nodding his head, for the old man had known what he wanted, and he'd gotten it.

As the truck rolled down Fifth Street he pointed a finger toward a sign that said Hotel Sleep-Tite on a four-story brick building that used to be The Heiser House way back when, and he tingled a bit remembering Mrs. A. T. Yarborough whose husband had been mayor, and whose afternoons had been open, up there on the top floor. Christ, she must've been forty-two or three, and him half that, but, geez, he'd learned it was true, pluck those seasoned fiddles right and they'll give you back the most sonorous tunes.

There was a new traffic light on Fifth, and after he stopped at it John X. stared over at Etta, who was definitely the wild card in his life right now, and he flubbed his lips as he considered how such a wild card might best be played.

Hell, who knows?

Let *that* sink in.

When the light flashed green he drove on and Anita O'Day sang "Let Me Off Uptown," and a big sly grin came over him as he listened because there'd always been a puff or more of steam clouding his thoughts on her, too.

Man, women were a different kettle of fish in those days.

At Voltaire Street he turned right and slid into the very heart of Frogtown, the neighborhood he'd come up in, then left his first family to. He drove slowly, for he wasn't in a big toot to get anywhere in particular, and it was passing strange to be in surroundings so familiar.

A long time back John X. had fingered St. Bruno in his rearview mirror, and had only breezed through town a few times since. Seems like he saw Tip play in a high school football game where some kind of trophy was at stake, and he was positive he'd seen Rene flog the burritos out of a Texican light-heavy in an eight-rounder at the Armory. But most of his life since leaving had been spent on the road where he sought out touted young hustlers whose one-pocket nerve he wanted to test, or old reliable strokers whose nine-ball inadequacies were obvious to him but obscure to themselves. And in between such sporting encounters he basically *stole* paychecks from day job suckers who thought they turned into pool wizards by night. There had been largesse and intrigue in most every one of his evenings back then, and hustling, dice, and an occasional petticoat pension had put him up in a hotel room life, downing a bottle a day to keep things fun, dining in raffish night spots, dressing like a corn-pone Errol Flynn, tellin' all the interesting gals he met that they had somethin' special that just sang out to him, and humpin' any of 'em who grinned shyly and hopefully said, Really? There had been a sweet string of years like that, up and down and here and gone years, the good years before he'd turned crazy for just one doll and ended up with Randi Tripp, the 'Bama Butterfly.

Oh, man.

Let *that* sink in.

Then, to complete his ruin, his eyes sold him downriver by going weak, and his hands joined the conspiracy by becoming shaky.

Oh, criminentlies.

And now Lunch would be searching for him and the kid, and that guy'd never believe the truth even if he told it to him, which he wasn't so sure he'd do anyhow. Huh-uh. Lunch can go piss up a rope—I've got a gun, too, right?

That's a choice.

As John X. cruised the streets of Frogtown his eyes alighted on reminders of his own life. He could remember these streets under water, with channel cat and alligator gar swimming in them. The big river had taken a notion and bathed these streets many times, and he could chart his life by the flood marks still visible on several of the buildings. The black uneven band left by the '27 Flood was the high-water mark, coming up just shy of third-story windows. Whole families had been shipped out to sea in that one. He had a clear memory of himself standing in drizzle on the roof of the tall Heiser House Hotel with his dad, his dad in shock, both of them watching the rush of water, looking for his mother. He recalled the sights and sounds, the cows bobbing by on the swift current, belly-up and bloated, cottages and upturned cars swirling crazily south, and the cries of frantic livestock, dogs, and people, and the wretched postures of dead livestock, dogs, and people streaming past like losing bets raked in by the victorious river. The flood was his earliest memory of life, and his only memory of his mother.

It was right about dusk, now, on a warm fall day, and he decided to cut behind Lafitte Street and drive on the cinder trail that ran beside the railroad tracks. The trail ran between huge coal bins made of withered wood and the back door of the corner joint he'd bet Monique still lived in.

They'd had some years here, in this brick rowhouse, and their boys had been raised up on this spot, mingling with the bums who flopped in the bins, learning to stay afloat by going headfirst into the big river fifty yards east of the tracks. Monique was likely in the place yet, on the ground floor, grinding out a living with three pool tables and a Dr Pepper cooler. Though the windows were small, he thought he spied her shape in there, perched on a high stool, blowing an elaborate chain of smoke rings his way.

John X. tipped an imaginary hat toward the window, then drove on. Down the cinder lane a block or so he came to a dirt alleyway and turned up it. He gently braked next to a wooden building that had stood up to some years. There was a rusted circle of tin nailed to the alley wall, and though the advertisement could no longer be clearly read, he knew it advertised the longtime gone Sulthaus Beer. The door of the tavern had a big sign hanging over it, and on the sign there was a debauched blue catfish standing on its tailfin, smoking a cigar while leaning against a lamppost, looking like it could use a pick-me-up drink and a piece of ass.

"My, my, how do you like that?" John X. said approvingly as he looked at the sign. "The boy has kept The Catfish afloat, if it's still his."

Etta came awake and rubbed her fists to her eyes.

"Huh?" she said.

The truck motor was idling and John X. was about to move along, when a sullen and mystical fella in a black shirt, white pants, and dirty white shoes, with a fresh pink scar over his brow, passed the mouth of the alley on Lafitte, and entered The Catfish.

John X. sighed, then hunched over and turned off the engine.

"That was one of your brothers," he said.

"Say what?" Etta said, and her mouth hung open. She rubbed both hands vigorously across her femme-flattop, her face scrunched up. She then swiveled her head around and looked down the rutted alley, across the hard-bricked street, then up at the degenerate blue catfish. "Dad, where *are* we?"

"Home," John X. said. "This here is home, Etta. Let's go in and say howdy, huh?"

"You're drivin', Dad."

They climbed out of the truck and stepped into twilight on Lafitte Street. The probably dead man's clothes John X. wore had been a decent fit on Grampa Enoch, who, when healthy, had been four inches shorter and thirty pounds heavier than himself. Gray slacks highwatered upstream of his ankles, displaying white socks that drained into low-top black sneakers. His shirt was sunset orange and what was either a plummeting stork or a pirouetting buzzard was sewn over the cigarette pocket. A rumpled shroud of green plaid jacket hung off him like a public act of penance.

John X. went to the door, paused, and peered up and down the old block, squinting at a physical world that seemed to have changed only slightly. It all looked and smelled and felt the same. He cupped an unsteady hand to one ear hoping he could still hear it, that fondly remembered din, the clang of youth against the world, and though he heard a faint trace of that redblooded racket he felt a certain sinking in himself, the unpleasantly sober sense of having been possibly bluffed by life. Suckered out of one way of living and forced to draw toward another. Perhaps there could've been more.

Aw, que sera and so on.

It's all choices.

Let *that* sink in.

He shook a cigarette loose and shakily lit it.

"I ain't the Aga Khan, kid," he said, "but I'll sure 'nough spring for some refreshments."

He then pulled back on the door to The Catfish Bar.

4

SINCE HE never had believed that love conquers all stuff, it was a much surprised big Tip Shade who found himself walking on his knees of late, having silently said "I give" to a yellow-headed field-hippie chick who'd come down from up in the mountains. Her name was Gretel Hyslip and she was way pregnant and alone, and he'd gotten the weak knees for her when she took a seat at his bar one morning and shyly asked for a Bloody Mary with extry stalks of celery since she was a feedin' two.

Big Tip had looked at her in the light of that morning, and said, "You ain't old enough, are you?"

"There's been some who think I am," she said.

"I mean to drink," he said. He came closer for a better look. She was a kid, more or less, with a skinny face and stringy yellow hair. A scar as wide as a whipped car aerial made a diagonal welter of proud flesh across her right cheek, but it wasn't nearly as unappealing as it should have been. A colorful butterfly was tattooed on her pale shoulder skin. Her hands were red and rough from farm work, and her eyes were gray like mountain mist. The baby she was carrying bulged her out huge.

"I ain't servin' no liquor to you pregnant," Tip said. "That's regardless of your age."

"No biggie," she said, eyes down.

"You don't want your kid to be born out of you with a hangover, do you?"

"No biggie," she said again. "It's not my baby anyhow." She rubbed both hands over the bulge. "It's done been sold off."

"Uh-huh," Tip said. "I see. You stayin' over here at Mrs. Carter's house?"

Gretel nodded yup and said yup both.

So she was alone, a kid, a yellow-haired kid of field-hippie heritage with a butterfly printed on her skin, staying over here at Mrs. Carter's house, which was a sad house full of sad girls who had cut sorry deals with motherhood, and there was that scar, that strange velvety slash on her cheek, and those gray highland eyes.

Tip said, "I'll tell you what, girl—I won't serve you no liquor, but what I will do is, I will let you set right there and for free drink soda pop 'til you splash."

"Make that Dr Pepper," she'd said back to him, "and you got yourself a friend."

Three weeks had now passed since thirsty Gretel had raised that first glass of Pepper to this friendship, and she'd been in the place about every day since, camped on the same stool, talking bashfully and bringing Tip to his knees under the tremendous weight of new feelings.

Tip Shade was a jumbo package of pock-faced bruiser, with long brown hair greased behind his ears, hanging to his shoulders. His eyes were of a common but unnamed brown hue. He tended to scowl by reflex and grunt in response. His neck was a holdover from some normal-necked person's nightmare, and when he crossed his arms it looked like two large snakes procreating a third.

He did his own bouncing.

The Catfish Bar was a place where plots were hatched. Hunkered over shotglasses and mugs, clusters of Frogtowners put their heads together and engineered simple B & E's, past-posting schemes, city hall payoffs, the stagecraft requirements of hanging paper, thefts of the new theft-proof cars, drug deals, and revenge. In this social set to have never done time was considered to be evidence of timidity, or genius.

Tending The Catfish had been Tip's all up 'til this odd romance popped in on him and romped all over his good sense. He just liked everything about Gretel, all the earthy scent he could pick up off her, her firm feel when he brushed her body squeezing by, and the many tender scenes he flat daydreamed about her, he liked those as well. She wasn't pretty in the manner of TV-pretty, and there was that pregnant aspect of her that might involve a questionable tale, but, man, she had a smile that kicked him in the belly, and the smell of a good garden.

After about a week he asked her if she'd like to do something sometime, and she said sure, and he said what is it you want to do, Gretel?

"I like things out of the blue," she told him. "Just spring it on me."

Big Tip sprung a flick on her, a corny thing about several pencilnecks and an infant, but she laughed at key moments. They went to a café for snacks and talk after, and this date was repeated more or less exactly a number of times. Over french fries and pork tenders he came to know a little bit of her story, which was mainly centered on her family life and pretty much off the beaten track. Zodiac and Delirium were words that came into the story every so often, but it took three dates before it dawned on him those were her Pa and Ma's hippie names. It seems Zodiac and Delirium had met at a Love-In or something like it that turned into a police tantrum, and out of resentment toward the laws of such society they had retreated far into the Ozark piney woods with the rest of their tribe and pitched themselves a different world right alongside the King's River. This fresh-made world was one of damned few rules and plenty of hugging and kissing and standing around naked and stoned before the eyes of various gods, but not much practical ever got done in the way of food or money or shelter, and when the third winter was whistling in, most of the tribe hustled back to the main road and thumbed toward central heating.

Zodiac and Delirium stayed behind and true to their different world, and when Gretel was born she was added to it. As Gretel grew she naturally grew weary of her parents' way of life and set out to find one that better suited her, but through a series of flukes and bad guesses that could only be called Karma, she ended up here, way down-country, lugging a baby to market.

That was the gist of what Tip knew about Gretel, and none of it lowered her in his eyes or heart. He never referred to the baby, or the facts behind it. He didn't want to know.

What he did know was that this girl, this Gretel, had buoyed him right up out of the narrow rut of his previous expectations.

And now, in the warm evening gloam of a fading fall day, she sat on her stool in The Catfish and read aloud from a tabloid she fancied because both the print and the stories were tall. Tip went about his business serving customers, and Gretel read in the halting, stumbling manner that was the result of her upbringing in a world that classed both schools and prisons as bummers.

She read with a speculative pause between each word.

"'The man in the moon is as reg-u-lar as you or me,' Mrs. Willow Henry said. 'Though his heads are set close to-gether as a double'—what's this one, Tip?"

Tip was drawing a beer but, as usual, he had time for Gretel and her self-improvement exercises. He leaned across the bar and looked where her finger pointed.

"Yolk," he said. "Like eggs."

"'Though his heads are set close to-gether as a double yolk,'" Gretel repeated, her spare hand rubbing at her belly. "'Else-where out in space this is likely con-sidered cute but it sure e-nough spooked me at first.'" Gretel lifted her eyes from the paper and smiled. "What do you think?"

"It's amazin'," Tip said, beaming. "You are really, really, really comin' along good."

The door opened and Rene Shade came in and bellied up to the bar. It was still quiet in the joint.

"Hey, Tip."

"Hey, li'l blood. The usual?"

"Just a beer," Shade said. He sat on the stool beside Gretel. "You ain't contagious, are you, kid?"

"Nope."

"How you doin'?"

"Mellow. Purely mellow."

"I been meanin' to ask you," Shade said. "Is that butterfly there a Monarch?"

Gretel grinned and nodded.

"It's life-sized."

The door swung open again, and, framed by the twilight of the out-door world, there stood a freakish little girl, and an old man with a strange fashion sense who looked odd but familiar. A cigarette slanted from the man's lips and he raised his shaky hands two-gun style, aimed a quivering index finger at both Shade and Tip, fanned his thumbs like triggers, then said, "Say, ain't you fellas sons of mine?"

Dark had fallen by now. The Shades were sitting at a small round table, getting sloshed as a family. The walls were adorned with athletic post-ers and photos, and ragged fishnets hung from the ceiling. The room was dimly lit, with shadows in the corners, and Catfish regulars were filling those shadows up. Tip's assistant, Russ, was working the bar, and Tip poured the whisky at the table near the wall.

A partly consumed triple order of frog legs sat on a platter in the center of the table. Etta and Gretel were drinking soda pop, taking turns playing the pinball machine at the back of the room.

Tip pointed at his newly discovered half sister and said, "So, we gotta add her to the Christmas list, or what?"

"Up to you," John X. said, a full glass in his hand.

Once again Tip pointed at Etta, with her flattop and purple nails and crucifix earring, and said, "John, that there is an out*landish* little kid."

John X. nodded slowly, his eyes shiny.

"All of mine have been," he said. "Far as I know."

"Uh-huh. I hear you." Tip winked at Shade, then poured more whisky into his father's glass. "So, Johnny, how the hell *are* you, anyhow?"

"My liver ain't turnin' out to be quite the organ I'd hoped for, Tippy," John X. said as he pulled the drink inside the corral his arm made upon the table. "But the thing about tears is they're salty, and salt ain't good for an ol' boy like me."

Shade sat slouched in his chair, studying his father as if trying to match him with a Wanted Poster in his mind. He'd run into him here and there over the years, but he'd never looked like this. There had always been resourceful vitality behind most of his Dad's handsome expressions, and this quality had consistently made more limp sorts want to be his friend, or at least acquaintance, to hear the colorful spectrum of his views, to lose money to him then take him home to get drunk with the wife. He'd slid through many a sporting year like that, but, man, the years had caught up and made sport of him. His hands shook, and his fingers looked like grubworms wigglin' on hooks. He was slim and all, but his skin had a bad yellow coat and his throat had deep, weathered creases in it. The old man had been tanned by the light of too many beer signs, and it just goes to show that you can't live on three decks of Chesterfields and a fifth of bourbon a day without starting to drift far too fuckin' wide in the turns.

Shade spoke up, saying, "You know, John, I've got to mention this—you really look different."

"Older you mean?"

"Not just older," Shade said, "but pretty much washed out, too. I mean, you always used to dress so spiffy—what happened?"

"Well, now, I always used to be a beautiful, flashy sort of fella," John X. said, then brought his hands together and made a diving motion, "but lately I've taken the big *plunge* into humility."

"That's what they call it in your circle, huh?"

"Look, here," John X. said, and held his arms spread wide. "I don't expect major hugs or nothin', but a friendly drink and a likewise bit of chewin' the fat oughta be in order."

"Hallelujah to that," Tip said with a smile. He filled all three glasses with Maker's Mark, a whisky that had long comprised John X.'s main food group. He then said, "So, Johnny, what kind of hustle is it brings you back to town?"

"It's no hustle. Hell, I'm done with that. What it is, is, it's a choice."

Tip, the eldest son, stared at his pop expectantly, waiting for some sort of punchline. When none came he said, "A choice, man? Whatta you mean by choice?"

A little sip of the sour mash oiled John X.'s throat just right and he said, "In life you're always gettin' into positions where you got to make choices, boys. Read me? You go this way, you go that way, you fall down in the middle and cry like a banshee, whatever. Them's all choices, and you want to be careful with them fuckers. Be ginger with them. Try to make 'em shrewd, 'cause in later years wrong ones you made can really loom up from behind and lord it over you."

"You mean like choosin' to be a wandering drunk and gambler?" Shade asked.

John X. gave his only blue-eyed son a flat stare, then nodded.

"Exactamunto, Rene. I should've made a choice to be a priest, maybe. The hours suck, but the perks are good, eternal life and whatnot." He raised the glass of whisky, held it under his nose, closed his eyes, and inhaled the scent. "That sounds nice to me these days."

"Huh-uh," Tip said. "*Noooo*, Johnny. If you'd've chose to be a priest, we wouldn't be here, now would we?"

"No, you wouldn't. Good point. You'd've both been sticky splatters on my sheets in the mornin', at best." He turned to Shade. "Did I make the right choice after all, son?"

Before Shade could make a response two grayheaded Catfish regulars sidled up to the table and said, "Johnny Shade, is it you?" And the old man said yes to them and they were off on a series of enthusiastic comments and shoulder slaps and grins. The balder buddy was Mike Rondeau, and the other Mr. Sportin' Life of 1947 was a burly red-faced fella named Spit McBrattle who was still active enough to get an occasional mention in the police blotter. Pop Shade seemed to revel in the reunion, and he kept a Chesterfield lit at all times, firin' 'em up with that same eight-ball Zippo he'd been carrying when he dumped the family, years ago. After a few minutes John X. told Mike and Spit that he'd be around, but now he wanted to talk to his boys, and Mike said how *long*'ll you be around this time Johnny, and the answer caused Tip and Shade to lock eyes, stony faced, because it was for good, fellas, I'm home forever.

Then the sports drifted and John X. turned back to the table and said to Shade, "So, you still with the cops?"

"Vaguely."

"Vaguely? What's that mean?"

Tip grinned and cut in, "It means some of the boys in blue, plus some of the dudes with pinkie rings, are all upset with li'l blood, here."

"Oh. I'm sick of that whole stripe of people, myself," John X. said. "But I guess it can't be good for you, Rene."

"They know where to find me."

John X. then gestured at the fresh pink scar over Shade's brow. "What happened there?"

"Little trouble."

"Little trouble, huh? I hope you got paid for it."

"'Fraid not."

"Criminentlies." John X. sadly shook his head. "I'll have to let *that* sink in. You want to get in trouble, son, you should get in trouble for profit, not just self-expression. Always remember that."

The trio of men laughed at this, and drinks were freshened all around. On the wall directly above the table, hanging from a nail, there was a framed photo of Willie Hoppe and Welker Cochran, cues in hand, exchanging sneers at the '39 Three-Cushion Billiards Championship. As the laughter faded John X. looked up at the picture and said, "Hell, Willie, Welker, I can't shoot a puppy no more."

Gretel came back from the pinball machine and stood behind Tip. She looked over her shoulder at Etta and said, "That girl plays that game tough."

"I imagine," John X. said.

"You sure do have you a nice aura," Gretel said.

"I do?" John X. said. "What's nice about it?"

She concentrated her vision on the old man.

"Why, the color. You have a purple fringe, Mr. Shade, and that's hopeful."

There was no audible response to her, and she stood heavily for a moment, then said, "I've got to head home to Mrs. Carter's now. It was good to meet you."

"I'll see her out," Tip said. "I think I'll call Francois, too. And grab us another bottle."

Tip and Gretel lumbered away, and Shade went silent, watching his father's face, a face that dragged him backward into history. On Saturday evenings in the years when John X. lived at home, and family life and liquor conspired to make him feel expansive, he would pack his three boys into the tight front seat of his already decrepit bullet-shaped '51 Ford, then slide in beside them, behind the wheel. Shoulder to shoulder, hip to hip, they rode around Frogtown. Daddy always packed six cans of beer, and the boys took turns lowering the church key that dangled from the rearview mirror, then gladly punching holes in the cans for him, the man at the wheel. Inevitably they cruised Voltaire Street where the bars and pool halls and tough guys were. Sighting a gang on the corner one day, John X. said, "Boys, I'm goin' to show you some hoodoo your daddy can work. I'm goin' to roll right past that knot of thugs over there, and I'm goin' to call ever last one of 'em an asshole, and they're goin' to smile and wave back at me." Then, with the boys big-eyed and fearful, he'd stuck his head and arm out the window, his hand holding a brew, honked the horn, and shouted, "Hey, assholes!" but slurring the words cheerily into a great, indecipherable, melted phrase, "Heyayasyarshehooooles!" The bug eyes of the Shade brothers fixed on the ducktailed boppers, who turned, looked at the car and their old man, and sure enough smiled at him, calling him Johnny. This became a game for the Shades alone, hurling smiley insults at hoods, red-lipped whores, hard-ass cops, thieves of all ages, and known killers, and eventually they got Greg and Slick Charbonneau, Mayor Yarborough, the Second Street Stompers, two of the Carpenter brothers, and on one occasion even Mr. B., to amiably raise a hand in acknowledgment of their salute. No insult was ever taken as John X. insulted the most dangerous folk in Frogtown, and always, as they drove on, he'd plant an elbow in the ribs of the nearest son and say, "You seen it, boys. Your daddy calls 'em assholes, and they're *happy* to hear it."

When Tip returned to the table with a fresh bottle, John X. pushed Shade's glass toward him and said, "Drink up, son."

Tip opened the new bottle and passed it around.

"I guess Frankie can't make it," he said.

John X. nodded.

"I never knew him the way I knew you two."

"Well," Tip said, "he says you've been a phantom too long to be anything else to him now. He's got some sort of grudge."

"No problem," John X. said. "He's a lawyer, right?"

"Uh-huh," Tip said. "He's doin' pretty good, too."

"Ah, well," John X. said, smiling, "I'm glad to hear that."

Etta came over from the pinball machine in the back of the room and sat on a wooden chair and scooted it up to the table. Her attire consisted of the same cut-off jeans she'd had on when they put Mobile behind them, and the same grimy green T-shirt, but the cooler air had prompted her to wear a black-and-white checked shirt of Grampa Enoch's like a sweater, and she'd ditched the thongs in favor of red sneakers. She plucked a frog leg from the platter and chomped into the meatiest part of it. Her lip color of *this* day was orange, and faint orange dabs had survived four frog legs and a soda before this, but now she smeared them off by wiping her mouth with the back of her hand. "Riv-vet. Riii-vet," she said, mocking her meal.

There was a strange, slim smile on Shade's face as he looked at this Madonna-wanna-be who had so suddenly been shuffled into the family deck.

"How'd you do on the pinball?" he asked her.

"I brung it to its knees," she said. "There's a hard tilt on that sucker, so I whupped it good." She grinned at him, and despite her attire and coif she looked ten years old. "Truthfully, it ate my quarters. I'm tapped out."

"Tapped out, huh?" Shade said, repeating the gambling term. "You're your daddy's kid, alright." He shoved a hand into his pants pocket and raised out a fistful of change which he plopped in front of her. "You're not tapped out, now, Etta. Go get even."

Etta dropped the frog leg, then used her right hand to slide the change to the table edge and held her left underneath to catch the falling coins.

"Thank you, Tip," she said.

"No, no—I'm Rene. *He's* Tip."

"Shit," she said, her head bowed. "I'm sorry."

Then she shuffled toward the pinball machine.

The bar was nearly full, smoke clouds hanging beneath the ceiling, guys in shirtsleeves and tattoos arguing about football, romance, and burglary. At the pool table in the rear a couple of young dudes in olive factory uniforms were jawing out three-foot puppy shots, then pointing at the cue ball and loudly bragging, "But look at that shape."

John X. kept glancing at them, sort of wistfully.

"Look, John," Tip said. "What're you and Etta goin' to do here? How'll you get by?"

John X. shrugged.

"I'll nibble from the big hound's bowl."

"You'll what?"

"I'll take a little from those that's got a lot."

The brothers' eyes met, then Shade said, "Okay, sport, you did it, you confused us."

"Huh. Didn't even break a sweat, neither." John X. lifted his glass and rolled it in his hands. "I'll just open a friendly poker game for me, and all the fellas like me around here. I'll offer a square gamble to old-timers, and we'll see what happens." He sighed. "I can hardly even run a single rack anymore."

"Well, hell," Tip said, his pocked face sincerely composed. "I've got room. You'n the kid can flop with me, Dad."

"That's a nice-soundin' stragedy," John X. said. "It has a nice ring to it."

Shade listened to this, and felt funny hearing it.

"You're really stayin'?"

"Oh, yeah, son. You bet."

Shade pushed his chair up close to the table. His eyes were honky-tonk red and he used both hands on his drink.

"Dad," he said, "now *why was it* you ran out on us in the first place?"

The old man's lips turned down in distaste. He glanced back to where Etta was pinging thousands of bonus points out of the pinball machine, then swung his eyes to the ceiling, then closed them.

He said, "See, fellas, long ago on a drunk night I lost my lucky penny, and ever since then I been on this endless pursuit of the one-armed man who found it and wouldn't give it back. But lately I heard on the grapevine he's turned up here again, back in the old hometown."

5

L UNCH PUMPHREY allowed himself exactly seven cigarettes a
day, and when he rolled off Rodney Chapman's wife, Dolly, he
immediately reached for his pack and put fire to Salem number three.
He hungrily inhaled the mentholated smoke, then collapsed onto a soft
porch chair that had a fabric depicting lush orchids. He smoked for a
moment, trying to get his breathing in order, his fingernails idly scraping at a lipstick smear below his belly button.

"Whew!" he said. "That sure ought've been a cure for *somethin'* or
other, huh?"

"Oh, it was," Dolly said. She was still on the couch, her left hand
covering her eyes, her right dangling toward the floor. Dolly was of
tender years with a sour face. She had store-bought blond hair hanging
in long lanks, and her body was lean from sheer youth and powdered
stimulants, with an all-over golden tan and black pubes shaved down
to a naughty pinch. She was ol' Rodney's young wife and she dug him
plenty, but if someone fell by with some good cocaine and a dick she'd
make the connection. "Boredom maybe," she said. "This could be a
cure for that."

Lunch said, "I think it's a ancient one for that."

They were on the back veranda of the Chapman place, perched
above the shoreline along the Redneck Riviera. Lunch got up to better
appreciate the setting, for the veranda was a point with a view to
offer, a vista, and he stared out across the Gulf water, squinting against the
afternoon sun, his line of sight going more or less toward Panama or

someplace of that type. He burned his cigarette down at a high rate, inhaling diligently, sweeping his eyes over a shimmery green expanse. There were a few motorboats and flapping sails out there. Tiny waves. Noisy birds of several sizes. Kind of interesting to look at, but not worth the real-estate prices by any stretch.

"Lunch, honey," Dolly said. "Can I get into a little more of your blow?"

"You betcha," he said. "Keep frisky."

Lunch looked like a self-portrait by an Expressionist who'd been skipping his Lithium. His face reflected a duality in that one half was clear and smooth as a babyass and the other half was bruise. His right cheek was still swollen along the jawline all the way to the ear, and in a gaudy stage of the healing process. Blue, black, yellow, purple—an awful selection of hues clashed on his face. His bodyskin was pale as fresh canvas, and numerous county-jail artists had used it as such. From his shoulders to his ankles there were perhaps six rough sketches and fifteen completed works on his skin. There was a heart with a pitchfork jabbed into it on his right bicep, a heart with a banner around it that said Yesterday on his left. Up and down his body there were skulls and lightning bolts and other sinister images that carried useful symbolic freight in the lockups of the world. At some point Lunch had caught on to the techniques of the Holding Tank School of Art, and with a needle and string and a bottle of ink he'd attacked the canvas of himself with no design at all in mind. One upper thigh read Repent upside down with a faint X through it, and on the other, right side up, it said Born to Raise Hell. His left forearm bore the inscription Cubs Win! His compact body was well adorned by this art, and though his interest in such artistry had resulted in an occasional infection, it had also given him many indelible memories.

The cigarette had burned down to the filter and Lunch flicked it away. He ran a hand across his sweat-dampened red hair and it stuck up in short spikes. He turned and watched Dolly hunker over the coke tray, her nose down, snorting up a drug-hog portion.

"Mmm," she went, her eyes shining.

"Uh-*huh*," Lunch said. He shook his head in wonder at her simplicity. She seemed to think he was merely colorful or raffish or strangely cute or some such, and, really, she should look deeper'n that. She should look deeper'n that and recognize a few terrible qualities in him, and right away, too.

She was still beaming when the front door slammed.

Her eyes started to spin in her head and she nervously looked to Lunch, who said calmly, "I expect that'll be your husband."

She let go with a long, high-pitched whimper of panic, and before the sound of it faded Rodney Chapman showed up in the doorway, an empty wine bottle held in his hand like a club, his hand shaking. He stared at her for a long second, then moaned and spun away, this spin bringing naked Lunch into view.

Their eyes met and Lunch said, "You should've just took my calls, man—you know I'm remorseless this way."

Rodney's eyes began to water. His mouth hung open. He said, "Lunch."

On the floor of the veranda was the black wad of Lunch's undies. He put his left foot over the wad, clenched his toes, and, with a display of simian dexterity, raised the undies to his hand. After he stepped into the bikini briefs, he said, "Where is he?"

"He? Who, he?" Rodney said. Rodney Chapman had rounded the age of forty a few years back, and he had a rounded shape, sparse brown hair, and a simple story. Until that fortieth year he had tended his mother as she died, an act that, owing to her moral vigor and pioneer genes, had taken nearly two decades to be finalized. Her strength just went down by the thimbleful from year to year, and Rodney had no special life outside the abject duty of tending her until mommy *did* bite it, leaving him behind in this world with only considerable personal wealth to compensate for the loneliness. Being a man alone in the world with considerable personal wealth seemed to change the way all the eyes on the planet focused, for suddenly he was no longer seen as merely a kind of patrician nerd, but a fascinating throwback to a more genteel era. Many a glossy gal heard his tale from himself or others and jumped on him with smiles ablaze and skirts lifted, relentlessly employing their charms. Dolly was one of the bronzed babes who saw him as the fabled main chance, and after a year he married her because she was the most inventively aggressive. In her arms he became a different man. Life brightened up and he acquired sensual vices. He grew a fluffy mustache and kept his fingernails trimmed down smooth. Now, on this sad afternoon, he looked at Dolly there on the couch, where she lay naked, crying gently, still wet from another man's kisses, and he felt the entire fantasy of his new self just fall to pieces and scatter on the veranda.

"Where is he?" Lunch asked again. "Where the hell is ol' Paw-Paw?"

Rodney deflated visibly, his shoulders sagging, chest heaving, head dropping. He wore a light blue sports coat over a deep blue shirt, with black slacks and shoes. He slumped to a soft chair, eyes down, and let the wine bottle fall from his hand.

He said, "Did John do that to your face?"

Lunch put his snap-brim black hat back on and said, "I ain't after pity, man—it's answers I'm here for."

Ever since Mother Chapman passed on Rodney had made attempts to be outgoing and upbeat and a man about town, more or less, but after a few months he'd narrowed the town he was about down to just Enoch's Ribs and Lounge. He sat at the bar there most nights, sipping Chablis, listening to the 'Bama Butterfly, gabbing with roguish John X., the widely traveled night bartender, for from three to six hours a visit.

"I didn't even know John was leaving," he said.

"He did it of a sudden I think," Lunch said.

Dolly sat up on the couch, found her yellow sundress on the floor, and pulled it on. She sniffled loudly several times, then stamped her bare feet on the floor, banging out a fleshy tom-tom solo.

"Why are you here?" she asked Rodney when her heels began to hurt.

"Pardon?"

"At *this* time. Why are you here at *this* time?"

Rodney looked at his wife, his face giving expression to queasy thoughts his mouth just couldn't quite get around to uttering. Finally, he said, "The neighbors."

"The *neigh*—bors?"

He nodded.

"The neighbors called me at the club because their children, their little-bitty children, could see you out here, you know, cavorting."

Dolly raked her hands through her long blond hair and growled.

"The neighbors! The neighbors! I'll burn their fuckin' house down, little-bitty children and all!"

Lunch was calmly standing there on the sunny veranda in his bikini briefs and snap-brim hat, apparently amused.

"Looky here, Dolly," he said, "don't go blaming your neighbors for that phone call, 'cause, actually, it was me." He pointed at Rodney. "You never returned any of the calls I made to you, man. You knew I'd be after ol' Paw-Paw, your pal, so your answering machine quit knowin' me."

Dolly helped herself to a Salem from Lunch's pack and lit up. She exhaled severely.

"When did you call him? I don't remember you goin' anywhere near the goddamn phone."

"You were in the shower, darlin'," Lunch said. "So you'd taste fresh—remember?"

The man of the house began to sob upon hearing this culinary detail, his rounded shoulders bouncing with each breath.

Dolly watched her hubby weep, then said, "You bastard. You son of a bitch. I used to think you were a nice little dude with a big unfair reputation hung on him, but now I know better."

"You still don't know the half of it," Lunch said. "But you might before I leave here."

Still sobbing, Rodney picked up the wine bottle. He chopped the air with it a few times, saying, "Why, I. Why, I oughta. Splat! Yes, sir. Why, I."

"Hey," Lunch said, "y'all can get into your conjugal boo-hoos later." He pointed at his clothes sticking out from the chair seat beneath

Rodney. "I don't want to tempt you by comin' over there, son—so just hand me my britches, huh?"

Rodney, still seated, raised the wine bottle like he might throw it at Lunch.

"Oh, no, don't," Dolly said. "Don't!" She scooted across the sun-dappled veranda and touched her husband lightly on his chest. "Don't do it, baby—Lunch'll kill you. He's known for that."

"That's good advice she's giving you," Lunch said. "I oft times *do* have a place in the life cycle, when money's at stake. So cool your jets down and drop that bottle." The bottle dropped. "Now be the gentleman you are, Rodney, and kindly hand me my Levi's. And pick 'em up by the belt loops, so you don't dump my pocket change all over the floor, here."

Dolly's fingertips were still touched to Rodney's chest. He looked up at her, then looked down and swatted her fingers away. She went back to the couch and he stood. He grabbed the belt loops and handed Lunch his Levi's. Then he handed him his shirt.

"Here's your shirt," he said.

Lunch started dressing.

Dolly was curled up in a yellow ball on the couch, her legs tucked beneath her, her head bowed. She said, "It's time to face up to it—I have a problem. A *serious* problem."

"So where is he?" Lunch asked.

Storm clouds had mobbed up out over the Gulf and were quickly rumbling toward shore.

Once again seated and moist in the eyes, Rodney said, "I don't really know. He's from over there in bayou country. The town is called, I think, St. Bruno. Upriver from N'Awlins. Some distance. When he said home, that's where he meant."

"I've heard of that place," Lunch said. "Reckon that's where he'd go?"

"It's a *serious* problem," Dolly said, "and the very first step is admitting that I have it."

"Who knows?" Rodney said. "It's all I can tell you." He looked at Dolly but spoke to Lunch. "I guess you just had to do this. You just had to ruin my life."

"Looky here now," Lunch said. Lunch had his pants on and his black shirt hung down unbuttoned. He was bent over, zipping up his half-boots, his black hat bobbing. "It's like the dyin' old men all over the world will tell you, Rodney—when you get aged and rackety and think back across your entire life span, why, it ain't the ones you do you regret, it's the ones you don't."

"Is that so?" Rodney said.

"It sure is." Lunch brushed lint from his pants leg as he stood up. "I mean, a piece of tail is a piece of tail, and your wife is purty cute, and she'd be one I'd sure 'nough regret someday if I didn't. You *could* take that as a compliment, you know."

"Honey?" Dolly said. *"Baby?* You know I love you, don't you? You know I love you, but I don't know if *you* love *me*, love me enough to help me fight this awful thing, my addiction."

Rodney turned to stare at her.

"That's what my problem is," she said. "My *serious* problem. I'm an addict—I couldn't face up to it before. But a thing like this, here, today, why, it's only my addiction that could bring me this low, bringing me to betray the love we have, honey, all 'cause of my sick, sick, sick addiction to nose candy."

Lunch got his cigarettes and coke from the table, pausing to grin a huge one down at Dolly.

Rodney kept staring at her.

"Drug troubles are tough to lick, but with you by my side I *could* fight this thing. Drugs *can* be beat, baby. Will you stand by me while I fight this thing?"

Rodney said, "You've just lain with Lunch, here, in *my* house, and you want to know if I'll stand by you?"

"It's a *disease*," she said plaintively. "What has happened here proves how *sick* I am from it. Sick, sick, sick." She brought her hands up to her face and began unleashing tears behind them. "I'm *addicted*—I *need* you, I *need* you, I *need* you, to help me fight it."

Rodney wiped a stubby finger at a tear on his cheek.

"We'd cut out all the *co*-caine?" he asked.

"Uh-huh."

"No more toot and brandy breakfasts?"

"Huh-uh."

"We'll stay away socially from bad influences?"

"Mmm-hmm."

Dolly was still sending forth tears from behind her hands.

"We'd have to do all those things," he said, "to have a chance. Any chance at all. And might as well kick beer, too. It's just a stepping stone. And French wines and pot—they'll have to go."

Dolly let her hands fall away from her damp sour face.

"French wines and pot aren't hurting anything much, honey," she said in an instructive tone. "The surest way is to *ease* out from under an addiction, not go cold turkey."

Real sharp laughter came from Lunch.

"Hoo, hoo, hoo!" he went. "Rodney, ol' son, I don't believe you can handle a gal like this one here. Hoo, hoo! She's from places like where *I* come from. She's fixin' to make herself seem codefendant with good blow, man—like she wouldn't've shook hands with me otherwise." Lunch adjusted the snap-brim hat on his head. "She's from the level I know well, which is one where you've got to be hard on her, or she'll just cook your ass down to mush, ol' buddy. You've got to whomp a gal like her to get any respect. Make her lips swell up tight for a spell." Rodney kept looking down, so Lunch cupped a hand beneath his pudgy chin and raised his face until their eyes met. "You've got to be a man, son—you can't let her bullshit you like this." He pinched Rodney's cheek to a red glow. "Be a *man*."

The storm clouds above the Gulf cut loose, and over on the couch Dolly clamped her jaws and looked fierce.

The condom Lunch had used was on the floor beside the couch and she picked it up, then twirled it like a slingshot.

"Hey, Lunch," she said, "Eat scum and die."

Lunch sensed something en route toward his head and turned enough that the projectile merely skimmed his hat brim, then swirled down to land on Rodney's shoe.

The contents oozed across the imported leather on his toes.

Rodney began to weep instantly. Ingrained manners caused him to promptly ease a white hankie from his breast pocket and clumsily wipe at his shoe.

Lunch stared down at Rodney, whose sobbing reaction displayed how little manly advice he'd absorbed, then shook his head in disgust, and threw his hands up in a gesture of defeat. He started stomping toward the door, saying, "Son, you are fuckin' *hope*-less!"

The parking lot at Enoch's Ribs and Lounge was empty except for a few beer cans and paper litter. A sign in the window of the dark restaurant said Closed For Remodeling.

Lunch parked his VW Bug in the shade of a large oak tree so the late afternoon sun wouldn't cook his bucket seats, then let himself into Enoch's through the front door. The front room was shadowy, with a musty odor in the air. Chairs were upturned and stacked on tables, and vast cobweb empires were expanding in the upper reaches of the room.

About halfway across the room Lunch heard the sound of cooking, and then the smell became distinct also. The grill was on in the kitchen. Lunch bent down to his left boot and came up with a two-shot derringer. He quietly crossed the lounge to the kitchen and slowly pushed the swinging doors aside, and there at the grill stood Short Paul of Tampa, spatula in hand, tending to a brace of T-bone steaks.

Short Paul looked at Lunch and said, "No potatoes? I searched all over and couldn't find none nowhere. Not even frozen."

"Huh," went Lunch.

"I'm a person who keeps it simple, you know—with meat, why, you have potatoes. Maybe peas or a salad or somethin', too, but those're extras." Short Paul was of a regular size but many times in his youth he'd come up short on his bar tab, hence the nickname. He had abundant gray hair brushed straight back from a jolly face that got him fast, friendly service from café waitresses with marital woes. A big-city growl snapped at the heels of his words, and he had the skin-tone of a beachfront condo owner. "But potatoes ain't an extra with meat—they're a must."

Lunch put the derringer in his front pocket, then calmly lit Salem number four.

"You here to lean on me?"

"I would never try to *lean* on *you*."

"You should make that never, never, never."

"Hey, now, be cool," Short Paul said with a quick grin. "Angelo and me, we just want our money."

Lunch looked at the T-bones cooking on the grill, then stared quizzically at Short Paul.

"No p'taters, huh?"

"None nowhere."

"That meat come out of my freezer?"

"Mm-hmm. You don't mind, do you?"

Lunch shook his head, smoke curling from his nostrils.

"Course not—help yourself."

After flipping the meat, Short Paul said, "That dude sure jacked your face up, Lunch. When will it be back to normal?"

"He japped me with a bottle, Short. Doctor said I was lucky nothin' broke."

"I guess," Short Paul said. "But, let me tell you, it don't look good, what he done."

Lunch eased over next to Short Paul, then flicked cigarette ashes on Short's yellow shirt.

"I need a ashtray," he said. "You'll do."

"Hey, hey," Short Paul said, backing away, swatting at the ashes. "Don't forget who I'm *with*, Lunch! Don't forget the people I'm with, pal."

Lunch wagged his head and smiled. "I'm only with my lonesome," he said. "But I still consider *me* to be the majority in most *any* argument."

"Yeah. That's what you're famous for." Short Paul downshifted in mood, allowing his composure to catch back up to him. The T-bones were sizzling so he raised the spatula and dished the meat onto a white plate. "So, Lunch," he said, "you still number your smokes?"

"Yup." Lunch was savoring the last puff of number four, leaning against the wall, letting the smoke float from his mouth only to be reinhaled through his nostrils. "Us smaller fellas has to keep our bad habits on short leashes. We can't run wild with 'em and still stack up in a pinch the way your moose–type of fella can." Lunch spit on the end of the cigarette, then dropped the butt. "Plus, seriously, there's nature, which I don't feel we should smoke all up just out of habit. Really, seven cigarettes a day is all you want, except out of habit."

Short Paul nodded, then pointed with the plate, gesturing toward the lounge.

"Let's grab a seat," he said, "while I have a bite. I gotta drive back to Tampa yet."

"Where's your Caddy?" Lunch asked as they sat at a table.

"In the alley."

"How'd you get in here?"

"Well, you have a window to fix, back there, by the alley."

Short Paul carved the meat from both T-bones into little mouthfuls, then started spearing them and eating them like he was being timed for speed.

"I found where the man might've gone," Lunch said. "His hometown was this place, you know, over in the bog country there, swamps and all that. I heard of it before, they call it St. Bruno."

Nodding and chewing in concert, Short Paul spat out, "Sure. Gamblin' town. Used to play cards up there."

"You what?" Lunch asked.

Short Paul, within sight of victory over his steaks, dropped his fork, then breathed deeply.

"I used to go there for the Hold 'Em games, years ago, when the snow pigeons had flown back to Ohio and stuff. I got to know this guy, dangerous sort of a wise guy over there, name of Ledoux. Pete Ledoux." Short Paul put both hands over his belly, then made a sour face. "If he wasn't dead I could call him, ask him if he knows this old man—Shade, ain't it?"

"John X. Shade."

"Pete was well connected up there." Sweat began to pour down Short Paul's forehead. His facial skin began to tune in to a less healthy color. "But a cop whacked him. Oh, man." He lifted the plate and sniffed what was left of the meat. His face bore a concerned and slightly green expression. "This smell right?"

Lunch leaned across the table and sniffed.

"Not exactly," he said. "A tad ripe, I'd say."

"It was in *your* freezer. Frozen solid."

"Yeah, well." Lunch shrugged. "The freezer was out for near a week. I just turned it on again last night."

"A week!" Short Paul raised the plate up high and hurled it across the room. He mopped his brow with a napkin. His pale green cheeks trembled. "You let me eat *rotten meat*?"

A smile played across Lunch's face. He turned his small shoulders inward in an almost coy manner.

"I couldn't be *sure* it was rotten," he said. "Course *now* I *am* sure, or purty close to it, from the look on you."

"You let me eat it!"

"I said, help yourself, that's all. And I meant it, like—eat at your own risk."

A very leery quality had taken over from Short Paul's normal jolly expression. He watched Lunch from the corners of his eyes.

"The meat was my mistake," he said softly. "Just get us our money. That's all we want."

"You'll get it, plus ol' Paw-Paw's head on a stick."

"Uhhh, forget the head on a stick. Angelo can get heads on sticks all day long, at wholesale." Short Paul choked something back down in his throat. "What he wants is his money, forty-seven K. When'll you be off to get it?"

Lunch touched a finger to his nose as if imagining his journey, then sprang from his seat, put both hands next to Short Paul's ears, snapped his fingers, and said, *"Poof!"*

With the sun sinking orange and fantastic directly in his path, Lunch cruised down two-lane blacktop, headed toward the big river that split the nation. He stayed well within the double-nickel speed limit, partly because it was a point of pride to never seem in a hurry, for any reason at any time, but also because he didn't like to put strain on his VW Bug. The Bug was red with a black interior, and he'd been driving it since his seventeenth year back in the Appalachian hills, when he'd been given it by a neighbor who didn't want any more of his hogs disappearing and figured that if the Pumphrey kid had some wheels he just might take to snatching shoats a little farther down the road.

The Bug had previously been in a smash-up, a one-car deal where a tourist from the low country refused to believe that the mountain lane he was on could possibly curve any more times in succession than it already had, and thereby missed one, shooting the Bug into a tree. Over a period of months Lunch lavished himself on the car, and tinkered it back into smooth-running shape. He polished it up 'til it glowed, and if his family had ever had anything that could by some stretch be called a *jewel*, then the Bug was it. The car fit him in every way; it was just his size, it cornered like a snake on those hillbilly highways, the colors of it spoke to him, and naturewise it was gentle on the world, with good mileage per gallon and clean exhaust.

Nature was a force Lunch felt compelled by, both as an observer and a participant. His fondest memories were of watching puppies and calves being born on the farm back home, and of the ferocious and sweet vibrations that hummed through his arms and legs, his brain and vital organs, the first time he'd killed a man. It had been for money, so that humming in his veins hadn't been venom or spleen, but an inner, almost musical sense of being connected to the natural order, linked very high up on the chain of things.

Like an owl, sort of, when it hoots in the dark.

When Lunch contemplated the life he'd been raised up in back among the Appalachians, it seemed like some dreamily remembered folk-ballad, a folk-ballad that was lunatic in spirit, for the way he recalled the years back there was that they were full of ominous moonscapes where phantasm hounds and poltergeist ancestors gave out unearthly cries from the nearby hollers, and voices of the congregated dead chewed the fat in his ear every night at bedtime, while his actual daylight life was oppressed by his grandma and aunt, who lamented his vile birth and administered constant Bible thumpings to his head to shoo away the evil he'd inherited.

Only his older sister, Rayanne, turned out at all well in his memories. It was Rayanne who would slowly check his head for lice, or lance painful boils on his childish ass, or bundle him and light candles for him when the electricity was shut off, or remember his birthday.

Even though Rayanne had often mocked or taunted him, she'd still come closest of anyone to being good to him, and when he was old enough he went to work pimping for her in Charleston, and eventually she arranged the first hit contract for him, sending him after a tavern owner in Marietta who thought he needn't listen to reason from a whore.

Man, Lunch thought, that hummin', that sweet music in the veins, it comes back over you at totally unpredictable times.

He lit Salem number five, and traced the present humming back a week or so, he thought, to the hospital and his visit to Enoch Tripp. He'd had questions for Enoch, but Enoch had had better questions for him. The old dude looked like hell, and the nurse said they'd given him something to take his mind away from all this. His eyes were wide but he hadn't seemed to recognize Lunch, his silent partner, at all.

Where are they? Lunch had asked, and Enoch had thrashed around a little and said, Second Grade. All in Second Grade now that Uncle Sam found his kittens. Do you get one?

There were tubes of oxygen going into Enoch's nose. His skin hung off him loose like a borrowed suit.

Where did ol' Paw-Paw Shade light out for? Lunch asked in a crooning voice. Where are they?

Would you sit by me? Enoch had said. Won't you set here by me and spell somethin' out plain the way you do?

Lunch had reached over and slid the tubes from the old coot's nose. Then he pinched the nostrils together, and Enoch's eyes got big, and bigger, then, of a sudden, they went peaceful, and he nodded.

Lunch let go, and the old man gasped until he reinserted the tubes. Enoch's eyes calmly followed him the whole time.

Maybe forty Japs I did in, Enoch said. Is that too much on account?

Forty? Shit, man, that's a lot. I was too young for 'Nam, and forty, man, that's a bunch in peacetime.

The old man's eyes studied Lunch from a far place.

Looky here, Lunch said, I *could* do you, 'cause I think you know I'm here, and why and all, but doin' you now would be for nothin'. Lunch leaned over Enoch, tugged his beard, and whispered, 'Cause, Enoch, nature is already killing you in a worse way than I could ever dream up. No, sir, I couldn't improve on it, not in a hundred years of tryin'.

Salem number five was down to the filter, and Lunch stuck it in the ashtray, then kept on cruisin' west in the Bug with that music still hummin' in his veins, unblinking eyes watching the golden sun smother beneath the black horizon.

Part II

Sinking in

6

"I t seems I've been backin' this same king-high nada all night long," John X. Shade said as Spit McBrattle pulled in another pot. "Time to change the game."

The deal had worked its way around the table once more, back into the control of John X. He named Draw as the game because, he said, he suddenly liked the very notion of having more than one chance to catch a winning hand. All of the old and unnecessary fellas sitting around the table nodded, winked, or sighed at his comment, for at their time of life the sweet dream of more than one chance was often indulged, though scenes in it sometimes deviated uncontrollably from the benign and lush toward the numbing and stark.

The cards were shuffled and dealt in the front room of Tip's bachelor heaven, a place of rough wood and stained rugs, set atop stilts near the river, with an oil-drum dock floating on the water. The summer was long gone but a straggling day of heat had strayed into early autumn and warmed the sunlit hours, and even at this hour of the night a nice summery breeze was breathed in through the screened windows.

"Criminentlies," John X. said as he folded his hand. "So much for extra chances." He leaned away from the table and stretched his arms. "Anybody for a beer?"

Spit, red faced and riding a good streak, raised his brown bottle and held it toward his host.

"I'm ready," he said. "Suds are goin' down cool this evenin'."

John X. took the bottle and held it out to his side. He looked over by the screen door to where Etta knelt on a rug playing Solitaire, her hair ruffling in the draft, her green lips pursed in concentration as she cheated the pee-waddy-doo out of ol' Sol, the lonely cardsharp's constant nemesis. Sol hadn't a chance the way the kid flexed the rules on him, and when she smirked in victory her lips looked like a twisted dollar.

"Angel," he said to her, and as she looked up he wagged the bottle. "One for Spit."

Etta hopped up and took the empty into the kitchen.

The kitchen of Tip's bachelor heaven was solidly square in shape, with the static atmosphere of a museum exhibit. Things gleamed from cleanliness and lack of use. The shelves were severely ordered, with canned goods in tight ranks, arranged in ascending value from pure vegetables, to vegetable soups, to basically vegetable soups with *some* meat, to meat soups with *some* vegetables, on up to the head of the parade, Spam. Next to the vintage stove a neat stack of white paper plates sat on the sideboard, but above the sideboard there were red-labeled cans brimming with congealed grease drippings, lined on the window sill like potted flowers that blossomed forth a porcine fragrance. The refrigerator was shiny white, huge, and of some historical interest but also defunct, so the beer was in a gray washtub on the floor, classically chilled by large blocks of ice.

Etta dropped a hand into the ice tub and fished out a beer. She wiped the bottle dry on a towel and twisted the cap off. When she set the bottle beside Spit, she used a new monetary term she'd learned, saying, "That'll be eight bits."

Spit held the dollar bill up and she snatched it from his fingers, then went back to her cards.

"That's three bucks to you, Johnny," Mike Rondeau said. "So shit or get off the pot."

"Guess I'll shit," John X. said, and tossed in three ones.

The players kicked two bucks an hour apiece to John X. for hosting, plus he had the concession business. Etta had made sandwiches modeled on the ones Dagwood ate in the funny papers and sold them for two bucks apiece, and that had added up, along with the beer sales. So far John X. was down about twenty from poker, but up fifteen or so overall.

On this particular hand John X. had stayed to the end with two pair, treys and eights, but lost to the three fives Spit held in ambush.

"Oh, man," John X. said with a groan. "I keep gettin' tripped up by the sin of pride."

"That's not the sin that used to trip you," fat Mike said, his bald head bobbing.

"No," John X. said as he lit a Chesterfield. "That one used to be hid so far down the list I didn't snap to it even bein' on there."

So this was the foreseeable future, hosting a weekly poker game for a pack of cranky old hounds who'd never quite caught up to the golden rabbit, but couldn't stop yapping about how close, how tantalizingly close they'd come. They'd all grown up in Frogtown during years long gone by, and most had done this and that when wars or trade carried them to various distant parts of the map to experience the life of other spots, but soon or late, for any or all of the possible reasons, they'd come back to this, the neighborhood of their youth, to live out the string.

The All Big Band radio station played constantly behind the conversational hubbub, and every second or third song one or another of the swing era swains would close his eyes and float off from this actual night, called away by the siren sounds of Kay Kyser or Les Brown or Claude Thornhill, catching slow boats to China in their minds, on sentimental journeys, having Sunday kinds of love.

And when the aged eyes of John X., Spit, Mike, or Mike's widowed brother-in-law, Stew Lassein, or Stew's widowed neighbor, Horace Nash, would slowly open once again to this place and time, they'd give their heads a shake and say something like, "Oh, *brother,* we had *music* back then."

The night air was warm as an illicit cuddle, and Spit was dealing Hold 'Em, his thick fingers flying like Benny Goodman's on a clarinet while that very instrument and man made music over the radio, and

John X., feeling the warmth *and* the music, said, "What the hell, angel—free beer all around."

Etta fetched the beers to the table, then, as the old fellas raised the bottles, she said, "Ice cold beer on a sweaty day sure 'nough proves there once was saints afoot on this earth."

Mike, fat, bald, and pale, looked closely at Etta, then said to John X., "Where's a kid get stuff like *that?*"

John X. winked at his daughter.

"Me," he said. "She's a little echo of my own words."

Etta put her arms around her old man's neck, her green lips near his ear, and said, "I got you memorized."

"That's a scary thought," he said. "I think I won't have it." He reached up and jerked a rat tail of her hair, pulling her head back. "Now go away, we're gamblin'."

"*Huh,*" she grunted, then went over to the couch and stretched out, watching him.

A little after ten the All Big Band radio station called up "Pennsylvania 6-5000" and changed the tempo of the night. The recently widowed Stew Lassein was on the receiving end of that musical number, and as it played he turned to fat Mike, his dead wife's brother, and said, "You remember? That was Della and me's song."

This song and comment came up in the middle of a stud hand dealt by Spit.

"I remember," Mike said, looking down.

Stew, a naturally fair man faded by age to the very edge of transparency, went misty in the eyes.

" 'Pennsylvania 6-5000,' she'd say to me, anytime we talked, on the phone, or at night, or, really, any ol' time, and it meant, 'I got your number, and you, you got mine.' " Stew turned his wet eyes on John X. and said, "But I guess you knew that, Johnny. I would guess you knew her favorite songs."

"Can't say that I did," John X. said. Certainly can't say that it was that one, specifically. Della did like music, and she liked to do everything to musical strains, from drinking coffee along with "String of Pearls," to chewin' the sheets in tune to "Sugar Blues." There always had to be a song playin' backup to the actions in the life of pretty li'l Della Rondeau, even after she became Della Lassein. "That was a popular song, though—every juke had it."

Stew wiped a finger at his wet eyes, then his lips drew back into a snarl.

"I s'pose I look like I believe that," he said. "I s'pose I look like the sort who'll believe anything."

"Are we playin' cards, or what?" Spit said.

"Aw, please, Stew," Mike said as Stew's eyes began to leak, "would you please quit it? Just stop it." He shrugged apologetically toward the other players. He turned his hands up. "Della only died this last winter. He's still kind of raw."

"Let's play around him," Spit said. "Your jack is high, Nash."

Horace Nash, Stew's neighbor, also widowed and lean and cranky, looked at the tears and said, "Fold."

At the part of the song where the band chants "Pennsylvania six, five, oh-oh-oh," Stew Lassein responded by trumpeting a muted sob solo.

Fat Mike grimaced. He hung his head, then said, "Johnny, you remember my kid sister, Della, don't you?"

John X. studied the tears running down Stew's face. He couldn't look away from them. They irrigated the dry old skin of Lassein's cheeks, the weeping and sobbing strangely taking years off the old man for a few seconds at a time. As the tears glistened on his reddening cheeks and his body lunged along with the sobs, the old man looked alive, and lucky in his ability to grieve.

"Sure I do," John X. said. "Her and Monique were close back then." His gaze did not shift from Stew's face as he spoke. "I remember Della as this short, dark, imported-lookin' sort of dame, who had a stylish way of smokin' a Sweet Caporal, and wore feathery hats cocked on her head like a double-dare. Mm-hmm, I remember."

"That's enough!" Stew said. His lips trembled and he pointed a finger at his host. "Enough! Don't say another thing you remember about my wife!"

Spit slammed his hand on the table.

"Look," he said, "I got eleven bucks in this pot, and if y'all don't quit your crab-assin' and *play*, I'm gonna call myself winner and rake it in. I mean it—I'm here to gamble."

Stew scooted his chair back from the table. He wiped at his eyes with a party napkin, then blew his nose on it.

"I remember she liked to go to dances," John X. said, "and she always showed up at 'em with Stew, here."

The radio had moved on to a new tune, some sort of discombobulatin' rhythm from abroad, probably Cuba. The brass section was agitated and the drummers pounded out a tropical war beat.

"There," Horace Nash said consolingly to Stew, "a new song."

"I told him," Stew said, repeating the finger pointing as he spoke, "not to say *another* word about her."

"Please," Mike said, shaking his head.

"I win," Spit said. "Time's up."

He started to pull in the pot, but John X. grabbed his hand.

"Huh-uh," John X. said. "I got seven bucks in there, too." John X. folded his hands on the table and sat up straight. "Alright now, Stew— what's your beef with me?"

"Look at him," Stew said. He tossed the damp napkin onto the table. "Would you look at him? Mister Blue-eyed Innocent." Stew stood up and angrily waved a hand at John X. "I can't be around you. I thought I could. I sure thought I could, but I just can't."

"What *is* your problem with me?"

"You know what! Mister Snake-hips! You always dressed like you were *so*, so special, peddlin' lies to every girl in town, actin' so handsome! Spendin' money like you didn't have to work for it—which you didn't!"

John X. lit a Chesterfield and eased back in his chair. His hands hung loose to his sides and he said, "I never felt like I had to apologize for bein' a *dream*boat."

This statement was at the heart of the matter, it rung true, and Stew fell back on weeping. His shoulders shook and he tried to stammer a retort but gave up after, "I, I, I..."

Horace Nash stood up next to Stew.

"I wish I missed my Luann like you miss your Della," he said. "Yes, sir, I wish I could work up some tears for that crocodile—if I could it'd mean my life once had *some* goddamned thing of value in it." As Stew jerked and moaned he patted him on the shoulder. "I envy you, buddy. I really do."

"Criminentlies."

"You and me'll split this," Spit said, then began counting the pot.

Etta had been dozing on the couch, but now she came awake and sat up.

"What?" she mumbled. "Who?"

"I just can't take you," Stew said. "I think you know why."

The old man was then led out the door by Horace Nash.

John X. watched the screen door smack shut, then said to Mike, "Hope he gets home safe."

Mike had a fresh cigar in his mouth, unlit, and he rolled it from cheek-to-cheek, talking around it.

"I never married," he said, "so I'll drive 'em on home." Fat Mike walked to the door and said "Sorry" as he went out.

Etta got up from the couch and stood before the screen door, taking in the night breeze. Bird noises sounded from high in the tall dark trees along the river. The breeze was scented with fermenting river stink.

"Dad," she said, "what's goin' on?"

Burly Spit tossed a wad of bills John X.'s way.

"There's your split," he said. He raised his bottle of beer for a long drink. "We'll get some players who ain't so temperamental next time."

"How's *your* wife?" John X. asked.

"Oh, she's dead, Johnny." Spit rose from his chair, stretched his back, and yawned. "Seven or eight years back. Pamela couldn't resist a bargain, you know, so she overdid the stingers durin' Happy Hour at The Oasis one night. It was foggy. She run the Buick right into the bridge pilings on River Road."

"Criminentlies," John X. said. "Sorry to hear that."

"Aw, hell, I rubbed a brick on it years ago," Spit said. He slowly stepped to the door, pausing at the screen to inhale deeply. "Ol' Stew should find hisself a good brick and give it a try." He shoved the door open and stepped onto the porch. "Catch you later, Johnny."

When the door smacked shut this time, John X. leapt from his chair and lunged for the couch and collapsed. With quivering hands he lit a smoke, inhaled needily, and coughed, his entire body arching as he hacked.

Etta sat on the couch beside him. Her little hand touched his knee.

Oh, but things were sinking in. Women you'd loved when they were young, had grown old and wide and infirm, and already died of natural causes. Women younger than yourself, and beautiful.

Criminentlies, but doesn't that make the ticking clock an ominous fuckin' bully to your mind?

"Dad, why ever did that man cry so?"

Thirty-five years back, him and Della, it was a summer thing, a summer fling, maybe part of the fall, and that one time the following year. He'd had a hideaway above Verdin's Grocery, a tiny room with a Murphy bed and a radio and a back entrance from the alley, up one flight of stairs. Della was sort of beautiful, prettier when she spoke 'cause she said the damnedest things, and somehow they got together and began to meet above Verdin's, usually in the afternoon while Stew loaded trucks at Bruns Van Lines. It was always hot, no fan, but plenty of music and slick sweaty skin. The day Della first tried to call it off the temp was a delta ninety-five, and they'd watered the sheets before laying on top of them. I shouldn't be here, she said. Monique is my friend, ever since grade school. Della was dark skinned and plentiful, full of sass and never pissy, and she lay on the wet sheets belly-down, her skin moist and available. I shouldn't be here. I don't know why I do this. And John X. had sucked an ice cube from his gin and tonic into his mouth, then leaned over her, his tongue pushing the ice cube down her spine, over the hump to the crack of her ass, and he'd held the ice cube there with his tongue and slipped a finger between her thighs, lightly fingering the slit. She growled, Oh, Johnny, and he swallowed the ice cube and said, You're rememberin' *why* now, ain't you?

Etta began to shake him.

"Dad? Dad?"

"What, kid?"

"Why ever did he cry?"

After two dismal, stalling puffs John X. patted her young, bony back, and said, "Kid, I'll tell you, when someone you give two hoots about goes away for good, why, it's a thing that can shake you hard and leave cracks behind in you."

While contemplating this, Rosetta Tripp Shade folded her bare arms across her chest, her big 'Bama browns staring out a screened window toward Europe, then said, "How far off is France in hours?"

7

THE LASSEIN home was small and square, painted white, bought on a lifetime plan, and not quite paid for. When Stew got out of his brother-in-law's car he didn't say good night, but walked briskly up the dark stone walkway and into his house. He began to turn on lamps, first one, then two, then all of them; six in the front room, three in the big bedroom, two in each of the kids' rooms, then the tall one with the fake fruit tree base and shade fringed by dangling green grapes that rose up from the kitchen table. Della had for some reason thought lamps to be perfect works of art, and affordable, and she'd made a hobby of their collection, haunting flea markets and church sales searching for lamps, the older the better, even if she had to rewire them herself. One corner of the garage was cluttered with two dozen lamps of all types, most hopelessly broken, that she had meant to repair but never had.

The lamps that worked certainly did light the place up, but the white glow they cast also illuminated dust bunnies and cobwebs and the wilting jungle of plants that Stew hadn't taken much care of since early in the last winter, starting that day the ice storm pulled down the power lines and Della'd slumped over dead after bringing in firewood.

Stew's reddened eyes noted the spreading disorder of his house and he sniffed, for he'd become negligent as a widower. In prior years his domestic surroundings had always been clean and tidy, perfectly presentable in case visitors arrived at the drop of a hat.

He put on a pot of midnight coffee and thought about where to start. It seemed logical to begin with things living, so he went to the closet and found Della's plant waterer, a red plastic pitcher in the shape of a heron with a thin beak for a spout.

Stew filled the heron at the kitchen sink, staring at the dusty family pictures on the ledge above. There was one of himself and Della, her in a hugely brimmed white hat and swimsuit, him in long white pants and shirt, with a wide gaudy tie around his neck. That must've been taken up at Hot Springs just after they'd married, when he'd loved her completely, with no fineprint of doubts at all. The other pictures were of their children, Cynthia and Donald, and in each Cynthia stood apart, withdrawn, while Donald smiled broadly, his lips spread nearly from one jug ear to the other.

When the heron was full, Stew set it down and poured himself a cup of coffee. He let the cup sit, for he preferred his java lukewarm.

Oh, my, but just the thought of Johnny Shade made him feel sick about his life. And hers.

He picked the heron up and began to move, tending to the living things. He went into the front room and began the watering. Philodendron, dracaena, Boston ivy, begonia, jade plant—he knew the names but he didn't know which was which. Green things they were, unknown green growing things that overran their pots—the kind of crap Della had liked.

Stew sat on a stuffed footstool in the bright room, the pail in his hand, his head slumped.

She'd lied to him, he knew that. Hell-fire, there was no doubt about that at all. She'd lied to him and he'd let it pass, he'd let it pass from her sweet lips and into his own mind, where this single nasty falsehood had taken root and spread, growing like evil kudzu, growing over every thought he had of her, every casual comment she made to him, until whatever truths she may have told were hidden from him, overrun by his pitiful knowledge of her single lie.

He'd had her. That son of a bitch had known the smooth skin and sweet lips and strong hips of his wife.

And she'd lied about it.

And he'd let the lie take root around his heart, until real love had been choked off and died lonely.

Time to water the hanging plants now. There would be no sleep this night, and this house needed attention.

For nearly forty years Stew had loaded trucks at Bruns Van Lines, eventually becoming foreman. He had a knack for order, for keeping things straight, and as foreman these qualities proved to be worthwhile rather than merely prissy. To travel safely, truck cargo had to be packed precisely, the load balanced to avoid shifting and breakage, and he'd excelled at this. He'd sit in his tiny office off the loading dock, sketching the trailer and its dimensions down to the half-inch, then chart the cargo into place, each box or crate or tube destined for a precise position. The boys would do the work, surly boys most of the time, and he'd crab at them if they deviated at all from his design. Let's do it my way, he'd say, and despite a few curses they would. As the boys toiled and the trailer filled, each item in its place, the cargo filling the trailer to the roof in exactly the order he'd charted, he'd chew gum and beam and think to himself—Now I know why those ol' Pharaohs got so carried away!

To be a Pharaoh in his personal life had been his desire, with every small or large domestic charm a building block to be stacked skyward toward a flesh-and-blood perfection, a monumental family harmony. But, no, if one key thing is out of place...

Monumental family harmony went unattained because of three words and a puppy, the puppy named Coral, the three words, "The bake sale." That was what she'd claimed, that's where she'd said she'd been. She baked terrific foods at home, but that's where she told him she'd been. She'd said it straight to his face, lying without any trace of effort, but her bag contained no bread, no pie, not even a single glazed donut, and because of Coral, their Beagle pup, the marriage was cracked, split wide, for Coral had slipped her leash and trotted off and he'd followed hollering for her, hollering up and down alleys and through vacant lots, the puppy lost to sight, and he'd come to the mouth of the alley down from Verdin's Grocery when he'd seen Della. He'd seen Della walking from behind the store, her hands held to her head, pinning her fragrant hair up, and he'd stood there watching, his throat dry from hollering and the whole terrible gamut of thoughts that immediately clutched at him, and he'd kept watching as she walked away, toward home, then Johnny Shade came from behind the store, in nearly the same footsteps as her, jauntily smoking a cigarette, but cunningly turning the opposite direction.

Stew had vomited against a fence, then gone off again after Coral. He couldn't find the pup in an hour so he'd gone home, and Coral was there already, with Della on the porch. "Where you been?" he asked. Della patted Coral and the puppy jumped up on her lap. "The bake sale."

After that he couldn't stop himself from asking that same question over and over, Where you been? Where you been? Where you been? If pretty Della went out to mail a letter, or get a quart of milk, or borrow sugar from Luann Nash next door, he asked the question by reflex on her return, without thought, Where you been? And of course she tired of this and began saying Where do you think I've been? and in years to come she either ignored the question altogether or came back flip, with some retort such as, Humpin' the Chinamen down at the laundry, or On a three-day toot with Frank Sinatra. He had tried to laugh sometimes, straining to find these comments funny, but more often he would suddenly become busy with the newspaper or start cleaning house, and say, Just curious is all.

Cynthia had been born the spring following the lie, and at first this had seemed a blessing, but the lie was loose in his mind now and not even a baby was safe from it.

These plants took more water than he had expected, so Stew went to the kitchen to refill the heron. While in there he knocked back a cup of coffee, then another. He intended to stay up all night cleaning. The time had come for it.

Just the thought of that man, that man and Della, and those three words of her answer, had ruined his marriage. Everything was affected.

He'd been a wrong father to Cynthia from the time her baby face began to take shape. She didn't look much like him, or Della, or any Lasseins or Rondeaus he'd ever seen. His uncle was blue-eyed, as was one of Della's brothers, but whenever he looked into Cynthia's big blues his chest would tighten. It was possible, just possible she was his, but by no means certain, and doubt is more evil than certainty, for a fact can be dealt with, got over, but doubt only feeds on itself and grows.

Donald was definitely his, for those jug ears and that goofy grin had stamped him as a Lassein more surely than a birth certificate. And Donald had been a happy kid—and why not, Stew had doted on him, giving him ninety-nine percent of his affections. Donald had grown up to be a confident sailor with a goofy grin, and was now a chief petty officer cruising the Indian Ocean.

Somehow Cynthia had known or felt his falseness with her. From babyhood she'd been shy, withdrawn, always watching, standing apart. He'd been gruff with her, never encouraging, and always short of temper. Several times he had spanked her too hard and once Della had smacked him for it. There had been tears shed in the dark over this, but he couldn't love her the same. Maybe not at all. When she was older she had told him his own feelings about her, right on the mark, in a ranting voice, saying he didn't love her, he never had, he only provided room and board.

She lived on the west side of St. Bruno now, in that sprawl of new streets and shopping centers out that way. Maybe three times a year he'd see her, and they'd have a drink and avoid the subject of their relationship, talking instead about new cars or gardening.

Stew set the water pitcher down and went to the phone. He dialed Cynthia's number, listening to the rings, hoping she'd answer rather than this beatnik what's-his-name she now lived with.

Like her mother before her, Cynthia had a weakness for shitheads. She married the first greasy rock 'n' roll shithead who asked, and after that shithead caught on with a NASCAR pit crew and split to work the racing circuit Cynthia had moped a while, then moved in with Wilkie, a much older jazz-buff shithead who could pay her bar tab and roll a tight marijuana cigarette. This Wilkie fella worked in radio as a late-night mellow voice, and whenever they spoke he called Stew Big Daddy.

When the phone was answered it was Cynthia, so he didn't have to tolerate that Big Daddy business tonight.

"Hullo?" Her voice was whisky deepened, and he could hear Wilkie's radio voice in the background.

"It's me, honey."

"Who? Who is this?"

"Your daddy. Stew."

"Oh. Dad. Shee! Dad, it's two o'clock."

Stew looked at the clock on the wall and saw she was thirty minutes ahead of the truth.

"I'm cleanin' house," he said.

"At two in the mornin'?"

"That's right. Why I called is, do you know which of your mother's plants is which? I've been waterin' them, honey, but I don't know their names."

The sound of ice cubes clicking came over the line.

"Are you kiddin', Dad? You called for that?"

"Well, they're your mother's plants, and I noticed they're not doin' so hot. I'd like to know them by name. Maybe I should play music for them—they like that, don't they?"

"Yeah, they like that." Cynthia laughed and spoke to someone else. Whoever it was also laughed, probably at goofy ol' Big Daddy's expense. "Dad, I'll come over Sunday and tell you their names. I gotta go now—you get on to bed, hear?"

She hung up. He didn't blame her. Maybe he'd do some sweeping.

He brought the broom in from the back porch and carried it into the front room. The lamp lights had revealed all these cobwebs on the walls, so he raised the broom and batted at the webs. As he swung the broom he thought of Mister Snake-hips, Mister Crooner of Deceit, and swung harder. They'd been friends once, a slick double-play combo on the sandlots of Frogtown, but Johnny Shade became a self-loving sport who left ruins in his snake-hipped wake.

One New Year's Eve, when the kids were in high school, Della had sat up by herself drinking gin, listening to old music on the hi-fi, dancing by herself, even singing along in a loud voice with certain songs. When finally she came to bed he'd sat up and watched her undress in front of the window.

She fumbled with buttons, and stumbled.

Della, he'd said, are you happy?

Della had yawned, then sat on the edge of the bed.

What do you think? she asked.

He'd watched her back for a moment, then lay down and pulled the quilt up over his face.

Pennsylvania 6–5000.

8

THE KID was almost always up first of a morning, so she'd pour the whisky and take it to him. She'd wait until her father let rip with a series of hacking coughs that signaled his awareness of the new day, then fetch him a glass of Maker's Mark to slow the shaking of his hands. Those shakes of his were awful to see if he didn't get his angel of sour mash right away, and on those occasions when he tried to pour his own, he made embarrassing messes.

On this morning Etta had fixed her face in the bathroom mirror, getting fancy with her kit of cosmetics. She put on eye shadow of a brooding black hue to match the crucifix hanging from her ear. No one color seemed to be enough for her mouth, so she'd used dabs of them all to make rainbow lips. Her dark rat-tail tresses were fairly well combed out, and she'd brushed the femme-flattop part of her hair to perfect level.

While John X. sawed logs on the couch in the front room, she sat cross-legged on her cot in the kitchen, the pink Joan Jett suitcase on her lap. She had the lid up to provide secrecy, and behind it her hands held five thousand dollars in fifties that she was counting for the ump-teenth time. Money that ran this high in amount had fabulous side effects, and as she snapped each bill onto the pile in the suitcase bottom her fingertips seemed to absorb greenback desires and rush them to her head. This much could buy: a CD player; one of those Ram-tough pick-up trucks; a cabin in Hawaii underneath a waterfall, like a cave, sort of, reached only by a secret bamboo ladder from below; an electric piano; a bass boat; a plane trip to Europe for her and Dad both.

But that last thing, the trip, was out. Mom had told her so, and told her so like she meant it. Randi Tripp, looking radiant in a sheer white dress, her black hair combed out and pulled back into a new look, had taken Etta by the hand and put the money into it. They were in the family Ford, pulled over to the curb near a highway ramp.

"He's your daddy," she'd said in a gust of peppermint breath, "and he cares for you, hon, but don't you *dare* let him know you have this money. Huh-uh. Under *no* circumstances. You keep it hid away, 'cause that's money for your college, baby."

Then Mom had put her out of the car and told her to walk from there to Enoch's Ribs and Lounge.

Etta closed the Joan Jett suitcase and slid it under the cot. She went to the window and stared out at the river, which was about the only hobby she had anymore. The wide brown flow surged south past the window and birds flew above it, high overhead.

Back home when her life had been regular she would be hearing songs by now. Possibly not whole songs but snatches for sure. Randi Tripp would be wandering about the trailer in her yellow robe working on her pipes, belting out a line or two about the way to San Jose, or little town blues, or impossible dreams the singer had. At any time of day Mom was likely to be singing, and if asked a question she frequently answered with a musical phrase.

If Etta wanted two dollars, the answer might be a growled, "Can't buy me love, oh, love, oh," etc.

Where's Dad? "Sooome-wheere, ov-er the rain-bow," etc.

On warm days Mom had liked to wash the Ford Escort on the little slab driveway next to the trailer. As soon as she came outside in her two-piece swimsuit, all the unemployed men in The Breeze-In Trailer Park, which was *all* of them but the one across the backyard, would rush out of doors to be handymen around their various trailers. The 'Bama Butterfly had a build on her that contributed greatly toward the general upkeep of the neighborhood, because she had a fetish about keeping that Escort spanking clean. She'd grab a big yellow sponge and squirt the hose and burst into song, turning the entire trailer park into a musical. She'd sponge the fenders clean and sing about the boogie-woogie bugle boy, or her and Bobby McGee, and when she rubbed the car down dry she shifted tempos and sang about strangers in the night, or whiter shades of pale. Once she had finished washing she would start rolling the hose up, and neighbor fellas would ask her to come over for iced tea, or beer, or champagne that'd been in the fridge since somebody's cousin's wedding. Randi Tripp never wanted any of what they offered, but she never was rude, she was nice, she smiled, she didn't step on their fantasies to the squashing point. No, she worked them like she would any other crowd, because to be a star they had to see you up there shining, so they could dream about you, but if they ever did reach up and actually touch a star and give it a squeeze, it'd just be revealed as a hot, hot rock and probably not worth a cover charge to see anymore.

That was the wonderful thing about Mom, Etta thought—she had her own fine opinion of herself and wasn't nobody could change it.

The twelve o'clock bells at St. Peter's had already sounded when John X. began coughing and harumphing into consciousness. Etta pulled the Maker's Mark down from the cupboard. She unscrewed the cap, then poured the whisky into a clear glass, filling it to the depth of four of her fingers. She raised the glass and smelled the sour mash and the scent caused her nose to wrinkle.

When Mom had been home she'd sometimes stop Etta from delivering these angels of whisky to John X. "You ain't a bartender, hon," she'd say. But Etta would listen to her daddy hacking in the other room and claim she didn't mind. Really. And, usually, after a few minutes more of hacks and groans, Mom would make a face like she'd broken another nail and say, "Oh, go on and coordinate your daddy, hon." Then Etta would take Daddy the whisky and his shaky hands would wrap around it, and not a word would be said until he'd drained the glass. Then he'd light a cigarette, and crack a joke that made her laugh, or tell a lie that interested her.

This morning on the river, in his son's house, was no different.

She carried the glass to his bed on the couch, and his hands trembled as he reached up and wrapped them around his morning angel of Maker's Mark.

John X. set the empty glass on the floor next to the couch. He patted his T-shirt where a cigarette pocket would hang on a button shirt, then grunted. On many mornings of late he could recall a ten-line conversation or a stolen kiss from back in 1949 in every detail, but could not find his cigarettes. He always seemed to be waking up in new spots for one thing, plus, those old acts and conversations came into his head so clearly that he sometimes wrung new meanings from them. Quite a few of the nuances and long silences that had baffled at the time now offered themselves up for interpretation in retrospect. They surely did. But that did not solve the real issue, which was, where'd I leave those smokes?

In this case the Chesterfields were discovered under the edge of the couch beside his eight-ball lighter and a full ashtray.

John X. lit one up, then grinned at Etta, who still stood there, just looking at him.

"Know why the crack in your butt goes long ways instead of sideways, kid?"

"So you don't go thump-thump-thump slidin' down stairs."

"Oh. I've told you that one, huh?"

"Mom did. She thought it was funny."

"I must've told it to her."

"Do you hate Mom?"

"Aw, please, no, kid. No, I don't really hate much of anything at all." John X. and his extremities were slowly pulling together. He was close to being together enough to stand and square up to yet another day. He looked at Etta with her thundercloud eye shadow and rainbow lips and said, "Ain't it about time for you to be in school, Etta?"

Etta sat on the arm of the couch.

"The school year hasn't started yet, Dad."

"It hasn't, huh?" John X. studied the burning end of his Chesterfield for a moment, then said, "I see these other kids with books and stuff—where're *they* goin'?"

"Oh, Dad," Etta said with a laugh. "Those kids go to Catholic schools, and I go to public."

"Uh-huh. When does public start? Seems like it used to start before the leaves all fell."

The black crucifix that hung from her ear was pinched between Etta's fingers, and she rubbed it.

"They don't make little kids chop cotton nowadays, Dad, so the school year is real different from when you went."

"Nah—they've all got machines now," he said. "So when *does* it start?"

"November," Etta said. She walked to the window and watched the endless flow of the big river. "I think ninth."

"Okay, then," John X. said. "November." He pulled his pants on without ever leaving the couch. "I'll see to it you're enrolled, kid. We got plenty of time." As he bent over to tie his black sneakers he saw the empty whisky glass. "School's a good thing for children," he said and lifted the glass. "Education." He held the glass above his head and tilted it to catch the bartender's eye. When he did, he grinned slightly, and said, "Another tiny angel, angel?"

When the workings of his body had come to seem totally familiar once more, John X. told Etta they'd grab a bite at The Catfish. He stuck his Balabushka cue under his left arm and told the kid that, while he wasn't precisely the Prince of Monaco, he figured he could finance a fish sandwich with a side of hush puppies.

Their walk through Frogtown to The Catfish Bar turned into a shambling guided tour, with John X. pausing to point out certain intersections or shacks or alleyways that he felt would be of special interest to his daughter. There was the corner he'd hung around starting at about her age; the alleyways he'd always preferred to open streets; the shack his boyhood best friend, Butter Racine, had lived in with his crazy old man, Crazy Racine, who was the first actual drug addict John X. could recall, with Butter becoming the second.

Etta's reactions to these points of interest were restrained, very low-key, and her audible response was either uh-huh or mm-hmm.

John X. called another halt near a busy corner that had a new gas station slash minimart on it.

"Right there," he said, pointing at the fuel pumps, "there didn't used to be a gas station. No, m'am. There used to be a little nite spot called Half-a-Heaven, with a sawdusted dance floor, and plenty of dark, moody corners."

"You liked to go there, Dad?"

"Oh, my yes," he said. "Everybody did. The whole world packed into that little joint on a good night." John X. lit a cigarette and stared at the gas station. He was still wearing clothes from a dead man's wardrobe, and though nothing fit quite right, somehow everything was comfortable. "Kid, let me tell you, women wore flowers in their hair in them days. To dances, bars, whatnot. Their hair would be long and hanging, but organized, you know, not running loose, and there'd be a big bright sweet flower of some sort planted in their hair. Just above the ear, usually, where a fella's face would nuzzle during a dance. They'd be red, or white, maybe yellow or pink — definitely sweet."

"Flowers?" Etta said. "I don't think that's cool anymore."

John X. looked down at Etta for a moment, then nodded once.

"Probably not," he said. "But it was not considered corny, then, kid, believe me."

They walked on down the sidewalk, and a minute later he added, "*Fetch*ing is more what it was considered."

The route to The Catfish led the old man and the kid past the intersection of Lafitte and Perry where Ma Blanqui's Pool House occupied the corner portion of a brick row house.

"That's where the mother of your brothers lives, kid."

"Are we goin' in?"

"Not today, kid. Let's get a move on."

As they walked past, Etta asked, "Did you do her like Mom done you?"

"I don't know. I guess. One mornin' I came to in Beaufort, South Carolina, and it was clear we'd drifted apart. I realized I was nowhere near done driftin', neither, and damn few wives can live with that."

"Mm-hmm. What's she like now?"

"She's an opinionated older woman, I imagine." John X. patted his daughter on the head so she'd follow him as he crossed the street. "Makes a mighty fine peach kuchen as I recall. Nice long hair to her shoulders. She raised your brothers up pretty decent."

The sign with the debauched blue catfish on it was now in sight.

"They seem sort of *rough*, Dad."

"Well," he said, shrugging.

"Tip cooks good coffee, though," Etta said.

"That's what I mean," John X. said.

John X. Shade, pool hustler in decline, was looking for a price on his Balabushka cue. Over the years he had hocked the cue perhaps twenty-five times, and on a few occasions left it temporarily in the custody of fellas who'd had his Number. He set the case on the bar of The Catfish and opened it. The cue lay in slots lined with green felt, and John X. rolled his hand along the fine pretty length of it. He rubbed his fingers over a slight score in the wood just below the ferrule that had already been there when he'd gotten the cue at a Johnson City Jamboree he'd played in back when his hands could form a firm bridge, and stroke smoothly, even brilliantly at times, and every honky-tonk or corner beer joint with an eight-foot table had represented a career opportunity.

"What'll you give me for this, son? You know what it's worth, don't you?"

Tip leaned over the counter from his side of the bar. He had a huge white apron on, and smelled strongly of after-shave.

"I know that stick is worth plenty to somebody who feels like payin' plenty for it," he said. "That person wouldn't be me, though."

"Why, hell," John X. said, "it's worth plenty to anybody with good sense. George Balabushka is dead, son, so this stick is like good earth as an investment—I mean, they won't be makin' any more of it."

This dickering with his own boy was not exactly fun, but fortunately there wasn't much of a crowd to see it. The lunch rush had passed. In the back two biker couples wearing Harley T's and tattoos lingered over their empty plates and full mugs to discuss the many traffic tickets they had earned but not paid, motorcycle maintenance, and similar domestic trivia. Three Catfish regulars, two of them older males, the other a squat, sulky woman in her thirties, sat nearer the door, each tippling at a separate table, though occasionally a few words were passed among them. Etta was down at the end of the bar sitting on a stool beside Tip's hippie chick, the kid eating hush puppies while Gretel read a tabloid.

Stew Lassein sat brooding over a beer glass two stools away from the girls. He was wearing white pants and a white shirt and a wide gaudy tie loose around his neck, appropriately duded up for an ice cream social that'd ended forty years ago. His normally pale skin was even paler, rinsed out, and he seemed in need of sleep.

That guy always was too square for this wicked round world, John X. thought. He actually liked Lawrence Welk and Kate Smith! And became a *foreman*, for cryin' out loud. He's now ending up exactly where the middle of the road leads you.

Let *that* sink in.

"This *is* a handsome thing," Tip said, looking at the cue. "I don't play much, or care to, but I can tell it's special." He lifted the butt from the case and hefted it. "Let me see you take a few shots with it, Johnny."

"No, no, now Christ, Tippy," John X. said, "I can't run six balls anymore. I might jaw out a hanger, even. It's terrible."

"Just shoot so I can see the stick in action before I put up money for it."

"Are you tryin' to embarrass me, boy? Is that it?"

Tip raised a hand to his long brown hair, flicked a stray strand behind his ear, then smoothed it back into greased formation. His face was down, as if studying the cue.

"Well, now, look," he said, "I'll hold this stick for you, Dad, and spot you fifty against it."

"Fifty?" John X. reached for the cue, then began to screw it together. The Balabushka had a blue twine grip, shiny brass fittings, and subtle cross-hatching on the lower shaft, but was otherwise austere and purposeful. "I need a hundred—maybe it'd help if you saw me run a few balls."

"I'll rack 'em," Tip said.

When John X. and Tip went toward the pool table, Gretel looked up from her reading. She'd been hip-deep into a story about a man in central Florida whose garden was attracting attention as a walk of fame because he had this weird knack for growing edibles, mainly potatoes and melons, that seemed to resemble certain movie stars, especially Curly from the Three Stooges and Shelley Winters, though he'd produced a far wider range of recognizably famous body parts, almost all of which were noses or breasts. There was a picture of a sweet potato that *did* sort of look like Curly, and the man held up two honeydews that had odd shapes for melons but perfect shapes for a starlet's breasts, and the man called them Marilyn. The man said the garden was a miracle, a pure gift, though the article seemed to poke some fun at him.

"Phooey," Gretel said. She then reached over and rubbed her hand across Etta's flattop, causing the hairs to bristle, and said, "I really do dig your hairstyle."

"My mom picked it," Etta said. "But I wear it."

"Don't you like it?"

Etta shrugged, nodded, shrugged again.

"I'm used to it," she said. She rolled another hush puppie through a puddle of tartar sauce, then popped it into her mouth. Gretel loomed over her, hugely pregnant in a red shift, her gray highland eyes looking resigned but alert. The scar on Gretel's cheek was fingernail wide, pink and mysterious, perhaps even romantic in origin. It started about an inch below the outside corner of her right eye, plowed a straight row at an angle across her cheek, and tailed off a fraction above the corner of her mouth. As Etta chewed the hush puppie she slowly raised her hand toward Gretel's cheek, stopping shy of contact. She swallowed hard. "How'd you get that scar?"

Gretel put the tips of four fingers lengthwise on the scar.

"Yah-weh hung it on me," she said somberly, "for not payin' atten-tion. I was s'posed to be steerin'."

"Yah-who?" Etta asked.

"Yah-weh. That's God in other places."

"Could I touch it?" Etta asked. "I'll take care not to scratch."

Gretel pulled her fingertips from the scar and raked back her blond hair.

"Help yourself," she said. "It's different."

Oh so lightly Etta touched her fingers to the scar, then slid them along the track of proud flesh. Her young face and bright eyes reflected her enthrallment.

"Wow," she said. "Holy freakin' wow! It's slick, ain't it? Slick like satin."

Laughing softly, Gretel leaned her face down to Etta's touch.

"I've come to love the feel of it," she said. "Spiritually, it's quite a reminder."

"It's slick like satin," Etta said again. Then: "Say, could I rub your butterfly, too?"

"Sure," Gretel said. "The Monarch just feels like skin, though."

In a gruff, tired tone, Stew leaned toward Gretel and said, "Tell me about it. Tell me about scars from not payin' attention. I got mine that very same way."

Gretel smiled at him, and Etta said, "Where is it?"

"What?"

"Your scar."

Stew held a hand to his chest, then tapped a finger over his heart.

"Uh-huh," Etta said. "That scar is what set you cryin' last night."

Stew said, "Your daddy doesn't love you, li'l girl. I feel I have to tell you that. Your daddy doesn't love nobody he don't see in the mirror when he shaves."

"Now that is harsh talk, mister," Gretel said. "You hush up."

"Li'l girl needs to know," Stew said. He was avoiding eye contact. "Things need to be brought out, you see."

"Hush up."

"It's for the good of all."

"Mom used to say the same thing," Etta said.

"Listen to your mom, li'l girl."

"I didn't believe her, neither."

"What do you call love anyhow?" Gretel asked. "Answer me that, mister, then I'll hear you out. But if you can't answer me that, you should hush up."

The trio fell silent at this, and went back to their individual contemplations: Gretel, the tabloid; Stew, the past; Etta, the number of faces in Dad's mirror.

Down toward the rear of the room, at the one pool table, John X. stood slouching with the cue in his hands, watching as a simple cut-shot on the nine missed the corner pocket by a full inch.

"Over-cut," he said. He lined up a cross-table bank on the three ball, and stroked it toward the side-pocket, but it went wide and skidded down-table. "Are these rails soft?"

"Maybe," Tip said. "That could be it."

John X. made two hangers in a row, though his stroke was shaky even on them.

"More like it," he said. Then he leaned over the table, his eyes watering, bridge wavering, and missed six straight puppy shots, not even slopping one in. "What'd I tell you, son?" He began to unscrew the cue as he led the way back to the bar. At the bar he put the cue in the case and snapped it shut. "Terrible. Fuckin' terrible. I'm cursed. The pool god hates me, and that's a spiteful, petty son-of-a-bitch when he hates you. I told you it was terrible."

Tip set the cue under the bar.

"You didn't lie," he said. "You told it like it was."

John X. rattled the ice in his glass.

"I'm cursed," he said. "I should've got a job forty years ago. Maybe fifty. That's right. A *job*. But I thought, Work? The only things that like *work* are donkeys, and they turn their ass to it. Where's the future in work when I could use that stick, there, and hold the table for three— four hours at a whack—know what I'm tryin' to say, Tippy?"

"Sure. You're cursed."

"Nail on the head, son."

Tip went to the register and slapped together some fives and tens, then spread the money on the bar.

"There you go," he said to John X. "And, Johnny, I ain't your mother or nothin', but you think maybe you should eat something?"

"Might be I'll eat a peach later," John X. said jauntily. He scooped up all the money but a twenty. He put the roll in his pocket, then waved the twenty overhead, swishing the bill through the air before slapping it on the bar. "Refreshments for all, Tippy! Set everybody up. Get those gorgeous gals at the end of the bar another of whatever they're drinkin', and give ol' Stew, there, a nice libation on me."

Stew snorted derisively.

"I don't want a lie-bation on you," he said.

John X. sidled down the bar toward Stew, but left a few feet of polished bar rail between them. He tapped out a smoke and fired up. "Somethin' wrong with my money, Stewart?"

"Don't call me Stewart. It's insulting the way you say it."

"That beer in front of you looks dead, Stew," John X. said with a shrug. "Hey, Tip, a couple of live whiskies over here."

Bent over the broad surface of the bar, with his white attire, white hair, and pale skin, his thin lips curled back from a mouthful of bright expensive teeth, Stew had the appearance of a truculent ghost. A ghost with a grudge.

"I won't take a drink bought with bad money," he said.

Tip set the drinks in front of the two old men, his head bent to hear their conversation.

"Now how can money be bad?" John X. asked. He spit on his hands, then ran his fingers through his wavy hair. "If it spends, it spends."

"This'll spend," Tip said, and picked up the twenty.

Stew snatched his drink aloft and dumped it to the floor.

"If money ain't worked for," he said, "then it ain't good."

The whisky made a puddle on the rough wood of the floor. John X. tapped the toes of his black sneakers in the puddle.

"Criminentlies," he said as he smeared the whisky underfoot, "that was a buck and a half, Stew. This ain't VJ Day anymore, slick. Drinks ain't a quarter no more, with a beer back and a pig's foot thrown in free."

"Your money is bad money," Stew said. "Which is the only breed of money a bad man spends."

"How bad a man am I if I'm buyin' you a drink?"

"There's guilt in you, Johnny."

"I think I'll pause to let *that* sink in, slick."

The bar was made of dark sturdy wood, and behind it there was a narrow passage backed by a small mirror, and a three-tiered display of liquor bottles. Sunlight came through the front windows and glinted off the bottles and the mirror.

"I *can* say I never *wanted* to be a bad fella," John X. said. He lifted his drink and held the whisky to his nose, inhaling the scent. "But, I've got to admit, sometimes opportunity was in such a lenient position I couldn't turn my back to it."

"I have it in mind to break your face," Stew said. He made no move, but stayed hunched over, talking into his glass of dead beer. "You always was Mister *So*-handsome—like there wasn't a man on earth handsomer'n you."

"Well, now, I always figured any man better lookin' than me was just a li'l *too* pretty—know what I mean? Like, say, Tyrone Power."

"And a funny talker, too," Stew said. "I never liked that about you neither. It's somethin' girls work at. I never liked it in you. Another reason to break your face. That makes two."

"Do you need more?" John X. asked. He tossed his drink back, and swiveled to face Stew. "Maybe I could tell you some more, slick, if you have this terrible need to add 'em up."

"I know your whole story," Stew said. "You used to screw about every third girl over ten years old in this neighborhood. Tell 'em lies, or true things they dream of hearin', then whisk their li'l cotton panties to their knees."

"Jealous?" John X. asked. He glanced toward Etta. "That's horseshit, anyhow." He smiled at Stew. "It's horseshit I actually wish was true—I could think back on such events and grin."

"Monique wasn't but about twelve when you married her, you rat."

"Rat? You better watch it. And she was *fourteen*—there's a difference."

"That's three," Stew said, then spun from his stool, and belted John X. with the bitter haymaker he'd been wanting to land ever since Coral the Beagle slipped her leash. This sucker punch landed on the button, and John X. was propelled from his stool and onto his ass.

John X. wobbled up from the floor, his eyes fixed on Stew. He spit theatrically, then raised his shaky old dukes.

"Why you sissy," he said. "I'll whup you 'til you pooch."

"Hah!" Stew barked. He then reached to his mouth and pulled his dentures out. He set them beside his beer. "Awl bwek oo flace!"

"Hey, hey," Tip said. He'd been pouring sodas for the ladies but now he rushed up the bar. "What is this shit, Johnny?"

John X. shot a pretty left jab plunk onto Stew's nose.

"Dinn hur!" Stew blurted, without the usual translation that dentures made. "Midda Wo-ansom!"

One of the bikers in the back laughed, then said, "Scope the old scrappers!"

Etta and Gretel got off their stools and stood watching the fracas, holding hands.

John X., in his comfortable suit of dead man's clothes, circled left, dukes held high, while Stew, in his apparitional attire, planted his feet and looked to land a bomb. John X. tried another jab but was short by a foot, and Stew lunged forward, his wild swing missing totally, but the two old noggins collided. Both men turned away, rubbing at their foreheads while making grunts of pain.

Tip wiped his hands on his apron and said, "Get him, Johnny. Kick his ass."

Stew recovered first and banged a right to John X.'s shoulder. John X. winced, then began to bounce on his toes, attempting lateral movement, but all the bouncing caused him some dizziness and he appeared ready to swoon.

"I got another reason for you," he said angrily. "Della told me I danced better'n you!"

"Huh-uh!"

"Oh, yeah, she did—at the Half-a-Heaven."

"Huh-uh!"

"On a slow dance, too."

Stew moved forward, his gnarled fists clenched and held low to his sides, and John X. stuck another jab to his beak, drawing blood, but Stew's low fists hooked to the belly, and John X. landed on his ass again, looking up.

Darting quickly to the bar, Stew reinserted his dentures so his insult would be intelligible. "That's the power of a *man!*" he said, then slipped the dentures out again and set them on the bar.

"Man?" John X. muttered as he stood. "Why, you're just a *baby* fartin' around in a *man's* suit. You always was, Stew."

Though his aching ribs caused him to hunch forward somewhat, John X. was slightly bouncing again, attempting to employ the tactical strategy of Billy Conn, his idol of yore. He slid left to right and back again, then pumped out a double jab, landing one on Stew's upper lip and nose. Blood spots began to appear on the shirtfront of Stew's apparitional attire, but suddenly John X. grimaced and crouched to one knee, from which position he vomited onto the brass foot rail of the bar.

Gretel and Etta had stood watching the old men fight, Etta rubbing her flattop nervously, Gretel massaging her pregnant hump. Now Etta pulled her hand free of Gretel and ran to John X. Instant tears appeared on her face.

"Dad!" She flung herself on John X. from behind, her arms around his neck. "Dad!"

Gretel said, "Can I stop this? Can I put a stop to this?" She approached Stew. "Aren't you ashamed?" she said to his face. "You're bleedin' bad—what's violence settle, anyhow?"

Some sort of retort came from Stew, but the words were mysterious and weakly offered.

"Fight! Fight! Fight!" the biker couples chanted.

"Here, Gretel," Tip said, and handed her some napkins.

Gretel took the napkins and began to swab Stew's bloody nose. He stood there and let her, making weird humming sounds as her fingers wiped his nose and lips of blood.

After a moment he pulled away from her. His eyes were wild and red. He slid his teeth back into place, his hands trembling and his breath shallow. He looked toward the door and shook his head.

"Oh, I don't know!" he said. "I don't know still!"

Then he walked past John X., to the door, and out.

When the door closed the ladies helped John X. up, then sat him on a stool. Etta clung to him while Gretel took a napkin to the vomit around his mouth.

"Maker's Mark," he said. "A double."

This entire event seemed to strike Tip as humorous, and as he set the drink before his father, he said, "As a dad maybe you have been a pretty sorry deal, but as an ol' fucker to get drunk with and have around, Johnny, you're a fistful of fun. Know it?"

"I'm touched," John X. said.

"What's his problem with your face, anyhow? I couldn't catch his drift about that."

After a soothing sip, John X. said, "See, son, in years gone by I always was your basic average citizen of the type who should've been arrested but only once in a while was. Folks of a certain sort *will* hold that against a man. I guess I did this, I did that, and now and again some other thing altogether. I wore flashy clothes for Frogtown, and my pockets didn't have no fishhooks in 'em, and the neighborhood girls liked that about me. And maybe not too many mirrors cracked when I looked in 'em, and I think girls liked that, too. Flashy clothes, no fishhooks in my pockets, and bein' a dreamboat were things quite a few fellas *did not* care for about me, but girls did, and girls that liked me, well, as a rule, I found things I liked about them, too. A nice shape, or lovely hair of any hue, brown eyes, blue eyes, green eyes, a wet voice, a cute gap in their front teeth — if they liked my style I liked theirs. Stew, for one, never could stand me for my bigheartedness."

"Long time to hold a grudge," Tip said.

John X. turned on his stool, and the ladies were standing close by. He stroked Etta's hair, while looking into Gretel's face.

"That scar is hard to get out of my mind," he said. "It makes you look like a woman of intrigue, a visitor from faraway places."

Gretel grinned and shuffled her feet.

"I wish," she said.

John X. raised his glass in salute.

"To you two gorgeous kids," he said, then tossed back the whisky. He stood and started walking toward the door, Etta hanging onto his coattail. He pulled the door back and stood in the opening. He looked out onto Lafitte Street, then up at the bright hot sun. "It may be that all I ever did with my life was to the bad, but, damn, son, I sure would like to do it all again."

9

As he'd driven up from the coast and through the night, Lunch Pumphrey had trusted totally to the map of geography retained in his memory, and thus ended up well away from his destination. The atlas in his mind had gotten foggy at the 'Bama border, but not scarily so, and he'd plunged on into the dark night only to finally find himself in an actual place that wasn't on his map at all. No way could he reconcile himself to this lost position. He hadn't seen any sign whatever of Memphis, and he was positive he had to pass through there before he hit the Big River. Or, if not Memphis, certainly Arkansas, or some such southern state whose name he'd blanked on entirely, but that would still be there to pass beneath his wheels anyhow. Yet Memphis had not appeared, nor had any expected state name known or blanked.

Early in the A.M., with merely a clouded moon above, Lunch admitted his lostness to himself and took to studying road signs so intensely that the Bug faded off the blacktop, through a ditch, then into a billboard that said See Rock City. The right headlight was blinked. Metal had screamed from the fender and rolled down to bog the front tire, which had been cut open and hissed angrily for a moment.

Lunch leaned his unhurt head to the steering wheel, and his lips kissed the horn.

"I'm sorry," he said.

It was very early in a new day but Lunch was already on Salem number three before he'd found a farmhouse and called a tow truck. The wrecker hauled the Bug into a place called Natchez, and Lunch found himself stuck there until Virgil or Bill, the head grease monkeys, could get around to fulfilling his mechanical needs.

As the sun rose Lunch learned that he had found the river, at least, and the town itself was one of those places that bubbled over with history. For a while Lunch stood around in Virgil and Bill's station, but there were others milling around there, too, which meant he had a long wait coming to him. So he set his snap-brim hat atop his head at a rakish angle and went for a stroll along a sidewalk on a bluff that overlooked the huge brown water.

The bluff was grassy, with rock-walled flower beds, and fallen leaves seemed to be picked up as they fell, for there were only a few on the ground. The day was weirdly hot. It should have been jacket weather, but it was bare skin weather, and Lunch sweated in his all-black attire. A kindly woman gave him one of the leaflets she'd been fanning her face with, and he found a park bench to squat on while he read it.

Before reading the leaflet he opened his eyes to the wide view of the river and let himself absorb the wonder of it. Only those immigrants who dive for sponges, or a South Seas type of person, could swim across it. The water was that wide, the current that strong. A shitload of birds flew above this majestic landmark, and a barge floated on it. Lunch felt that he might possibly come to where he could care for a body of water like that. Especially when these birds are strung all along above it, and others fill the trees on the banks, which makes our feathery friends seem like they are an audience swooping to take seats at an upcoming event of a pleasing sort.

"That's a river, ain't it?" a man's voice said.

A man and woman in their thirties sat on the next bench. They'd been at Virgil and Bill's also.

"Good view," Lunch said.

The leaflet was on blue paper, and he picked it up to read. The whole thing concerned Natchez and the Natchez Trace. There were suggestions on where to go, where to eat, where to sleep, what times the seven-dollar horse-drawn carriages took off, and what special spots they trotted past. The few lines about history had a section that stood out, and Lunch read it twice: "John Thompson Hare, the hoodlum, was among the first who shrewdly saw the possibilities of banditry on the Trace. The Trace made him rich, but moody. In its wilderness he went to pieces, saw visions, was captured, and hanged."

"Damn," Lunch said. "This place makes you think."

The man on the next bench said, "It's got a bizarre history that's awfully attractive."

"Our forefathers," Lunch said, "were a rugged bunch."

"Oh, yeah, buddy," the man said. "The dudes down here in historical days were truly some rough cobs. No doubt about it."

"Some of it's sad, too," Lunch said.

He stood and approached the couple and held his hand out to the man, who was large. They shook, then Lunch extended his hand to the woman, who was knitting away at a ball of red yarn. She took his hand and slightly over-held it.

"Rich Moody," Lunch said, "pleased to meet you."

"Our name is Smith," the man said, then the woman said, "John and Mary Smith," then they both said, "and we ain't kiddin'!" This bit was well rehearsed, and the Smiths giggled at the end.

"That's cute," Lunch said.

"Thanks," said John Smith. "We hail from corn country, north of Cedar Rapids, south of Waterloo."

"Uh-huh. I saw you at Virgil and Bill's."

"That's right. We saw you there, too. Is that bruise on your face from your wreck?"

Lunch touched his fingers to his face.

"Oh, yeah," he said.

"We were in one, too," Mary said. "We got blindsided by a local resident."

"That's true," John Smith said. "We've been on vacation, but, as it turns out, we've made money on the whole deal." He inclined his large form toward Lunch. "The other driver was tipsy, see, but well-to-do, and her family paid off in cash an hour ago."

Mary reached into her handbag and held up a flat thick booklet of money.

"This'll spend," she said, and her husband went "Hee-hee."

At this moment Lunch decided to scrutinize John and Mary Smith.

John Smith had the complete barnyard of personal characteristics: ox-sized, goose-necked, cow-eyed, a hog gut, probably mule-headed, and clearly goaty of appetite. His hair was black and worn in the style of an early Beatle. He sported a thin decadent mustache that suggested he just might have a few perversions he wouldn't *insist* on keeping private. Possibly John Smith would pass for kinda cute at an I-80 truckstop.

The distaff half of the Smiths from corn country acted meek but talked from the side of her mouth. Her fingers were diligent, clicking those needles, knitting something red that would surely be warm. Her hair was the color Rayanne's had been, the color of corn ready for harvest, not too long, pulled back into a ponytail. Mary Smith's hips were thin, maybe even skinny, but somehow her breasts were huge presences behind a white T-shirt that advertised The Old Creamery Theater.

"This heat," Lunch said. "Whew! Could I interest y'all in somethin' cool to drink?"

Mary looked up at him and smiled, then turned to her husband.

"I *love* the way they talk down here."

"I know it," John Smith said. Then, to Lunch, "Hell, yes, little buddy, lead the way."

"That's a problem," Lunch said. "I just got here. I don't know the way."

"Oh, well," John Smith said, "we've been here two days, so we'll think of a spot."

"The saloon," Mary said, still knitting. "The old one under the hill."

Lunch pulled a wad of cash from his pocket.

"I'll get the first round," he said.

John Smith clapped his hands together.

"By golly, it looks like you can afford to," he said. He patted Lunch on the shoulder. "Follow us, little buddy."

The Smiths walked Lunch to Natchez Under-the-Hill. They pointed out several antique houses and lampposts that dated from the era when the town was jammed with river men, whores, bandits, slumming gentry, and assorted frontier ruffians. It was the memory of those lively times that prompted tourists to come here and gawk at surviving reminders of that rough-and-ready past.

The tavern they chose was called the Under-the-Hill, and it had been opened originally back when the very term Under-the-Hill meant buckets of grog, long knives, loose women, expansionist dreams, and sudden endings. The walls did seem to give off some faint echoes from key events in the lives of people who'd been dead a century or more.

The threesome sat at a table near a window, the river in easy view.

"We were here yesterday," John Smith said. "What're you drinking, Rich?"

"I'm a Bud man," he said, "and a Cub fan."

"He knows our motto!" Mary exclaimed, not addressing Lunch directly.

"I heard it," said John Smith. "Everybody back home is a Cub fan— I didn't know they were down here."

"Cable," Lunch said. "When Harry Caray says somethin', he speaks for me, too."

"Grrr-eat," said Mary. "I think I'll have a Bud with you guys."

Over three bottles of beer Lunch got the story of John and Mary Smith's lives, which were, though dull in the telling, extremely detailed. The details were relentlessly tacked on to the main body of the dull narrative, and there were several sidetracks in the tale where the Smiths took shots at each other over minor domestic disputes. He didn't pick up his socks, or do dishes, or cook anything but red-hot chili and spareribs, while she irked him by buying cheap beer instead of good beer, letting her sister visit for up to six weeks at a time, and by singing Patsy

Cline songs in such a horrible manner that they were ruined for him as tunes, even when Patsy herself sang them. Late in the tale Lunch found himself appointed as the final judge in a wrangle that the Smiths had kept going for most of their marriage, to wit: should coffee be electro-perked and taken black so it tasted like *coffee* (him), or dripped and taken with milk to avoid throat cancer (her).

Three beers and no sleep had Lunch ready to feel like a judge, and he ruled on the coffee case by saying, "Electro-perk it, and serve it black, but make sure he gets ten minutes or more of titty-suck per diem, and that should make things *just* all around."

For a moment the only sound was knitting needles clicking. Then Mary looked directly at Lunch for a change. Her eyes were green and hot on him. She said, "That is an interesting answer. Black coffee and titty-suck—we never thought of it, but it's good."

John Smith had his head tilted back, and a lopsided smile put a kink in his mustache.

"Hee, hee," he went. "She's got the titties for it, doesn't she?"

Lunch glided his beer bottle along the wet spots on the table.

"No gentleman would answer that question," he said. "But she damned sure does."

Mary laughed and said, "He's the *cutest* little man."

John Smith again made the noise of "Hee, hee, hee." Then he said, "Let's us all go for a carriage ride—what say?"

They caught a carriage on Canal Street. Lunch and the Smiths spread across the seat, with Mary in the middle, still knitting. The carriage was open to the air and hot sun, pulled by a dark horse that didn't seem anxious for the work. The driver, a pudgy young man in regular modern clothes, except for a funky period hat, called out the landmarks and special memories of the town in a loud voice and tended to get a mite hysterical about old-timey architecture and certain ancient bloody deeds.

Lunch found the ancient bloody deeds to be especially interesting. The Natchez Trace had been nicknamed the Devil's Backbone, which was a phrase so strong it belonged in a song, perhaps as the chorus. The Devil's Backbone had been run all up and down by bottom-born, forceful types of fellas who Lunch wouldn't've minded drinkin' a few Buds with. Their criminal actions, and the still remembered drama of their bloody lives, spooked feelings awake and made them flit about in Lunch's deeper parts.

The carriage rattled past this old house and that old house, all of them with the proper names of people, and the horse and driver cut around pick-up trucks hauling pumpkins, RVs of the retired, and Japanese automobiles. Only Mary really liked the house stuff (this was the Smiths' third carriage ride in two days), while Lunch and John Smith both studiously blotted their minds with the historical gore and all its fine points.

When the carriage ride ended the trio went into a tavern called Mike Fink's. Mike Fink was another riverfront legend, one who had apparently talked a whole lot of boastful trash that had been passed down. His daddy was an alligator, his mammy was a hurricane, he ate gunpowder for breakfast, and whipped whole armies with his farts, and so on. Several of his allegations in this vein had been painted on weathered boards and tacked to the walls.

Lunch and the Smiths stuck to Bud, with the addition of burgers, the Smiths buying, since, as it now came out, they had thirty-six hundred dollars on them.

Though she didn't seem to look at him much, Mary made some observations about Lunch. For one thing, she said the bruise on his face looked older than from last night. Lunch answered by saying the human body is a funny piece of work. A while after that she pointed a knitting needle at his feet, then his hands.

"He has the itsy-bitsiest hands and feet—have you noticed?"

John Smith made that hee, hee, hee sound again, which was becoming an irritant.

"Haw, haw, haw," Lunch said, as an antidote.

"Well you *are* small, little buddy," John Smith said. "Like Little Harpe, who was the brother of Big Harpe, who as brothers murdered and robbed countless travelers along the Devil's Backbone. I've read up on it."

"Little and Big who?"

"Harpe," John Smith said. "One was known as Little and the other as Big, and the different gangs along the Devil's Backbone considered both the Harpes to be beyond the pale, just too darn strange in their crimes. There was a freaked-out style to the way they murdered and carried on that shook these other murderers up to where they avoided Little and Big as much as possible."

The thing Mary was knitting had begun to take shape as a sturdy knee-sock. From the side of her mouth she said, "Tell him about the baby, and the bodies."

"The Harpes had some women with them, little buddy, and naturally they ended up with kids. But Big was real uptight, and when a baby, his *own* baby, mind you, bothered him by squalling and keeping everybody awake, why, Big snatched the baby up by its heels and smashed its head against a tree trunk."

"No shit?" Lunch said. He was listening raptly, as if to his own family history. "What'd Little do?"

"I think they all went to sleep," John Smith said. "The squalling was over. Their great talent, though, was the disappearance of bodies. The folks they murdered didn't get found very often. See, the Harpes were farm boys, mean farm boys, and they'd learned some things slaughtering animals back home. You take a body of a person, hee, hee, hee, and you split it through the gut, the tummy, scoop out the innards and toss in rocks, see, then kick it in the river. It won't come up. The gas escapes through the split as the victim rots, instead of ballooning up, and with the rocks in the tummy, it just sits in the riverbed and bottom-feedin' fish nibble away all evidence of the crime."

"Gee," Lunch said. "History is really okay."

"History was always my best subject," John Smith said.

"Mine was recess."

"I guess that's why I'm tellin' this, and you're hearin' it."

"I guess." Lunch checked the clock on the wall. "Those sure were wild times."

"That they were, little buddy," John Smith said. "I must say I think it'd've been a real adventure to be down here in those days. I really do. I expect I could've handled myself among that sort pretty well. I've got the size, plus, I can *fight* if I got to."

Mary said, "You ain't been in a fight since you smacked Alice Buchtel's boy for throwin' a snowball at your Caprice."

"But in *those* days, hon, I would've had to be in them all the time, which would improve my hand-to-hand skills. I *can* fight when I have to. And when I've *had* to I've ended up on top as a rule."

"Oooh," Lunch said. "I can't imagine such violence. A little fella like me, why, it wouldn't do for me to mix in violence like that."

Mary said, "You know his tiny boots look like they'd fit *me*."

"Please don't wrestle me down and take my clothes from me, ma'am. Especially my boots."

"He's cute. He's the *cutest* little man."

When the trio had finished their burgers and Buds, Lunch wowed them by showing off his left forearm tattoo that read Cubs Win! They gushed about that for a moment, then Lunch said he had to go check on the status of his Bug at Virgil and Bill's. The Smiths needed an update on their Caprice, so they all walked to the station together.

Neither Virgil or Bill wore name tags, but for some reason Lunch thought it was Virgil he talked to. This possible Virgil said that Lunch had lucked out, and at a nearby car cemetery they'd found a fender for the Bug, though it was a flat black color. A new tire had been slapped on, balanced, and aligned. The dents in the front bonnet had been pinged out fairly well, but not perfectly.

"I'll see to that myself," Lunch said. "What do I owe you?"

With the tow charge, the tire, the fender, the labor, and the inscrutable miscellaneous, the total bill was equal to the take from three convenience-store robberies. But the immediate future seemed so rich in prospects that Lunch paid up without any complaint.

The deal on the Smiths' Caprice was less certain. It was set to roll as soon as a side door was put on, but the side door was on order from Vicksburg and late in arriving.

"This lazy ol' river has slowed these people down," Mary said. "I want to go back to the room and get some rest. My eyes hurt."

"I hate to see good folks like you turn spiteful on the region," Lunch said. "Folks down here are nice as pie. I mean, the sun'll set in two hours, and my car is runnin'. How's about I carry y'all to dinner in the country? A mom-and-pop place out at the crossroads. The moon'll be on the water."

"Well," John Smith said. He looked at Mary, who nodded. "It's a date, but only if you let us pay, okay?"

Lunch waited mostly on a park bench for the sun to set. He did some scurrying around the grounds. A snort of cocaine added flaky clarity to his thoughts. For amusement he had the river and the birds in view. Pretty soon he needed to push on to St. Bruno, which he'd learned was an easy drive away. But first, dinner with the Smiths from corn country. When it was dark he went into action.

He drove the Bug at a slow speed toward The Cromworth Motel, where the Smiths had a room. Their room was off the road, and as he cruised back that way he saw them, standing in front of room one eleven, both holding pink wine coolers, staring at the small swimming pool in the courtyard.

Lunch parked a foot short of their kneecaps. He leaned his head, hat and all, out the window.

"Howdy, howdy," he said. "Feelin' hungry?"

"Famished," Mary Smith said. She had her blond hair fanned out around her face, and she wore a short red cocktail dress that showed her fit, firm gams on one end, and a mile of creamy cleavage on the other. "I could eat your black hat with ketchup."

"We can do better'n that," Lunch said. He kept the clutch put in and revved the Bug engine. "This mom-and-pop place Virgil told me about *special*-izes in catfish and chicken."

"Big platters, I hope," John Smith said as he opened the passenger door.

"They serve family style," Lunch said. "You'll get your gut stuffed alright."

"Hee, hee, hee."

The Smiths tossed their wine coolers into a trash can, then climbed into the Bug. Because of his size John Smith crawled into the back seat, which he needed all of. Mary rode shotgun, her large bag of knitting resting on her lap.

"In case I get bored," she said, tapping the bag.

"You won't," Lunch said.

Lunch pulled away from The Cromworth Motel. At the main drag he guessed south. Streetlights and assorted neon lit the way, and Lunch drove slowly through sparse traffic.

"This thing seems to be luggin'," John Smith said.

"All this weight," Lunch said.

At the edge of town Lunch kept going. There were still pockets of houses along the way on one side of the road. A big yellow harvest moon was hung in the sky, casting a terrific golden glow that seemed peculiarly invented, perhaps by some lone nut spiritual figure, or else rigged up by Hollywood technicians to bathe a love story in. Once in a while the river burst into view between rows of trees, the brown water golden in the night.

"Are we lost yet?" Mary asked.

"It's a little further out this way," Lunch said. He saw a gravel lane in the high beams, a lane that turned toward the water. "I think this could be it."

He turned off the paved road and onto the gravel.

"It sure is dark," John Smith said.

"Dark enough?" Mary asked.

"Yup."

She reached into her knitting bag and raised out a nickel-plated revolver. She pulled back the hammer and put the barrel at Lunch's head.

"If you want to stay cute, li'l man," she said in a jailhouse tone, "you'll stop when I tell you to."

"What the hell is this?" Lunch said.

"Banditry," John Smith said. "Hee, hee, hee."

He leaned forward from the rear seat and touched a hunting knife blade to the side of Lunch's throat. "Welcome to the Devil's Backbone, you redneck punk."

The lane abruptly ended at the river's edge. High beams from the Bug shone way out across the water.

"Stop," Mary said. "Or I'll bust a cap in your fuckin' face."

"Hey, now," Lunch said as he braked. "Don't shoot me, Mary. Please. I'm a harmless tiny fella."

"You are now," John Smith said. "Where'd you do your time?"

"What time is that?"

"Oh, cut the comedy," Mary said. "You're a jailbird if we ever seen one—were you fixin' to rob us?" She leaned across and tapped the pistol barrel to his bruised cheek. "You cute tiny man—did you figure you could take *us* off?"

"Hee, hee, hee."

"Leave the lights on," Mary said. "And get your ass out that door. You run and I'll drill you."

"She can do it, Rich," John Smith said. "I've seen her."

"Y'all ain't from Iowa," Lunch said. He kept both hands firmly on the steering wheel. "Corn country don't behave like this."

"The hell it don't," John Smith said. "Hee, hee, hee. You need to travel more."

All three of them got out of the Bug.

"Stand in the light," Mary said. "And toss that big wad of cash you got tucked in your pocket on the ground there, Rich."

As Lunch emptied his pocket of cash, John Smith kicked at the gravel, spraying tiny rocks about.

"This stuff is too small," he said sadly.

Mary came into the light, her red dress brilliant in the glow, shiny pistol glinting, her blond hair gleaming like Rayanne's used to do when she'd just finished washing it.

"One thing," she said, "would you say our skit worked, Rich?"

"Skit?"

"The knitting, Rich. The knitting and the corn country yucks—did it make us come across as lovey-dovey hicks, ripe for pluckin'?"

"Totally took *me* in," Lunch said.

John Smith grabbed the pistol from Mary, then they kissed briefly.

"We just love the outlaw life," he said, waving the pistol. He did a little dance on the gravel, his large body bouncing. "The way we live it, it could go on forever."

"There aren't too many couples like us, Tiny Baby," Mary said. "We're gonna make this romance last."

"There it is, Gina," Tiny Baby said. "Shared interests bind."

"Your names ain't John and Mary Smith neither, huh?"

"Not exactly."

"This is devastatin'," Lunch said. "I'll never fully trust a blond slut and a big fat slob again."

Tiny Baby said, "I doubt you'll be meetin' any more, Rich." He smacked the black hat from Lunch's head, then shoved Lunch toward the river. "I'll bet that water's *just right*."

When Lunch was shoved again he fell, and while down he slid the derringer from his boot.

"I'm scared," he said. "I'd like to pray." And as Tiny Baby swaggered toward him, smirking, he raised the derringer and shot the big man, catching him in the throat. Tiny Baby staggered back into the light, blood spraying from his neck. The pistol fell from his hands, and he sunk to his knees. Lunch said, "Crawl, you dirty dog!"

Tiny Baby gurgled blood, wheezing on his knees, his head bowed to the ground.

"Well, I got a heart," Lunch said.

Then he put the derringer at Tiny Baby's temple and pulled the trigger. The big man dropped, face down in the gravel.

Gina screamed once, her hands held to her chest, then she whirled and ran into the canebrake that grew tall along the riverbank. Her flight was heavy footed and noisy, canes cracking and twigs snapping to give away her trail.

Lunch picked up the nickel-plated pistol Tiny Baby had dropped, then retrieved his black hat. He set the hat on his head at a Bogartish angle, then began to follow the woman. The golden light cast by the harvest moon imparted a magically real quality to the night. A beautiful light more real than real illumination. As Lunch followed Gina he inhaled deeply, and paused to savor the scene. This river, that moon, this light, those goofy people—yet more evidence of Nature's fantastic production values!

The path Gina had blazed through the canebrake made Lunch's task simple. He slowly followed in her own footsteps until her red dress gave her away. She was trying to hide, all rolled up low to the ground, but the red dress was so brilliant the entire maneuver was a waste of time.

"Hide and seek," Lunch said. "I *see* you!" He stood over her and gave her a soft kick. "Come on, Mary—let's negotiate."

"Don't kill me. Oh, don't."

"You know what? You *look* a lot like my sister, Rayanne, and you *act* like her, too." He grabbed a handful of her blond hair and pulled her up. "Let's check on Tiny Baby."

She walked weakly, her knees all rubbery. Lunch shoved her along, back to the Bug and the headlight beams. When she saw Tiny Baby laying there, bloody and inert, she collapsed beside him.

"I'll do anything you want," she said. She rolled onto her back, the light in her eyes, and looked up at Lunch. "I do great french—anything you want, please, please."

Lunch watched her for a moment, then said, "It's weird—you really *do* look like my sister. She had hair like yours." He squatted beside her, then reached a hand to the top of her red dress and pulled down, baring her breasts. "Whew!"

"Please, please. Anything."

"Too weird!" he said. "So much alike." He put the pistol barrel against her chin and forced her head back. Then he lowered his lips to her left breast and sucked. He circled his tongue around her nipple. "Sweet," he said. "Hers weren't this big."

"Please, pl—"

"No beggin'!" he said. He ran his fingers through her blond hair, tangling his fingers in the long fine locks. "Did Tiny Baby say something?" he asked, and as her eyes swung hopefully toward Tiny Baby he pulled the trigger, and blew her face away in a red pulpy mist. The sound of the blast ran up and down the river, spreading over the water. "So much for forever, sis."

Lunch tossed the pistol into the river, listening to the echo the splash made. He searched Tiny Baby's pockets for cash but found none. Then he found his own cash on the ground, rolled the cash tightly, and tucked it in his pocket. He walked back to the Bug and opened Gina's knitting bag. The thick booklet of money they'd flashed was in there, and he carried it to the headlights to examine. He fanned the bills in the light, and quickly saw that it was a Michigan Roll, five twenties wrapped around two inches of cut paper. All of this for a C-note! What fakers!

His heart sank. He doused the headlights, then stood slouched against the fender of the Bug and smoked Salem number six, exhaling wistful trails of smoke. Another part of the blue leaflet Lunch had read earlier in the day popped into his mind. It dealt with days like this one. The passage was to the effect that the actual river, as well as the river of life, was festooned with innumerable shoals, sucks, snags, and sawyers, all of which posed dangers, both seen and secret, to the craft that floated down them. That was all of the passage Lunch could recall for sure. There may have been a solution or remedy mentioned farther down the page, but he'd just skimmed that part.

When the Salem was burned to the filter, Lunch flipped it into the dark. He opened the bonnet of the Bug where the storage space was on these things. He reached in and grunted loudly as he heaved three large rocks onto the gravel beside Tiny Baby and Gina. "His," he said, then started heaving smaller rocks onto the black graveled earth. "And hers."

Part III

Choices

10

R ENE SHADE had started his evening off in the community center gym, sitting in the bleachers with his father, watching a bar league basketball game and trying to plumb the depths of his strange love for the power forward in red. Nicole Webb, the high scorer for his affections and on the court, was leading the Peepers, the team from Maggie's Keyhole, against the much feared ladies from Barb'n Bob's Bowl'n Brew. Shade sat impassively next to his father, only occasionally pointing toward the court as the woman in his life flung elbows at ribs, kicked at shins, set vicious moving picks, dove for loose balls, and got into shoving matches with burly, emphatic spinsters as if she wanted this sport and its attendant violence to make a personal choice for her.

"Your lady friend is good to watch," John X. said. "She ain't afraid of contact."

"She doesn't usually play this rough a game," Shade said.

"Well, you're a lucky fella, son. She runs the court very nicely for a pregnant gal."

Out on the hardwood the sweat and curses and jump shots were flying. Nicole's skin had flushed to a temperamental pink, and she'd picked up three fouls and one new enemy in seven minutes of rough play. The expression on her face was as intense and bellicose as it had been earlier, when the subject of the future had come up between Shade and herself. The discussion had been held over cups of coffee at Maggie's Keyhole where Nicole was bartender, and it had been a friendly, open discussion for the first minute and a half. Then Shade had said the routine things about feeling pressured and somewhat roped, and she said a caustic thing about his predictable comments, and from there they went at it in a strained, snapping, he-said-she-said squabble that eventually ended with a to-each-his-own proposition being coolly stated by her, seconded by him.

"I couldn't even guess what marriage to her would be like," John X. said. He lit a Chesterfield and smiled. "The women I've attracted always ran more to the type that are fans instead of players."

Shade said, "Marriage hasn't even been mentioned, Johnny. Lots of other shit has been, though."

The Peepers had a fast break going down-court, and the twenty-five or thirty people in the bleachers made an appreciative murmur as Nicole caught the pass out on the wing and drove toward the hoop, curling around one opponent, then going body-on-body with another as she skyed for the lay-up, and drew the foul. Both women fell to the floor, and when her opponent offered a hand up, Nicole shook her head. She got to her feet and trudged to the foul line, small trickles of blood below both knees.

"She *is* knocked up, ain't she, son?"

"Yeah. Yeah, she is. But don't start stockin' up on cigars just yet."

Watching Nicole from the bleachers, seeing the way she muscled into the paint for rebounds and whipped those hard elbows around, Shade wished he could take back over half the things he'd said to her. The Peepers' jerseys were red with blue lettering, and Nic had on black shorts and bright red sneakers. When she raised her arms to rebound or shoot, lush tufts of dark pit hair were displayed. She moved from hoop to hoop with gangly grace, fluffy ponytail flopping down her back. Her jump shots were fluid and deadly below the key, and she fought for all of the garbage under the basket.

Probably she *would* make a fine mother, if that was the point.

"Well," John X. said, "I guess you don't have to get hitched these days just because she's pregnant. Plenty of women who are pregnant don't want to either. So they don't. Nobody throws rocks at 'em nowadays."

"What if *I* want to get hitched?"

"You do?" John X. stubbed his smoke out and dropped it between the slats.

"Could be. I don't know."

Down on the court the contest was slipping away from the Peepers. Nicole sat on the bench to take a blow, and the inside game of the large Bowl'n Brew ladies asserted itself. The Peepers began to laugh helplessly on defense, and with the ball they were dispirited and failed to set up any offense other than individual attempts to execute the fabulous. By halftime the Peepers were down by fourteen points. The two teams huddled at opposite ends of the gym. A few voices were raised to shout advice to the desperate. Players from both teams took turns walking slowly to the water fountain.

"I think I'll head for the shed," John X. said, stretching his back. "Not much of a game anyhow." He put his hands in the pockets of his dead man's coat and looked at his son. "But listen, Rene—there always was two things I wanted to never ever do in my life, and I did 'em both. That's right. One was gettin' married, and two was gettin' married *again*. Both times I found myself locked in jail by wrong choices, see. I would've had to draw a picture of Betty Grable on the wall and crawl out the crack to escape."

"What're you saying? You're *legally* married to Etta's mom?"

"Of course I am."

Shade just stared at his dad. "Shit, you mean you've added bigamist to whatever *else* you are?"

"Why, I don't think so, son."

"That's what it is, when you're married to another woman, besides Mom."

"Not besides, son—married *after*ward."

"What are you talking about? That's not what Ma said. You two never got divorced."

"Really? That's what she said?" John X. shakily lit another smoke. "Geez, that's awful romantic of her, son. I can see where she could make it vivid to you boys. I don't mind much. It was one of her talents, you see. But actually, she divorced *me* after I hit the road. Why, the papers finally caught up to me the night I saw you at that fight of yours in Tampa. You must've told her I was comin'.'"

"I might have," Shade said.

"Criminentlies, remember that fight, son?"

Shade raised his fingers to his broken nose. "That was when I hooked up with that kid they had down there then. Wolburn. Tom-Tom Wolburn. He was quick, but he tired late."

"I remember," John X. said. "He was a will-o-the-wisp type of fighter. He painted your face up pretty gaudy with that jab of his. Pop-pop-pop. He had that mitt on your nose all night long."

"Shit," Shade said. "I busted his guts. He stayed in the hospital for two days pissin' blood. I beat his belly to fuckin' jelly."

John X. shrugged.

"I thought they could've seen it as a draw."

"Draw? I *won* that fight."

"No."

"*I* thought I won it."

"No," John X. said, shaking his head with certainty. "You didn't win it, son, by no means, but they could've called it a draw."

Smoke curled above the two men.

Then, Shade nodded his head, smiled, and said, "His fuckin' jab was a beautiful punch. I couldn't do nothin' with it, and there was no way to hide from it. Bob, weave, peek-a-boo, it didn't matter, the fuckin' jab found me."

John X. inhaled a long slow draw of smoke. As he exhaled he flicked the cigarette down through the bleacher slats. "We saw the same fight, after all, son. Honesty can siphon off a few regrets and resentments if you tap in to it. Let that sink in." He half weaved as he stood, and Shade heard the creaking of his father's knees. "Bleachers are hell on old men." John X. patted Shade's back, then shuffled a few feet down the bleacher aisle. "It's your choice," he said. "See you around, kid."

The second half was more of the same, but Shade kept watching until Nicole fouled out with three minutes to play. The Peepers were down by twenty-three points so he left the gym and began to walk through Frogtown. The sidewalks were dark and uneven. Here and there small piles of leaves had been raked into the gutter and set afire, imparting to the night the smoky, wistful smell of another year gone.

On North Second Street Shade came abreast of the Sacred Heart Academy and took a seat on a bench at a bus stop there. The Sacred Heart encompassed a full city block, and inside the tall iron-pike fence that surrounded it there were beautiful parklike grounds. The night was warm and fallen leaves scuttled in the breeze. Birds roosted in the bare trees, and Shade could see a few sisters strolling past gas lamps that lit the paths inside the fence. Though he'd lived in Frogtown all his life, he'd only been inside the Sacred Heart grounds twice, both times when he was a child, for reasons now forgotten.

For fifteen minutes Shade stared through the pike fence, watching as nuns from the Sacred Heart took their evening stroll, listening to the cadence of their steps and occasional laughter. He resumed his own stroll then, and headed toward Nicole's place on the fringe of the neighborhood.

Frogtown, the oldest quarter of St. Bruno, had been founded by the flocking of outdoorsy miscreants who saw business opportunity in the swamps and the river and the parade of suckers who boated down that treacherous brown flow. It was by now a neighborhood of row-houses of brick or wood, shotgun apartments, small weary stores, robust vice franchises, and abundant dirt alleys that made for excellent escapes from the scene of the crime. Small backyards were strung with clotheslines from which flapped the work clothes of the occasionally employed, a work force that generally punched the clock on various nearby stools where they drank at the bar, toked in the alley, and gambled upstairs with their cut of the take or this month's disability check, and when that was lost, the last smoke ashes, and the bottles only glass, they posted themselves to the street with their empty pockets held open wide, faces turned to the sky, on a red-eyed alert for that much ballyhooed trickledown of wealth.

Nicole's place was a frail frame house on Perkins Street. Shade went up the steps of the front porch, then took out his key and let himself in. As the door opened into the dark front room, bells tinkled gently against the glass, and he called out a questioning "Nic?" to announce himself. The light from a street lamp fell through the lace curtains on the tall narrow windows of the living room, casting paths of faint blue light across a worn Persian rug. Shade walked through the shotgun apartment, heading toward the back until he saw light seeping out from beneath the bathroom door. He rapped his knuckles gently to the wood. "It's me," he said. He heard water lap against the tub. He pushed on the door and slipped into the small, steamy bathroom that he and Nic had painted a startling shade of peach one Saturday afternoon in the spring. She was lying in the deep water tinted blue from the bath salts she used, her toes curled over the enamel lip of the old clawfoot tub.

"If you half close your eyes," she said, "it's like Cozumel."

"Tough game," he said. Nicole released a long heavy sigh, then, blue water slishing past her breasts, she leaned forward, her hair falling around her face as she stared down into her lap. Shade sat on the edge of the tub, picked up the bar of soap, and began to wash her back with long, unbroken strokes of his hand.

"I been thinking," he said.

When he finished her back and rinsed her with long pours from a plastic beer pitcher lifted from Maggie's Keyhole, Nic pulled the plug chain with her toes, then stood silently, and he handed her a towel. Her knees were scraped, and swollen red from hot water, and he made out the beginning of a long yellow bruise on her upper left thigh. Nic stepped out of the tub, as water cascaded to the tile floor. For a moment she buried her face in the towel, muttered something indecipherable, then padded into the dark bedroom leaving a wet trail of footprints behind. Shade pulled another towel from the rack and kicked it toward the puddle on the bathroom floor. He still kept his own apartment—a tiny bachelor pad in the upstairs of his mother's pool hall—but most nights he curled up against the perfect fit of Nicole's buttocks, in her bed that was, in practice, theirs.

She had dropped herself like a sack of groceries, flat out, face down on the bed. He turned on a night-light on the bed stand. It was a fifties lamp, a plastic cylinder depicting Niagara Falls, with a couple standing beside an overlook above the blue and white waters churning below. "I've been thinking," he said, as he reached for a tube of Ben Gay next to the lamp, then sat down on the bed, and pressed some cream into the palm of his hand.

"Thinking what?" she spoke into the pillow folds.

"About a honeymoon." He rubbed the Ben Gay between his hands. "We could go to Niagara Falls. Something like that." He leaned over her and began to knead her shoulders and her shoulder blades.

"Oh geez," she said with a groan, but it was unclear to him whether she was saying no or saying yehess to his massaging hands. He worked his hands in circles over her ribs, then down to the small of her back, and she released a long, yielding moan.

When she spoke, however, her voice was monotone. "You want to get married now?"

"I've been giving it some thought," he said.

She tilted her head forward so he could knead the nape of her neck. "Why do you think you want to get married, Rene?"

"It could be the right way to go," he said.

"I'm asking *why*, Rene."

"Well, come on, you know I'm Catholic."

"You're *what*—"

"I'm Catholic. That's what I was baptized."

"Oh, Christ, you're not doing this to me. You're not going to say the Catholic Church is why you have to marry me."

"Okay, okay, forget the Catholic. I don't go anyhow. But maybe I just want to then. I was just sort of spooked before. I was caught off-guard. Here I am on suspension and all—it just seemed at first like *one more thing* that went wrong, and smacked me in the head. I sort of panicked at first, okay? But now I'm getting used to the idea, and if you think about it, I mean, where *are* we going, Nic, if we don't eventually get married and so on." Shade pressed his hands back and forth across her rib cage, then began to knead the muscles in her buttocks.

"I don't know," she said, drawing the words out as he massaged. "You're pretty good at *this.*"

Shade moved down to her thighs, and Nicole groaned as her hamstrings stretched with his fingertips. "Thank Chester Anderson for this stuff. Chester taught me everything I know. That old man could draw the pain out through his fingertips. Best rubdown man a fighter like me could ever hope to find."

"Rene," Nicole said through a mouthful of sheets, "you don't even have a job."

"I'll be back with the cops," he said. He slid down on the bed to reach her calves. "This idleness is just temporary."

"You're through with the cops, Rene. You're through. Unless you say you're sorry, or something. Tell them you'll be happy to be their bagman from now on, and knock off anybody they tell you to. Unless you knuckle under you're through as a civil servant." She sighed, and he turned his attentions to her feet.

"Look, Nicole, if I have a family, I *will* provide."

"Oh great—great! I'm not going to be the excuse for you to become evil. I'm just not *fucking* going to be that excuse for you."

"Hold still," he said. "You like the feet part best."

"Rene, Rene, Rene," she said. "What about me? I mean, I never planned to end up in a place like this, a little grubby town where everything gets dirty just hanging in the air. What will I become? I'm a bartender, for chrissake. I could be something different. I just never planned to sling suds forever."

"You never planned anything," he said. "That's why you're a bartender." He rubbed the ball of her foot, but her foot was taut, resisting him. "So you're a bartender, anyhow, so what?"

"I wanted to go back to Europe, especially to Spain," she said. "Could we go live in Spain? I mean, what do you care about St. Bruno, anyway?"

"Spain?"

"Barcelona. Costa Del Sol. Ibiza. There's a world of blue water out away from here."

"You gonna keep drifting all your life?"

"I like new places. I'm a traveler."

"Yeah, right. You oughta talk to my dad about that. About travel-ing." He let her foot drop to the bed. He stood over her prone body.

"I love you, Nic. I want to marry you. I'm asking you to marry me. Have the little thing. Crumb snatcher crawling on the floor. Drool-ing and squalling, I can handle that. Not just one, though. It's bad to have one kid. If you're gonna have one, have—three. Three's a good size."

"*Three?* You're out of your fuckin' mind, man," she said. She sat up and pulled on a robe. "My God, you *are* a Catholic—a frigging Catholic—"

"So what's it going to be? Do you love me, or what?"

"Or what? Or what? I love you," she said, "but I've got to think." She looked at the blue night lamp. Inside there was a fettered wheel above the bulb, and when it heated up enough the slatted wheel turned round and round causing an illusion of white water roiling upward from below the falls. They had picked up the lamp at a flea market for fifteen bucks. It seemed like a lot for celluloid, but they liked the notion of an idealized Niagara Falls forever cascading inside the lamp, so they bought it anyway.

"We're not going to Niagara Falls," she said. "I can tell you that."

"What does that mean?" He took hold of her shoulders and pulled her face closer. "What does that mean?"

"It means I'm not going to act impulsively. We're talking about deep shit here, Rene. The rest of our lives. If we're lucky we'd still be kickin' when our little ingrates would go off to the state university, or the vo-tech, or maybe just down to the corner for a few zillion drinks."

Shade leaned to her until he could smell the faint scent of jasmine and musk in her hair, then he brushed his lips across her forehead just below the hairline. "So you're going to think about it?"

"Yeah. I'm gonna think about it *all*. You bet I am." She patted his rear end the way two athletes do between plays. A dismissal of sorts. "You'd better sleep at your place tonight," she said. "I've got things to sort through."

As Shade came down Lafitte Street, walking through a light mist, he saw that the lights were all on in Ma Blanqui's Pool Room, which meant his mother had customers. When he reached the door he saw his brother Francois's white Volvo parked down the block, the shiny import seeming to gleam amid the domestic heaps.

There was some straight pool education going on at the front table, the lessons being taught by J. J. Guy, who lived in a flop across the street, and absorbed by Henry DeGeere, a neighborhood fella who had, by local standards, gotten rich off the gas business, but who still couldn't run six balls to save his life.

"J. J.," Shade said. "Henry."

Both of the older men nodded and said, "Rene."

There were two teenaged boys at the center table playing eight ball, no slop, call your pocket, and though Shade had seen them all over the neighborhood he knew them only as the Freckle-Faced Kid from around the corner, and the Four-Eyed Chubby Kid who lives where the Pelligrinis used to. They both knew him, though, and Freckle-Face said in a mocking drawl, "What's happenin', off-i-cer?"

Shade stopped, and said, "What you *want* to happen?"

Freckle-Face got interested in his next shot. He kept his face down, scrutinizing the green felt.

"Nothin'," he said.

"That sounds right," Shade said, and walked on toward the back where he could see his mother on her high stool behind a red Dr Pepper cooler, a wide cooler that his younger brother was now leaning against.

Francois, the tallest of the Shade brothers, was a lean man with carefully styled dark hair, and the sartorial flair of a Latinate dandy. He was an Assistant D.A. and lived in Hawthorne Hills in a landmark home his wife, Charlotte, had inherited. The suit jacket he wore was of a smoked silver color, over a pale blue shirt now open at the collar, a gray striped tie dangling from a jacket pocket.

"It's your birthday, Ma," he said to Monique, "just tell me what you want."

Monique had her long gray hair braided and pinned up like a crown. She wore horn-rimmed glasses that magnified her eyes, a black cigarette dangling from her lips. She was dressed in khaki trousers, a green army shirt, with pink fuzzies on her feet.

She was looking at Rene's approach as she said, "How's about world peace, and a river of beer?"

Shade leaned against the cooler beside Francois, who said, "We'll save that for Christmas, Ma."

"What's up?" Shade asked.

Francois patted him on the shoulder.

"Trying to get her to confess on the subject of what she *really* wants for her birthday."

Monique turned her magnified eyes on Shade, pointing at him with the black cigarette.

"One thing I want is for you to be good to Nicole, you rat." She jabbed the smoke in his direction. "You hurt that girl, son, and I *will* take a fuckin' skillet to your head."

"I love you, too, Ma," Shade said. "Now butt out."

"What's up with Nicole?" asked Francois.

"Nothin'," Shade said.

"Hah," went Monique, "that's a man talkin' there."

"Oh," said Francois. "I think I get it."

At the front table Henry groaned loudly over some sort of pool injustice, and Shade looked that way.

"Saw the old man tonight," he said. "He doesn't look too good."

"How could he?" Francois said. "He's been holed up in a bottle for thirty years, at least."

"He don't look too good, but he can still be pretty funny," Shade said.

"Don't I know it," Monique said. "His sense of humor got you boys born. Tell me about this daughter he's got now."

"Well," Shade said, "she's a weird kid."

"I always wanted a daughter," Monique said, smoke clouding around her face. "It just wasn't to be."

Shade turned to Francois, and said, "You ought to drop in on the old fart. He's stayin' over at Tip's. This girl, her name is Etta, she's half your sister, Frankie."

"No," Francois said. He spun away, his eyes on the pool players. His clean teeth scraped at his lips. "He's a phantom to me. That's all—a fuckin' phantom. I don't want anything to do with him." He raised his left arm and looked at his watch. "I'm late. I've got to get home." He smacked his hand on top of the cooler. "See you for your birthday party, Ma."

He patted Shade's shoulder once more as he walked toward the door.

When the door closed behind Francois, Monique asked, "So what's this li'l girl of Johnny's like? Is she pretty?"

"That's hard to say, Ma. Her hair is cut funny, and she's been taught to use, like, Crayolas on her face. She's a sight."

"L'il girls are different, son."

"This one sure is," Shade said. He yawned and stretched his back against the Dr Pepper cooler. "I'm crashin' upstairs tonight."

Monique regarded him coolly from behind another black cigarette. "That's interestin'," she said.

"I'll tell you what's interestin', Ma," Shade said. "You know how you always told us you'n Dad were still married, legally? How he was just a runaway husband and daddy, runnin' for all these years? Well, the way he tells it is *you* divorced him *years* ago. Years and years, actually."

"That so?"

"Yeah. Why'd you keep tellin' us you were still married if it wasn't true, huh, Ma?"

From her seat on the high stool Monique leaned forward and planted her elbows on the cooler top. Her eyes looked huge behind her glasses. She raised her chin to a belligerent angle, then blew smoke at her son.

"Why, it should be obvious," she said in a caustic tone. "I wanted to fuck with your head, pure and simple."

11

MRS. CARTER had a number of rules. A tallish woman of considerable age, Mrs. Carter was usually attired in a calico dress and plain black shoes, and though the expression on her pinched face suggested an inner, ineffable sadness, she was diligent in the performance of her duties. When new girls came into her house, she sat them down and ran off a short speech to them that explained her various general rules: "A healthy child is what folks want, and it's what they pay for, too. That means we'll have zero vices here. No drinkin', dopin', cigarette smokin', or godawful eatin' habits. You'll eat vegetables in this house. You'll eat lean meats, all varieties of vegetables, lots of fruit and milk, and you'll have no sex. Don't get outside here and meet up with some boy who is just dreamy to you, and his arms are so very, so very, very warm to you, and his tongue darts quick in your mouth and you plumb blow it out your mind that you are fatter'n a blue ribbon pumpkin because you are *preg*-nant, girls. There's a child in you. So, no carnal relations—hear?"

Mrs. Carter's house was ranch style, basically, everything on one floor to avoid the strain of stairs. Gretel and the four other girls didn't do much around the place but languish on the soft furniture and expand. They nibbled at trays of fruit Mrs. Carter set out and watched television from the early morning agricultural reports right up to the late local news, the end of which signaled bedtime. Three of the girls were from the area, with Gretel and one other being the only out-of-state recruits.

The girls talked quite a bit of worried talk about the birthing of their babies. There were rumors of tremendous pain in the delivery process. The girls talked about it like Marines in a foxhole talk about being taken alive. Gretel was quietest on this subject because she'd seen field-hippie women have babies while lying on Navaho rugs in Delirium's kitchen, and they'd come out of it fine, healthy, sometimes joyous.

Mrs. Carter's house was well known in the neighborhood, and once in a while it would be the site of a disturbance. Ex-boyfriends might drive up drunk, screaming insults, or parents would arrive to lecture one of the girls about their deep disappointments in her, then escalate in their anger. Sometimes after dark young boys on spider bikes mooned around on the sidewalk and front lawn, calling out enticements and lusty claims to this household of girls who clearly would *fuck* if they could be lured into the bushes.

The bedroom Gretel slept in was farthest from the kitchen, which discouraged snacking in the early A.M. hours, but it had a window facing onto the street, and studying the view soon came to be her hobby. Gretel shared the room with Lori, an older woman of twenty-two who'd lived a life of rancid nothingness down on the south side of town, but because of the positioning of the beds, she had the view to herself.

Three houses were constantly in sight, and if she craned her head to wider angles two more houses and a garage were visible. The men of these houses seemed to lead lives similar to those Gretel had been told about by Zodiac and Delirium. These men went off in the mornings fresh-shaven and in crisp clothes but came home around supper time all tore down by soulless work of some sort, their clothes sagging, their faces weary. Two of the men nearly always carried six-packs of beer to kill their evenings with. The various wives were about perfectly split between going away to work or staying put at home. So many children ran around the worn lawns that she wasn't sure which houses which ones belonged to.

The way these people lived was so weird. They were under the thumb of society to the extent where they probably thought they had it good. Would Zodiac mock them if he was here? For sure he'd flip his gray ponytail at them and bark. He'd bark and grin and sing a song about their humdrummery as loud as he could and possibly do the Pawnee Dance of Doom on the trunks of their cars. Zodiac spent *his* days doing whatever he wanted, the only thumb he came under was Nature's, a fairly ferocious thumb at times, but one he found agreeable. The crop he tended was an Afghani strain called Razorback Red that he'd grown for years on government land, an ungreedy stand of twenty-five plants budding in the Mark Twain National Forest. Generally Gretel and Delirium handled the chores around the house. Delirium gardened and sewed through the daylight hours, then, as darkness fell, she turned to her poetry, which was all concerned with her childhood back in Tarrytown, New York. The poems, some rhyming, some not, spelled out how this childhood in privileged circumstances had turned her away from the shallow urge to own and destroy, and toward the hidden part of herself that society would kill, the part that was best expressed nude, under bright stars, with a reefer in one hand and the laughter of freedom pealing from her lips.

When darkness fell on this street, the people of all five houses closed in around TV sets. They didn't come out again until their alarm clocks made them.

Weird. But interesting.

Gretel was sitting cross-legged on her bed, letting her skin breathe, watching the street, when Tip slowly drove by in his big ol' gas-eater car. She rolled carefully off the bed and went down the hall to the bathroom. She ran some water and splashed her face. She slipped into a green dress, brushed her hair, then went into the front room. The other girls were all gathered there, ignoring the sitcom on the tube, making jokes about Tom's child.

"Tom's child is kickin' this evenin'," Lori said.

"Tom's child is healthy," said Carol.

"And so damn cute!" said Dorothy.

The four of them giggled, their big ripe bodies wallowing on the soft furniture. This Tom's child business was the house joke, a variety of unwed mother humor. All of the girls had wearied of explaining who they knew or thought or hoped was the father of their baby, and after a few bull sessions Carol had loftily claimed that the man responsible for her condition was none other than Tom Cruise, the cutest dude in the galaxy, and after a moment of silence, Gretel had said, "Well, me, too." Pretty soon it developed that all five women believed themselves to have been knocked up by the very same movie star dick, and from there on all referred to their common burdens as Tom's child.

"I'm takin' Tom's child to a movie," Gretel said. "Show him his daddy, maybe."

"You take good care of my man's child," Carol said.

On her way out Gretel encountered Mrs. Carter on the front porch. Mrs. Carter smoked a pack and a half of Marlboros per day, but, in keeping with her own rules, she only smoked on the outside porch.

"Where you goin'?" she asked.

"A movie."

"Seems like you've been goin' to a lot of movies."

"I enjoy them. I hardly saw any back home."

"Uh-huh. Where do you get the money?"

"The movie money?"

"Uh-huh."

"Today—a man gave it to me."

"Ah." Mrs. Carter stuck her cigarette in the big sand ashtray she kept on the porch. "Why'd he give money to you?"

"I watched his dog."

"His dog?"

Tip's car was not in view.

"While the man shopped. At Krogers. His dog has run away twice this week, and he didn't have a chain with him, so I said I'd watch."

"Uh-huh."

"It was an Irish Setter." She looked down the street. "Named Bono."

Mrs. Carter lit another Marlboro. She flicked the dead match on the lawn.

"You be home early."

Gretel went walking down the sidewalk, occasionally placing her hands under her belly and hefting. One of those dirty little boys trailed her on a spider bike for a minute, wheeling up close to her side and breathing heavy, but on his own like this he didn't have anything foul to say, and soon pedaled away.

Around the corner and halfway down the block Tip was waiting on her. The night was warm, his windows were down, and she could hear his radio tuned in, as always, to a Golden Oldies station, blaring "White Rabbit," a song Delirium had often sung to her when she was young.

When Gretel slid into the car Tip started the engine, grinned at her, and pulled away from the curb.

Pio's Italian Garden was a spot of make-believe Brooklyn, a loving re-creation of the joints Pio had known during his childhood back in the Red Hook section of what he often called "the old country." The authentic touches in this decorative homage were the vast scenes of Neapolitan kitsch that were painted on the walls, the small square tables with red-and-white checkered cloths, the DiNobili cigars in the glass case below the cash register, and the jukebox on which Ol' Blue Eyes was the boss songster, backed up by a goombah choir of underboss songsters mostly named Tony.

One painted wall depicted a spectacular scene wherein a Naples tenement was built at an angle that extended far enough over the bay that a chubby mama with a big toothy grin could fling a platter of linguini from a third floor window across the sailboats and yachts to a wedding group dining al fresco on the Isle of Capri.

Tip leaned back in his chair, pulling away from a plate of savory manicotti he was too nervous to eat. Gretel sat across from him, slowly chewing a meatball, her eyes intent on the wall painting. Despite all the spice in the air, he could smell her, her certain scent. She smelled so sweet, but not of perfume. This fragrance of hers couldn't be bought in a bottle. It was a scent that must rise from the spirit or soul, then waft from her pores, her hair, that huge bulge, or perhaps that scar. He raised his nose and sniffed.

Gretel turned her face from the wall, and said, "I don't believe that's accurate."

"The mural?"

"It's not like that abroad. Zodiac's been everywhere."

In his red shirt with black buttons, black sports coat and slacks, with his glistening brown hair swept back and hanging to his shoulders, big Tip looked potentially dangerous but sincerely spruced. A series of curious smiles kept coming to his pocked face. These smiles were small in stature, but quick and relentless.

"I'd like to take you there," he said. "Rome."

Chewing, Gretel pointed a fork at the wall, then swallowed.

"It won't look like that. Don't get your hopes dashed."

"By boat, maybe," he said. Three quick smiles. "Or do you get seasick?"

"I don't know," she said. She touched four fingers to her scar. "On curvy, hilly roads I *can* get carsick. Maybe the sea is different."

"By plane would probly be best," Tip said.

"I haven't had better food," Gretel said, her fork wrapping up a wad of spaghetti. "I like these meatballs, even though I realize animals have personalities. Spirits, even."

Tip smiled. "I couldn't see me livin' on vegetables alone."

"Some say cows are sacred. Did you know that, Tip? That cows are sacred?"

"Smothered in Pio's sauce, they're even better'n *that*," Tip said, smiling, laughing, tapping his fingers on the table.

Gretel made a happy face.

"You're funny."

"You're beautiful."

"Come again?"

Tip planted both elbows on the table and leaned forward.

"I haven't kissed you, but you're so *beauti*ful, Gretel."

"I feel good inside. I try to have up vibes, and not down vibes."

"No," Tip said. His big hands went to his hair and messed it up. Long slick strands flopped over his face. "What I mean is, I want you to stay after your baby is born."

"That'll be soon," Gretel said. "It's s'posed to be another month— but I don't think so."

"I want you to stay with me."

"Sure." Gretel raised a napkin and wiped her mouth. "I could likely use a place to crash by then—I won't be welcome at Mrs. Carter's no more."

"God," Tip said. He looked around the restaurant, not really seeing anything. "I don't mean to crash—I want you to marry me, Gretel."

Her fork dropped. "That's too far out."

"I can't imagine living without you."

Tip's face showed doubt, and fear, and nervous hope. He was smiling too much and knew it, and rather forcefully asserted control over his features, composing his face to meet possible disaster.

Gretel said, "Marriage is ownership, Tip. Domination. There's a pretty flower in the forest, let's say, and what is marriage but the pluckin' of that flower so's it can be worn in a buttonhole. Like a decoration. A plucked flower in a buttonhole can only wilt, man, and it won't never bloom again."

"I guess I don't follow," Tip said sullenly.

"It's murder by ownership," Gretel said.

The clock was pushing toward ten, and the Italian Garden was fairly quiet. Near the front window from which a red neon pizza beamed onto Fifth Street, a silver-haired gent in a tasteful linen suit split a meatball grinder with a golden-haired boy in street leather. The organizers of a just-ended Knights of Columbus fund-raiser were relaxing at a big table in the center of the room, and Monsignor Escalera was pouring the beer. At the back of the room, in their regular booth next to the pay phone, a couple of Frogtown boys loitered over plates of mussels and glasses of rosé, studying tomorrow's nags in the Racing Form.

"I make decent money," Tip said. He picked up his fork and rolled the manicotti on his plate. "I've got a comfy set of wheels." He forced his fork down on the pasta tubes and chopped them. "My house ain't much, but I own it *outright*."

One of the K of C crowd dropped some quarters in the juke and punched in Ol' Blue Eyes. The first song was "Summer Wind," and the wistful lyrics got to Tip. With nervous fingers he wrecked his hairdo altogther, then sighed.

"I'm sorry you feel this way," he said.

"Tip, marriage and all that—it ain't the way I was raised."

"You'd be taken care of good."

"Freedom is what we value. It comes from *within*. Society, and rules, and all that is what takes it away." Gretel leaned forward. Her face had an earnest expression. "I can't get into marriage, Tip, but I've been wantin' to live with you. I've had it in mind for a while now."

Tip's pocked face raised. He looked into her eyes.

"You have?"

"Uh-huh."

"Well that'd be alright," he said eagerly. "Give it a try, anyhow."

"I do dig you," Gretel said. "We've never got naked together, but I've thought about it some, and I think we'd fit."

"When *I* think about it we sure do," Tip said. He stretched his huge arms and sighed with relief. His face relaxed. "And I've thought about it plenty, though we ain't even kissed before."

"We will," Gretel said. One of the many Tonys was now singing "Jeepers Creepers," raising the spirits all around. "But there's a few things I want in my future. In the place I live, I mean."

"Name them, Gretel. I want what you want."

She took a sip of her soda, and lowered her eyes.

"This is embarrassing," she said, "but at home we don't have flush toilets. Delirium always says the simpler life is the better, but I think I'll have flush toilets from now on."

"Well, hell—I've got *flush* toilets."

"You do? That's primo to me. I've got used to 'em at Mrs. Carter's."

Tip waved his hand in the air and leaned back in his chair.

"Electric lights, gas stove. I've got all that. My fridge ain't too good, though."

"Air-conditioning?"

"Huh?"

"I like air-conditioning, though I know it just enriches the greed heads."

"A window job," Tip said. "It does pretty good. I could get another one."

"I'll buy it," Gretel said. She patted her belly. "I should clear right at fifty-two hundred dollars the lawyer says."

Tip shook his head, long slick hairs flying.

"That's none of my business," he said.

"I won't be afraid to spend it, neither."

Her hands were on the table, and Tip reached his own across and grabbed them. He held tight.

"This is great," he said.

After a few more minutes of silent happiness, Tip and Gretel left Pio's, Tip leaving a ten-dollar bill for their waitress. They walked together out to the parking lot. A light mist was falling and the moonlight was diffused by the clouds. They held hands, ignoring the fine drops, shuffling slowly to his car.

"What about showin' me that house," Gretel said. "You've never took me there before."

Tip pulled his keys out and jangled them.

"Comin' right up," he said. Then he threw his arms around her, pulling her to him sideways to avoid her belly. She turned her face up to his and they kissed, standing in the rain. The first kiss was so swell it immediately led to another. Tongue met tongue, and Gretel put a hand on his ass, then slid it around, squeezing. "Oooh, Gretel," he said, "let's go."

He started to open the car door, but she said, "Wait." She raised her left hand, spread her fingers, and crooked her pinkie. "Tip, give me your finger." He raised his hand, and they entwined pinkies.

Gretel squeezed and said, "That means as much to me as any piece of paper."

12

THE HOUSE was dark, though no one was asleep. Etta lay on her cot in the kitchen, Tip's transistor radio near her ear, tuned to a rock station, listening to George Michael sing "I Want Your Sex," while John X. lay on the couch in the front room, *his* radio playing "Apple Blossom Time" by the Andrews Sisters.

To keep his mind off of the many possible or certain disasters in his future, John X. was fantasizing, conjuring up an earlier version of himself poised over a regulation Brunswick table, running racks of balls, sinking table-length cut shots, three-ball combos, sophisticated bank shots, constantly drawing the bright white cue ball into perfect shape for the next stroke. This remembered self was having a great time back there in the past, dazzling a crowd of faceless sports and dames, these memories thick with smoke and musk and derring-do. Glorious runs of sixty to ninety balls were routine but fully imagined.

In the midst of a fantastic run, with his former self drawing the Balabushka back from the cue ball, the tip raised to apply top, one of the faceless sports in the crowd stepped forward, into John X.'s line of sight, and suddenly had a face.

John X. jerked up on the couch. His ribs ached from Stew's punches, and now his gut ached with anxiety.

"Criminentlies," he said. "Lunch."

He reached to the side table and turned on a lamp. He could see the kid in the kitchen, curled on the cot, her back to him. He lit a Chesterfield, then walked across the room to the telephone. He sat on a straight-backed chair and dialed information, got the number he needed, then punched it in.

After four rings his call was answered.

"Chapman residence. Mr. Chapman speaking."

"Rodney? It's me—John X. Can you talk?"

"Okay. Yes." Rodney's voice was strained, uncomfortable. "I don't know where you might be, John, and *please, please* don't tell me, but you better be hidden well."

"He's after me, is he?"

"Yes. He was here. He basically *raped* Dolly, looking for you."

"Aw, shit, Rodney—I'm sorry. That's terrible."

"We've begun to see a counselor. The whole thing was awful. It wasn't really your fault, John, but I can't help blaming you."

"I'm sorry, believe me." John X. sucked on his cigarette. "I guess he was brutal, huh? Did you tell him anything?"

"He might've killed us, John. It wouldn't have bothered him to do it, not at all."

"Oh, I know that. Lunch is a killer. But did you tell him anything?"

There was a pause, a telling silence.

"I don't know where you are, John, and I don't want to, but if you and Randi and that girl of yours should happen to be in a town called St. Bruno, well, I think I'd be moving along very promptly."

"Shit!" John X. shouted. He slapped the phone down, slamming the receiver into the cradle. He bowed his head, groaned, and rubbed his temples.

When he raised his eyes, Etta stood before him. She wore boxer shorts and a white tank top, her right hand twirling the black crucifix that hung from her ear.

She said, "What now?"

"Aw, kid—Jesus—do you know what fate is?"

"Uh-huh."

"You *do?*"

"Yeah," she said. "Like if your mom is chubby and crosseyed, probly you'll be chubby and crosseyed, too."

"That's something else," John X. said. "Fate, see, is a black fuckin' cloud that's always pissin' and moanin' *exactly* over your head. You can't shake it and it won't butt out. That's what fate is, kid, a Nosey Parker that meddles with you from the cradle to the grave."

The kid backed to the couch and slumped down.

"You know something about that guy Lunch," she said. "Don't you, Dad?"

He raised his eyes, looked at her, and nodded.

"You're a smart kid, Etta. I must've been sober when I made you."

"Huh. Not likely."

"Watch your lip, angel, I got quite a bit of Sluggo in me tonight." John X. stood and began to pace. "Tonight, you don't want to goad me." He took a few steps toward the door, stopped, clenched his fists and shook them overhead, then turned to his daughter. "We gotta run again, kid."

"Oh, Dad, no!"

"Yeah, kid. I hear the call of the open road again."

"I *like* it here!"

"We better heed the call, kid."

"But Dad," Etta said stridently, "there's family here! We've got family here!"

The old man lit another weed, then sat beside the girl. His hands weren't too steady, and his aching ribs required him to sit hunched forward. His breaths all finished in muted sighs.

"Now kid," he said, "for people like us *the family* is only just a resting place between adventures. You'll need to adjust yourself to that. That's how it is. That's the way us types live."

"But, Dad," Etta said, "Tip is tough. Rene is tough, too, so why do we got to run from Lunch?"

"Aw, kid—Lunch is a ferocious fella. He's a gunman."

"Dad, that guy's only about this much taller'n *me*. You already knocked him out once, all by yourself."

"I got lucky."

"Now you got Tip and Rene to help."

"My trouble ain't their trouble."

"They'll help."

John X. searched for the ashtray, then stubbed the Chesterfield out.

"We're gonna be broke soon, anyhow," he said. "This poker game ain't gonna bring in the bacon I'd hoped for."

"Uh-huh."

"We can't get by on it."

"I hear you, Dad."

Both radios had continued to play, and John X. and Etta sat together on the couch, sagging, sighing as two very different kinds of music fugued badly, grating on the nerves, Dick Haymes singing "Little White Lies," while Van Halen threw "Jump" into the musical mix.

John X. said, "I need to think—go turn that crap off."

"It's not crap."

"Turn it off anyway."

Etta sat there, hugging her knees, twisting the black crucifix absently, staring at the floor.

"Turn it off, kid—it's janglin' my thoughts."

"Okay, okay," she said, then lurched forward and walked across the room, slapping her bare feet to the floor. She turned the radio off, then got on all fours and pulled the Joan Jett suitcase from underneath the cot. She flipped the lid, carefully ran her hands past Grampa Enoch's bass lures, past her few clothes, to the money hidden in the bottom of the box. She looked at John X. on the couch, then quickly grabbed a handful of cash.

"Dad," she said as she returned to the front room, "I didn't tell you a lie."

"Did I say you did? About what?"

The kid leaned against the wall, poised on one leg, rhythmically swinging the other foot lightly over the floor.

"What I mean is, you never asked, so I never lied."

"That covers an awful lot of ground," John X. said. "Questions I never asked you."

She slowly walked toward him, hands behind her back, her pale girl legs seeming preposterously long beneath the white boxer shorts. When she reached him she brought her hands from behind her back.

"This is from Mom," she said. "It's my college money. You have to pay after the twelfth grade."

John X. snatched the money from her hand. He reared back on the couch, his eyes narrowed.

"A conspiracy, huh?" he said. "You and Randi cooked up a deal. A deal that cut *me* out."

"I just now cut you in, Dad," Etta said.

She stood there, waiting for some sort of punishment, not knowing what form this punishment might take, or even what was possible, since he'd never spanked or smacked or yelled at her much. "You never asked."

The night was warm, quiet, the eternal murmur of the big river and the radio announcer's voice were the only sounds. The voice was going on and on about world events, reciting the latest news at the top of the hour.

"This hurts," John X. said as he counted the money. "Kid, it really hurts — do you like her more than me?" His fingers snapped each bill onto the cushion beside him with a flourish, the flourishes becoming broader as the count went higher. "Don't answer if you don't want to."

"No," she said.

"Ah, ha — there's nine hundred and fifty bucks here, darlin'!" He began to laugh. He slapped his thigh. "This calls for a drink, angel — where's my bot —"

Steps creaked on the porch, and John X. anxiously looked toward the door. He placed a finger to his lips, motioning for silence. A footstep sounded, and as it did he raised a cushion from the couch, dropped the money in, and brought Enoch's Bulldog .38 out.

"Get in Tip's room," he whispered. "Hide. Don't come out no matter what you hear." His blue eyes were wide. "You've been a great kid." His daughter hadn't moved yet, and in a harsher voice he said, "Now!"

Then she was gone in a light rush of pattering feet. John X. cocked the pistol, his hand wavering, and slid to the dark screen door. When the steps came closer he aimed, then said in a low, confident voice, "Do you believe in miracles?" He shoved the screen door open, the pistol raised for a point-blank shot. "'Cause it'd be a fuckin' miracle if I missed you from here."

The figure on the porch was dressed in white, carrying a shotgun. Stew Lassein said, "I don't know why I brought this." He held the shotgun with one hand on the barrel. "I s'pose I've been considerin' killin' you, Johnny."

"You ain't got a chance, Stew. Set that duck gun down right there. Drop it."

The shotgun clattered to the deck. Stew calmly looked at the pistol barrel trained on his face, smiling as if it were an ice cream cone or a strange carnation. John X. backed into the house, the .38 held high, and Stew followed him into the dimly lit front room.

"Criminentlies, but did you give me a start, buddy. I thought you might be somebody else." The light cast by the one lamp illuminated a ruined Stew Lassein. His attire of apparitional white was now soiled, and blood had dried into dark streaks on the shirtfront. He was very pale, and black circles had formed under his eyes. His upper lip was swollen to thumb size. A strong fetid smell wafted from his clothes and body. "Oh, man," John X. said, "have a seat. You look like shit warmed over, buddy."

Stew fell to the couch in sections, like a cargo carelessly unpacked, and sprawled across the cushions.

"Go on and shoot me, Johnny," he said. His chin touched his chest. "My life was finished last winter, the day that ice storm hit."

"I don't want to shoot you. That's a sad fuckin' statement for a man to make, anyhow, ain't it? 'Shoot me,' I mean."

"I just don't care. I ain't been to sleep since the night before last. Since the poker game."

"Well, no wonder."

"I can't. I can't sleep."

John X. took a seat beside Stew on the couch. The pistol sagged in his hand.

"I know you hate me," John X. said, "but I don't know why."

"You know why."

"Sure, there's water under the bridge, but we ain't in it, face down. That's the main thing, right?"

Stew snorted. "That's nowhere *near* bein' the main thing."

"I see. I'm full of shit?"

"Just shallow. So damned shallow. Life is about nothin' but creature comforts to you, and the many like you."

"That's shallow?"

"It's damned shallow."

"Are fuckin' and drinkin' and gamblin' creature comforts?"

"Oh, yes. Yes."

"Then you're right—I'm one shallow S.O.B."

For a moment Stew was quiet, his eyes open but his mind lost in potent remembrance. A Glenn Miller medley sounded from the radio. When he came out of the past and turned to John X., he made eye contact for the first time since sitting down.

"So, tell me," Stew said, "was Della a good piece of ass?" John X. merely looked at him, unmoving. "I mean it—was Della a good roll in the hay, by your standards?"

"Aw, please, shut up. Don't speak that way about the dead."

"She was my wife, and I thought she was so pretty."

"She was, Stew. A gorgeous kid."

"I never had your gift with the gals, Johnny. I never bowled 'em over the way you did. In high school I screwed a few yaller gals over at Reena Lovett's place, the one she had in that big ol' house by the park."

"A splendid whore house," John X. said. "Reasonable prices."

"And one night I walked home from Uncle Dot's Café with this girl from around here—Olive Thiebault—did you know her?"

"I don't think so."

"She invited me in, and we sat in the kitchen for a while, then we smooched for a while, then she told me it was that time of the month and she couldn't screw, so right there at the table, with her daddy snorin' in the next room, she pulled my thing out and sucked it. I groaned so loud I expected to be murdered before I could get out of there."

John X. laughed, then lit a cigarette.

"How about a drink?" he asked.

"Maybe a week after that I asked Della to go dancin' with me." Stew sighed. "And that's it. That's all the women I ever knew that way."

"Really? Criminentlies—you're gonna make me cry, Stew."

"So you see, I can't make comparisons the way you can. Huh-uh. That's why I have to ask this to know for sure—was my wife a good fuck?"

"Aw, Stew."

"If you said she was, compared to the many, many gals you've humped, Johnny, why, I think it'd cheer me up. I could say, Hey, Stew, you spent most of your life rollin' in the arms of a special piece of tail." Stew slowly stood up from the couch. His weak legs sagged. "That'd be good to know, uplifting." He loomed over John X., his white arms fluttering up and crossing over his chest. "Just the thought of you ruined my marriage. You put a shadow over every kiss I ever got from my own wife."

John X. couldn't raise his eyes. He nervously tapped his cigarette and squirmed on the couch.

"So, Johnny, please, tell me—was Della a special bit of poontang?" His voice raised, cracking. "Was she a nice hump? Good piece of tail?"

"Aw, shut the fuck up!"

"Or just a little on the side, somethin' to pass an hour with while her husband busted his ass at work?"

Stew uncrossed his white arms, placed his hands on John X.'s shoulders, then began to slide them toward his neck.

John X. sat perfectly still, his pistol hanging down, limply, between his knees. He softly said, "Keep it up, and I'll *give* you an answer, buddy."

"Please, tell me."

The hands of Stew Lassein began to slowly close.

"She was really put together," John X. said. "You know that. Nice figure."

"Yes?"

"She smelled good, great kisser, and if you rubbed her titties she'd..."

"Oh! Oh!"

Stew fell over backward, his body thumping hard to the floor, not getting even a hand down to break his fall. He sprawled on his back, lips sputtering, eyes closed, his fingers digging frantically at his chest, breath wheezing. Then, with foreboding swiftness, he was still, and a long, long, long breath of air rushed from his body, whistling an acute, sad song past his false teeth.

John X. stayed on the couch, not bothering to look at Stew. He sat in stunned silence, smoking, then lit another cigarette from the butt of the last, and smoked it down. He dropped this butt into the ashtray, then slid off the couch, and bent over Stew. He looked down at the dead man's face and nodded.

He squatted on the floor, touched the back of his hand to Stew's cheek, and said, "You wanted to know."

When the voices in the front room had quieted, and stayed quiet for what seemed like a long time, Etta cracked the door open and peered out. She could see her dad's head above the couch back, tilted down and unmoving. There'd been some hot voices audible through the door, and one loud thump, so she didn't know what on earth might have happened. She slowly began to move toward her dad, in the lamp-light, stealthily stepping in bare feet, her fingers pinched to her boxer shorts and pulling out the slack to avoid telltale rustling.

The man in white, the man who'd cried during poker and claimed to have a scarred heart at the bar, was on his back. Not breathing. And there was Dad, squatting beside the corpse, squatting still as a stone.

Etta came closer and looked at the dead man's face. His mouth was yawned wide, his eyes were narrowly open.

"Oh, Dad," she said, her voice sounding strangely mature and disappointed. "You killed him."

John X. did not raise his head, but he shook it.

Quick confident footsteps came up the stairs, across the deck, and to the door.

Tip's voice sounded, saying, "It's not a bad place, Gretel. The river floods, but there's a good feeling here. I call it home. I like it. Mainly, I guess, because it's paid for."

The screen door jerked open. Tip and Gretel came in and immediately stopped.

"No, not here!" Tip said. "You had to kill him in *my* house?"

John X. looked up.

"I didn't kill him," he said.

The Bulldog .38 was in plain view.

"You shot him, didn't you?"

"He had a shotgun, son, but I didn't shoot him. It's out there in the dark."

Gretel looked suddenly weak and weary. "I've got to sit down," she said. She sat on the couch.

Tip knelt beside the body, then rolled the corpse over twice, searching for blood.

"He ain't shot. You didn't shoot him."

"I told you that," John X. said. "Heart attack."

"Mrs. Carter is gonna take a switch to me."

Etta took a seat on the couch beside Gretel.

"I can't stand this," she said.

"Dad," Tip said, "we've got to get him out of here. You and him were known enemies after that fight today. There could be a stink if we call the law."

"I hadn't thought of that."

"We could take him into the swamp..."

"No! No way." John X. shook his head, then raised his hands and rubbed his eyes. "Let's just take him home—do you know where he lived, son?"

★   ★   ★

Tip lugged Stew out to the orange truck in a fireman's carry.

"Whew!" he said. "This guy smells."

John X. trailed his son.

"It's been rough times for him, lately," he said. "But they got worse."

Tip laid the body in the bed of the truck. A light rain was falling, and the night wind was whistling off the river in a creepy falsetto.

John X. got behind the wheel, Gretel slid into the middle, Tip took the window with Etta on his lap. Enoch's truck was slow to start, but finally the engine rolled over and the pistons began to make bickering noises.

"Dad," Etta asked, "what is it you want me to do again?"

"Just knock on her door and tell her who you are. Tell her I'm drunk or something and you need a place to sleep."

"She'll let you in," Tip said. "Ma's okay."

The orange truck rolled through the rainy streets of Frogtown to the corner of Lafitte and Perry. John X. pulled to the curb and Etta hopped out, Joan Jett suitcase in her hand.

"I'll be down to get you tomorrow," John X. said. "Be good."

"Tomorrow's Ma's birthday," Tip said.

"That's strange," John X. said, then drove on, following Tip's directions to Stew's place.

The Lassein house was all lit up. When Tip lifted Stew from the truck bed he was sopping, inert and heavy with rain. He quickly carried him to the porch.

John X. tried the door.

"It's locked," he said.

"Try his pockets," Gretel said.

With Tip holding Stew upright, John X. rummaged through the dead man's pockets. He found the key in the front pocket of Stew's wet white pants, and opened the door. A large stuffed chair was in the corner of the front room, surrounded by newspapers, a pair of slippers on the floor beside it.

"That looks like it could be his favorite chair," John X. said. "Let's put him in it. That way whoever finds him'll think he died kind of happier than he really did."

"Whatever," Tip said.

He hoisted Stew into the chair with the body slumped sideways. The corpse looked freshly showered, cleansed, white hairs boyishly slicked down its forehead.

"Try to set him up with dignity," Gretel said. She grabbed Stew's shirtfront and pulled the body upright. "We've got our own Karma to consider here."

Tip said, "He was just talkin' to you, then crashed over dead, huh?"

"That's right."

"What'd you say to him?"

John X. lit a cigarette and looked around the house. Could I have lived like this? Could I? Would it have been better, richer, in any way finer to be a solid citizen like this? Was it for him? Criminentlies.

"History," John X. said. "My history, mainly, a lot of which is lies."

"I don't follow."

"Oh, son, see, a fella gets out in the world and things will happen, and naturally you *will* react, and pretty soon another thing happens and you react again, and after that you got a history you are known by. A bunch of shit concernin' your reactions to things that happen that follows you around by word of mouth. People who don't really know you know what they think is your history, and in my case that ain't so good."

Gretel had Stew's palms turned up to study them. She said, "Yellow nails — that's no good. Plus, his heart line is crossing his head line with a deeper rut. That won't get it for a happy life."

"Uh-huh," Tip said. Then he turned to John X. His brown eyes were bright. "What was it — did you have a thing with his wife?"

John X., the cigarette slanting from his mouth, took a long look at Stew. He could remember when he'd first married Monique, and as darkness fell he had to call her in from the street out front where she'd be playing with other fourteen-year-olds, smacking a tether ball, or dealing old maid, or shaking up soda bottles and squirting root beer into the air. He would stand on the concrete stoop and call for his young pregnant wife, calling her to come in from play and fix her husband supper, and so often Monique would call back, Come-ing, then show up with one or two of her little friends, saying they would help her cook this special dish or that, some dish he would enjoy, and more often than any other her apprentice wife would be Della, Della Rondeau, the cute, cute dark kid who'd lived in these rooms for forty years, with a man who loved and feared her.

"Oh, I've got to go," John X. said. He walked to the door, pausing to cast one last look at Stew Lassein. His benediction was simple: "Que sera and so on, slick."

13

LUNCH PUMPHREY put his tiny black boots on the windowsill
and sat back with his hands behind his head, trying to put an exact
number to the deaths he'd administered. The room was on the fourth
floor of The Hotel Sleep-Tite, and from the window Lunch gazed out
into the black night and wet streets of St. Bruno. A surly wind had
kicked up, and rain howled against the window, spattering violently,
the raw weather perfectly attuned to Lunch's mood.

Number One had been the tavern owner in Marietta whose last
words were "Wake up, Mac—closin' time." Number Two was the
auxiliary cop who'd caught him coming out of an electronics store
window at two A.M., and Number Three was the woman who'd gone
to the twenty-four-hour laundromat in the cool of the night and accidentally seen him blow the head off Number Two. She'd been holding
a wide wicker basket of clean clothes, standing on the sidewalk, and
when he approached she'd begged, which he hated, he hated begging,
fear was in order, sure, even resistance, but begging merely made a victim's last moments shameful, which is not the emotion you should want
on your face when you are returned to Nature.

After Number Fourteen, an Italian fella in Daytona who'd been a
thorn in the side of Angelo Travelina, Lunch lost interest in the arith-
metic of murder. What was the point in adding them up when there
would surely be more, possibly many, many more deaths to be har-
vested by him? At least one more of them, soon, too. Ol' Paw-Paw. He
was here, Lunch could feel it, hear the old man's death song hummin'

in his veins. And most likely Randi Tripp, the 'Bama Butterfly, would be a bonus crop, and whew! but would he have that thrush warblin' a few new tunes! And if that gaudy li'l girl was standing there, lookin' like some sort of freak dwarf from the future, well, just call her dessert!

Lunch stood and stretched, looking around the hotel room. The room was decorated in Flophouse Classic, with lamps screwed to tables, tables bolted to the floor, and faded paintings of one clown in several poses nailed to the walls. This clown had a red nose, a tattered top hat, and grimed cheeks and clothes in each of the paintings, but in one he had a neckerchief bundle on a stick over his shoulder, in another he held a hand of cards, all jokers, and in another he drank an unknown beverage from a rusty tin can, the serrated lid still attached to serve as a handle.

Lunch shook his head at the squalor of the joint and decided that whisky and cocaine were in order. This place too closely resembled home, home with Granny and Aunt Edna, and anyplace that reminded him of home made him desperate to get high.

He patted a small bottle from his pocket, opened it, and pinched out a snort of blow for each nostril. He hoovered the powder and began to pace. He never should've let thoughts of home into his mind, for any jail he'd ever been in was kinder to him than home, more affectionate even—except for Rayanne. Rayanne—now he needed whisky to wash that name from his mind.

Lunch picked up the door key and his hat and left the room. The Hotel Sleep-Tite had a lounge on the first floor, and he'd fetch a bottle from there. He took the stairs down four flights, crossed the cruddy carpet of the lobby, and went into the lounge. There was a narrow bar and a bunch of tables with plastic chairs, and the lights were low and blue. The bartender looked about the age of a schoolboy, with curly blond hair, and his T-shirt sleeves were short so his muscles were on view.

"Give me a bottle of Johnny Walker Red," Lunch said.

"We don't have it," the bartender said. "Wrong neighborhood. Plus, I'm not supposed to sell by the bottle."

"State law?" Lunch asked.

"Profit motive, I think."

"Ah." Lunch pulled out a twenty and laid it on the bar. "Give me a bottle of what you got."

"Ten more."

"Ouch!" Lunch said. "But okay."

He forked over another sawbuck.

The bartender set a bottle of House of Usher Scotch in front of Lunch. He leaned forward, and said, "You need a broad to go with that, amigo?"

"How much?"

"Fifty for normal stuff."

"Room four ten," Lunch said. "I'll pay the money to *her*. And tell her to bring a magazine."

"A magazine? What kind of magazine?"

"Any kind, it don't matter. But tell her to bring one."

"Twenty minutes," the bartender said.

Lunch went back to his room.

Back in his room, as the rain battered down, Lunch went deep into the blow and Scotch, constantly pacing, drinking straight from the bottle, getting higher and higher until he felt like he was six feet overhead, hovering aloft with no wings, looking at himself from above.

"Rayanne," he said.

Candlelight would be more appropriate, and historically accurate, but he didn't have a candle so he tossed a Sleep-Tite towel over the lamp to soften the light. If he had a radio, he'd tune it to a shit-kicker gospel station, like the one back home, and listen to nasally delivered musical sermons on the topics of eternal love and eternal damnation, while banjos strummed and fiddles whined as an accompaniment.

Whew, but would that make his whole scene percolate!

When his door was knocked on, Lunch opened it. A black gal stood there, maybe nineteen, but she could pass for less. She wore white knee boots that glistened, and a snug red miniskirt. Her face was lean, and her eyes were big round browns, which was all fine, but what made her seem like a sign from the other side was her hair, which was cornfield blond and not long, but plentiful.

"Oh, man," she said, "is that a birthmark on your face?"

"Bruise. Car wreck."

"Well, hi, then," she said. "I'm Lushus."

"That's nice," Lunch said. He staggered a little, waving the bottle. "But could you answer to Rayanne tonight?"

"Rayanne? Let's see your money first."

Lunch pulled a roll of green from his pocket.

"I got plenty," he said. "Now what's your name?"

Lushus came inside, then kicked the door shut with a white boot.

"Sugar—it's me, Rayanne."

"You got the Sears Catalog?"

"No, I ain't got no catalog."

"I said for you to bring a magazine."

"Oh." Lushus unslung her shoulder bag and reached inside. She pulled out a copy of *Vogue*. "I got this, sugar."

"Well, now," Lunch said giddily, "that's the new Sears Catalog, Rayanne."

"Just tell me what you want," she said. "I think you have a certain story you want to think you're in. That's fine with me. Just tell me what you want."

"Take a shower," he said. "Leave your hair damp, but come out smellin' of soap."

"This is gonna cost."

"I can pay. Here's a C-note."

Lushus snatched the money.

"Just tell me the story," she said as she began to undress, "and I'll be in it."

"You'll be in it," Lunch said. "Don't worry about that."

Lunch looked away as Lushus stripped. When she went into the bathroom and turned on the shower, he sat on the bed. He pulled out the bottle of powder and snorted. He could hear the whore sudsing away in the shower. He bent over and unzipped his boots and slid them off. Then the shirt, then his trousers. Socks and bikini briefs stayed on. He lay across the bed, belly down, his face over the edge, the magazine on the floor before his eyes.

When Lushus came out of the shower, she asked, "What's next?"

"We're in a farmhouse," Lunch said. "Way back off the hard road, down a rutted lane. Total boonies. Granny can't pay the electric bill, so all we got is this candle. Now come here and cuddle on my back. *I* always turn the pages in the catalog."

Lushus slid onto the bed.

"Lordy, but you sure got plenty of pictures on your body!"

"Not at this age I don't." Lunch opened the magazine. "Looky here, Rayanne—new clothes!"

Lushus spread herself over his body, skin on skin. She smelled of soap and her bones dug into his back.

"So pretty," she said, not even looking at the pages. "I want one of those."

"Rub through my hair, Rayanne. Pick through for lice."

"Lice?"

"I don't have lice at this age—I did then. Do it."

The whore began to pluck her fingers through the killer's hair.

"There's one," she said, and pinched his scalp.

"They made fun of me at school today."

"Who did?"

"The Cranston brothers."

"Oh, those boys are mean."

"And Abel Young."

"Him too? Why they make fun of you for?"

"You know why, Rayanne. My shoes and stuff."

"Now that's awful."

"They said I wore stinky clothes and had head lice."

Her fingers pinched his scalp again and again. "I'm killin' them lice, sugar."

"Looky here—cowboy boots."

"I'll get you cowboy boots—see if I don't."

"You always say that."

"I will, sugar. I want things, too. Nobody ever says a nice thing to me neither."

"I know."

"I'm pretty, ain't I? I'm a pretty girl."

"Uh-huh."

The whore lay her face to the killer's neck, her hands at his shoulders.

"But I can't sing good enough for the choir, so they won't have me in it."

"Someday I'll kill them for you."

"I know you will, sugar."

Lunch reached a hand back and began to slide it over the cheeks of her ass.

"Can we?" he asked. "Granny's asleep and Aunt Edna won't hear us in this room."

"I mean, listen here, I have feelings, *too*."

"Blow the candle out."

Lushus reached across and flicked the lamp off. In the dark, Lunch pushed up from beneath and rolled her over. He spread her legs, then lowered his lips to her left breast and began to suck. His lips sucked gently at her nipple, his lips moving softly, his little hands cupping both breasts.

"Let me slide you in, sugar."

"Nuh," he said. "We don't do that. We just lay like this together."

He continued to suckle at the whore's breast while rain rattled the window, and her hands came up slowly in the blackness, clasped behind his head, and held on.

"We'll always be together," she said. "Always and always."

Lunch greedily sucked and sucked, until it began to sound as if he were crying. Suddenly he pulled his mouth from the whore's breast.

"Please, Rayanne, don't never turn state's evidence on me. Please, sis, don't never do that."

"Never," Lushus said. "You're too dear to me. You and me are all we have."

He dropped his head onto her chest. His breath was warm on her skin.

"I'd have to kill you if you did that."

His lips found a nipple in the dark, and Lushus once again held his head in her hands.

"Oh, sugar, this story is gettin' too sad."

The rains had ended during the night, and as a gray, pearly dawn arrived Lunch came awake, his senses sharp, and saw Lushus standing at the bureau, stealing his roll of green.

Her white knee boots shined, and her red dress fit her like a sheath. Her golden hair hung to her shoulders. She had the entire roll in her fist, preparing to take it all.

"Lookin' for a match?" Lunch asked. He spun off the bed, shook loose Salem number one, and lit it with a butane lighter. "I can give you a light."

"I'm not *stealin'* this, li'l brother," Lushus said. She kept her back turned to him. "I thought I'd pay Granny's 'lectric bill, sugar."

"How nice of you."

"Then," she said, turning to look him in the face. "I was fixin' to fetch breakfast for my *favorite* brother."

Lunch nodded. All he wore was his black bikini briefs, his many tattoos on clear display, and as he advanced on the whore it was like a small private collection of bad art swaggering forward.

"Brother?" he said as he reached her side. "I look like a nigger to you?" He sidled close to her, then punched her in the belly. "If you were kin to me, I'd be a nigger."

Lushus took the punch pretty well, then raised her fists and swung back at him. Lunch smiled, and punched her again. She sagged, and the money tumbled from her hand, fluttering to the carpet.

"You're all the same," he said. He grabbed hold of her blond hair, flicked his lighter, and held the flame to her thick locks. The hair ignited, and blue fire spread up the strands, crinkling, smoking, stinking.

"Evil!" Lushus shouted. Her hands rose to her blond hair, but the fire was too hot. She closed her eyes and ran to the bathroom, smoke and stink hanging in the air. She jumped into the white tub and put her head under the faucet, kneeling, and turned the water on. As the water doused the flaming hair, soaking her, the whore murmured and hissed.

Lunch stood in the doorway, calmly smoking, watching as the whore's hair became a strange new, two-tone color: blond and burned.

"I ain't got no sister," he said.

14

O N S UNDAY mornings when the spirit was in her, a questing, vengeful spirit, Monique Blanqui Shade slipped into grungy clothes, heavy boots, and a frayed straw hat, and tromped down the tracks toward the Marais Du Croche swamp to slay a few serpents. There were rituals to the hunt. First she'd set the heavy black skillet on the stove, fry a mess of eggs in butter, layer Bermuda onion slices and mayonnaise on bread, and slide the eggs aboard to make hearty sandwiches. She would put the sandwiches in a sack and tie it to the belt loops on one hip, then place three cold beers in a plastic bag and lash it to the opposite hip. Then she'd select a sharpened cane from the collection in her closet, flip the Closed sign on the front door of the pool hall, and head for the dense thickets and muckish terrain where snakes abounded, slithering and hissing, just asking for it.

As she fried the eggs on this Sunday morning, her birthday, Monique stood before the stove, her long gray hair down, not yet braided, brushing against her ankles, and stole looks at the rollabed in the pantry where Etta lay, the girl already awake, but feigning sleep.

"You about awake?" she asked gruffly.

The girl kept her eyes shut and breathed steadily in a fair imitation of true sleep.

"Get up," Monique said. She was stout, sturdy, and her brown eyes were large behind the lenses of horn-rimmed glasses. "These eggs are practically done."

The girl's eyes fluttered, and she sort of tossed on the bed, as if only now nearing consciousness.

"I raised three boys," Monique said, "and all of 'em was better fakers than that. Get on up, Etta."

"What time is it?" Etta asked, almost sourly.

"Time to get up and kill a snake, girl."

"What did you say?"

"I said it's snake killin' day, girl, and I'm up for it. Want to tag along?"

"Criminentlies," Etta said. She spun off the bed and began to dress.

"Wear old clothes," Monique said. "It'll be muddy from the overnight rain."

"I only got these clothes, ma'am."

"Wear 'em, then. And I told you to call me Ma."

When the girl had come to the door during the night, Monique had turned on the front door light, looked at the girl standing on the stoop with a pink suitcase held to her chest, and known who she was before they even spoke. She'd given the girl milk with banana bread and butter to calm her, for she was fidgety and shyly evasive. They'd sat at the table and talked in sentence fragments for a half hour, then turned in. Monique had gone to bed thinking, she looks like a Shade, like a Shade girl, which is what I wanted, but never had.

The sandwiches made, Monique sat on a chair and began to braid the witchy length of her gray hair, braiding the strands into coils that she pinned up like a crown. Bright morning sun blared in through the small east window, shining on her back. A long black cigarette dangled from her lips.

Etta came into the kitchen, sniffed the sandwiches, then slouched against a wall.

"Do you really kill snakes?"

"Yup."

"You ain't shittin' me, are you?"

"I see John X. has passed his potty mouth on to you, girl."

"He says words like that are part of our language."

"Your dad says more ridiculous shit than any three lunatics do."

"Maybe. Sometimes he's right."

Monique began to pin the final braid into place.

"It's only fair to admit that, I s'pose." She stood and opened the closet door. "Look here."

On the inside of the door snakeskins were nailed to the wood and hung down like pennants, rustling as the door yawned wider.

"Wow!" Etta said. She advanced on the door, slowly approaching the slightly swaying snakeskins. She carefully raised her hands and began to feel the skins, and as the initial sensation was pleasant, she ran her fingers up the long dry length of the various copperheads, cotton-mouths, and one stray rattlesnake. She leaned into the skins and smelled them. There were over a dozen faded, vanquished serpents nailed to the door, and the smell of them was neutral, but their colors and designs were exotic, fetching, and she pulled them to her face and pressed her young unpainted lips to the brittle, brilliant scales. "Ma—you killed *all* these?"

"Yup."

"They're so pretty—are they poisonous?"

Monique blew a cloud of smoke from the side of her mouth.

"The poisonous ones are *always* the prettiest."

"Gee, that's too bad."

"I s'pose, but it's something good to know."

The back screendoor squeaked as it was jerked open, and Nicole Webb walked into the kitchen, wearing a black T-shirt, washed-out bib overalls, and high-top sneakers. Her expression was vague, not quite awake, and her dark hair was amok.

"Coffee," she said. She had taken a chair at the table before she became aware of Etta. "Who're you?"

"Nic," Monique said, "this is Etta—Rene's half sister."

"I was gonna guess that," Nicole said. "How're you, Etta?"

"Peachy," Etta said. "You're Rene's girl?"

"That's right," said Monique.

"Approximately," Nicole said. "Where is he, anyhow?"

"Still asleep."

"Good."

Monique lashed the necessary bags to her belt, then pulled three long sharp canes from the closet. She passed the canes out, keeping her favorite, a cracked pool cue that had been converted to a snaking instrument. She put a straw hat over the crown of her hair, cupped a hand to her ear, cocked her head, and said, "Can you hear 'em, girls? Their forked tongues are callin' me."

North along the railroad tracks the steady thump of Monique's heavy boots set the pace. Church bells were tolling in the far distance, the clanging bells causing the winos and bums who flopped beside the tracks in boxes and upturned rowboats and other makeshift suites to come awake. The derelicts pissed in the weeds or vomited or picked up nearly empty jugs for an eye-opener. The three generations of woman-hood kept marching, stomping along to the pace set by the oldest among them, tapping their canes to the railroad ties in rhythm with their steps.

When the snakers were abreast of a slough, a slough in the midst of a foul but alluring thicket, the thicket rich in serpent potential, Monique turned off the tracks and down a slender path. Horseweed grew beside the path, taller than the tallest head among them, and though the weeds were beginning their autumnal wilt, they blocked from view any step but the next step. Nearly bare cottonwoods towered overhead, while limbs of the more squatty chinaberry, catalpa, and unknowns closed in snugly around the path. The path was clear but muddy, and the wet earth seemed to suck at footsteps.

After leaping over a small felled tree that had splayed across the path, Monique halted. She jabbed the sharp point of her pole into the mud, her eyes surveying the lush thicket, the fallen leaves and limbs and ancient muck of the swamp.

"It's fall," she said, "and they could be in their holes. Or this warm weather could have them out still—sunnin' on rocks, lyin' in wait— let's beat 'em into the open, girls."

"It's *your* birthday, Ma," Nicole said. "Hope we find you a present."

The snakers, their sharp tips down, began to poke into dark corners, tangled vines, mysterious holes, jabbing with their canes, driving the bladed tips into likely spots. They snaked roughly parallel to the river. They swung their poles, slashing through vines and under bushes, cracking weak branches, sweating, joking, cursing, thoroughly enjoying the hunt, eyes alert for anything poisonous that might slither into view.

"Have you killed any?" whispered Etta to Nicole.

"Not really. Ma's skinned quite a few."

"Seventeen," Etta said. "I counted."

As they went deeper into the swamp they splashed through shallow water and soft marsh mud. Grime clung up to their hips. Eerie cypress grew in these wetlands, their trunks swollen, and fluted. In the shallows cypress knees, some a few inches in size, some several feet tall, rose above the water, each supported by a vast root system, root systems that frequently tripped the snaking women. Every few slashes of the canes seemed to occasion unseen plops into water—a bull frog, perhaps, or a water turtle, or muskrat, or maybe a cottonmouth as thick as a grown man's arm.

Near a cypress knee, gnarled and indomitable, Monique stood alongside Nicole, and lit a smoke.

"How're you feeling?" she asked. "Any mornin' sickness?"

"Sort of," Nicole said. "More like constant confusion."

"Uh-huh. Yup. Girl, all I can say to you is—don't count on *him* to know what's right."

"The trouble is I don't trust *me* that much either," Nicole said. "I'm not exactly sittin' on top of the world."

Etta was spearing the thicket ahead, and Monique started to follow, but after two wet steps she called over her shoulder, "Sure you are."

After two more snakeless hours the women were hungry and thirsty but had seen only a single black milk snake, already dead and partly consumed.

Monique pried the tip of her pole under the snake and flipped it into the brush.

"Not much of a present," she said. "I think we should eat."

Monique led the way down the path to the river's edge. A huge white rock dike protruded into the wide flow, and the snakers picked their way out onto it. Mud covered them to the waist, their arms, necks, and cheeks splattered with dark swamp muck. Monique and Nicole, knowing the rituals, stood on white rocks and undressed, peeling down to their damp skivvies. Etta watched with suspicion for a moment, then did the same. The women squatted at the water's edge and rinsed the mud from their various shirts and pants and socks and overalls, then spread the clothes on rocks to dry in the sunlight.

"I believe a beer would refresh," Monique said, her eyes shadowed beneath the rim of her frayed straw hat.

Then the three snakers, clad only in underpants, their bodies open to the air, squatted on rocks, unwrapped the bags, and began to picnic.

Monique passed a beer to Nicole, then, after a brief hesitation, passed one to Etta. Nicole popped the top and chugged.

"I'm definitely drinking," she said.

"I hear that."

When Etta popped the top on her brew, foam flew out. She licked the suds from the rim on the can, her eyes shining, licking carefully, coolly, as if she'd done this before.

The egg and onion sandwiches were distributed, and the women sat there, lunching beside the river, looking like a nude illustration of three crucial stages in a woman's life.

Etta ate her sandwich with big bites, her eyes straying to Nicole's interesting armpits, so full of hair, and Ma's huge heavy breasts that drooped toward the roll of fat around her belly.

"My mom has terrific knockers," Etta said. "Does that mean I'll have 'em like that, too?"

Nicole laughed, looking at her own smallish breasts.

"Don't ask me."

"Maybe," Monique said. She took her glasses off and wiped the lenses on her skivvies. "I'll bet *he* was fond of 'em."

"Huh?" Etta said. "I don't want 'em—they get in the way for sports. Mom couldn't even throw a baseball without makin' a face."

The noon bells at St. Peter's sounded, ringing faintly through the warm air.

"Why'd your daddy send you to me?" Monique asked.

"I can't talk about that."

"He told you that?"

"No. I just don't *know* why. That's why I can't talk about it."

"Was he drunk?"

"Well, just the normal."

"Mm-hmm."

Half of Etta's beer was gone, and she was buzzed, her eyes suddenly fluttering.

"You ever wondered what would've happened if they hadn't killed Christ for our sins?" she asked. "I mean, if instead they'd just dragged Him out back and slapped Him around some?"

Nicole and Monique raised up from their private thoughts and looked at her steadily.

Nicole said, "Now that is a morbid thing for a girl your age to say."

Monique grunted amiably. "She *ain't* sayin' it—that's Johnny Shade talkin'."

A cool peal of laughter came from Etta. She tapped a finger to her temple. "I got him memorized," she said.

"I better take some of that," Nicole said, and took the beer from the girl. She swished the beer in her mouth and swallowed. "My tummy is dry."

Monique nodded and said, "I think maybe you've made your mind up."

With the sandwiches eaten and the beers drunk, the snakers lay back on the rocks and silently sunned. After a while Etta sat up and said, "Hey! A tugboat!" The women came upright. "There's a man on deck lookin' at us!"

Nicole shaded her eyes with a flat hand.

"Oh," she said, "he's a little bit cute."

She stood, watching the man on the tug, and stretched her arms overhead.

"*Nicole!*" Etta said, "he'll—"

Then Monique stood beside Nicole, and, as the tug drew near, they turned their backs to the man on deck, bent over and rolled their undies to their ankles, shining contrasting moons across the river.

"Criminentlies!"

The man on deck called out something cheerful. Then another man rushed out to join him. They both waved frantically, and did flagrant pelvis bumps.

"Fuck you, too," Monique hissed under her breath. "Monkeys."

The tug whistled twice as it pulled away downstream.

Etta jumped up, now, and offered her own tiny hairless moon for view. She was giddy, bent over with her head between her knees, her skimpies stretched from ankle to ankle.

"Can they see this? Can they see this from there?"

"Maybe," Monique said. The old woman laughed. "You're okay, li'l girl. You did swell on the hunt. I watched you. You've got all kinds of Shade qualities."

"This is fun."

Soon after the tug disappeared, the women dressed. They put the trash into the bags, lifted their poles, and walked on up the path toward home. They stuck to the trail through the thicket, no longer pausing to thrash for snakes. On the railroad tracks Monique put an arm around Etta's shoulders. She held her close, then rubbed the girl's hair.

"You're one of us," she said. "No matter what might happen, Etta, we'll do what we can for you."

The sun beat down, and overhead a small band of late migrating birds scurried south.

"I'll let *that* sink in," Etta said.

When they reached the back door of the pool hall Monique unlocked it, pushed it open, and the tired women went directly to the table and collapsed into chairs, their poles clattering to the floor.

Monique Blanqui Shade slumped in her chair, her chin low, eyes on the snakeskins draped from the open closet door. She sighed.

"No snakes today," she said.

Part IV

Que sera and so on

15

THERE HAD been a time in river country when the sky from delta to headwaters blackened into one solid thunderhead, then busted open, punishing the land with far too many inches of rain in short order, and the big river, swollen by the runoff from the heart of the country, jumped its banks and kept on jumping, forever changing the face of the downriver world. The flood was named for its year, 1927, and in its wake towns became sloughs, riches became forlorn memories, and whole families were washed to the Gulf, never to be found. The swamps were flushed by the surging water, and all who lived there were forced to seek the haven afforded by higher ground, where they huddled in Red Cross camps and met the world that existed outside their own.

This was the first peek at life beyond the swamp for most of the refugees, and as the weeks in the camp went by many of them came to like what they saw. When the big river calmed and the swamp settled back to level, families that had known no life but the swampy decided that the allure of wild rice ranching and nutria trapping was overshadowed by the grand tales they'd swallowed of city life, a place where sugar-cured hams were free so long as you bought a potato, pigeons were fat and sleek and tasted like shrimp, cash was doled out twice a month, and there was an endless supply of liquid cheer and hoochy-koochy bonhomie. The flood pushed these folks from the remote life of the swamp and into the bullshit embrace of the bluff, winking city.

John X. looked out the dusty bathroom window of Tip's place to the brown river wending its endless path through the night. He wedged his elbow against the sill to hold himself steady, then finished off the whisky in his glass. Among the families forced to flee before the flood were the Blanquis, who fled from a place with no name, deep in the swamp. They'd come to town in the summer of '27, three months after the flood, and it was because of that rushing water that he had, later on, met a certain fourteen-year-old Blanqui girl, whom he'd wooed with spontaneous ditties on the subject of his desire, and ended up married to. And though that terrible flood had killed his mother, her drowned body never recovered, it had also round about brought him a wife and progeny.

John X. leaned back from the window, and when he turned he saw a drunken face in the mirror over the sink and sadly realized that drunken face was his own. Criminentlies, he hadn't had his little angel to pour his whisky today, and on his own he'd made a mess. His little angel knew just the right size that an angel of whisky should be. On his own he had this problem with portions, and he'd been drunk since shortly after he'd come to on the couch at noon. His pale grizzled face was a blur in the mirror.

He looked blurrily at the blurred image of himself, and decided to shave. He opened the cabinet and found Tip's razor and shaving cream. The foam hissed into his palm, and John X. lathered it to his cheeks. He leaned closer to the light, then dropped his jaw and pulled the razor down as it cleared a wobbly path from his cheekbone. Two red dots of blood bloomed immediately. He was trying to be at Monique's for a seven-thirty dinner, but he'd seen the damn clock from a screwy angle and been thrown off on his reading. Two hours off. He'd believed it to be a quarter of six, which left plenty of time, only to look again in ten minutes and find that it was nearly eight, and he had to hurry. He flattened his lips and drew the razor rapidly over the bump of his chin. When he finished, thin furrows of whiskers that the razor had missed bristled up, and tiny bits of reddening toilet paper hung from the nicks he'd made on his skin.

He dressed in the front room. He selected the handsomest threads from his suitcase of dead man's finery. He struggled with the buttons, but overcame this new test of his dexterity. Unfortunately black sneakers were his only shoes, and he bent down to tie them. When he raised up, Lunch Pumphrey was standing in the doorway, all in black, his hat brim pulled down, one little hand stuffed in the pockets of his Levi's, the other little hand holding a Colt .45.

"Paw-Paw, I've had Enoch's orange truck staked out for hours," Lunch said agreeably. "I got tired of waitin' for you to show yourself."

"Hey, sorry about that Lunch—" John X. said. "Say, what'cha drinkin'?"

"Oh my head's still poundin' from last night, Paw-Paw. I don't think I want to drink none."

John X. straightened the collar on his shirt and stood up straight, sneaking a glance toward the couch where Enoch's pistol was hidden. "I'm gonna guess pain is in the forecast for me, huh, Lunch?"

"You don't gotta guess, Paw-Paw."

"Well," John X. said, "that forecast calls for a drink." He lurched across the room toward the kitchen and his bottle of Maker's Mark. "I guess I half figured you'd be showin' up."

"You know I'm relentless this way," Lunch said.

John X. pulled the cork with a flourish, and took a deep sniff of the sweet sour mash, then raised the bottle neck and drank deeply.

"Where's the money?" Lunch asked.

"Oh, hell, slick, all that's left of that money is a *beautiful* memory, and nine hundred bucks. I had myself a time blowin' it," John X. said, shaking his head. "Yeah, Lunch, it all went to good causes, if you call bookies good causes. I'm gonna guess you don't."

John X.'s wrinkled face took on the mobile features of an animated raconteur, and he waved his arms with a sloppy charm.

"Looky here, Paw-Paw, you're sayin' nine hundred bucks is all you got left from forty-seven thousand dollars?"

"Well, really, nine hundred and fifty," John X. said, waving his bottle around. "But I'd like to keep a fifty so's I could slip it to ol' St. Pete—it might make the difference."

Lunch Pumphrey's dark, sepulchral eyes narrowed, and he eased his snap-brim hat back from his face.

"What you did to me proves you're in-sane. I might as well hear the details."

"Randi was furious with me, and at Pascagoula she jumped out with the kid and split. So, bein' alone, I decided I'd take that money of yours and run it up to where I was a millionaire!" He shook a cigarette loose, then flipped his eight-ball lighter open, and lit it.

"See, I took the advice of the pigskin experts, Lunch, and I put fifteen K down on them wily 'Bama boys. Saturday last, they lined up against a team from Florida whose star quarterback and favorite wide receiver had just been carted off to jail on rape charges. That oughta be an edge, right? Short of a fuckin' jailbreak that game *had* to be a lock for the Crimson Tide. But as you might know, late in the fourth quarter their stud runnin' back, the one that beat that burglary rap back in the spring, coughed it up inside the Florida ten-yard line, and that Florida linebacker who'd just come off suspension from that summertime assault beef the papers were full of, jumped on the ball and kept 'Bama from coverin' the spread."

John X. sucked on a cigarette, shook his head, and said, "Makes you wanta puke, don't it?" The old man looked at Lunch's face and grimaced. "Criminentlies, that's what I did to your face, huh? Nothin' broke?"

Lunch leaned against the wall, tapping the barrel of the pistol to his thigh.

"Just a bruise," he said. "Some pain."

"Randi told me I'd fucked up bad."

"Randi's a smart chick," Lunch said. "So where's the other thirty-two grand?"

"Oh, Slick," John X. said. "It gets worse." He flapped his elbows and gestured to the sky. "I doubled up to get the money back."

"Shit, that's stupid," Lunch said. "That's the same way I lost it to Short Paul in the first place."

"But that's what happened," John X. said. "I mean, can you believe Notre Dame could get beat by the Air Force Academy?"

"That was a shocker," Lunch said.

"Course then I spent another grand or so eatin' and drinkin', you know. I like good whisky."

"Good whisky an' bad luck, looks like to me," Lunch said. "You know I'm gonna kill you, don't you?"

A cigarette in one hand, a bottle of Maker's Mark in the other, John X. raised his arms wide over his head.

"Que sera and so on."

"Gimme what you got," Lunch said. "And forget holdin' out that last fifty."

John X. pulled the roll of greenbacks from his pocket. He swayed loosely as he leaned toward Lunch, and handed him the wad.

"I hope you had fun," Lunch said, "cause your fun is over."

"I know," John X. said. "I should be halfway to Dallas by now."

Lunch briskly tapped down the brim of his little black hat, then pointed the pistol out the door.

"Let's take a little ride in my Bug," he said.

"Sure," John X. said, lifting his bottle expansively. "Feelin' the call of the open road, huh? That's always been my downfall, too, Lunch."

There were a handful of flowers he'd pulled out of a neighbor's yard resting on the kitchen table, and as John X. passed, he paused to break a blossom off and insert it in his lapel. "I don't know what these are," he said. "Do you?"

"Might be tulips," Lunch said.

They crossed the wooden deck, their footsteps echoing out across the water, then down the slab steps to the gravel drive. Gravel crunched underfoot as they walked to Lunch's VW which was parked discreetly at the end of the drive. John X. took a deep breath of the autumn night air, then looked up at the bowl of stars above his head. Lunch's pistol prodded him in the back when they reached the VW.

"Open the trunk," Lunch said.

John X. pushed the button in and raised the bonnet, the hinges groaning loudly in the silent night. He looked down at three huge rocks on the bottom of the trunk.

"What are the rocks for?" John X. asked.

"Now, don't you worry about them, Paw-Paw." Lunch raised his pistol and planted it squarely at the back of John X.'s head. "Get in."

The old man crawled inside, and curled into a fetal position on top of the rocks. He looked up at Lunch.

"Look all around you, Paw-Paw. Notice *every* little thing. Appreciate it all at once — and say good-bye."

The birthday party was haunted by a white plate that set empty on the table. Monique Blanqui Shade hunched in her chair, smoking a long black cigarette. She wore a flower above her ear, a dainty gesture Etta had talked her into, and now she pulled the yellow rose from her hair and tossed it beside a dirty plate. Dinner had been eaten, and a jug of red wine was being passed around. All the children were gathered here. Rene and Nicole were avoiding eye contact, pointedly not talking to each other beyond banal courtesies, Nicole topping her wine glass with every passing of the jug. Big Tip, lonely since Gretel had been grounded by Mrs. Carter, shoveled in cake and smiled regularly; Francois, with his sports coat elegantly hung from the chair back, sat with his wife, Charlotte, a blonde of robust physique who smiled a lot, but always shrewdly studied the family as if her visits were part of a sociological inquiry. She'd expressed the keenest interest in meeting John X. Shade.

"He's halfway to Dallas by now," Etta said, looking at the empty plate. She propped her chin in her hand. "Mom predicted this."

"I don't care," Francois said. "He was *always* a phantom to me."

"Can I play pool with his cue now, Ma?" Etta asked.

Monique Blanqui Shade raised one long gray eyebrow, then gazed at Tip.

Tip shrugged, took a sip of wine. "Why not? I brought it back for him. Try it out, kid. Sure. Why not use the best? It's how he liked to do."

Etta got up from the table and went to the adjoining room where a pool table sat under a hanging lamp. She unlatched her father's black cue case, then lifted the sleek Balabushka from the slots lined with green felt. Then Rene was at her side.

"Pretty, ain't it?" Rene said. "Here, let me show you how the pros do it." He took the two pieces from her, then screwed the halves together. Rene picked up a square of chalk from the table edge and rapidly buffed the cue tip. "That's how to chalk the cue," he said. "Chalk between each shot. Always." He slid the Balabushka appreciatively through his fingers, and leaned over to break. He smacked the cue ball low and drove it into the rack, spreading the balls around the table. "Yeah, Ol' Johnny won hisself a lot of dough and free drinks with this piece of wood, kid."

"Grampa Enoch told me Dad was real good once."

"He sure was, kid," Rene said. "Course you spend fifty years at this game you *oughta* get pretty good."

Etta looked up at her half brother, twisting the crucifix in her ear. "He said his eyes got bad."

"He used to have good eyes," Rene said, "and a steady hand and the nerve of a back-door man."

Rene handed Etta the Balabushka cue. She leaned over the pool table. "He never let me touch it before," she said.

The party was breaking down along gender lines, Nicole and Charlotte remaining at the table with Monique—Nicole swirling the red wine in her glass, but looking deflated somehow; Charlotte saying, "What a lovely time this is," but looking at her gold wristwatch; Monique sitting there, her eyes unfocused, her attention somewhere else. A couple of birthday presents lay opened on the table—a teapot in the shape of a fish, a green silk blouse, one used bass lure.

From time to time there was a loud clacking of balls on the pool table.

Rene, Tip, and Francois congregated over at the window, looking out at Lafitte, the dark cobblestoned street they'd spent their youths on and never left far behind.

"I guess I believed him this time," Tip said.

"Sucker," Francois said.

"But that was before I knew he had nine hundred bucks."

The three sons stood in a rank, looking onto the black empty street, and finally Rene cupped a hand to his ear and said, "You hear it?"

Tip nodded slowly and said, "Honk, honk—"

Then, recognizing the prelude, all three sons hoisted the glasses in their hands together, raised them in salute toward the dark street as if seeing a certain bullet-shaped '51 Ford cruising their way, and said in unison, "Hey, assholes."

DANIEL WOODRELL was born in the Missouri Ozarks, left school and enlisted in the marines the week he turned seventeen, received his bachelor's degree at age twenty-seven, graduated from the Iowa Writers' Workshop, and spent a year on a Michener Fellowship. He is the author of eight novels, the five most recent of which were selected as *New York Times* Notable Books of the Year, and *Tomato Red* won the PEN West Award for fiction in 1999. He lives in the Ozarks near the Arkansas border with his wife, Katie Estill.

MULHOLLAND BOOKS

Reading Group Guide

THE BAYOU TRILOGY

Under the Bright Lights
Muscle for the Wing
The Ones You Do

by

DANIEL WOODRELL

A conversation with
Daniel Woodrell

It's been almost twenty-five years since Under the Bright Lights *was first published, and twenty years since the publication of* The Ones You Do. *What was it like to revisit the trilogy after so many years? Did the re-publication process stir any fond memories from the early years of your career as a novelist?*

I do not read my own old novels much. Once in a while there will be a reason to search one, primarily when I want to be sure I am not repeating myself. I had great fun writing all three of these novels, gave them all I had to give, and rereading them I find myself pretty happy with what came out of the ol' ink pen.

The lively Cajun town of St. Bruno, with its changing ethnic makeup, abundance of crime, and systemic corruption at the local level, is a fictional bayou town entirely of your own creation. What was it like to invent a city from the ground up? Is there a specific reason you later decided to make the switch to setting your novels in the Ozarks?

I did not expect myself to write Ozark novels when I started. I've lived quite a few places under various circumstances, and wanted to create a setting that would allow me to explore anything that appealed to me without any concerns about puny ol' conventional reality. The purely invented scenes are often the best. I want my writing to start in realism, but not to end up as mere realism. The switch to the Ozarks was not something I anticipated—I am very well aware of how disinterested the country as a whole is in places like this, so I knew it would mean taking a vow of poverty, but this is what started coming out, and I have kept on with it.

When you look back on the trilogy, do you note any stylistic differences among the three novels that surprise you? Are there any elements or attributes of these novels that strike you as stepping stones toward the writer you are now?

A lot of verve and energy are apparent. My love for pulp and for other forms of fiction seems obvious on every page. I was and am much taken with the sort of language that can hold high and low expression in the same sentence. Rough and refined. Oddly, I see more scenes of a faintly or strongly autobiographical nature in these early novels than I remember.

If you had to pick one favorite scene or moment from all three of the Rene Shade novels, what would it be, and why?

When Rene and Nicole have oral sex in a wading pool in the backyard.

Your most recent novel, Winter's Bone, was made into a motion picture directed by Debra Grank that was a critical success, won the Grand Jury Prize at the 2010 Sundance Film Festival, earned five Academy Award nominations, and has become something of a cult favorite. What did you think of the production, and to what extent were you consulted? Grank has mentioned in interviews that you showed the crew locations that had inspired you in helping them set the film.

The film came out very well. Awards out the wazoo. I think it telling that our culture will award and award a film that faithfully sticks to the book, but the book was completely left out of the awards and benedictions. I did show the film folks around, extended every courtesy, took them on the river, introduced them to the terrain and people, fed them when they showed up unexpectedly and hungry (fed them my own supper, in fact), etc.

You left high school to join the Marine Corps and ultimately ended up with an MFA from the Iowa Writers' Workshop. What led you from point A to point B?

I wrote all the time and had already been doing nothing else much for five years before Iowa. The Iowa Writers' Workshop was the only program to which I applied, and, quirk of quirks, I was admitted. A couple of faculty members would later loudly regret that I had been admitted, but I got through and learned what I needed to know.

Your style has been described as "southern," "gothic," "country noir," or all three. If you had to classify yourself, where would you say you fit?

All labels are a form of prejudice—so said Chekhov, and, as usual, he knew what he was talking about. "Regional," "gothic," "noir," "mystery" are all terms meant to segregate us from a true evaluation—no need for the literary world to even look at the work, since you are sub-literary by category, and the categories are very dumbly applied in many cases.

What books, music, and art inspire you? What are you reading and listening to now?

I still pay close attention to McGuane, Lehane, Hemingway, Edna O'Brien, Bruen, and Faulkner and Flannery. I read a lot of poetry, Kinnell, Merwin, Brigit Pegeen Kelly, Vallejo, Trakl, many others. I love Cézanne, Charles Burchfield, Chaim Soutine, and on many days Bonnard. Munch and van Gogh are so obviously an influence I usually forget to mention them, same with Twain. I like the Drive-By Truckers, Pieta Brown, Bo Ramsey and Greg Brown, Leona Naess, Malcolm Holcombe, and too many others.

Questions and topics
for discussion

Under the Bright Lights

1. *Under the Bright Lights* opens with the quote from prizefighter Joe Frazier: "If you cheated on [your preparation] in the dark of the morning, well, you're going to get found out now under the bright lights." How does this epigraph prefigure the story to come? What do you make of Rene Shade's years as a semiprofessional boxer? Why is it, as Shade remarks, that nobody remembers seeing the fights he won?

2. The Shade brothers—hard-drinking policeman and former boxer Rene, bartender to criminals and lowlifes Tip, and criminal prosecutor Francois, all started in the same broken home in a bad neighborhood of St. Bruno and ended up on different paths and with different positions in the social hierarchy. What do you think each of the three brothers represents in their varying approaches to lawfulness, morality, and social standing?

3. Alvin Rankin, the murdered African American city councilman, is described as a man who could have been the first black mayor of St. Bruno if his life had not been cut short. Given the motives for his murder, what does his death signify? What would his continued ascension have symbolized?

4. The denizens of St. Bruno are reluctant to disclose any information, however minor, to Rene or any part of the police force.

Why? Considering Woodrell's representation of St. Bruno's legal system and law enforcement, does it do them more harm or good not to trust the system to work on their behalf?

5. Many of the characters in *Under the Bright Lights* make racially disparaging comments, or bemoan the changing racial profile of St. Bruno. What do you make of all this overt racial tension? What correlation, if any, do you think race has with the crimes depicted?

6. *Under the Bright Lights* closes in a moment of violence and tenderness among brothers Rene and Tip. Does Woodrell's novel posit that both impulses can coexist among family? Among men? Or must one eventually win out over the other?

Muscle for the Wing

1. *Muscle for the Wing* invokes issues of class in its very first sentence, as Emil Jadick pushes himself shotgun-first through the door of the Hushed Hill Country Club to avoid the possibility of "a snub." Does class play a significant role throughout the novel? If so, to what end?

2. Fire-topped Wand Bone Bouvier is the only associate of the Wing to survive the events depicted in *Muscle for the Wing*. Considering the age (sixteen years old) at which romance brought her into close contact with a life of crime, do you consider her a victim of the men who worship her? Are her crimes or her involvement with criminals excusable, or is she to be held accountable for the violence waged on her behalf?

3. What do you make of the police force's cooperation with organized crime in hunting down the Wing and putting an end to their armed robberies? Is justice still served when mixed with the vengeance of villains?

4. Rene Shade and Shuggie Zeck were once extremely close friends as teenagers and got into more than their fair share of trouble in

their younger years. How would you characterize the relationship between Rene and Shuggie when the novel opens? In the moments before its conclusion?

5. Woodrell writes that Wanda Bouvier knows her body to be "a taunt that [sends] would-be Romeos off on quests for Love Oil and ceiling mirrors and nerve." Considering what happens to and around Wanda in *Muscle for the Wing,* would you say Wanda's sexuality generally places her at the mercy of male aggression, or is her body principally a weapon used to gain leverage over the men who desire her?

6. What would you say causes the Wing's undoing? Shuggie's death? Wanda and Rene Shade's survival?

The Ones You Do

1. John X. Shade, father of Rene, Tip, and Francois, is no longer the man he used to be—by his sons' observations as well as his own. In what way does Woodrell characterize the effects of aging on the kind of masculinity John X. represents? Has age softened the edges of John X. or just made him sloppier?

2. The first part of *The Ones You Do* is titled "Criminentlies," a colloquial exclamation that stems from "criminy," which in turn is a stand-in for "Christ." Do you think the root meaning of this word, much used throughout *The Ones You Do,* has significance for the events portrayed? What, in your estimation, does the term signify to those who use it?

3. In the most general sense, *The Ones You Do* is the story of a return home—a narrative trope that extends all the way back to the Greek classics. What does it mean to return home in general, psychological terms? And for John X. in particular? Does John X. return in defeat? In triumph? In search of reckoning?

4. Relationships between lovers play a primary role in the last novel of Woodrell's Bayou Trilogy: the wayward John X. and his runaway wife, Randi Tripp; Rene Shade and his longtime lover, Nicole; Tip and the pregnant Gretel. In the cases of Rene and Trip, what draws each brother to these vastly different women, and vice versa? What does the promise of a union represent to each brother? To the women they would have?

5. In chapter 11, Gretel reflects on "normal" domestic life from her perspective as the child of highly alternative parents. Does her characterization of the average American household ring true to you? Is her free-form existence preferable to "normal" domesticity in any way, or simply tragic? To what extent has Gretel rejected the nature of her upbringing, and to what extent has she embraced her parents' ideals?

6. *The Ones You Do* introduces the youngest member of the Shade clan, Etta, and features many scenes of the young girl interacting with her elderly father. How does Woodrell characterize their relationship? Would you say John X. is a mostly good or poor father? Does his parenting seem much changed from the role you envision him having played in raising Tip, Rene, and Francois?

The Bayou Trilogy

1. What changes, if any, do you see in Rene Shade over the course of the trilogy?

2. Has the Shade family changed for better or worse as a result of the events depicted in these three novels?

3. In the end, is St. Bruno on the path to betterment, or has the character of the city only continued to degrade?

Also by Daniel Woodrell

WINTER'S BONE

"A stunner. A bleak, beautifully told story about the inescapable bonds of land and blood.... Contemporary fiction at its finest."
—Kathleen Johnson, *Philadelphia Inquirer*

"Profound and haunting.... The lineage from Faulkner to Woodrell runs as deep and true as an Ozark stream."
—Denise Hamilton, *Los Angeles Times Book Review*

"As serious as a snakebite.... In *Winter's Bone* Daniel Woodrell has hit upon the character of a lifetime.... His Old Testament prose and blunt vision have a chilly timelessness that suggests this novel will speak to readers as long as there are readers."
—David Bowman, *New York Times Book Review*

"Woodrell is a stunningly original writer.... Ree Dolly is one of the most memorable female heroes in modern American fiction."
—Associated Press

"Sometimes brutal, sometimes mordantly funny, sometimes surprisingly sweet.... I just didn't want *Winter's Bone* to end."
—Harper Barnes, *St. Louis Post-Dispatch*

Back Bay Books
Available wherever paperbacks are sold

MULHOLLAND BOOKS

What's Coming Around the Curve

You won't be able to put these Mulholland books down.

APRIL

GUILT BY ASSOCIATION *by Marcia Clark*

THE BAYOU TRILOGY *by Daniel Woodrell*

MAY

A DROP OF THE HARD STUFF *by Lawrence Block*

JUNE

THE WRECKAGE *by Michael Robotham*

FUN AND GAMES *by Duane Swierczynski*

JULY

BLOODLINE *by Mark Billingham*

AUGUST

TRIPLE CROSSING *by Sebastian Rotella*

HELL AND GONE *by Duane Swierczynski*

Visit www.mulhollandbooks.com
for your daily crime-fiction fix and excerpts
from forthcoming titles.